10/21/09 Donated by Author $16.95

BENEATH THE SHADOWS

LEE ANN NEWTON

JAMES A. BENSON

Cold Tree Press
Nashville, Tennessee

The characters depicted in this story are fictitious.
Any similarity to persons living or dead is merely coincidental.

Published by Cold Tree Press
Nashville, Tennessee
www.coldtreepress.com

Beneath the Shadows

*is humbly dedicated
to the*

Lost Heroes

*who so nobly gave their lives, near and far,
that we might enjoy the freedoms we have today.*

They ask only that they not be forgotten.

ACKNOWLEDGMENTS

LEE ANN NEWTON

As with any great endeavor, there are those along the way who help us swim up the rapids. I have learned that God is always one step ahead of me; putting those people in place and that his vision is grander than I would ever dare to imagine.

First and foremost I must thank my co-author Jim for his friendship and patience.

My parents, Paul and Margaret Kunkel, are the stalwarts of my life, always there, always supportive, never changing; as dependable as the seasons of the year. I love you both.

My daughter, Emily, for believing in your Mom and her dream.

My son, Michael, whose birth signified many new beginnings, including the writing of Beneath the Shadows.

My daughter, Sarah, whose determination is a shining example that encourages me on my darkest days.

My husband of twenty-three years, Greg, your love is the lighthouse of my life; always shining and guiding me safely back to our family harbor.

My in-laws, Aileen and Jim Newton; Aileen for always believing it would happen; Jim, for always showing me the kindness and generosity of your Kentucky lineage.

My lifelong friend Sherri Rawson, for inviting me into your family so many years ago and showing me the true heart of the Cumberland Gap and its people.

Mona and John Eversole are friends of the heart and their early enthusiastic reading of the manuscript was pivotal.

My publisher, Peter Honsberger, CEO of Cold Tree Press; for your excitement, hard work and dedication. You took "Beneath the Shadows" from my life and offered it to the world.

My editor and friend, Sheri Swanson, for your enthusiastic edits, conversation and coffee.

For all of you who have encouraged, cajoled and touched my life along the way. I thank you with a most gracious and humble heart.

JAMES A. BENSON

Well, it's my turn to thank you to all near and far, intimate and stranger.

To my wife Joanne and daughters Kathryn and Samantha who hung in there while ol Dad, as their grandpa used to say, battled writing demons, advancing age, and dementia.

To Lee Ann for saying, "yes" to co-authoring on that ubiquitous morn. "Oh my Lord," I said to myself after she agreed. "Now what?"

To a zillion folks with whom I spoke at a dozen battlefields, airplanes and airports, restaurants, before/after worship (sometimes during), and a sandbox full of places betwixt and between. They inspired me and filled me with heritage and personal journeys, many of which are sewn between these covers.

To Chaplain Phil Conner who told me of a distant CW

descendant who exclaimed desire to be buried in a hickory coffin so that when hell beckoned, he'd enter poppin' and snappin'.

And there's this other chaplain, a Tennessean, called Robert Vance Brady, who suggested in the winter of '98-'99, "Hey, Jim, why don't you write a novel about the bullet that kilt yer uncle William Wright at Resaca, GA." Thanks, Bob. Great idea minus the bullet thing. William Wright was a Yankee like me (with roots in Crockett, TX); Bob's a Johnnie Reb. Matter of fact, so is Phil. And so is Chaplain Brady Eggleston. My Wright clan of the 105th Illinois was infamous (along with a wagonload of more Union boys in The March to the Sea) for burning their way to Savannah, and as one of their trophies—the Eggleston farm. Nevertheless, and in spite of my ancestor's Yankee war of Northern Aggression, the Egglestons then and now represent the soul of American spirit-hood; Jacob can attest to that.

To my liege, the master of the universe, a direct descendent of near every royal in eastern and western Europe, his highness and Vail-ness, Chaplain (Colonel) Thomas Claire Vail—a friend indeed. For through the millennia, my English, Scandinavian, and French ancestors have tilled his Vail-ness' soil. This Royal, of the Army Medical Department Center and School, has kept me sane.

To Chaplain (Colonel-Retired) Edward K. Maney, an anomaly of the Chaplain Corps, a visionary through and through. Though junior in age, he was/is my mentor. Born a Lion, he met this Tiger and offered friendship. There are none better than he. None.

And lastly, to the Lord.

Amen.

BENEATH
THE
SHADOWS

LEE ANN NEWTON
JAMES A. BENSON

"Did you get him, Jacob?"

"Yeah, I got him."

He had shot at least six times and his aim was good, but that Yank didn't flinch. And with another dozen in the hunt, the big bastard lasted long enough to pick off a dozen of theirs. He made up his mind to check on the Bluebelly himself once the sun went down.

THE PROPHECY

*In the Days of the Darkness,
the Spirit came and they called the Spirit, Pangari.*

*The Shadow of Pangari shall be cast upon the seventh daughter of
the seventh daughter of the seventh son.
To the hundredth generation shall the Shadows come.
When the moon's fullness embraces rebirth,
the Chosen One must leap into the great Darkness.*

*If the Chosen One should fail. If Pangari's seed is not sown,
before the moon wanes in winter's dawn,
mankind will be destined to live beneath the shadows.*

*When the Darkness has been purged from the new land,
when those who suffered its burden remain no more,
the last child born of Pangari shall step from the recesses
and cast its light upon a weary world.*

PROLOGUE

I turned thirty-five years old that spring of nineteen hundred and thirty-nine. My soul was dead, my dreams withered like the days of my youth.

It was a bone-chilling spring in the Appalachia Territory. The rains were heavy and frequent but despite the cold, rebirth came just as surely as the sun would rise and set on the days of my life. It came for me and the world surrounding me. I wasn't looking for it. I was content in the way miserable lonely people become content; living out my day's one by one, complacent and uncaring, ignoring the ever-approaching horizon. I wasn't looking for change, but the Ancients were searching for me.

I was a teacher at Pine Ridge Settlement School, the only teacher for at least twenty miles around. The children left home before daybreak, traversed mountain and stream to reach the school by nine. Those that lived too far away to walk, boarded with us throughout the winter months when the crops were in and their bounty preserved. It was the only time their parents could do without them.

I never wanted to be a teacher, but I was needed and for some bitter-resented nobility I stayed. The mountain people looked to me to take it over, expected it. That was their way. So I stayed.

Stephen left, Callie Dawn left, they all left. Some walked out of these mountains, some went by horse and then by train. My hearts' rose withered on the vine.

Seemingly overnight the cold spring gave way to a disturbing oppressive summer, with long hot days melting into even longer, muggy nights, fraught with thousands of buzzing mosquitoes. We were thankful for last year's abundant corn crop as it provided us with many cobs for the much needed gnat-smokes in the evening. The thick lingering smoke had a pungent odor that proved most effective in holding the tiny black, biting gnats and mosquitoes at bay. This allowed us precious time on the front porch in the cooler evening hours to sip sassafras tea, chilled in the cold mountain water that ran through the springhouse. When night had fallen, we would retreat into the hot stuffy house for a few hours of restless slumber.

Despite our best efforts there was little sleep to be had, and what I was able to obtain was often interrupted by the most horrifying nightmares, flashes of blue and gray and the permeating stench of death and black powder. When the nightmares began to surface during my waking hours, I attributed them to sleep deprivation and any other excuse I could think of. I was not one to give credence to the Shadowlands.

However, my beliefs would be challenged as never before that summer of thirty-nine. For it appears that just when we think our lives are beyond change, safe in the world of complacency, fate deals us a new hand and puts us back in the game.

My journey began with voices from beyond the grave.

ONE

▓▓▓))) ⊃ ⊃ ● (((((

I think to lose Kentucky is nearly the same as to lose the whole game.
—Abraham Lincoln, September 22, 1861

Perryville, Kentucky
1862

GOD'S CREATURES FLED the intrusion of thousands of marching boots trampling autumn's splendor. Private Caleb Wright missed the melodies of sweet songbirds, now gone from woods stocked with soldiers. The only noise was the clamor of hundreds of men preparing for battle, it was anything but a routine morning, and they all knew it. The men were quieter than usual, some sat reading letters or looking at pictures of loved ones. Caleb woke, along with the rest of the Eightieth Indiana Volunteer Infantry Regiment, to bugle's pre-dawn revelry—he gathered his gear and longed for a hot cup of coffee but fires were forbidden this morning—the enemy was close and there was no time.

He listened for the last morning trills of a whippoorwill, but the woods were dissonant and quiet. Any creature fool enough to stay had found itself stuffed into some lucky soldier's haversack.

He'd heard tell of more than one barn rat falling victim to a soldier's grubstake and after having nothing but salt pork and hardtack three times a day for the last week, roasted rat didn't sound half bad.

The Army had never been inundated with such large numbers of new recruits, and the logistics of providing the most basic necessities to them, was for now, a near impossibility. Blankets and rubber mats were still in short supply, and the drought-ridden earth gave little comfort to a body weary from walking upwards of thirty miles a day. Months without rain had left little water to support the thirsty soldiers as they quick-marched toward Bardstown. Despite the fact that is was October, Kentucky was in the grips of a devastating drought and the heat was as brutal as the worst August day.

They suffered their first casualties on the hard march, not from rebel bullets, but heatstroke. Caleb had marched past three such comrades yesterday, leaned sallow and serene against a tree, he had wondered if there might not be a sliver of God's breath left within. His inquisitive mind led him often to question the assumptions of others. Shallow graves and makeshift crosses dotted the roadside while others, like these three, waited for someone to put them to rest. Shards of paper were pinned to their clothing. They noted the day of death and any known personal information. "He died a hero," would write the commander. There was no time to tarry and consider the loss; battle loomed.

When the Rebel Army claimed Lexington and began pushing north to the state capitol of Frankfort, Lincoln had put out an urgent request to defend Kentucky at all costs. If Kentucky was lost, it would equate the loss of crucial supply lines, and so Caleb, along with thousands of new, largely untrained, troops from Indiana, Ohio and other western States, rushed to fill President Lincoln's request.

The Army of the Ohio, under the command of Major General Don Carlos Buell, of which Caleb and the Eightieth were a part, had been ordered to meet and push back an invading Rebel force led by the formidable Confederate Generals Edmund Kirby Smith and Braxton Bragg. The Generals' reputations preceded them and evoked terror in the hearts of the Yankee greenhorn recruits. The Rebels, mostly from Arkansas and Tennessee, were already battle-tried and trained and they had tasted victory at every turn since their push into Kentucky began. They were living up to their reputation of being half-hoss and half-alligator capturing the Union garrison at Munfordville, taking Lexington and now the state capitol of Frankfort.

A volunteer, Caleb enlisted for only one reason; he could not stay and watch his heart's desire proffered into a loveless marriage by her greedy despot mother. Caleb was neither Catholic nor of German descent and as far as Adel Weldishofer was concerned; he was a Protestant heathen and a one-way ticket to hell for her daughter.

His father, Charles, often spoke to him about forbidden love and its disastrous results—tales meant to dissuade him from his heart's pursuit, but Lydia distracted him as fervently as the clanging bell on the front door of Father's mercantile.

Helpless to change the age-old beliefs of their families, they caressed with their eyes and met in their dreams. However, fantasies were at the bottom of Charles Wright and Adel Weldishofer's priority list. A son had to provide, and a daughter needed to make a good union; neither should even consider the holy estate of matrimony outside their prospective Church.

Grandma Hannah was the only one who understood Caleb's heart. She understood and agreed that one should marry for love—convention be damned. She also understood his tender heart for

God's creatures. The relentless teasing of family and friends had taught him early to keep his mouth shut and his soft underbelly hid. How ironic, that he now sat among soldiers, was in fact, a soldier himself, ordered to kill not bird nor beast but man. What would the others around him think if they knew his weakness?

Caleb checked his gun and rolled the flag-quilt Grandma had sewn for him before he left home. She spoke admirably to him of the reason he was going off to fight—to free the Darkies. A veil of pain swept over her face as she said, "You must do what you can to rid our precious nation of slavery, Caleb. Perhaps then you will be able to help me put things right before the good Lord calls me home."

She wiped the moisture from her eyes, removed her butterfly necklace, and placed it in his hand. "It has seen me through many a tough time, and it will do the same for you. Like an invisible cocoon, the angels will protect you until all danger has passed." She took his strong calloused hand in hers. "When you find the one that mends your wounds, touches your soul, and speaks to your heart, give the necklace to her."

Grandma had a gift for seeing things before they happened, and that made him more than a little nervous. How he was to find a girl out here, in this sea of men, was beyond him, and of what wounds did she speak? The officers were pensive this morning, checking and rechecking, sending out scouts, receiving messages and that did little to calm his nervous stomach.

His thoughts were of Lydia and he wished he had a tin-type of her, but what did it matter? She'd marry the old bastard tomorrow anyway. He could still see her pleading blue eyes—the day Adel brought her into the mercantile to purchase silk for her wedding gown. The gown was not for him to see, but for the one with the thousand acres. She had cried that day, begged her Mother to let her marry for love, she had looked at him, her eyes beseeching him to intervene, but he had done nothing.

Instead, he answered Lincoln's call for volunteers, had in fact, been the first in line to join the ranks. Hesitating but a moment, he signed his name, and spent the rest of the afternoon defending his decision to enlist, to his angry, disillusioned family. Having taken all the tongue-lashing he could stand, he packed his gear early and left before supper to say goodbye to his one ally, Grandma Hannah. As always, she knew what he was going to do before he did and she had the stars and stripes quilt ready for him to take along for his bedroll. He intended to stay the night with her and leave first thing in the morning but Grandma's premonitions and cryptic words kept him awake, so he told her goodbye and spent the rest of the evening riding around the countryside of his youth, trying to muster up enough courage to stop by the Weldishofer farm and tell Lydia goodbye. They had never spoken, except for a few words here and there, but their attraction was obvious, to them and everyone else, and he was desperate to gaze into her blue pools one more time; transfix her image in his mind to take with him to battle and beyond. Halfway out the door to war's salvation, he felt confident that he could withstand Adel's barbed tongue one last time.

Caleb rode up to the front gate; his stomach swarmed with butterflies. He could do this; he was a man now, a soldier even. He dismounted and tethered his horse to a flawless white fence held captive beneath a fragrant thicket of red roses. He plucked one for Lydia, it pricked. He bled.

His palms perspired as he opened the gate, took a deep breath, and strode up the immaculate walk. A lace curtain drew back on an adjacent window, and he heard clipped footsteps cross the foyer. The door opened a few inches casting a yellow triangle of light onto the clean swept porch.

Caleb doffed his cap. "Good evening Missus Weldishofer."

"Mister Wright, are you aware of the hour?"

"Yes Ma'am," he stammered holding the rose behind his back. "I'm sorry it's so late. I was hoping to speak to Lydia before I go."

"Lydia is none of your concern. She has retired for the evening."

"But I..." The woman inhaled his words.

"Good evening, Mister Wright."

The door slammed on his fallen face. He stared at the door and clenched his fists. He threw the rose down and ground it into her precious, unblemished porch. What had he expected? *Please come in, Mister Wright. I'll fetch Lydia for you?* What a fool he was.

From an upstairs window, fingers tapped. He walked down the steps and looked up, his breath dissipated. Lydia stood in the window with candle in hand, ivory skin against a blue silk dressing gown. Her sapphire eyes shone misty in the soft candle light and strands of flaxen hair were matted to her damp face as long blond curls cascaded over full breasts. Caleb's eyes paused on luscious cherry lips—lips he would never taste, never know.

She raised her hand; he tipped his hat and committed her beautiful vision to memory. He rode away that night without looking back, leaving his shattered heart bleeding on Adel Weldishofer's manicured lawn.

In his pocket was Grandma's silver butterfly necklace that he had hoped to give to Lydia that night. Grandma knew of Caleb's dreams. Their singular bond began on a morning when he was three and she found him in the front yard crying.

"What's the matter, child?" she had asked.

He had pointed to a bluebird's mangled form, brought down by his brother's slingshot.

"We all have our time, Caleb. You will have many choices. This creature of God had none." She had pressed his head into her old tummy, and together they mourned the lost life and buried it in the freshly tilled garden soil.

The rest of Caleb's family rarely visited her. They claimed she was a black mark on the family name although they would never explain what it was she had done. As far as he could see, without Grandma's choices, none of them would be alive today.

He went to see her once or twice a week, to cut her wood, and do repairs on the farm. Mostly, he went to eat her delicious food while she told him wonderful stories. He missed her already.

With the necklace was Father's silver pocket watch, given to him that last afternoon with words he was just now beginning to understand. "It's not what you think, Son. There's no glory in war." Father had pressed the watch into Caleb's hand and cupped it between his own. "Time will stop for me until you are safe at home again." Caleb watched his Father walk away and swipe a handkerchief across his nose.

A piece of white silk held Caleb's treasures—hopeless romantic, his brother would tease. But no one knew these things; they were the ghosts of the battlefield, the private ruminations of a soldier.

Army life was nothing Caleb could or would have conjured; sleeping on bare ground, eating monotonous food, and drinking coffee three times a day did little to boost his sagging spirits. Cannon retort echoed in the distance, in the direction they now marched. Caleb's boots kept time while his mind shifted homeward to Mother's porch where he often sat after breakfast and watched her churn the fresh milk. Magically, she transformed the thick white liquid into a daily fare of butter and cheese and later fashioned the leftover cream into secret sauces, wondrous aromas, and sumptuous flavors.

Caleb's breakfast of cold coffee and salt pork rang hollow. They were wakened before daybreak, bludgeoned by Sarg's profane expletives to march double-quick toward the enemy and hell.

The Eightieth's intrepid journey landed them on the periphery of Perryville, Kentucky. Lydia pranced in his thoughts while cannon rumbled in the distance; he stood in the front line at a right angle to a line of thick trees. Was it only two weeks ago that he peeled apples at Grandma's table? What in the Lord's holy name was he doing here?

"What's done is done," Grandma would say. So it was. He stood in line with anxious comrades. They shifted and shuffled, whispered and joked in a false display of bravado until an order careened up and down the ranks. "Shoulder arms!" Cannons continued to belch smoke, and explode in the distance.

Sergeant Ben Decker, Caleb's new found mentor, and Top Soldier Vail were the only ones with battle experience, both from the Mexican War. Ben was rough and crude; his mass of thick black hair and pencil-lead eyes bore holes through innocents and sinners alike. No doubt about it, Sarg showed no partiality. He treated all comers the same—bad—damn bad. The noncom seldom shaved, but washed when he could. Not that it mattered, there was precious little water to drink, let alone bathe with.

Caleb watched Sarg study the distant Rebel tactics. All the boys were scared of him. Whispered stories of his Mexican War exploits were enough to keep them out of his sights. For reasons unknown to both parties, Caleb and Sarg had taken a general liking to one another. Always out of Sarg's earshot, the other boys whispered, "Too bad for you, Wright."

This general liking had earned Caleb the moniker of Storekeep, or when Ben was angry, Shithead, accompanied by a litany of profanities. The boys tried to get Caleb to give it back, but he wasn't too keen on the idea of getting a boot up his ass. Caleb soon discovered that Ben's influence on his churchly upbringing was profound or one could say—profane. While he strove to maintain some of who he was, the Army's code of behavior centered on killing and survival. His hard-assed tutor couldn't teach "turn the other cheek" when twenty thousand Rebs were marching north to meet them, and they weren't coming for a Sunday social, but for a pound of flesh and retribution.

Sarg woke him each morning, an hour before revelry, with a swift kick to the ribs. Profanities were exchanged, and Caleb rolled out to another day of merciless drilling in weaponry, stealth, and positions. Such a day was always good for Sarg, but his favorites were the days he centered instruction on his weapon of choice, a nine-inch steel blade sharpened on both sides. "Bleeds 'em," he would say matter-of-fact. Caleb thought of hog butchering day— squealing pigs pulled up by their hind leg; jugulars sliced; blood caught in a washtub.

Caleb coursed his parched tongue over dusty lips. The sun scaled the horizon bearing all the signs of another scorcher with no water in sight. Captain Challand had sent a scouting party out to look for some, but they had yet to return. Caleb's canteen was nearly dry, and the little slosh it contained was murky. They had found only stagnant pools of water from which to fill. Two weeks ago, he would have thought it certain death to drink such water, but two weeks ago, he wasn't a soldier living off the land. Nevertheless, with thousands about, Caleb felt fortunate to have the brackish brew.

Rumor had filtered down that the fight had started around three that morning when a reconnaissance team reported small pools of water in the Confederate-held Doctors Creek. Some God-Almighty Union general ordered the water and the hill seized. Scuttlebutt had it the Arkansas Rebs, surprised by the pre-dawn attack, were driven back.

Twelve-pounders, the artillery type, exploded far-off and rifle fire popped like roasted chestnuts in the distance. Men stood to

Caleb's left and right waiting for their turn. The Fiftieth Ohio waited to their rear. A field lay before them, a corn stubble landscape of foreboding spikes.

Across the field and meadow beyond, the Thirty-third Ohio marched to form a skirmish line and hopefully seduce the Reb's itchy trigger fingers. Caleb checked Father's pocket watch as the Ohio boys advanced. It was two-fifteen.

The Rebs let go with a few warning shots, nothing more. They're saving it for the turkey shoot, and we're the turkeys, Caleb thought. He had hunted rabbits in open fields but at least they were small enough to hide in the stubble and stand a chance. Now he was going to be the target, with no cover in sight. *God forgive me for my sins.*

The sweat that ran down his backside had little to do with the heat and more to do with an acute case of first-timer's syndrome. He looked to Sarg for reassurance, but his mentor was focused on the distant smoke. Ben's every muscle was taut and his right hand nursed the form-fit handle of his killer blade. He reminded Caleb of a wild cat poised to pounce on unsuspecting prey. The sounds of battle exploded in front and to their left. *God let me fight in Ben's shadow.*

Down the line, Top Soldier Vail yelled intermittent threats and vulgarities at his fidgety recruits. His authority, like Ben's, was unquestioned. "You want my job?" he would say. "Name the time and place. You win and the job's yours. You lose…" He'd pause and stare through his audience. "…and it'll be the last load you'll dump in my honey wagon."

Caleb tried once to get Ben to give Vail a go-round. "A badger will bite yer heels if ya walk by. Pick it up by the tail and it'll claw yer eyes out," was all Ben said.

Vail strutted by. "Get ready, you mama's boys. Drop your

haversacks and bedrolls, the elephant's getting ready to thunder this a-way."

"When are they gonna charge, Ben?"

"You'll see em soon enough, Shithead."

"What do I do?" All the instruction, all the knowledge Ben had imparted vanished with the approaching storm.

The days-old beard did not conceal Ben's agitation. "Damn it Boy. Top's gonna hear yer whinin' and chew my ass." Ben glanced over his shoulder and saw his student's pale sweaty face. "Shit," he muttered and spat tobacco juice. He motioned Caleb up. "See Harris' battery over there?"

Caleb nodded.

"Once the Ohio boys get back, Harris' chillun will lay into them Tennessee Rebs. Then, it'll be our turn but we'll let em get a tad closer. Make it count."

Vail raised his sword. "Check your loads and say your prayers. Look a-yonder boys. It's Judgment Day."

Caleb looked at the gray swarm pouring down the slope. Their Rebel cry sent fear scurrying up and down his thin skin. His thoughts ricocheted. Did Ben say to aim high or low? Was his gun loaded? Did he remember the cap? What about powder? Did he load the powder? The gray was taking shape; he saw figures. Bayonets gleamed. Caleb heard Father's voice, *It's not what you think. There's no glory in war, Son.*

The Rebs fired into the first waves of defense. Screams of Union pain and cries of Rebel passion truncated the air. The laughter and small talk ceased, and the Indiana boys stole wide-eyed glances at each other. The Ohioans advanced to fill the gaps in their line. Down range, Rebs marched toward them with relentless precision. Like a scythe to wheat, the Reaper cut his harvest.

"How do you know they're from Tennessee?" hollered Caleb above the ruckus.

"Damn it to hell Boy, use yer eyes." Ben's powder-stained finger pointed in the distance. "Ya see them flags and those Ohio boys bout two hundred yards out?"

Caleb's squinted to try and see the flags through the smoky haze. The Ohioans were scattering for cover behind a riddled barn and firing around the corners in a steady barrage.

"Here we go, men," commanded Vail. "Stand ready."

Caleb moved out of formation to piss.

"Wright," Vail shrieked. "Get back in line!" Vail turned his ire on Ben. "Sarg, keep em in the goddamn line!"

Ben's neck hairs bristled. Caleb would catch hell later if he lived that long.

An occasional stray missile buzzed overhead. Some kicked up dust at their feet. Vail didn't flinch. He turned his attention to Caleb. "Look like ya seen a ghost, Wright." His eyes welded, "I'll shoot anyone that goes yella on my watch." He looked down the ranks. "And that goes for the rest of you Greenhorn."

The Rebs landed fire into the barn, and it was ablaze within minutes. The Ohioans scrambled for fresh cover but none was to be had. Caleb watched in horror as rebel artillery mowed them down. The turkey shoot had begun. Life's crimson wine flowed.

Harris' battery stood ready. Caleb's mind convulsed, *Why aren't they firing?* As if in rebuttal, Union artillery let loose and made fillet of attacking Rebs. Hundreds of Rebs rushed to fill the gaps left by Howitzer reports.

"Advance," Vail bellowed.

Caleb's line moved forward. Confederate Bars and Stars flayed. Black and white signal flags waved. What remained of the Thirty-third Ohio retreated through their ranks like Satan was on their heels. Terror glistened in their eyes. The Tennessee Rebs, in hot pursuit, descended on the Eightieth's lines like an army of screaming banshees.

Urine streamed down Caleb's legs. He aimed his gun into the Rebel onslaught. Hell had arrived, but the damn demons looked just like him.

"Fire," Vail boomed. Smoke exhaled from thousands of black musket rifles, the shrieks of dying men pitched on the air. The Rebel yell grew louder.

Caleb's ears rang with the repercussion of artillery. He fired into the smoke, reloaded, fired, and reloaded in practiced repetition. The world fell away in the Rebel charge. Rifles fired, and desperate men stormed their way, bayonets slayed the frightened and the fearless. Some went down without a sound, some screamed as arms tore away in artillery's fury, others grit their teeth and charged again, maimed and mangled until they could charge no more.

The battle temper surged beneath the callous heat. Caleb knelt to reload, his mouth parched beyond measure. He thought of his canteen. There was no time. His rage kindled; he leapt to his feet and fired at a charging Reb twenty yards away. He aimed high, his bullet left a gaping hole in the Reb's face. He went down bloody and screaming. Caleb couldn't move, couldn't look away. It wasn't supposed to be like this—this Reb still alive, clutching his devastated misshapen face.

Ben darted left and right, in and out, up and down, firing and fighting with deadly accuracy. "How ya doin' Storekeep?" he yelled, gutting a charging Reb with his Bowie knife.

The scene was surreal as the battle raged in all directions. Comrades screamed and fought, killed and were killed. A renewed Rebel yell jarred him from his stupor. Good God, how many were there? Panic began to spread through the thinning Yankees. A twelve-pounder exploded a few yards in front, tearing apart several of his comrades and sending hunks of their precious flesh flying into his face. Enough! He threw down his gun and began to run back to the safety of the tree line, past the fallen and the fearless. Faster and faster.

A steel hand caught his collar and jerked him from his feet. Caleb revolted against his captor, his shirt ripped; as the hand spun him round. "Where ya goin', Shithead?" Ben held him with one hand and shot a Reb with the other. "Where's yer gun?" Caleb didn't answer. Ben shoved him toward the fray. "Get a goddamn rifle!"

Caleb knelt to retrieve a Reb's gun and ammo pouch. The warm sweet odor of torn flesh and spilled blood made his stomach lurch and breakfast bile spewed with immobilizing ferocity and sweat ran down his sallow face.

"Git it loaded," Ben ordered.

Caleb wiped his mouth. His hands shook as he loaded the weapon in a nightmare trance.

Ben jerked him to his feet. "The fight's out there, Boy."

"I can't."

"Livin' takes some dyin', Yella. I'll call ya soldier when ya stop waterin' yer britches, look ol Satan in the eye, and kick him in the balls." A Reb broached their line. Ben tossed his pupil aside, drew his knife, and drove it into the Johnnie's receptive belly. The Reb let out a dead man's groan and fell in a heap to the dusty ground. "Come on, Shithead, we gotta get in behind em. That means runnin' upstream."

Caleb knew he had one more chance with Ben. "I'm right behind you."

Ben took off like a jackrabbit dodging Rebel lead. Caleb watched him but an instant, then threw down the Reb's Enfield and ran in the opposite direction. *To hell with this.* Just inside the tree line, he saw a woman beneath a pile of brush. Their eyes locked. *What the…*

Within that instant, Ben caught the draft of Caleb's cowardice, turned and fired, sending a mini-ball into the back of Caleb's thigh.

Caleb's leg gave way and he was thrown headlong to the ground, a protruding rock silenced his thoughts.

"Worthless sum-bitch." Ben spat brown juice and looked into another wave of Gray. There were Rebs to kill and water to gain and no time to ponder the deed.

Reinforced Union regiments laid into the Rebel onslaught. Soldiers, green as fresh mowed hay, fought the elephant, a tough and worthy foe. Thousands on both sides fell. Some abandoned their cause. Most held true.

Caleb woke to the sound of thousands of footsteps marching in the distance, along with cannon report and the popping of heavy rifle fire, all the sounds of a heated battle. Was he in the land of friend or foe or was this hell? His sight was fogged, his brain muddled and pounding like a son of a bitch. One thing was sure. He was alive.

He rolled over and tried to sit up. His head swam, and fresh blood trickled down his face. His leg burned like it was immersed in fire. He felt for the wound, his trouser was soaked, and his hand covered with bright red blood, lots of it. He was bleeding bad. He pulled the strip of silk from his pocket, dumped out the watch and necklace, and used it for a tourniquet.

He had no idea how long he'd been unconscious. He looked at Father's watch; it must have busted when he fell, the hands were frozen at three forty-five.

Rivulets of sweat and blood stung his eyes and his thirst was unbearable. A dead man's canteen lay within reach. He heaved himself to it. It was empty.

His distorted vision could not deny the destruction and death that lay in all directions, a landscape devastated, strewn with bodies, dead horses, guns, cartridge boxes, and all manner of accoutrements. Torrents of lead and missiles had stripped the trees of all but the largest limbs. Their debris lay heavy on the ground, a token burial for some.

At the sight of a broken ambulance, Caleb's heart fell. They had come for the wounded and left him for dead. Damn them. Damn him. He was Charles Wright's son, but on this day it was not Father's brave blood that flowed through his veins, it was that of a coward. He picked up Grandma's necklace and Father's watch in his bloodstained hand. He felt a welcome presence. There were two choices he could make, and the second one was for two time losers.

Hoisting himself upright with a dead-man's rifle, he stuffed the necklace and watch back in his pocket and began to limp across the desecrated battlefield, past hundreds of fallen heroes, some already bloating beneath the brutal sun. One poor sot clutched a small gilt-edged book with a gold cross on the front. A brass clasp secured the covers. What calamity befell him? Caleb sat and searched the man's uniform. He found a picture of a woman holding a baby. He sat there for a while, staring at the picture, and thumbing through the worn pages of the German Bible. He thought of Lydia.

Artillery lambasted the hallowed landscape. Time was wasting. He could be a soldier, with killing as his trade. He tucked the Scripture inside his shirt, put the picture back in the dead man's pocket, and again pulled himself upright with the rifle.

His head thundered. He needed water. *Keep going, keep going. You can't die a coward, you good-for-nothing. You'll not tarnish your ancestors' good and fearless name.* He stumbled toward the nearest Union lines still three hundred yards off, wrestling his will with each step.

Across the quiet chaos of the battlefield, Caleb tried to make sense of his yellow deed; there was no reckoning. He remembered a time when he watched father dive into a drunken brawl to save a friend. He was just a boy then but watched Father toss men like sacks of grain. Charles Wright never flinched, never retreated. He came away with a few busted ribs and a black eye but the scolding he got from Mother was the worst. He heard his father's words as if he were standing right behind him. *Never quit, Son. You are a Wright and a Wright never leaves a job undone.*

Caleb lopped across the field toward the sounds of battle until he reached a massive lone oak on a gentle rise. To his right, two hundred yards away, a company of Rebs fought a regiment of Union men. The boys in blue were being slain, pinned down in a lethal crossfire. Caleb had a clean shot, and the blood bath below gave him rise to use it. He was a soldier and he would act like one, all the way to hell if that's what it took.

Propped against the hardwood, Caleb loaded the rifle with slow precision and rested it on a broken limb. He took aim like Ben taught and put his sight on a Reb near the end.

"This one's for the Wrights."

He fired. *Finish the job, Son. I raised no cowards.* One Reb fell, and three looked his way. A conical round screamed. Caleb loaded and fired again.

"Shoot the Piker on the hill. Kill that bastard!" Reb's shouted.

Caleb laid another onto Kentucky sod.

"He's pickin' us off!"

A dozen Enfields siphoned his way. Damn them to hell. Caleb beaded another.

In the Rebel line they placed bets on his blue-belly head. "Give ya a Yank sawbuck if you shoot off his cap."

Bullets tore his garments; their metal stingers bit. His shame expired. Chunks of bark splintered from the tree. Rebel lead reigned, but Caleb's metal barked back with equal ferocity. He loathed his cowardice as much as the Reb's disdained his resistance.

Arkansas and Tennessee Rebs joined the game to slay the lone Yank on the hill.

A new firestorm of lead hail pelted his coat. A Reb with a score to settle aimed at his hat; the bullet's aim was true and creased Caleb's skull. He spun and fell to unforgiving earth.

"Did you get him, Jacob?" yelled one Reb to another.

"Yeah, I got him."

"Want me to go finish him fer ya?"

"He's already finished." Jacob shot at least six times. His aim was good, but that Yank didn't flinch. And with another dozen in the hunt, the big bastard had lasted long enough to pick off a dozen of theirs. He made up his mind to check on the Bluebelly himself once the sun went down.

C H A P T E R

TWO

)))) ▶ ● € € (((

Our common country is in great peril, demanding the loftiest views,
and boldest action to bring it speedy relief.
—Abraham Lincoln, July 12, 1862

I T HAD BEEN two weeks since Lydia's brothers burned the
chicken coop as a nighttime diversion to help them escape their
mother, Adel, a tyrannical German immigrant that ran her
home, children, and husband with unparalleled resolve. They left
Lydia to her fate and sought refuge with the Fiftieth Ohio
Volunteer Infantry Regiment. She could forgive Ethan and Ren
but not Theo. He was her twin and second skin. How could he
abandon her without a word?

Lincoln's call for volunteers came in September. Within days,
Lydia's life emptied of brothers, cousins, and friends. Caleb Wright,
the man who strolled through her dreams, deserted her as well. The
only men left to her were Papa and Mister Brenham. The first she
would die for, the second, she would rather die than marry.

She was happy for her brothers, yet Theo's absence stole the
sun from her days. He was her best friend. They shared all their
dreams and deepest secrets. Or so she had thought. She wondered if

he felt guilty for leaving without telling her, or was he just reveling in his newfound freedom? If one could call the Army freedom.

Adel favored her boys, and Papa favored his baby girl; it was obvious and always had been. Lydia loved exploring the outdoors, riding her prize mare, Dolly, and working in the flowerbeds and gardens, but Mother was determined to keep her daughter's skin the color of snow, and kept her in the house most of the time doing worthless needlework and learning proper etiquette. The one indoor activity Lydia did enjoy was reading, but Mother thought there was no need for that either. Thankfully, Papa shared Lydia's passion and snuck her a book every chance he got.

Mother was raised with wealth and prestige in the German homeland, and she married Papa after he came to work for her father. She presumed he would always work for her father, move up in the company, and eventually take her father's place at the helm, but Papa had other plans, and within a year of their marriage he bought them passage to America. She never forgave him for it, but she was determined to establish herself in the new country and regain the status she had lost. Mother was formidable and had done an amazing job of accomplishing her goal. Lydia was her crown jewel, to be given to the highest bidder. The only one in the running that fit Mother's bill was Bradford Brenham, a widower with five children and a thousand acres that abutted the Weldishofer farm.

When Ethan, Ren, and Theo left home to join the war effort, Adel confined Lydia more than ever, peering over her shoulder to make sure she completed the needlework for her trousseau; her marriage vows were a mere two weeks away. Lydia had to dine with Bradford when he came calling, which to her consternation was nearly every night.

Before yet another supper with the bloated man, Adel made Lydia don one of the new silk dresses newly arrived from Paris. One was kitten-tongue pink and the other the blue of an October sky. They were gorgeous, but with the corset laced up tight they showed half of her breasts. Mother didn't seem to mind, but Lydia certainly did, and Bradford didn't need any encouragement. Lydia tugged and pulled at the bodice to no avail.

During dinner, the dumkopf barely took his eyes from her cleavage. She gave Mother hateful looks throughout the evening, and then to make matters worse, Mother insisted they take a carriage ride. "It's such a nice evening. It would be a shame to waste it. Don't you agree, Josef?" Papa had not answered but lit his pipe and walked out to the porch and his rocking chair.

Bradford acted the proper gentleman in front of her parents, save for staring at her breasts, but this was the first time they would be alone, and Lydia had her doubts.

The moon was full, pale and waxy just like his skin. Lydia sat on the farthest edge of the buggy seat, turned slightly away, listening to the rattle of the harness and the steady gait of the horses. She watched the countryside pass by. Tall maple trees lined the road, like ancient sentinels. Each beat of the horse's hooves seemed a drumbeat closer to the hell that would be her life. Bradford's pasty fat face made her nauseous, and the thought of his sausage fingers on her body was more than she could bear. How could Caleb leave her to this?

Bradford turned off the road into a moonlit meadow on the backside of his property. A doe and two spotted fawns gazed at them a moment before bounding off into the trees. This was a lover's moon, and Lydia's thoughts were not of Bradford Brenham but of tall, handsome Caleb Wright. He reined the horses to a stop beneath the haloed moon, and with nary a breath of warning, lunged for her cleavage. Fat lips rooted across her breasts and clammy fingers tugged at her laces.

"Stop it!" she screamed, slapping his balding head as hard as she could. He ripped her bodice open and yanked the fabric down. Greedily, he covered her tender pink nipple with his fat lips, sucking like a half-starved babe. This beast was no stranger to a lady's charms. He pinned her between the surrey's canopy and padded seat. Expert hands rummaged beneath her dress groping her petticoats. A wrestling match ensued. Lydia bit, scratched, twisted, and pounded anywhere she could.

His breath was sleet on winter's windowpane. "I am sick of your pretentious ways. I'll fight you every night if I have too, but I will have my way with you. You will be my wife in every sense of the word."

Bradford's hand dipped beneath her petticoats. Lydia struggled to get at his ear, when she did, she bit as hard as she could.

He jerked his hand from her skirts and slapped her hard across the face. She gasped and reacted in kind. His anger was apparent in his brutal grip as he moved into position; she seized the fool's folly and thrust hard with her knee; the widower's mouth gaped. She rolled from his weakened grasp and out of the rig, but her dress caught on the brake handle.

Bradford grabbed a handful of pink silk.

"Let go of me!" she shrieked.

"Even the finest filly gets bred," he spat.

Lydia jerked as hard as she could. The silk ripped and before he could react, she darted for the safety of the woods leaving half her dress behind.

When she finally stopped to look back, the buggy was gone. So be it. She covered herself the best she could and started through the woods. The four miles home would give her time to plan her escape. There was no one in heaven or on earth that could make her marry that man. Papa would see what Bradford Brenham had done, and then he would stand up to Mother. He had to!

Adel glanced at the pink blur that bounded in the door and up the steps. Josef's worried eyes looked to his wife. Adel rolled hers and took up her needle. "She'll find out soon enough what marriage and men are really all about."

Josef ignored the inference and went upstairs.

A knuckle knocked on Lydia's door. "Punkin, anything the matter?"

Lydia sat on her bed staring at her reflection in the tall beveled mirror. A bruise in the shape of Bradford's hand was beginning to turn blue and her eye was swollen.

"Can I come in?" Papa's voice was soft and worried.

Lydia donned her robe and opened the door.

Josef's hazel eyes sparked. His fingers trembled with restrained fury as he traced the swollen handprint on his Punkin's face. He pulled her close.

"Oh Papa, I can't marry him." Lydia burst into tears. "Look what he did to me. I hate him!"

Josef patted his daughter's back. He would kill Brenham if he ever lay foot on Weldishofer land again. Adel be damned.

"Papa, I can't stay. I can't!"

Josef's throat constricted. Damn Adel for driving their children away—first the boys and now his heart's treasure. To think of a life without them, to live alone with Adel, he would rather be dead.

"Where will you go?" His voice was sad and defeated.

Lydia detected a ray of hope amid her despair. She stepped back to gaze into his watery gray eyes.

"I don't want to leave you, Papa, but I can't marry him. I just can't, and you know Mother will never leave me alone if I stay."

Josef looked at the bruises on his precious flower. "Where will you go?" He asked again.

"Kentucky. I can find your renegade sons. Cousin Vera told me after Mass that she saw them signing up for the Army. I could look after them, cook, and do their laundry, and if they got wounded, I would write to you and let you know where we are and what's happening."

Lydia hoped that once she got there, she could convince Vera, her favorite cousin, to join her adventure. Vera had no reason to leave Aunt Esther, Papa's only sister was a nurturer and a loving mother, but maybe she would come.

Josef winced internally at the possibility that his sons might be injured or worse. He hadn't heard from them since they left and he knew Lydia would write. What choice did he have? His time raising the children was finished. They must choose their own paths now. He prayed God would keep them safe.

"Tonight, after your Mother is asleep, dress in Theo's field clothes and tuck your hair up. If you're going alone, you need to look like a man."

"Josef?" Adel's shrill voice bit the air.

He ignored her; his voice low and determined. His gaze never wavered from his precious daughter's eyes. "No one will approach a man riding unless they have a reason but a woman…"

"I understand, Papa."

"I'll come for you at midnight. Now hurry and start gathering your things."

Lydia wrapped her arms tight around his neck. She breathed his scent, of earth and sweet tobacco—felt his strength and his frailty. Her kiss lingered on his soft stubbled cheek.

"I love you, Papa. I will always love you no matter where I am."

Josef's eyes watered. "I know you do. But remember—don't let your guard down for anyone—ever. Understand?"

Lydia nodded and stifled the sobs that were rising within. "I promise."

Josef trudged slowly down the stairs while Lydia snuck off to her brother's room to gather his field clothes. She slipped on his boots; her tiny feet swam. She would wear her own. No one would notice from a distance.

Back in her room, she put the gray wool breeches on over her cotton petticoats. Thankfully, Theo wasn't a large man yet. She packed her corset in her small black trunk with extra undergarments and paused in front of the mirror to admire her voluptuous breasts beneath the airy camisole. Some girls talked of binding, but she saw no need to hide what God had blessed her with. Theo's double-breasted shirt fit just fine over her camisole even though the buttons protruded in all the wrong places. She decided to take Ren's tattered sack coat to cover her secret should the need arise. She braided her thick blonde hair, coiled it into a bun, and secured it with her favorite silver comb— a gift from Grandmother Rose in Germany for her sixteenth birthday. She plopped on Theo's floppy felt hat and tucked up the few stray strands.

Her reflection was no longer a teenage beauty but a scallywag boy off on an adventure. She scanned her childhood room, spotless as the rest of the house. Grandmother's flower-embroidered quilt covered her four-poster bed. Thick brocade curtains hung from the windows, and a Persian rug warmed the floor.

She opened the double doors of her spacious chifforobe and ran her hands lovingly through an array of silk dresses. How she hated to leave them. The autumn blue dress trimmed in delicate lace had yet to be worn. She laid it on the bed with her favorite wool cloak, and in a flurry of indulgence rolled them up in Grandmother's quilt.

The house was dark and quiet when she tiptoed down the stairs to the kitchen to fix a knapsack of Papa's sausages and Finia's dark rye bread. Finia had been with them for three years; she was an escaped slave from Kentucky and a marvelous cook. She loved her job and would stand up to Mother if it was for the better efficiency of the household. She could get by with it because if there was one thing Mother coveted as much as money, it was efficiency.

Lydia stuck the tea tin in her knapsack and wrapped one of Mother's best china cups and saucer in a kitchen towel. If she would have no civilities, she would still have tea.

Josef came to the door as promised. He wished he could go and fight for the country that had given him a second chance, but he was too old, too weak, and too tired. He shouldered the trunk, and carried the bedroll and saddlebags. He was proud of Lydia's bravery and determination; it came from the same well of courage he had used to leave the old country, despite Adel's vehement displeasure.

It was a cool breezeless night as Lydia watched him walk to the barn. The autumn moon's ambient glow bathed the fields of weeping grain in a somber serene light.

Josef fitted Dolly with Ren's best saddle and led her into the moonlit night. Dolly snorted softly and nudged her mistress' hand in search of a treat. Lydia kissed her soft muzzle and gave her the expected apple.

"You're giving me Ren's saddle?"

"If you have to ride like a man, Punkin, you might as well use the best."

Lydia hugged him. Her hand memorized the hills and curves of his dear sweet face. This might be the last time she ever saw him, she hadn't thought of that until now. Tears sprang to her eyes, and she embraced him once more.

"I love you, Papa."

Josef put a small leather pouch in Lydia's hand. "Take this so I won't worry." His heart was breaking.

Lydia clutched the bulging bag—Papa's rainy day money no doubt. There were no words. She kissed him again and slung into the saddle as she had often done, away from prying eyes, when racing Theo across the meadow. Papa smiled his approval and bound her belongings tightly behind the saddle.

"Write as soon as you can."

"I will, Papa."

Josef watched her disappear into the darkness. He leaned against the fence post and wished he could cry, but heritage dictated otherwise. The orchard needed pruning and he would be hard at it by first light.

Lydia was accustomed to men's attentions and stolen glances. To her dismay, she soon realized that as a bedraggled waif, she received none. The disguise worked too well for her taste, and she missed the admiring stares. She remembered how Caleb's cheeks flushed every time she swished her skirts at him in the store or on the boardwalks of New Alsace. She thought he would fight for her, but with a tip of his hat and nary a look back, he had ridden out of her life.

She rode all night, finally stopping to nap late in the morning in the seclusion of a deep wood by a soothing stream. The next day, she rode hard through the afternoon and spent the night on frosty ground, wrapped in Grandma's quilt. She hardly slept at all and when dawn's light whitened the sky to gray, she saddled Dolly and rode on to the Ohio River and the bustling town of Lawrenceburg.

She needed a place to change unnoticed. There was but one—
Aunt Marie and Aunt Francis's comfortable boarding house. They
were Papa's sisters and had immigrated as soon as he could send for
them. Neither ever married, and they loved doting on her.

Lydia knew they would be delighted to see her and equally
alarmed to hear that she was traveling alone. She would have to
fabricate a story, or they would telegraph Mother.

She tethered Dolly to the post in front of the house and
stretched Theo's hat down as far as it would go. Unlashing the
trunk, she hoisted it to her shoulder as Papa had done and walked
up the front steps.

Aunt Marie came to the door. She was a striking woman,
tall and thin with porcelain features and wisps of silver in her
coiffed hair.

"Welcome young man, do you need a room?"

Lydia was surprised that she didn't recognize her and decided
to play the ruse. She nodded.

Marie stepped back to let her pass through the foyer and into
the dining area. The stairs were just ahead.

"We're just now serving lunch. You're welcome to join us. The
meals are included in the boarding fee."

Lydia smiled beneath the uneven hat. Every table in the
dining room was filled with soldiers in new blue uniforms. Aunt
Marie took the lead and headed for the stairs. "You shall have the
room for a pittance as the others have. It is the least we can do
before they march all of you off to Kentucky."

Lydia felt like a child playing a practical joke and she wished
she hadn't done it, but it was too late to turn it around now. She
would have to play it through and confess later. She followed
Auntie up the walnut staircase to the third room on the left with a
number seven marked the door. When she stayed on visits with her

family, they slept on the third floor in the large guest rooms.

"There's fresh water in the pitcher and towels in the dresser. I'll put a plate back for you. When you're ready to eat, come on down to the kitchen."

"Thank you," Lydia mumbled in as deep a voice as she could muster.

As soon as the door closed, she stripped out of Theo's farm clothes and poured water into the basin. She knew she must look a sight from her travels, and the mirror quickly confirmed her assumption. She immediately set to a thorough bathing. When she was finished, she polished her dusty boots, buttoned them snug and donned her corset. It was such a comfort to be back in proper undergarments. She untied the bedroll and shook out the blue dress. It was a bit wrinkled, but it would have to do she thought, as it fell cool and silky over her head. Mother did know how to shop and she still had a standing account at her favorites in Paris. Evidently, she and Grandma shopped there a few times each year until Papa brought her to America. If Mother wasn't so hateful, Lydia might find some empathy for her. No matter, she thought, lacing the bodice up tight. Her smooth white hills were front and center; no question about it, the French certainly knew how to display a lady's charms. She tugged at the material to cover more but it was hopeless—she was overtly blessed and the cut was low. Oh well. She took a deep breath, powdered her breasts and spritzed on a bit of French perfume. Nearly ready for act two, she sat at the small dressing table, brushed her hair to the sheen of a midday sun, swept it up into a lavish French roll and secured it with Grandmother's comb. She wished she had the hat that matched the dress, but one could not very well carry a hat box on a horse while pretending to be a man. She checked her reflection, pinched her cheeks for color and smoothed her eyebrows.

She stood and twirled. The silk spun a whirl of blue about her before falling perfectly over her polished black boots. Carefully, she opened the door and peeked out. The dining room was still a buzz. The scrumptious fragrance of a fresh apple cobbler permeated the vacant hallway as she tiptoed up the stairs to the third floor and down the back staircase outside, the private entrance.

Several soldiers occupied the rockers on the front porch as she came around the house. There was an audible pause in conversation as they stood and swept off their caps.

Lydia smiled coyly, "Good afternoon, gentlemen."

There was a collective, "Ma'am," from the soldiers.

She gathered her skirts and walked up the steps, past the men to the door. She smoothed her dress, checked her hair, and knocked.

Aunt Marie answered the door and let out a flourish of words. "Francis! Francis! You'll never believe who's here." She swept Lydia into her arms. "Whenever did you get here? Is Adel at the mercantile and what of Josef? Probably buying some lumber for that new chicken coop?"

Awestruck, every man stopped mid-bite to gaze. A sudden, feigned busyness prevailed, silverware clinked, coffee cups rattled on saucers and there was a clearing of throats and shifting of chairs. After a moment, they resumed their meals and tried not to stare, but Lydia caught a few sneaking glances between bites. She adored it. That sort of behavior would have driven her brothers wild, especially the oldest, Ren.

Aunt Francis emerged from the kitchen wiping her hands on her flour-dusted apron. She was petite to Marie's height, her hair a deep auburn with a few strands of silver mixed through. She still maintained her hourglass figure and her feet, the size of a child's, peeped in black button boots from beneath the red calico. Francis loved pinks and reds and no matter what people said about them clashing with her hair, she wore them often, and in Lydia's opinion, wore them well. They fit her bright bold spirit.

"Bless my soul, Lydia Weldishofer, what brings you to grace our home? Where's Josef?"

"I'm alone." She watched the predicted shock shadow their faces. "It's rather a long story, I'm afraid. I'll tell you all about it over a piece of that apple cobbler I smell."

"Of course you will, Dear," replied Aunt Marie. "Right after dinner, and it's not apple cobbler you smell but Francis's infamous apple dumplings." Marie gazed at her wayward niece, and a hundred questions flowed through her mind. "I have so many questions."

The next morning after breakfast and answering most of her Aunt's worried questions; Lydia took some of Papa's dollars and bought a simple green calico dress and bonnet from the local mercantile. It was amazing to be free to roam the streets and shops at her leisure without Mother watching and directing her every move. She felt very grown up shopping alone, making choices without consult. It was heaven. She desperately wished Caleb were here so they could finally have a real conversation, without inhibitions.

As she came out of the store with her brown paper package, she noticed a crowd gathered in the town square around a raised wooden platform on which stood a terse little woman, dressed all in black and holding up a sign which read, "Sanitary Commission Fair. Support the Union Soldiers." People were donating barrels of flour, sauerkraut, slabs of bacon, quilts, bolts of cloth, and all manner of chattel. Lydia watched some men packing dozens of eggs into barrels filled with sawdust.

Perhaps, she thought, she could join the Sanitary Commission and get to her brothers that way. Feeling quite grown up, she took a coin from her pouch and made her way through the crowd.

"I would like to make a donation, Ma'am."

The woman took the money and unceremoniously tucked it in her apron pocket as she continued her litany to passersby. "Do you have a son on the line? A husband? Winter is coming folks, and these boys need blankets, coats and food. They will soon meet the loathsome traitors. Do you want them prepared? Bring everything you can spare and some you can't. Show God where your heart is. What is a little sacrifice from your nice warm home? They are sleeping in the elements, eating cold salt-pork and hardtack."

Lydia felt let down and watched the hawker wheedle coins from the people better than a preacher-man. She made her way back through the crowd.

The woman continued her patter. "You say you can't help. Are you going home to a hot meal? Are you sleeping in a warm bed tonight? We can't win this war with cold, hungry, tired boys. They need to be strong. They need to be prepared."

Lydia thought of her brothers and decided to give it another try. "I want to help," she shouted over the crowd. The people turned to see who spoke and the crowd parted to let the fancy lass through. Still dressed in her finest, Lydia walked poised and self-assured to the woman's platform although she was trembling inside. She had watched Mother play the part all of her life—putting the face forward that would gain her what she desired. Those life lessons were about to be put to good use.

The diminutive lady looked cross at being interrupted and peered over her pointy little nose at Lydia's earnest face. "Turn around," she demanded.

Lydia spun a circle.

"What is it that you think you can help with? These boys are going to war, not a Sunday social."

The crowd snickered.

"I can sew and cook."

"You are a little fool." The rude woman scanned the crowd for affirmation. "The battlefield is no place to look for a husband."

The crowd enjoyed the game at Lydia's expense. She flushed.

"And that goes for the rest of you young ladies. Look for a husband when they return victorious in a few months. For now, go home, and knit the men-folk warm stockings, and bring them to me. I will see that our soldiers get them."

"No Ma'am. You misunderstand." Lydia's German temper seeped into her words. "I have three brothers with the Fiftieth Ohio, and I intend to help them the best that I can, and that does not mean sitting at home knitting. If you won't take me, I will find someone who will."

"I'll take her!" a heckler shouted. The crowd laughed.

The woman pursed her lips. "You have no color to your face, no calluses on your hands. You say you have three brothers in the field? They are dust particles in the masses. I need women who know how to work, that can do with privations. It is obvious that you are a pampered young lady. Now go home where you belong."

Chuckles confirmed that some agreed.

A handsome doctor approached and smiled empathetically. "I'm afraid she's right Miss. The battlefield is no place for a lady of your sensibilities." He turned his attention to the woman. "Miss Crask, may I have a word with you about these medical supplies?"

The woman gave no more notice to Lydia. "Of course, doctor."

Humiliated and embarrassed, Lydia pressed back through the crowd. A man in a top hat and frock coat stood nearby on the boardwalk. He gazed at her and puffed his cigar before turning his attentions to the group of men with him. "I heard Hardee's Rebels are gathering around Harrodsburg, and General Buell's on his way to cut them off. There's gonna be a fight boys, mark my words."

Lydia took her package back to the house and spent the rest of the morning fuming at Miss Crask's audacity. She wished she could tell someone, but she didn't dare trust her plan to anyone. She was sure some of the boarders were in that crowd, and she would have to leave town before they gave her away.

She went into the kitchen where her Aunts were busy with lunch preparations and made two sandwiches while chatting with them. She excused herself and went upstairs to change and pack her knapsack with the sandwiches and a couple of apples off the tree in the backyard. She left two coins and a note of apology on her pillow, closed the small trunk, and snuck with it down the back staircase.

When she came around the house, four gracious soldiers vied for the privilege of carrying her trunk to the livery, where they saddled and packed Dolly for her. Lydia walked Dolly from the stable and to their astonishment and delight, swung into the saddle like a man. She adjusted her skirt but her pantaloons still showed. "Which way to Harrodsburg, Gentlemen?"

"You don't want to go that way, Miss," said one who was certainly stirred by her undergarments. "Things are heatin' up down there. Matter of fact, our Sergeant says we're headed there ourselves come morning."

"Perhaps I shall see you there," she smiled. "Now which way did you say it was?"

He smiled at the sweet damsel's grit. "I didn't, but if there's a chance I'll see you again, it's southeast."

She smiled again, "Thank you."

"Be careful, Miss."

"I will. Thank you, gentleman, see you in Kentucky."

Lydia gave a tap of her heels to Dolly's flanks and abandoned the humiliating town in high canter. Dolly sensed her mistress's determination and responded in kind, her hooves echoing a repetitive beat on the parched earth.

Within a few hours, the hot October sun seared Lydia's dark calico dress. Beads of sweat trickled between her breasts. The Kentucky countryside rolled brown with not a single blade of green grass in sight. Months of heat and drought had taken their toll. The day would be hot and long, leaving her plenty of time to think about what to do next. She had no destination in mind except to keep traveling south toward Harrodsburg.

She spent the next several nights in little towns along the way—Sugar Creek, Owenton, Monterey and finally Frankfort, which was held by Confederate forces. She spent the night in a boarding house there, where many Confederate officers had also taken rooms. She tried to glean information on their movements, but the talk was mostly of a possible move North to Indiana and how they would have old Abe licked inside a month.

She left town early the next morning, spent nights in Alton and Salvisa before finally making it to Harrodsburg. The town was swarming with Union troops but finding no face she knew; she spent only a night and continued south.

It was the seventh of October but could have been August with the heat. As the sun climbed the sky, Lydia sought a shady place with water to wait out the hotter part of the day. She finally stopped beneath a tall shady oak tree, parched and exhausted but there was no water in sight. She took two long drinks from her canteen and poured the rest into Dolly's mouth.

When she remounted, she thought of Papa's instruction about animal instincts and let Dolly take the lead with hopes she'd bring them to water. Within the hour, Dolly delivered. A small spring bubbled forth and flowed like soft music amid the arid landscape, a narrow stream dancing over emerald reeds. Lydia's shadow cast away the sun as she peered into the luscious cool liquid; an alarmed crawdad skittered beneath a stone.

She unsaddled Dolly and removed her bridle. Dolly dipped her muzzle in the cool water and tore at the fresh green shoots flowing beneath. Lydia looked around. Brown rolling hills lay before her and a deep wood behind. She seemed to be in a world alone. Perhaps it was the freedom of making her own decisions. Perhaps it was the heat. Whatever it was, Lydia did something she hadn't done since she was a child. She stripped down to her petticoats and camisole and hung her damp dress on a tree branch to dry. She inched her toes into the cool stream; it was heaven. Casting propriety aside, she slipped off her corset and lay down in the wondrous water. Holding her nose, she ducked her flushed, sweaty face beneath the cool dancing spring. Oh, wonder of wonders, had anything ever felt this good? She lay there a long while, relaxing, not thinking, just feeling the water flowing over and down her thinly clad body while the sun beat down.

When she was thoroughly refreshed, she left the water and spread Grandma's quilt in the shade of a magnificent maple tree where dappled sunlight danced. Feeling suddenly famished, she opened the saddlebag that was stuffed full of provisions she had purchased in Harrodsburg and removed a crisp apple and a hickory-smoked ham sandwich.

With her thirst and hunger abated, she lay back and quickly fell asleep. She woke to Dolly's soft muzzle nudging her.

"What is it girl?"

Her hair and clothing were completely dry, and she wondered how long she had been asleep. The sun had clouded over, and she sensed that they were no longer alone. Dolly shivered her withers and snorted in agreement. Lydia sat up and listened. There was a commotion down stream, with hundreds, perhaps thousands of male voices. She scrambled up, dressed in haste, saddled Dolly and strapped her small trunk tightly in place. Quickly, they rode into the thick woods. Twigs snapped behind them. Someone or something was following them. Lydia tapped Dolly's side with her feet. They moved faster. Dolly's ears perked when they reached the forest's edge. Lydia could scarcely believe her eyes. Lines of gray stretched to the horizon, thousands of Confederate soldiers were marching, the stars and bars, waving in the breeze.

Lydia turned Dolly back into the woods and cut straight across with a southward bent. She was certain they were still being followed, perhaps by a Rebel scout. She couldn't see anyone, but she didn't breathe relief until they emerged on a road and saw the stars and stripes waving tall and proud, amid endless lines of blue, sabers gleaming. She paused just long enough to slide her leg back over the saddle and take up a sidesaddle position. Her heart swelled with pride and apprehension at the magnificent sight of the Union army. Unit guidons were unfurled to the shallow breeze. She would serve these men, and no Miss Crask would stop her. Dolly pranced in place, waiting for her mistress to loosen the reins.

The rear guard spotted her as soon as she started down the road behind them and rode back to meet her.

"Whoa there, Miss. Where are you going?" the dusty soldier asked.

"I have information," she said with authority. "I saw the Rebel army."

"Did you now?" The two soldiers looked at each other. "And where might they be?"

"On the other side of those woods. About three miles to the north."

The guards gave each other a look of doubt.

"You don't believe me? Why would I concoct such a story?"

"Calm down, Missy. I never said I didn't believe you. I just find it hard to believe that you spotted the entire Rebel army when our scouts have seen nothing for two days."

"I happened on them by accident. I had detoured to find water."

"And I suppose you found that, too?"

"Yes, as a matter of fact, I did." Lydia held up her sweating canteen as proof and offered it to the hot dusty soldiers.

They both took a deep drink before handing the container back. "That's real good, Miss, thank you kindly. Not to doubt you but how do we know that water didn't come from some farmer's well round here?"

"Are you calling me a liar?"

"No Ma'am, just doing my job."

"I'm a nurse on my way to join the hospital corps. You may need my assistance sooner than you think. The entire Rebel army is but a few miles away, and I believe one of their scouts followed me through the woods."

"And you led him right to us. Thank you kindly for that."

Lydia was becoming irritated. Her brothers had teased her relentlessly and it had left her with a bit of a short fuse for such things.

"Gentlemen, do you intend to continue this charade or are you going to inform your commander?"

The soldier who had been questioning her swept off his hat and placed it over his heart in exaggerated gallantry. "You are so right, Miss. We would be remiss in our duties if we did not escort you to our commander. Please accept our apologies and follow us." The other soldier smirked. They were enjoying their pretty diversion.

They'll get theirs, she told herself as they moved toward the mass of blue, just as soon as their commander finds out I speak the truth. Dolly followed the soldier's mount while the other took up the rear. A chorus of hoots and hollers erupted down the lines as the trio passed. Amid their pining, Lydia searched in vain for a familiar face.

The Captain rode back, shouting orders at the hecklers.

"Eyes forward!" He looked at Lydia's rosy cheeks and tipped his hat. "Sorry about that Miss."

"Sir," her escort interjected, "this lady says she found water and has information about Rebel movements."

Lydia extended her hand. "Thank you, Captain."

He took her hand. "If you don't mind my asking, why ever is a lady of your graces traveling alone?"

"I heard there would soon be a battle down this way and I am determined to become a nurse for the Union Army. My brothers are serving in the Fiftieth Ohio and I intend to be available to them, should they be wounded."

An amused smile crossed the Captain's too handsome face. Lydia found that she was immediately irritated but was determined not to show it.

"While I am sure that my men would be delighted to have you for a nurse, I cannot permit you to travel any farther. However, I would be most grateful if you could tell me where you found water. My men and horses are in a desperate way."

"I will do better than that, Captain. I will show you where the water and the Rebels are."

The officer looked to her escorts.

"She says they're on the other side of these woods and north a few miles."

Lydia extended her canteen to the Captain.

"Thank you, no. I'll not indulge until my men are taken care of. Privates, send a scouting party with her and report back to me as quickly as possible. We will continue south."

Lydia's temper flared. "Captain, you can turn your army around right now, get your water, and engage the enemy."

"If you will pardon my saying so Miss, I can hardly turn an army of ten-thousand around on your say so. Now if you will kindly show my men where the water is, we would be forever in your debt."

"I understand Captain, but at least let them rest here until you can substantiate my story. Why march them further south when they'll just have to turn around in short order?"

He looked at the sassy lass for a moment then back to her guards. "Privates you have your orders."

"Yessir," they saluted.

Lydia was undaunted. She considered these thousands of men as if they were Caleb or her brothers. "Captain, would you concede to allow the entire Rebel army escape, while they are right beneath your nose. I wonder what President Lincoln would think of that, or for that matter, your Commander."

The Captain cleared his throat and raised his ass an inch.

"I would not want to be you when he finds out that you knew of the enemy's position and told him nothing."

The Captain, searched the lady's eyes, she could certainly hold her own. He wondered if perhaps she was a Rebel spy sent to slow them down. He had heard of the Southern Belle's tenacity and she certainly fit that description. However, if what she said were true, Colonel Webster would want to know immediately. But how was it possible that she could spot the whole Rebel army when they had seen nothing since they left Indiana? *Damn.*

"Privates, escort this lady to Colonel Webster." The Captain's eyes spoke volumes to his subordinates. "I want you to accompany her personally. Do you understand?"

"Yessir!" They saluted and moved to each side of Lydia's horse.

"What are you doing?"

"We're taking the reins, Miss."

"You most certainly are not!" Lydia wrapped the leather straps around her hands.

The Captain intervened. "The truth of your story remains undetermined."

Lydia glared.

"Please allow my men to do their job."

Lydia tossed the reins at them. "Very well Captain, but I will expect a full apology when the truth comes to light."

A thousand eyes surveyed the female landscape as she was led up the line to the Commander's regimental colors.

"Colonel Webster." The Private saluted.

The Colonel returned the salute and moved his horse from the marching masses. "Private."

"Capt'n Morris had us escort this lady to you. She claims to have found water and says she saw hundreds of Rebs back a few miles down the creek."

"Thousands." Lydia corrected.

The Colonel surveyed the beautiful lass and tipped his hat.

"Is this true?"

Lydia sat straighter. "It is." The Colonel seemed like a nice man. "I did see the Confederates. They have gathered by the creek on the other side of those woods, a few miles to the north."

She waited for a response. He gave none. This was the

opportunity she needed. "I'm on my way to serve as a nurse for the Fiftieth Ohio, my brothers' regiment. I want to tend to them should they be injured. I could cook for you if you'll let me travel with you until I find them."

The Colonel's response was matter of fact. "This is an army of men, Ma'am. There are no women here, and there are plenty of reasons for that."

"Then, Colonel, you are in a desperate way. I am so glad I came. I make a wonderful apple pie."

The Colonel raised his eyebrows and perused the comely lass. What lay beneath the brazen façade and why, he wondered, was she traveling alone?

"Your offer is tempting, however, we will soon engage the enemy and if what you say is true, it is imminent. Therefore, I must insist that you allow my men to escort you back to the safety of Harrodsburg."

"I understand your concern Colonel, but if you could please send the scout out right away to validate my story, you might have a change of heart. If, as you say, battle is imminent then you will soon be in need of my services."

Colonel Webster smiled. He liked this gal, but war was hell and choices difficult. "I thank you for your concern, truly I do, but I must insist that you leave the management of this army in my capable hands." He turned his gaze to her escorts. "Privates, do as your Captain ordered."

"Yessir!"

Colonel Webster tipped his hat to Lydia, saluted his privates, and put spurs to his horse.

Lydia's heart sank as she watched him gallop back up the line. She had lost her argument and her chance to stay with the army and find her brothers. The soldiers led her back past the long lines of admiring eyes. She sat straight and indignant. If they thought she was going back when she had come this far, it was they who would be played the fool. Why would no one look beneath her appearance and give her heart and hands a chance to prove their worth? Miss Crask saw her as a husband seeker, the Colonel as a threat to the very men she sought to give care, and Mother kept her from the sun—pure and white, to be auctioned off to the highest bidder. Did no one care about what was under the seamless veneer? Did they think she had no heart, dreams, or desires of her own? And what of her opinions? If they mattered for naught, why did God give her a brain to think with and a heart to break?

Papa valued her for all that she was, and he taught her how to fight with words and brain, as fierce as her brothers fought with brawn and brute strength.

The privates saluted their Captain. "The Colonel ordered us to escort her back to Harrodsburg."

"Then get to it and take Schantz and Kunkel with you. They can check her story and report back while you escort her the rest of the way." He looked at Lydia. "I'm sorry Miss, but your safety must come first."

Lydia said nothing. *Be patient, Lydia. Be patient.*

An hour into her humiliating retreat, the soldiers looked at each other and then back to their charge. "Our apologies, Miss. We know you meant well, but this is no place for a woman."

"It's a little late for that gentleman. If you are truly sorry, you will let me be on my way. I can assure you that within a fortnight you will be in need of my services. Look over there."

The scouts looked at the cloud of gray in the distance. "Holy shit," Schantz exclaimed. "We'll ride back and let the Colonel know! Come on Kunkel." His voice pulsed with excitement as they turned tail and galloped down the road like they were on a mission from God.

Her escorts looked like whipped puppies. It was time to take the advantage. "There is a place a short ways from here, by the stream where we can't be seen. I have some nice ham sandwiches and delicious red apples. We could have a picnic and cool ourselves."

"We would like to do that Miss, but we have orders."

"I am fully aware of your orders, gentlemen. Now that you know my story is true, the least you can do is give me a chance to rest and take nourishment before we continue. Riding sidesaddle is not a comfortable proposition for long paces."

The privates looked at each other. "I guess we could stop for a bit," one conceded.

"Have to eat sometime," his comrade agreed.

"Perfect," she purred. "May I show you the way?"

A look of doubt crossed between them.

"Gentleman, I am a lady riding side saddle. Where would I go and why should I try? You would catch me in no time. Now please..." Gently she loosed the reins from their hands and took the lead. Dolly sauntered slowly while her mistress removed her bonnet. "I am truly suffocating in this heat," she said undoing the neck buttons of her dress. "I wish I was wearing my summer white. Perhaps I could change once we get to the creek." She released the pin from her hair and let it fall loose down her back. She looked back at her captors and dislodged another button.

They shifted in their saddles.

"Ah, there it is gentlemen. Shall we dine?"

Lydia nibbled an apple and chatted with them as if they were her brothers. They soon forgot they were her guards, and for a brief hour or two, they were spellbound by the aristocratic lass who shared the contents of her knapsack.

When they were fully relaxed and showing fatigue, Lydia began to unlace her boots. "Would you be so kind as to help me off with these boots?"

The soldiers stole glances at each other and eagerly did as she asked. She was leading them by the nose now. She stood and hiked her petticoats to her knees, rolled down her stockings and took them off. Delicately she slid her feet into the cool stream.

"Oh, it's heavenly, just heavenly. You really should try it. I bet your feet haven't been out of your boots for days."

"You're right about that," said the dark-haired lad.

"Well, it isn't good for your feet you know. They need to breathe, and as your self-appointed nurse, I insist that you take better care of them. So, I'll go over here and change into my summer white, and you two give your feet a nice cool soak."

The young men smiled at their beautiful champion. Lydia picked up her shoes and stockings, and waltzed over to Dolly's tether and pretended to untie her trunk. They whispered and smiled with an occasional glance her way, and it wasn't long before they were leaned back on the bank, hats over their eyes and feet in the water.

She waited a while longer until they were obviously asleep and eased into the saddle with her skirts tucked high. She sat like a man and quietly disappeared into the thick forest.

Some latent sense of soldiering soon woke them.

"Shit, Virgil. She snookered us."

"Where'd she go?"

"Hell if I know! Come on!"

Groggy and agitated, they pulled on their boots and took off after their escaping charge.

Dolly navigated the twine of the Kentucky woods. The whereabouts of Rebs or Yankees remained unknown until they emerged onto a massive rolling meadow. Within minutes, her guards crested a hill about a hundred yards away.

"There she is!" Virgil shouted. Lydia's duped escorts put hell to their mounts.

A few yards into the meadow, Lydia saw them riding at full stride. "We've got company Dolly. Show them what you're made of girl." Dolly jumped to her mistress's call and took off across the vast expanse of meadow, her muscles pumping without restraint.

The soldiers behind barked commands, leather smacked and hooves pounded. They were gaining, their faces flushed with anger and determination. Dolly's withers foamed, but Lydia spurred her on. The soldiers closed the gap to a mere fifty yards by the time Lydia reached the next wood. When Dolly dove in, Lydia ducked, her heart pounding to the tempo of Dolly's hooves. Still the soldiers came.

Out of the woods, a pasture separated by low stone walls and a whitewashed fence beyond them came into view. A pristine village of tall, small white buildings gleamed in the distance, surrounded by acres of pasture and fields. Lydia kicked Dolly's withers, and they galloped quickly across the pasture sailing over two stone walls and the whitewashed fence into a garden where a woman was gathering herbs.

The woman looked up just in time to see Dolly crest the four foot fence. Within minutes, the soldiers were at the fence on their heaving beasts. The woman calmly sat down her ample willow basket and wiped her hands on her apron. She looked at Lydia, then at the infuriated soldiers.

Lydia patted Dolly's wet neck and glowered at the men. They in turn eyed her pantaloons and hoisted skirt. She held her head high and slid back to a sidesaddle position, shaking her skirt down over her legs. They smirked.

"Why don't you just go away and leave me alone?"

"We have orders to escort you to Harrodsburg and that's what we intend to do."

The woman interrupted. "What is your business with this woman?"

"We have orders to take her back to Harrodsburg, Ma'am."

"If she wishes to go with you, she may. If instead, she seeks sanctuary, she shall have it."

Virgil took off his hat, wiped his brow, and reseated it. "Ma'am, we have orders from Colonel Webster."

"Your orders can be changed, can they not?"

"Ma'am, that woman there…" He removed his blue cap and aimed it Lydia's way. "…has disobeyed a lawful order and fled our custody."

"Everyone is fleeing something, my good men."

"With all due respect, Ma'am, we intend to take her back to Harrodsburg as the Colonel ordered." He moved to dismount.

"Soldier," the woman broke in, "we are a God-fearing community and bear no weapons. As such, we may grant this woman sanctuary if she wishes. Our orders come from a higher authority than your Colonel. We care for all who are in need, Union and Confederate, and we will continue to do so until the need is no more. If you are dismounting for rest and food, please proceed and you are welcome, however, if you dismount for dishonorable reasons then I must insist that you turn around and go back to your unit."

The woman turned to Lydia. "Do you claim sanctuary with the Believers of Pleasant Hill?"

Lydia looked at the flustered soldiers. "It is true that I ran from them, and according to Colonel Webster's order they may take me back." She turned her attentions to Mary. "However, I am not in the Army and only offered my services and information on Rebel movement to the Colonel. I have traveled many days to find my brothers and to serve the army as a nurse. I will not be forced to return when I am so close. So, as I see no alternative, I claim sanctuary."

The soldiers glowered.

Mary addressed them. "It is done. You must remember that God accomplishes all intentions, good and bad, to His will."

"Ma'am, we can't…"

"You shall return without your charge. God has brought this lost soul to us and she is my sister in Christ. All will be well with you upon your return."

Like hell, they thought. The soldiers swapped a glance and without further exchange, tipped their hats, wheeled their horses, and rode away.

Lydia watched them go and felt a twinge of guilt as she wasn't angry with them, but with their orders. They were two of the soldiers she had come so far to serve, and she hoped they would never need her assistance.

"Thank you," Lydia said to the woman.

"Thank the Lord, not I." The woman extended her hand. "You are here by the will of God."

Lydia took the woman's calloused hand and slipped from the saddle.

"Let me get you some refreshment, and please call me, Mary."

"Thank you Mary that sounds lovely, but I need to take care of Dolly first."

"The Brothers will tend to her at the stable."

"Thank you, again."

"There is no need. A Christian can do no less."

Lydia marveled at the articulate simplistic design of the immense white buildings as they strolled down the shady lane. The entire settlement was pristine, an oasis in the storm that was her life. Almost immediately, her body and spirit began to relax.

"It's so beautiful, Mary."

"What is your given name?"

"Lydia Weldishofer. I'm from Indiana."

"A beautiful name. What are you running from, Lydia? You are so young to be traveling alone and so far from home."

"My brothers are with the Fiftieth Ohio. I had hopes of being a nurse for their regiment. That's why I came. Those soldiers and their commander wanted me back in the safety of Harrodsburg, away from the fighting. If I was worried about my safety, I never would have come."

"You speak a partial truth."

Lydia looked into Mary's brown windows of wisdom.

"What do you mean?"

"It is Providence that brought you here. I know this because you are the answer to my earnest prayers."

Spirit sparks rippled through Lydia's soul. "I'm not sure I understand." In some strange way she felt like she had known Mary all of her life.

"It is not necessary. It will be revealed to you in time."

They left Dolly in the capable hands of a solemn bearded Brother, and Mary took her over to the immense kitchen in the main hall. Lydia had never seen such an organization. Massive cast-iron kettles simmered over fires while Sisters of the society in their pale blue gowns with white triangles pinned over their bodices and blue caps kneaded dough in three-foot wooden bread troughs. The smell was heavenly. They spoke little but everyone seemed to be in good spirits and content with their present task.

Piles of squash, turnips, potatoes, parsnips and carrots filled bushel baskets along the wall. The next room served as the bakery where dozens of loaves of bread rose on a long wooden table covered in flour and two brick ovens filled an adjacent wall. The heat was stifling and the Sisters working the bakery were bathed in perspiration, yet their faces portrayed a peace of heart Lydia was just beginning to understand. They seemed satisfied in one another's company, taking the dictation of bread making, simple ingredients and the labor of their hands.

"How many people live here?" Lydia asked Mary.

"Nearly three-hundred."

"Are they cooking for everyone?"

"Yes and many more. We have been cooking and baking non-stop since the troops began coming through last week. It has taxed everyone to keep up."

"Have you seen Federal troops?"

"Yes, many thousands."

"Which way did they go when they left?"

"Most of them left yesterday down the Mackville road, but there are still a few hundred camping by the creek. They have plans to leave in the morning. A battle is surely imminent, and that is why I believe you are the answer to my prayers."

Lydia followed Mary down a flight of steps to the largest stone cellar she had ever seen. The fall bouquet was a comforting mixture of sweet apples, persimmons and the musky earth scent of potatoes; rows of shelves were weighed down with summer's preserved bounty and barrels of fresh cider filled the rest of the room. Mary popped the lid on one and ladled the sweet cool nectar into two tin cups.

Lydia quenched her thirst with the first cup and savored the full sweet flavor of the second. "Mary, this is as good as my Papa's, I didn't think it possible."

"We use all of the bounty that God gives us; the bruised, imperfect apples make the sweetest cider. We also have many special varieties that have been propagated by the Brothers over the years."

"I wish I could send Papa some seeds. The orchard was our special project."

"I am sure that could be arranged."

"Do you really think so?" Lydia could hardly restrain her excitement. She would be able to send Papa a special gift he could get nowhere else.

Mary smiled a motherly smile and led Lydia out of the cellar and across the compound to a building set apart. "This is where our new arrivals and guests stay. If you should find yourself in need, ring this bell and someone will come to your aid."

Lydia looked at the cast iron bell mounted on top of a tall white post. A long rope knotted at the end hung within easy reach. She followed Mary inside. The room was immaculate though austere. All that occupied the eight-by-ten enclosure was a narrow bed, a blanket chest, a nightstand with a simple glass lantern, and a washstand. The white porcelain pitcher was filled with cool fresh water.

"Take your rest and I will come for you in an hour to break bread with the community."

"Thank you, Mary. Thank you very much."

Mary smiled and left her to the peaceful quiet of solitude.

Lydia removed her dress and washed her face and neck. Her trunk had been delivered to her room, and she retrieved clean undergarments and wished she had a clean dress beside the blue silk. She definitely could not wear the silk; perhaps Mary would let her borrow a dress so that she could wash her own.

A single waist-high window provided light and ventilation. From it, Lydia looked down upon the remaining Union troops camped along the creek. Despite the drought, water flowed through the village; it seemed amazingly charmed. She would go down to the troops after dinner and look for her brothers.

Lydia woke an hour or so later to a soft tapping at the door.
"Who is it?"
"Mary."
"Come in."
Mary opened the door.
Lydia quickly got up and began to don her soiled gingham. "Do you have a gown I could borrow tomorrow? I'm afraid mine is in desperate need of washing."
"Of course, I'll bring you one after dinner."
They walked to the dining hall where long smooth, walnut trestle tables overflowed with autumn's bounty. A multitude of windows were open on either side of the great hall to allow optimal airflow across the room.

Lydia took a seat next to Mary. Striking hand-hewn wooden serving bowls sat before them, heaped high with snowy mashed potatoes, fried apples and summer squash. Heavenly aromas emitted from the large platters of braised vegetables and thick slices of juicy pork, studded with garlic and seasoned with rosemary. There were gravy boats filled to the brim with smooth brown gravy and wood cutting boards with fresh-churned butter and loaves of fresh-baked bread.

A white-haired gentleman said grace over the feast. Lydia watched to see how others served themselves and followed their example. The brethren ate in silence. She didn't mind. She was famished and ate with relish, consuming more than she thought possible.

After dinner, Mary took her to the apothecary garden. Lydia was again amazed at the neat rows of herbs and flowers, many she knew and many she did not. Wonderful scents filled the air as her skirt brushed against the aromatic plants.

"Many will be in need of our assistance very soon and I have so much to do to prepare. Would you help me with the medicines?" Mary asked.

"Of course. You have so many plants I've never seen before. I would love to learn what they are used for and how to prepare them."

"Wonderful!" Mary handed Lydia an armload of peppermint, lemon grass, bee balm, valerian, and several other herbs. "We have much to speak of, but there is no time to tarry. While you slept, the remainder of the Union troops received word to leave at once. It seems that the Rebel army was spotted setting up camp near Doctors Creek over by Perryville. It is likely that the battle will begin before sunrise. Therefore, we must prepare the medicines and leave as quickly as possible."

"I wonder if the stream I showed them was Doctors Creek." Lydia mused out loud while she followed Mary into a small building where large bunches of herbs hung drying, suspended upside down from the ceiling.

"Your role is of no consequence. This war was preordained many years ago when the first white man took the first black man into bondage. You have come to me on the wings of a prayer and resurrected dreams from my youth with your determination and bravery."

Bravery? Was that what you called a girl who fled her Mother because she was too scared to fight?

She came to find her brothers, it was true—but what she should have done was shimmy down the roof and follow Caleb when she had the chance.

What would Mary think if she knew the truth?

THREE

Pine Ridge Settlement School
Spring 1939

T HE REPEATED RAPS of Grandma Lydia's cane on the banister woke me before dawn. I crammed the pillow over my head and drifted back toward restless sleep. Just as the haze settled over my brain, she thumped the pine floor with renewed fervor.

"Matilda!"

Her voice was old and shrill and sent my nerves screaming. I threw back the covers and stared at the barely visible flaking plaster ceiling. Damnable old woman. My reluctant body rolled out of bed like a thousand times before, my toes curled when they touched the chilly floor. I hauled on my old flannel robe in the predawn light, poked my feet through worn-out slippers, and shuffled to the top of the stairs. The percolating confab was waiting below. Would she never run out of years?

"I've been at my desk for some time, Matilda." She began before I was halfway down. "There are some parental inquiries that you neglected to mention."

"You woke me in the middle of the night to talk about that?" I snapped.

My indignation fueled Grandma's.

"Matilda Ann Wright, how can I give you the full responsibility of this school when you continue to act irresponsibly?"

My patience frayed at the seams. It was too early for this. I put my backside to her remark and shuffled toward the kitchen. "I'm going to make tea," I grumbled.

"Bring a few of those plum kolaches I made yesterday."

Go to hell, my thoughts burned, and yet my actions were resigned to our age-old routine. I stoked last night's embers in the ancient wood-burning range. Grandma's words echoed. *How can I give you the full responsibility of the school when you continue to act irresponsibly?* I added kindling and a piece of ash to the coals and slammed the damn iron door. I was her stooge, and everyone knew it. Teacher in residence, handmaiden to all, I begged for every blessed penny to run this joke of a school. Grandma would never relinquish the purse strings. Our pre-morning battle was simply another ruse to make me think otherwise. We beat this habit to death, and the clash would never cease until one of us was dead, and by the look of things, that would most likely be me. At ninety-four, Grandma showed no signs of stopping: up at five, in bed by seven, seven days a week, three hundred and sixty five days a year. She was a veritable antiquated timepiece, a goddamned time bomb—ticking, ticking, ticking. Before long, she would blow me right out of my mind.

I loitered in the kitchen as long as Grandma would tolerate and a few minutes more. Tea tray in hand, I entered the parlor and glared at the back of her head. The queen waited upon her needlepoint chair, sitting as proper as her ancient bones would allow. To my annoyance she wore a lifetime of creases with gentle grace. At thirty-five, I had failed to master an ounce of poise.

Grandma's watery blue orbs bespoke an insurmountable spirit as she watched me pour the tea. The liquid amber swirled in the translucent pink china decorated with hand-painted butterflies inside and out. The tea service was an anachronism in these rugged hills and came with the rest of the inheritance years ago.

My eyes moved to wavy windowpanes through which morning's light silhouetted our coronet of lush mountains. To most, they gave comfort, a feeling of being nestled in earth's womb. For me, they were a symbol of the isolation I felt inside and out.

"Mattie, I want you to have this." Grandma's shaky hands removed the butterfly necklace she had worn since time began. "Take it and wear it. You will need it to gain entrance to sights and roads you have yet to travel."

The butterfly quivered and blinked in the first rays of sunlight as it dangled from her trembling fingers. What was the crazy old bitty up to now?

"What is this all about, Grandma?"

"You must unravel my threads and put them right, Mattie. I should have given it to you long ago."

More riddles. "Grandma, I am honored that you would entrust your necklace to me, but I don't want to fix your past. I can't even run my present, as you have so aptly pointed out. And if I wanted to help, which I don't, I wouldn't know how. You've told me nothing about your life beyond this valley."

"My time is short, Mattie."

Play another tune, Grandma. "Did you have another dream about Grandpa last night?" *Did I care?*

Grandma placed the necklace in my hand and folded her hands over mine. A bolt of lightning shot through my body and memories flooded my mind. Grandma's face began to fade from view. *What was happening?*

"Do you hear the thunder, Mattie?" she said softly.

I was viewing a winter's day when I was ten.

"You are the lightning within." Her voice was distant like it was coming down a long narrow tunnel.

The blizzard was raging, and I was tired of being housebound. I remembered it like it was yesterday. I hadn't thought of it in years, and when I did, it had always been foggy like a dream—this was running like a picture show. I was begging Grandma to let my best friend, Callie Dawn, come over and play. She told me for the umpteenth time that the snow was too deep and the wind too mean for Callie Dawn to cross the hollow that separated her and Levi's tiny cabin from Grandma's spacious home. I knew Callie Dawn was going stir crazy, over there in that tiny shack, with Levi whittling and singing.

Grandma was in a mood and had scolded me time and again for being underfoot. When she finally busied herself with lunch preparations, I snuck into her bedroom. Being around Grandma was like being pecked to death by a chicken, and it had the distinct effect of making the most angelic child do something naughty—not that I was ever angelic.

I climbed the footboard of her enormous feather bed and somersaulted into downy bliss. I locked eyes with the handsome soldier in the portrait that hung above Grandma's pillows.

"Hi Grandpa, do you want to play?"

Was it my imagination or did his steel-blue eyes flash amusement? I scampered from the bed, yanked Grandma's magenta silk robe off the hook and twirled in it for Grandpa to see.

"Do I look pretty?"

I swirled the second time and something caught my eye. There was a slender door beneath the wooden peg that had held the robe. I looked back at Grandpa. He seemed to concur with my curiosity.

The door squeaked when I drew it open, and a cool breeze brushed past. Dark, dusty stairs beckoned. Where was Callie Dawn when I needed her? She was the brave one. My feet defied my hesitation, and slowly they crept up the gloomy stairs, taking me with them. Afraid of spirits, afraid of Grandma and spiders, I tiptoed about, peeking beneath sheet ghosts that filled the attic. Treasures abounded: a baby buggy, beveled mirror, rocking chair, and untold sealed crates and trunks of various sizes and description. I squealed with delight when I uncovered a mannequin dressed in a regal silk wedding gown. Unable to reach all of the buttons on the dress, I pushed the mannequin over, and it toppled with a thud. Floor dust jumped.

Within minutes, I had it on and stood admiring my reflection in all of its silken beauty. I waltzed about the attic. The floor jiggled. I stopped. The floor liquefied beneath me and I began to sink toward faint unfamiliar voices, like whispers from the back pews. I screamed.

Grandma's face came back into focus and I relayed what I had seen.

"All these years I thought it was just a dream. Was I really sinking into the floor?"

"You were sound asleep on that big old feather bed. The mannequin was on the floor, and the dress was lying in a heap nearby. When I woke you, you told me the same story. You had a gift for telling fantastic stories, you know."

"The stories were true. You just never believed me."

Grandma's eyes went hazy with that faraway look that was so common these days.

"I know that now. I could not accept it then."

"Accept what?"

"Your stories. If I believed you and what you saw, then I would have to believe that you were communing with the dead and that was beyond my grasp. Papa often said, "Gone is gone. You can move forward or not at all, but you can never go back."

"What are you talking about, Grandma, and what does it have to do with me?"

"After the war everything was so different. Levi tried to tell me time and again about your Gift, but I refused to hear. I didn't believe in his voodoo. I believed what I could see and touch. Germans are a practical people. We believe in the work of our hands and the prayers of our soul, nothing more."

"Grandma, I don't understand. What Gift?"

"Open your heart, Mattie. Listen for the whispers that you have heard all your life."

"I've been listening for thirty-five years, Grandma. Listening to everyone's reasons for leaving, listening to your reasons why I must stay. Listening for answers to prayer…" *A tiny grave beneath thick wild roses flashed in my mind.* My voice caught. "…answers that never came." I forced it away. "You're born and you die, and there's a whole lot of hurt in between."

Grandma's eyes were unwavering. "You were young and innocent then and that was the beginning of your journey. Khalidah tried to make me understand, as did Levi. I refused to listen, to see, to believe. In doing so, I hampered your journey Mattie, and for that I am truly sorry. But now it's time for you to look at your life, what it was, is, and can be. So much rests on your shoulders Mattie. You are all I have now. You are all the school has."

Old feelings stirred, anger leached; I forced them down and swallowed hard. I didn't want to have this conversation. I didn't want to relive or remember. All those years, she had admonished my imagination, scolded me for making up stories and telling lies. The strange images and dreams never left me; I just quit talking about them. I was afraid I had some kind of head sickness and that Grandma would send me off to some insane asylum if she knew. For her sake and mine, I lived two lives; the one everyone saw, and the one I knew. Only Levi and Levi's mother, Khalidah, understood, and I sought them out day after day to assure me that I wasn't crazy. *No. It was too late to change, too late to start over.* I turned to Grandma, my arms crossed and my face defiant.

She read through my granite facade.

"You must move forward, Mattie."

"I tried. You wouldn't let me. It's too late now." Resurrected ghosts rose like mountain mist from the depths of my soul. "I don't want to move anywhere, not anymore. I have no husband and no children to call my own. I have lived alone and I will die alone, and that, my dear Grandmother, is the way that I want it. My baby lies cold and dead just like my dreams."

"You have the children of these mountains to consider, Matilda. Our lives are never our own. Open your heart and embrace them. They need you as much as you need them. I was wrong to admonish your Gift. I know that now—you have so much time left, Mattie, embrace your destiny."

Once again, I saw Khalidah's dark-skinned face, the urgency in her green gold-flecked eyes—eyes like Levi's—like mine. I felt the urgency in her hand as she grasped mine—saw her slipping away from me—the only gentle woman in my life. I heard her last quivering words, just as I did on every sleepless night of the full moon.

"Child, you are the Chosen. You must step into the great darkness and bind-up the threads of time…"

Khalidah knew my defiant ways.

"If you refuse…" Her voice came hard as she used her last breaths to try and make me understand. *"…if the seed is not planted…the*

portal will close forever." She held my hand, emptying her life's force into mine with a power that was unbearable and terrifying to a ten year-old child.

"The future rest in your hands… your destiny is the world's only hope, Mattie."

Her strength vanished with those words. Her hand clung to mine even after death.

Levi thought I forgot. I never did.

Sorrows of a lifetime weighed upon me, an emotional tidal wave that threatened to sweep me out to sea. "No, Grandma. All of these years, you've harped on me, kept me at arms length when I needed your touch, and now you want me to just open myself up? Well I can't. I won't."

"Matilda, you must." Grandma's voice sounded like Khalidah speaking to me and for a moment I saw Khalidah sitting where Grandma sat.

"No," my voice cracked, fear spiked, and I was ten again. Life's heartaches threatened to purge themselves from my soul. "I won't!" I ran from the room and out of the house as images tumbled in vivid relief: the wedding altar, abandoned woodland paths, suffocating hills, and many, far too many, cold gray stones. What had Grandma done? I didn't want to examine my worthless life. I didn't want to finish her unfinished business. I ripped open the garden gate and fell to my knees beside Mama's yellow rambling rose. The floodgates opened and raindrops poured from my desolate soul, as un-tethered emotions ripped up and out. The sounds that emanated from my mouth were foreign and grotesque, the mortal pain excruciating. I wanted to die.

I clutched the rose canes, their thorns pierced deep, I wanted the pain, something I could control. "Mama…"

FOUR

Pine Ridge Settlement School
Spring 1939

S INDBAD PURRED AND pushed his way beneath my
body, up to my tear-stained face. I buried my face in his long
black fur and wished the cuddly creature could talk. I picked
him up, and together we walked around the garden.

Hundreds of red jewels blinked from beneath emerald foliage.
At least twenty quarts of strawberries needed to be picked. I could
envision the thick red jam boiling while I stood for hours on my
feet to keep up the relentless stirring it required, until finally hot,
red liquid would flow down both sides of the large wooden spoon
to form a single sugary gem. Then it would be poured into jars,
sealed with paraffin and stored for winter's use. If that wasn't enough,
gangly blooming peas begged for support with their tendrils
grasping at thin air, the potatoes needed hilling and the carrots
needed to be planted. Against the garden shed sat the newly hardened tomato plants that were ready to be set out as well. My soul
compressed with the weight of responsibility.

With a resigned sigh, I put Sindbad down. He brushed against

my legs. "Time to get to work, Sindbad. It's just you and me."
I retrieved the large chipped, red-rimmed bowl that hung from the
garden post. It had been Mama's, and thirty years later, it was still
doing the job. I walked to the first row of strawberries and knelt in
front of the beckoning ruby gems, the dew soaked through my dress
as the damp earth molded to my knees. I had to force myself to pick
the first one, knowing that once I started it would be a very long
day. I thought of pictures I'd seen of people vacationing along the
ocean, boating and swimming. I had never had a vacation. How
could you get away in the summer? Once the garden started it was
work, work, work until the snow was flying again. A solitary tear
slipped down my cheek.

I wiped away the tear, ran the sleeve of my housecoat across
my sniffling nose, and pushed Sindbad off my lap. With practiced
efficiency, I began picking the exuberant berries. They made a
popping sound as I plucked them by the handfuls and plopped
them in the bowl. Busy hands, quiet mind, Grandma always
said. Within minutes, my bowl was overrun, and I began to fill
the lap of my nightgown. When that was overflowing, I gathered
my nightgown about the berries, grabbed the bowl and stumbled
to my feet to head back to the house and breakfast. I paused by
Mama's creamy yellow roses at the garden gate and inhaled their
scent, soft as first light. Years of growth had draped the blossoms
like a blanket across the faded wood fence where they remained
a threshold to my past.

I remembered a summer's day long ago when Mama and I were
tending this same rose; it was in full bloom, its fragrance strong and
heady. We paused in our pursuit of perfect blooms for the dinner
table, to watch my baby sister, Ruthie. She was in a squat with her
thick diapered bottom touching the ground, and giggling at the

kittens rolling and wrestling on the warm sunny earth. She poked a dimpled finger at them, and without missing a beat, the black one, an ancestor of Sindbad's, wrapped its legs around her chubby little hand and bit and kicked it as kittens do. Ruthie was mortified and squalled like Armageddon was upon her. Mama rushed to her rescue and swept her up, kissing away her fear. As the memory faded, I looked down at my blood and juice stained hands; the thorns had done their damage. How I wished Mama were there to kiss it all away.

I walked back to the house, dumped the berries in the stone trough beneath the water pump, and went inside to change. Grandma's litany would never cease if I came to breakfast looking like this.

Biscuits and gravy, Levi's special recipe sausage, fried potatoes and a bowl of fresh sugared strawberries greeted me when I came into the kitchen. Grandma made no acknowledgment of our earlier dispute and I prayed she'd leave me be.

We said grace in good Catholic fashion and began a quiet meal. I sipped the object of my addiction—rich dark coffee. Grandma preferred tea, but I needed coffee in the morning, especially, this morning.

"The strawberries are lovely, Mattie," Grandma said, taking two large spoonfuls. "I believe this is the first time they've produced so heavily and so early in the spring. That manure Levi put on in the fall must have done the trick."

The manure had been my idea, but it was useless to mention it. Let Levi get the credit, he deserved it, putting up with Grandma all these years.

My thoughts wandered to the summer of my fourteenth year. I wanted Grandma's love in the way a starving animal wants food.

Other than the token peck on the cheek that I gave Grandma each night, I had no physical contact with anyone, except for an occasional hug from Levi. Of course at the time, I didn't realize it was nature working with my biological clock. I was convinced that if I could uncover the heartaches of Grandma's past, I might be able to figure out a way to open her heart to me. She sealed it shut the day Daddy left for the Army after we buried Mama and Ruthie.

Seemingly overnight, Grandma became a woman of all work and no play. The school gained her undivided attention and she became a model of efficient determination. The mountain people loved her, not because she was lovable, but because she worked so hard to improve their lives. She believed to the depth of her soul that education could cure the world's ills.

Callie Dawn was a year older than I and lived with Levi. He found her in the woods one morning when he was squirrel hunting. Someone had obviously left her there to die, as she was only a day or so old, cold and hungry. He stuck her inside his shirt and took her home. Grandma tried to take her, but Khalidah and Levi insisted that God had given her to them, or so the story goes. Levi wouldn't talk about it, and Grandma said I snooped too much but I questioned them to death that summer. An abandoned baby, who happened to be my best friend, was to good a story to leave alone.

Callie Dawn didn't want to talk about it either, but then there were a lot of things she wasn't talking about, I soon found out. In the full blossom of womanhood, she channeled her interests elsewhere that summer, trying her wiles on any mountain boy that would look her way—and plenty did.

Disgruntled and bored, I channeled my energies into unraveling the mountain lore of Grandma's past. Grandma portrayed herself as a woman without a past and for all intent and purposes managed to keep it that way. However, I was blood of her blood, and with that came determination. I delved into the mystery that was her life. I talked to everyone and anyone. I wrote letters to my relatives in Indiana. I spent days in the cemetery on the hill and read the epitaphs over and over. Most of them were clear enough, except for the single gray-blue stone that leaned against the giant oak in the center of the cemetery. It had a carved butterfly in flight in the upper right hand corner and across the stone was the simple inscription, "I love you."

My search continued for two dark inquisitive years. I visited Mama in the cemetery nearly every day, asked questions of her silent stone, and cried often. I could still see baby Ruthie tucked into Mama's arms before they sealed the coffin and lowered them into the cold April ground. Twenty locals had fallen victim to the fever the spring of 1909. I was no exception but I managed to live. Daddy was the local doctor and despite his heroic efforts, he couldn't save Mama or Ruthie. He barely managed to save me.

Not long after that, he went away to Cuba. There was a war on there, and he thought he could help—or at least that was his excuse for leaving. Everyone knew how heartbroken Daddy was, and I overheard Daddy tell Levi that he hoped a bullet would find him and put him out of his misery.

I was only five and I thought that somehow it was my fault— that if I had died and Mama and Ruthie lived, it would have been different for Daddy and Grandma.

Grandma was devastated by Mama and Ruthie's deaths, but she didn't shut down until Daddy left. The school became her everything and it stole her energy, her money and her love. There were no more hugs and bedtime stories, no more long walks looking at butterflies and such, unless it included the other school children. It was quiet in the house at night, and she rarely talked, other than to tell me it was time for bed.

Daddy wrote once a month for a while and then a couple of times a year and finally the packages and letters stopped. I never knew what happened to him and if Grandma did, she never said.

When I turned sixteen, I stepped away from childhood strife and embraced the handsome mountain boy from the north ridge. Stephen became my newest investigation, a foray into the heart and flesh.

I recoiled from those salacious memories and cleared the table. "I hear the children, Grandma. I'm going on over to the school. I'll finish the strawberries this afternoon."

"Alright, Dear."

CHAPTER

FIVE

Pine Ridge Settlement School
Late spring 1939

I T WAS THE last day of school and the squawking of fifty children was excruciating to the pounding in my sleep-deprived mind. They wiggled, squirmed, and talked while eating their lunches at their desks. Despite my efforts in elementary etiquette, they ate with mouths open and lips smacking. At times, it seemed that I could hear head lice scurry through their filthy matted hair. My stomach churned at the sight of ten-year-old boys with tobacco-stained teeth.

I considered their fathers and thanked the fate-god that I would never birth another child. What were they in these God-forsaken hills but the drippings of men's sexual appetites and afterthoughts, nothing but walking, talking parasites, inhabiting every crevice of our ill-conceived portal of practical education. Grandma saw hope. I saw despair.

Nothing would change the outcome of their lives. They were trapped by poverty and ignorance as surely as I was trapped by responsibilities that I neither wanted nor invented. Unlike me, the children didn't seem to mind their predisposed fate, the desire for a better life, had gone extinct from their gene pool. The harsh realities of mountain life were all they knew and from what I could see, all they cared to know. The boys talked of hunting, the girls talked of babies.

Last night's tumultuous nightmares, amidst the near daylight of a planter's moon, had left me no mind with which to teach. I freed the children early as they had energy to spare and no concentration left in their "last day of school" minds. Planting season was upon us and their help was needed at home.

I gathered my things and went in search of Levi. By following the repeated raps of a hammer, I found him supervising two of my older students in the repair of a corncrib. He said nothing to me but sensed my need to talk and after a short while, sent the boys to check on the expectant heifers in the lower pasture. They had plenty of work at home but they enjoyed helping Levi. I waited until they were out of earshot and began my woeful tale.

"Levi, I don't know what Grandma wants from me. I can't get any sleep these days and when I do, it's full of nightmares. I wake up more tired than when I went to sleep. This morning, I hadn't been asleep but a few hours when Grandma woke me up with that damnable cane, rapping on the banister, just to tell me how irresponsible I am at running this school. As far as I can see, the children couldn't care less about school. All the girls talk about is getting married and having babies, and all the boys can talk about is hunting and fishing and who's Pa makes the best shine. Why should I try to do more? We could close this school down for all the good it does."

Levi rested his hammer; his jade eyes bore into mine. "You is a spoiled selfish young-un. Dis school was Miz Lydia's dream and it has served dese people well. You is da one has brung it down, Miz Mattie. You gots no vision."

"Vision? Of what? I never wanted to run this damn school and you know it."

Levi waved a long wrinkled finger in my face. "Nobody made you stay." Levi picked up a nail and put another between his thick burgundy lips. "You talk of obligations. You stayed cuz you is a-feard of Miz Lydia." He began to pound the nail.

"I'm not afraid of her. It's just that she puts so much guilt on me, about everything..."

Levi cut me off. "Your Grandpa Caleb, Ben and me, we stood by her troublesome ways. Her heart's good and she cares about dese folks. You could do worse."

"It was your choice to stay. I had no choice. It was expected, demanded."

Levi drove the last nail home. "You chose to give up yer dreams, too weak, too tired, too full of excuses to fight. Just look at Callie Dawn. I did'en want her to go but she went. It was her choice and she made it. Gone. Jus' like yer Daddy."

Levi's words stilled my heart and blossomed forth another memory. It was the day my rainbow colored dreams dissolved beneath a myriad of gray shadows, a day of grief and accusation, a day I had hoped never to remember.

"Callie Dawn, where were you this morning? You promised to go to Hazard with me and help me pick out my wedding silk."

Callie Dawn met my eyes. "Did you find some?"

"I did, but that's not the point. Where were you? You promised."

"With Isaac," she mumbled.

"Isaac who?"

She stared into my eyes. I saw the truth, and my stomach twisted.

"Old man, Isaac?"

Callie Dawn withdrew a cigarette from her ample bosom and wrapped her lips around it like it was a candy stick.

"What were you doing with him?"

"You know the answer, Mattie. So go ahead and tell me I'm stupid, that yer disappointed in me." She lit the end and inhaled deeply. I didn't even know she smoked but to inhale like that she'd been smoking a while. Where had I been? She tilted her head back and blew a funnel of smoke into the cool evening air. Who was this person? When had she started lurking in night shadows, hiding from her Dawn? What had become of my friend, a girl of laughter, adventure and beauty whom I admired more than any other?

"Why Callie? Why on earth would you want to sleep with Old man Isaac? It makes me sick just to think about it."

"God, Mattie, ya sound just like yer ole Gram-ma. Can't ya think fer yerself?" She took an agitated drag and blew the smoke in my face.

I coughed and waved it away. "What's happened to you? When did you stop talking to me? When did you lose your virginity, and what on earth possessed you to give it to Isaac?" I screamed out the last words and stared into Callie's glacial eyes.

"He paid me for it," she declared, threw the cigarette down and ground it out with the toe of her shoe.

A chasm opened between us, her words ricocheted through my mind and turned me inside out. "You're his whore?" I asked in disbelief, staring at my childhood playmate—the one with whom I shared all. She had been my only friend. I had not been hers. The realization hit me like a landslide. Levi had allowed Callie Dawn to play with the other children to become part of the mountains, free and wild and rough-edged. Grandma saw to it that my edges were sanded clean.

The eyes that looked back at me were none I knew and in that moment of self-realization, my naïve illusions shattered with an internal explosion of unfathomable magnitude.

"I don't care whatcha think. I want out of these mountains. I want a life. I want to see the ocean. Hell Mattie, I want to go to Paris. How's that fer a dream. And I'll get there or die tryin'. I'll do whatever it takes to get outta here. Thar ain't no other way fer a woman to break free… lest she's got money. And thar's two things a man will pay fer, booze and sex." Callie lit up again. "I'm not proud of it, but I ain't ashamed neither."

"Why didn't you ask Levi for the money, or I could have asked Grandma?" I watched the nuances play over her face, once so familiar, now those of a stranger.

"Oh, that's rich." Her laugh was laced with venom. She leaned into a tree and dragged a fiery long ember. "Ya really think ole Levi would give me money to leave him? He'd hog tie me to the kitchen table to keep me here. The way he acts, you'd think he couldn't live a day without me. He's suffocated me fer years, and to tell ya the truth, I can't wait to shake the dirt of this God forsaken mountain from my feet. I ain't ever comin' back! It'll be a relief not to hafta see yer ole Grandma lookin' down her nose at me. Yer such a baby, Mattie. You'll never get outta here. It's just a stupid dream fer you. But not me. I'm goin'. I'm goin' just as soon as I get enough money, and Isaac pays me good."

My eyes burned. My throat swelled. My heart broke.

"Oh, shut your gapin' mouth, Mattie. Go on and marry Stephen, but you ought to know that I've been with him too, lot's of times. You'll have his babies, and he'll spend yer money and sleep with everything that moves while he's doin' it. Not me… no sir… I'm gettin' out!"

Callie turned her back to me and walked into the shadows of the forest. Her smoke lingered as the bright orange glow moved away.

I screamed after her with bitter tears running rivulets down my face.

"Whore! You're nothing but a worthless whore!"

My wedding was a week away. Callie Dawn was supposed to be my Maid of Honor. She didn't show. Why would she? I stood alone at the altar and felt the baby flutter for the first time. I waited for my knight to rescue me. He never came.

SIX

)))))))))((((((((

Pine Ridge Settlement School
May 1939

"GRANDMA, DOES ANYBODY know who gave birth to Callie Dawn?"

"Some ghosts are better left alone, Mattie," Grandma replied and continued shelling peas at the kitchen table. The late afternoon sun cast a homey glow through the window.

I couldn't wait to steam the peas with some new potatoes and pour my buttery cream sauce on top. It was my springtime favorite, right up there with strawberry shortcake, topped with a mountain of fresh whipped cream.

"It's a little late for that, don't you think?" I asked, rinsing the new red potatoes.

"Perhaps."

My head throbbed. Maybe Grandma was right. Maybe I didn't want to know. If I stopped asking questions, life might get back to normal, what ever normal was for me. Back to pretending was more like it. My memories and emotions had been jarred awake and the questions kept coming, unwanted, unbidden but they came, nevertheless. Why did she think she could pick and choose what she told me and what she didn't? I had to make her understand that it was all or nothing.

"What woods did Levi find her in? Was it near a house?"

"That is a question you should ask Levi."

"Why won't you tell me? You wanted to tell me everything else this morning."

"Perhaps Matilda, I would, if you could allow me to have my say."

"Allow you? You always have your say, Grandma. What about my say? What about my questions? If I hadn't listened to your say, I might have left these mountains before Stephen left me." I didn't know why I said it. It just fell out.

"Stephen left because I paid him to leave. You were so young, your eyes so full of stars. You couldn't see him for what he was."

My mouth turned to parchment. "What did you say?"

"Stephen didn't love you, Mattie. He was after your inheritance." Grandma set the bowl of peas on the table and went to the sink to wash her hands. "He did his homework, I'll grant him that. He made a trip up North to my land, digging around, asking too many questions. I still had friends."

I stared at Grandma as I had stared at Callie Dawn. She was a stranger to me, and yet I knew every line on her face. An angry tear trickled down my cheek, a friendless drop from a dangerously full well.

"Do you remember when he said he was going to visit his sick aunt?"

"It's a lie."

"No, Mattie. He was the liar. I knew his type. He was a charlatan. The South was full of them after the War."

"It's not true." Stephen was a melancholy of images in my

biased mind, sultry hazel eyes, delicious kisses, the seducer of my body and soul. He had sown his seed in fertile ground.

"He could have stayed and married you, Mattie, with the condition that he would never gain control of your inheritance. I would maintain the finances until my death. The inheritance would go directly to your children. He would get nothing. Not then. Not ever." Grandma came back and sat down. "He accepted my payment to leave—without hesitation."

"He loved me."

"No, Mattie. Only you loved."

I felt nauseous.

"You should have told me."

"Perhaps it was a mistake to keep it from you." Grandma finished her tea. "I thought you would forget him. Go on with your life."

"Forget him?" My voice was an unfamiliar high pitch. "I loved him."

"At the time, I felt your infatuation would pass."

My body trembled with a building rage. "Infatuation? We were to be married!" Memories charred. Friends and family gathered in the little stone chapel, where huge bouquets of mountain laurel and lilacs scented every crevice. Soft afternoon light streamed through the westerly windows. Grandma sat in the front row, her face set like stone.

"My God, you knew he wouldn't come, that he had already gone."

Grandma's eyes never wavered.

"How could you just sit there and watch me be humiliated like that? What kind of beast are you?"

"It pained my heart to see you hurt, Mattie, but it was one day of humiliation or a lifetime of misery."

For a moment, there were no words as lost images seared my mind and Grandma's words lay bare on the altar of betrayal. I began to tremble as the anger pushed out like molten lava.

"My life has been a void," I said through tight lips. "I never stopped loving, Stephen. I never knew why he left me."

Grandma rose and moved deliberately toward the parlor and her ritual nap. I moved in front of her.

"Did you stop loving, Grandpa?"

She looked weary. I didn't care.

"What Caleb and I shared can in no way be compared to the unrequited love you had for Stephen. Ours was a rare butterfly, pure in intention. We could never love another. Not ever."

How could she be so matter of fact about her deceit, and as far as I could tell, unrepentant of the wrong done to me? She moved slowly away. I stormed from the house and let the screen door slam—a rant Grandma hated. Thunder clapped, and a cool wind whipped through my hair as charcoal clouds rolled up and over the mountains tops. They suited my mood. I strode through the meadow, past Levi's cabin, and beyond his mystical bamboo forest. He sat on the porch smoking his pipe, watching the approaching storm. My back warmed beneath his questioning gaze, and I began to run before he could call to me. I ran until I was deep in the seclusion of the forest beneath a canopy of spring leaves and transient shadows. Grandma's secrets screamed inside my head as I moved deeper into the forest; the rich scent of mountain laurel lambasted my senses, songbirds chattered, squirrels scampered from limb to limb above me, gathering material for their nests, preparing for their young. All of these spring happenings were abominations to my bitter heart. I was desperate to escape myself, and ran down the mossy path of my youth.

I collapsed by the old weeping willow, the one that shaded my childhood swimming hole in Troublesome Creek, years of restraint unleashed in a cascade of betrayal and acidic love. I was oblivious to all, and finally my exhausted body and tormented mind fell to dream. The miserable day disappeared, and Callie Dawn and I swam beneath summer skies.

The deep rumble of thunderheads woke me. The forest was eerily dark. My thoughts were filled with images of Callie Dawn and happier times, perhaps the last I had known.

Callie Dawn sent me one letter after she left—to tell me she was training to be a nurse and had married an Army doctor nearly three times her age and that he had lots of money. That was the end of our correspondence. My subsequent letters came back, address unknown. She relegated me to her past just like everyone else. There was a time when I thought friendship counted for more than that, but time had proven me wrong.

It was the silence I hated most, and the lonely life that loomed ahead.

"Come on, Mattie! Ya in't scared, are ya?"

Callie Dawn's ten-year-old mirage taunted me from down the familiar path of our childhood rambles, and I followed her toward Pirate's Cove.

In the gloom of the impending storm, the mammoth rock overhang shaped like the bow of a ship loomed into view, a tangled mesh of rhododendrons and grapevines camouflaged our old hideout, a deep cave beneath the rock. It's numerous catacombs were the bowels of our ship—yesteryear's grand adventures.

"Whatcha 'fraid of, Mattie? Yer ole Gram-ma?"

The past mocked in vivid relief. I, the spectator, cringed at my weakness and remembered my feeble response.

"I'm not afraid, but we gotta go back," I whined. "It's going to storm."

"You're such a baby, Mattie. Never wanna try anything." She ran ahead. "Hurry up. I wanna show you somethin'."

A sharp clap of thunder shook me from my delusion, and the wild scent of storm-driven rain rode a chilly foreboding wind. An eerie green ambiance blanketed the forest. Fear gripped. The last time I saw this atmospheric quirk, several years before, was now revered as the Day of the Twisters. I pushed Callie Dawn from my mind and ran toward the forbidden cave as giant raindrops began their assault on the tender spring growth.

"Callie Dawn, I told you we should go back. Now, we're stuck out here."

"Quit your bellyaching, Mattie. I wanna show you somethin'."

"Where?"

"In there." Callie Dawn pointed in the cave. "I found a skeleton."

"I don't want to see a skeleton! I'm not going in there."

"Would you go if I had a lantern?"

"But you don't," I replied. *Idiot,* never call Callie Dawn's bluff. Why hadn't I just said no? Callie Dawn reached behind a tree and retrieved Levi's new barn lantern.

"What are you doing with that?"

Callie rolled her eyes and retrieved a kitchen match from her pocket. A big grin plastered her face as she lit the stolen prize. She grabbed my hand and dragged me into the cave and down a bat-filled catacomb.

I screamed. She laughed.

The memories dissolved as the storm's fury unleashed, and I struggled through the tangle of vines into the cave's stony mouth. Damp rock and dry earth permeated my senses as torrents of rain penetrated the forest canopy, ripping new leaves from ancient trees.

I shivered. I was just wet enough to be chilled and the cold air of a cool front came in with the storm.

Thankfully, the cave was dry, and I gathered a nice pile of dry leaves and twigs that had blown in from storms past. Luckily, I always kept matches in my pocket to light the kitchen stove. I struck one on the rock wall. The tiny orange flame sprang to life for a brief moment and then went out. Darkness adhered to my shoes.

I lit a second; it flared and was quickly blown out by a cold breeze that came up out of one of the catacombs.

"Still soft and warm..." hissed a voice.

The hair stood on the back of my neck as a man's wicked laughter echoed through the cave. Memories slithered forth with the white vapor that seeped out of the deep catacomb that held the skeleton, its ethereal tongues flicked at my feet. I wanted to scream, to run, but my body was frozen in terror. The mist coiled and spun about me until I was engulfed into a chasm of madness.

When my eyes opened, the vapor had vanished and I was no longer in the cave but lying face down in a crunchy carpet of dry leaves. For a moment, their woodsy scent was familiar and reassuring. I pushed myself to my haunches and peered through the thin waxy haze that blanketed the forest.

A bullet whizzed past my head and splintered the bark of a nearby tree.

"Don't shoot," I screamed and dove into a pile of nature's

debris. *What in the hell?* A hailstorm of lead answered my thoughts, and a stampede of men ran past. Some leaped over my hideout.

"I'm hit," yelled one. "Shit."

I lifted my head. A handsome young man saw me. He opened his mouth to speak, but his words were silenced by a bullet. He went down hard. A protruding rock gashed his head. Blood spewed. I darted from my leafy hole to give him aid. A buzzing projectile exploded. Shrapnel cracked through the trees and sent me scurrying back to my cover.

"Stay down," a man yelled.

Horrific explosions and massive gunfire reverberated through the forest. Sulfurous smoke saturated the air. I curled into a ball and buried my face into the folds of my skirt, holding my ears while the battle raged into endless pandemonium.

When the mêlée finally stopped, bone-chilling screams echoed through the smoky calm. Something warm dripped onto my hand. I looked up through the brush pile. The glazed eyes of a young man, little more than a boy, gazed into mine. A thread of blood trickled from his nose and mouth.

My mouth gaped in horror, I wanted to scream but no sound would come; desperately I clawed free of my sanctuary and met the face of another corpse, his jaw and chest a mass of bloody mangled flesh. The smell of fresh kill brought bile rushing up my throat.

Wake up, Mattie. Wake up! My brain re-connected to my feet, and I began to run, dodging bodies, crawling and jumping over felled trees and limbs. As I struggled through the woods, my voice returned. "Help, somebody help!" I screamed time and again. Finally, I stumbled free of the woods onto a trampled cornfield— an inconceivable sculpture of death. Hundreds of dead and wounded men lay in every direction, along with dead horses and broken wagons. My eyes came to rest on the prostrate body of a child a few yards away, his dirty hands still wrapped around a bloodied drum. I rushed to his side. He was so still. With trembling fingertips I rolled him over. Tears filled my eyes as I stroked his brown dusty curls and looked into unseeing hazel eyes. I scooped him into my arms and clamored to my feet. Hundreds of hands reached for me, soldiers begging for water and aid as I maneuvered the labyrinth of the battlefield. It was a nightmare unlike any other. I trod onward across the death field toward a distant farmhouse.

When I finally reached it, wounded men lay on every available inch of yard. Agony saturated the air and screams rang from the house. I jumped when a young woman came from behind and touched my arm. I clutched the child to my breast. She was fair-haired and fairer-skinned, her eyes that of an angel, she wore a long black dress with a white apron stained bright red.

"May I help you?" she asked in a gentle German lilt. I showed her my silent bundle. Her brilliant blue eyes swelled.

"What has happened here?" I asked, begging reply.

The woman caressed the child's hair. "May the Lord's angels carry you home," she whispered. Her arms cradled the child from mine and into those of a large black man. She kissed the child's dusty forehead, and the dark man vanished into the approaching mist.

"Please, tell me what has happened here?"

She seemed to no longer see me and without reply moved on to tend others in the thick fog.

Lines of wagons and men stretched into the distance. Those at the front walked or limped into the swollen yard. Others were carried by comrades.

The clapboard house, a family home, had been turned into what I guessed to be a hospital. Soldiers carried live men in and dead men out. The house must have seen the worst of battle, for its doors were missing, windows broken, and its veneer splintered.

Panic raged through my soul; where was I? *God, please wake me up! Rouse me from this nightmare of bedlam.* I ran around the house looking for someone, anyone who could see me or save me. I saw a soldier standing inside an open upstairs window. I ran toward it, yelling and waving my arms to get his attention. Not seeing what lay beneath, I fell headlong into a deep pit of sawed off appendages. He tossed an arm from above and plunked me on the head.

"Holy b'Jesus."

The soldier leaned out the window and stared down at me. He yelled back to others inside. "There's a goddamn woman in the pit."

SEVEN

)))) ● (((

Our common country is in great peril.
—Abraham Lincoln, 1862

"YOU ALIVE, blue-belly?"

A bayonet probed Caleb's backside. His foggy mind struggled to conjugate the question; the words were out there like wind-blown leaves. The bearer poked at his wounded leg.

"Well, I'll be damned. I thought Yanks bled yella." He rolled his victim over and examined his coat; it looked like a damn sieve but there was no blood and no holes on the shirt beneath, just powder burns. *How in the hell?* He'd seen his share of battlefield quirks, but this beat them all to hell, hands down. If there was anything left living on this hill, he had damn sure planned on finishing it. They'd killed his brother this morning and he was aiming to get revenge. But it looked like something a might bigger was on this Yank's side and he was having second thoughts about running him through.

They'd rained lead at this man, and he never flinched. Instead, he reloaded and took methodical aim time and again.

They blasted into the mirage, a mirage that fired back with deadly accuracy. The Yank took no cover, was an unremitting mark, and culled a dozen of their best. It took a shit-load of Enfields to lay this man down, and still he lived. Jacob had expected to find a battered bloody body.

If he killed this Piker, no doubt, a curse would follow him clean to the grave. He'd best leave it be and tell the rest of the boys that the bastard was dead a hundred times over or one of them would be sure to finish the job.

Caleb moaned.

"I can't believe yer still breathin', Yank. Hell I shot ya at least six times myself." The Reb's voice was almost a whisper.

Caleb was alive, and with living came feeling. Hordes of Johnnies scavenged in blurred moonlight, their arms full of dead soldier's clothes, boots, and haversacks. Caleb moaned as he fought to sit up. He'd been shot to hell and felt sure that a six-mule wagon had run him over.

"I wouldn't do that if I were you. Yer head has a price on it and there's plenty around that'd take great pleasure in takin' it off."

Caleb heard an ugly groan and turned to see a Reb twenty yards off shove a bayonet into a boy in blue. He proceeded to steal the boy's boots and put them on his own bare feet.

"Bastards." Caleb spat with all the venom of a fly and swung at his foggy foe.

The Reb chuckled. "Yer awful feisty fer a dyin' man. Don't worry, I ain't a-gonna finish ya. It ain't worth cleanin' my knife fer, besides, from the looks of ya, the devil'll be along directly to escort ya to hell." The Reb pulled on Caleb's boot.

Caleb groaned.

"Sorry bout that, but ya ain't gonna need these where yer a goin'," said the Reb.

Caleb tried hard to swallow, but his mouth was as dry as a desert. He hadn't counted on being field dressed before he was dead.

"Now Yank, ain't no cause to be sore. You'd do the same in my place. Winter's comin' and I gots no shoes, no blanket, and my uniform's thin as Federal skin."

Caleb swung again. The Reb chuckled.

"Yer a damn sight Yank, layin' here a waitin' on the devil to collect yer blue-ass soul and still thinkin' ya can take me."

Caleb's arm fell heavy to the ground. "Finish me or move that pig-sticker," he mumbled.

The Reb looked at his bayonet poised over the Yank's crotch and moved it aside. "Don't reckon you'll live to pleasure that again."

The Yank's face was smudged black, stained red and pale as Christmas snow.

"I'm no coward, Reb."

"Ya mean that hole in the back of yer leg? After what ya gave us today, don't reckon anyone thinks ya are." The Reb stiffened his crumbling resolve and looked for tobacco and jerky in Caleb's pockets.

"Had to come up here myself and see if ya was real. I sure as hell didn't expect ya to be breathin'."

Caleb's words came hard and slow through parched, cracked lips. "Take what you need... but leave those things in my pocket."

"I reckon I'll make that choice myself."

The Reb removed a watch from Caleb's pocket and after reading the inscription, stuffed it back in. "I gots no need fer that. Sides, that'd be sacrilegious, it bein' from yer Pa and all." Jacob withdrew a deer-handled knife from a fringed sheath. "See this here knife? My Pa made this fer me from the horn of my first whitetail. I'll be damned if anybody besides my boy gits it when I'm gone."

"You got any water?"

"Some. Ain't had no good water since y'all run us off that creek." The soldier opened his canteen and gently lifted Caleb's head. "It ain't much but it's wet." Caleb eagerly gulped the brackish liquid.

"Easy Yank, easy."

Caleb coughed and drank more.

"What's yer name, Yank?"

Caleb's breath was labored and ragged. The Reb eased him back. "Caleb."

"My name's Jacob. Jacob Eggleston, First Tennessee. I'm from down Memphis way where I got a wife and two young'uns."

Caleb's mind was going cloudy; Jacob's voice drifted.

"Tell ya what, Yank. I'll set ya against this here tree and if they come lookin' fer ya, they'll be able to see ya."

Jacob grabbed the miracle man behind the collar and dragged him to the tree. He thought the Yank would shout out with pain but he didn't make a sound. It was a bad sign; he likely wouldn't make it through the night, but then he had survived the worst they could give. He was in God's hands, that was sure. Jacob stuck his canteen in Caleb's hand—couldn't hurt—just in case anyone important was takin' notes.

"I'll git me another. We've got the water again anyways, did ya know."

Caleb muttered something unintelligible.

"Well, I gots ta go."

Jacob gathered up his booty. Night was falling, and so was the temperature. He put Caleb's hat back on his bloody head, took a few steps and paused. He put down the boots, took off his coat and threw it over his enemy. "Reckon it's the least I can do seein's how you've been so generous, given me yer boots and all.

"See you in hell," Caleb mumbled.

Jacob smiled. The Yank just might make it. "Could be, Yank. Could be. Stay awake and ya just might live to see another day. Somethin tells me ya got lots to live fer."

The hot day folded into a cold star-filled night. Caleb shivered while his wounds sang harmony with the dying and Jacob's canteen ran dry. As the hours inched by his leg numbed, and death's cloak stole over the battlefield. Men's echoes began to subside.

Rebel fires ensconced the battlefield and the smell of a thousand pounds of sizzling bacon and vats of coffee brewing floated across the decimated landscape. Around the crackling fires, soldiers chewed bacon fat and whispered of sweethearts, while just beyond lay blood, death, and decay.

There would be no rescue tonight.

Caleb wished for the warmth of home or heaven. His Father would hear the story of how his eldest son made a stand, and he would be proud.

EIGHT

*Blessings on the brave men who have wrought the change
and the fair women who strive to reward them for it.*
—Abraham Lincoln, April 18, 1864

THE SUN ROSE invisible behind heavy gray clouds. A cold drizzle kept the soldiers hunkered over hissing coals and sizzling salt pork. Ben sat alone and tried not to think of his messmate, the one that never burned the bacon.

A scout burst into the camp. "They've skedaddled. Them damn Rebs lit out during the night!"

The boys let out a whoop and took off running for the battlefield, with high hopes that their fallen comrades were still alive.

"Best go find your kid, Sarg," said Vail.

Ben poked at the bacon with his killer blade and ignored Vail.

"Damn it Decker, that wasn't a request. It was a goddamned order."

Ben kept to his task and the few eyes left in camp watched the battle of wills and quietly placed bets.

"I'm fixin' vittles. Don't reckon no dead coward will keep me from it."

"Coward?" snorted Vail. "Haven't you heard? Your Storekeep went back to the line and picked off a bunch of Johnnies before they laid him down."

Ben looked up. "Who tells?"

"The story is your Shithead found himself a hill with a big ass tree on it and started firing into a fray of Arkansas Rebs. Reckon the least we can do is bury him."

Ben watched the bacon burn.

"Your boy might have started yella but he didn't end that way. I'll be proud to tie his streamer to the Eightieth's colors," Vail said. He patted Ben's shoulder and walked toward the rest of the men. "This ain't no church social." Vail's voice pummeled the gawkers. "There's recovery to do. Get cracking men."

Ben gathered his gear. "Harley," he snapped to one of the soldiers leaving camp. "Yer in charge till I get back. I'm goin' to find Storekeep."

Private Harley Johnson was a tall quiet man about Ben's age, and he spent many evenings around the campfire with Ben and Caleb. He wasn't a talker, but he could trim a man's nose hairs from two hundred yards.

"Need help gettin' the boy?" Harley asked.

"Nope." Ben thrust his Colt under his belt and tucked his blade in its sheath. "Save me some coffee, I done burned the bacon."

Ben smelled the battlefield long before he saw it. It was something he never got used to—the unmistakable odor of rotting flesh. The Rebs had left their scavenger mark on the Union dead. It was a bitch to see, but with winter coming and no supplies, he would've done the same.

Yesterday's dusty desert was today's cold, desolate wasteland littered with bloated bodies, dead horses, and battle debris. The skies were crying. Ben had seen it many times before. After a battle, the weather would turn off bad. Angel's tears, his Rosita used to say.

Others wandered the field looking among the dead for friends, comrades, and brothers. Buzzards hopped and pecked, while along the perimeter of the battlefield, feral hogs feasted on the country's finest. Ben walked past it all, toward where the Arkansas boys had been yesterday afternoon. He checked his pistol and walked up a hill toward a lone battle-scarred tree. From what Vail said, that had to be the one.

Caleb lay in a grassy meadow watching butterflies frolic about. He reached for one. It fluttered just out of reach.

"Grandma, help me catch it," he begged.

"Not so fast, Caleb, you have to move slowly. Watch how Grandma does it."

Little Caleb watched mesmerized as his grandma, knee-deep in swaying alfalfa coaxed butterflies to light on her hands.

Ben spotted his bloodied pupil propped against a tree, grasping at the air.

"Caleb?" boomed Grandma.

The boy was confused. It didn't sound like Grandma.

"Caleb?" Ben jostled Caleb's shoulder. "Can ya hear me, Storekeep? It's Ben."

"Grandma, look. Ben's a butterfly."

Ben knelt and raised his canteen to Caleb's parched lips. "Take a drink, yer talkin' drunk."

Footsteps approached. Ben popped like a broken mainspring, Colt in one hand and canteen in the other. The soldier's hands went up.

"Easy, Sarg. Just came to see if you needed some help. You have the only live one around here."

Ben checked his weapon.

"Ya shouldn't sneak up on a body like that. It's a good way to get dead. Seein's how them damn Johnnies stripped our boys last night, half the Rebel army's gotta be wearin' blue. How do I know yer not one of em?"

"Do I sound like a Reb?" The man's German brogue had a familiar ring, and Ben's watch-works relaxed.

"Ya sound like an asshole to me."

The soldier laughed. "There are plenty that would agree, but I'm no Reb," said the man.

"Grandma," blabbered Caleb, "Ben's brought more butterflies for me to play with."

The man looked at Caleb. "Is that the crazy man I heard-tell of yesterday?"

"Yep." Ben held out his hand. "Ben Decker, Eightieth Indiana."

Caleb's hand waved aimlessly.

"Ethan Weldishofer, Fiftieth Ohio." He took Ben's hand in a firm shake. "He sure looks familiar, but then it's hard to tell out here. Don't believe I'd recognize my own brother if he'd been through all that."

Ben looked at Caleb's peppered body. "Ya say yer with the Fiftieth Ohio?"

"We were behind you," Ethan said.

The battlefield was a web for rumors, and Ben heard-tell that one of the Fiftieth's Captains threw one of his own wounded soldiers back into the fracas while he hid his yellow ass behind the poor boy's tree, and their Colonel turned tail and ran. Without their leaders, the Fiftieth stuck their heads up their asses and laid low. Greeners didn't have a clue without someone giving them orders, and who could blame them.

"Hey lady," Caleb mumbled, "you like butterflies, too?"

Ben poured more water into Caleb's mouth.

Ethan looked at the holes in Caleb's coat. "Why isn't he dead? What did those Reb's bullets do, bounce off his brass balls?"

Ben laughed. "Hell if I know. I expected to find him in pieces."

Ethan looked at Caleb's coat and the splintered tree.

"You're right there. It'll be a damn shame if he doesn't make it after all that."

"How far to the hospital?"

"It's a good mile, Sarg. How about we get them to dump that dead wagon over there."

Caleb pawed at the air. "The butterflies are talking, Grandma."

"You think he really held off two hundred?" asked Ethan.

"Damn right," gloated Ben. "Trained him myself."

"Ben? You think that woman caught any butterflies?"

"Oh hell, lots of em, Shithead." Ben waved Caleb's hands aside. "Gimme a hand, Ethan."

Ethan helped Ben heave Caleb to his feet, and Ben hoisted his babbling friend over his shoulder.

"Reckon there's plenty others need tendin' to." Ben looked across the battlefield. The Rebs had left their dead behind. "See they get a decent burial. They sure as hell earned that much."

"That they did," Ethan replied. "I got a brother out here somewhere. With Brass Ball's here surviving, maybe there's hope yet."

Ben shook Ethan's hand and walked off toward the dead-wagon. "Hope ya find him."

The wagon's crew was reluctant to unload the dead for one about to join them. "Listen here, Sergeant," yelled the lead teamster, "you have no call to order us.

Ben withdrew his Colt. "Like hell. Now dump em."

The driver grunted, "Now see here. We've got our orders and that's to get these men in the ground. Throw him up top, besides, he's not far from six-foot under anyway."

The hammer of Ben's Colt locked.

The teamster stared into Ben's black eyes and turned to the soldiers. "Listen up, men," the teamster ordered, "Toss these poor devils out. Looks like we'll have to come back for them."

Ben watched emotionless. He'd be damned before he put Storekeep with the dead. Besides he liked to see men work; it was good for their constitution.

After a "thank ya, boys" Ben laid Caleb in the bed and climbed aboard. "Ged-dap." He snapped the reins and headed for the hospital.

The ride was agonizingly slow. For churning butter, it'd be a good ride, but for a body trying to die, the bouncin' made it easier. When they reached the Mackville Road, the wagon came to a halt behind a glut of horses, carriages, and chewed-up men. Ben hauled Caleb off the commandeered buckboard and slung him over his shoulder. He'd make better time walkin', and the way his Storekeep looked, there weren't minutes to spare. He walked strong and steady, nodding to some, ignoring most. If battle was hell, the aftermath was Armageddon.

"Storekeep, you better make good after all this. Yer a son of a bitch to carry."

"Where's that woman? She was in the brush."

Ben ignored Caleb's crazy talk and concentrated on the farmhouse fifty yards off.

The yard was full of the suffering and those tending them. Ben saw a bare spot under a tree and gently eased his friend down and rolled him to his belly. He cut the trouser leg away from the wound he'd inflicted. God-Almighty, the leg looked bad, black with blood and swollen with infection. For the first time in a very long time, Ben felt a pang of regret.

He re-rigged the silk tourniquet and wondered where in the hell Caleb had found a piece of silk on a damn battlefield. But then, Storekeep had a knack for surprises, like the bullet holes in his coat with only powder burns beneath. Ben had seen plenty of strange, unexplainable shit happen on battlefields, but nothing like this.

"Soldier," Ben grabbed a passing private. "Ya seen a sawbones round here?"

The soldier pointed to a two-story, white clapboard house. "In there."

Ben put his cap over Caleb's face to keep the flies away and walked over to the hospital. The place was buzzing with the vermin and the operating room looked worse than a slaughterhouse. One soldier tossed a leg with a boot still attached past Ben's head and out the window. He watched a doctor take the saw to a young soldier's arm while the kid lay screaming on a bloody, straw-covered door propped up on two oak barrels. The floor was a red sticky mess.

Ben's stomach knotted. "Bastards," he muttered.

The boy's face grayed and thankfully he passed out. Two more swipes and his arm was lopped off, quickly bandaged, and he was moved off to make room for the next poor soul.

The doctor dipped his saw in a bucket of bloody water.

"We take better care of our meat on butcherin' day," grunted Ben to no one in particular.

Two soldiers carried a dead comrade past. Ben watched them toss him onto a wagon, with a host of others stacked like cordwood and destined for a mass grave—no one to mourn, no one to pray them into heaven. He thought of their kinfolk. By the time they heard the sorrowful news, if they ever did, their loved one's rot would be mingled with a hundred others.

Lost heroes.

"That one's gone." A doctor pointed to another. The weary soldiers moved in to carry him out.

"Oh God," squealed a soldier. The doctor was sawing again, this time a leg just above the knee.

Ben's steel stomach somersaulted and the vicious memory resurrected, his innocent young wife begging him for death while he held her down for the bastard sawbones to cut out the baby. The doctor had killed Rosita and failed to save their son.

Ben's hand fondled his knife. "Nurse," he barked above the ruckus. "There be a nurse about?"

Two soldiers carried another dead boy past.

"Look in the yard."

Ben glanced at the sawbones and decided the smell all round was better outside. He walked back to where Caleb lay face down on the grass—unmoving. Ben's heart gave a twang. "Is there a nurse about?" he barked again looking around. His mind was raw with Rosita's memory. Someone tugged at his sleeve.

"I'm a nurse."

Ben spun around. A blonde-haired, blue-eyed lass carrying a ladle and bucket of water met his fiery eyes. The white apron over her black dress was smeared with blood. What was such a delicate rose doing amidst all these thorns?

"Well, at least I'm learning to be."

Ben glanced at his dying friend. His countenance reloaded. "Are ya or ain't cha?"

Color sparked to her face. "I will try to help your friend the best I can. I only arrived this morning."

Her voice had a tinge of foreigner like that Ethan fella back there. "He's in a bad way. His leg's festered somethin awful, and he's got a couple a head wounds."

The nurse knelt and gingerly pulled the cloth back from the leg wound. It was repulsive and full of infection. She knew enough in the few hours she had been working that the doctor wouldn't waste time trying to save his leg. "The doctor will want to amputate."

"Don't reckon he will," growled Ben.

"Then he will die," she said with equal fervor. "It is full of infection and gangrene will soon set in."

Ben's face solidified.

"I assure you soldier, Doctor Kenton will do what he can for your friend, but he will want to take the leg. As you can see, there are hundreds yet waiting a turn on the table and more coming."

Ben raked a hand over stiff whiskers and looked up the road at the long line limping in. "Reckon he can have a look but I'm stayin' with him and makin' sure he leaves the leg."

"He won't like it," she said.

"Yer sawbones can kiss my ass."

The nurse looked at the hard man. She could see that scolding would only encourage his crass ways. Papa always said that you catch more flies with honey. "Soldier, your friend will die before the sun sets if he is not tended to. Please put aside your differences with the doctor and see that he is cared for. With thousands about, you are his only hope."

Ben eyed the spunky lass. "I'll see to it."

She nodded at him and continued on her rounds. She hoped his friend would make it but there was little time to ponder. The need was unfathomable, the urgency and misery beyond counting, a human travesty that existed here and only here.

Ben put his cap back on and hoisted his friend up and over

his shoulder.

"Nice voice." Caleb's words strained.

"So, ya speak, Storekeep. No more butterflies?"

"Listen to her." The sentence was barely audible.

"It'll hurt like hell's fire."

"Let them take the leg," whispered Caleb.

"We'll see bout that, Hero." Ben wished himself a praying man.

"Ya gonna give him some of that painkiller medicine, doc?" Ben asked.

"Don't have any more until the supply wagon arrives, and he can't wait. Besides, he's unconscious. Now get out of here while I do my work."

"I'm a stayin', sawbones. Gonna make sure ya don't do no sawin' on this boy."

"Private, get this soldier out of here."

The noncom touched Ben's elbow.

"This way, Sarg."

Ben rooted to the floor. His hand moved instinctively to the handle of his Bowie.

"I'll be stayin'."

The doctor's Adam's apple bobbed.

"Now see here, soldier," he sputtered. "I'll do what I can to save his leg, but it's full of poison. Leaving it may well cost him his life."

The Private advanced like he was gonna dispatch Sarg. This time, Ben's hand didn't do any fondling. The blade came up without a sound.

"I'll dump yer innards, Boy."

A familiar hand touched Ben's shoulder. "Let it be, Sarg." It was Harley.

Ben knocked his hand away. He looked at Caleb, back to the

doc and then to Harley.

"Let's wait outside, Sarg."

Ben's beady eyes locked on the Privates.

"If'ns he so much as touches that saw, ya best come fer me. Ya hear?"

The doctor glowered and cut the tourniquet.

"Private, wipe my face!"

The private hesitated.

"Boy," repeated Ben, "I said ya come fer me. Understand?"

"Yessir."

Ben sheathed his knife and stepped out the door with Harley on his heels.

The Private sighed relief and wiped the doctor's brow.

"Fool," mumbled the doctor.

All the Private could think was that Doc Kenton was a fool to challenge a killer like that.

Ben picked a misshapen apple and plopped beneath the tree's shade with a dozen other soldiers. Harley went back to help inside and left Sarg to his thoughts. Ben sat amongst the wounded and listened to their banter. Some spoke of the Indiana soldier that wouldn't die—the one among them that stood alone firing a thousand rounds into a thousand screaming Rebs.

"They said his coat was full a holes, but none went through the skin. Can you imagine that?" a young soldier boasted. He broke a twig and chewed on the end.

"If there's another fight, I wanna be near him," said another.

Ben's chest swelled. He sent a silent awkward petition skyward. Light steps broke his thoughts. The spunky little nurse was back.

"How is your friend?"

"He's with the doc."

She smiled sweetly and offered Ben a drink from her near empty pail. "You did the right thing."

Ben drank deep, got to his feet and took the pail. "I'll fill it fer ya."

Her heart warmed to the burly sergeant.

"Thank you." She walked beside him. "Where are you from?"

"Kentucky, round the Cumberland Gap."

Ben hooked the pail to a long rope and dropped the bucket toward Hades. It was five feet within the end of the rope when it finally hit water.

"Wonder it ain't dry."

"I hope it lasts. I don't know what we'll do for these men if it gives out." She retrieved another bucket while Ben hoisted the other.

"Is your friend from Kentucky as well?"

"Nope. Up Indiana way. New Alsace."

Her heart lurched. "What's his name?"

"Caleb."

"Caleb Wright?" her voice rose.

Ben looked into her panicked eyes. "That's right."

"Holy Mother of God," she gasped. Pail and ladle flew. Before the water could slosh to the ground, she had disappeared inside the house.

Ben's curiosity was piqued. He refilled the bucket, handed it to a passing soldier, and went back to the house.

When he walked in, Caleb lay face down and the doctor's saw was poised over his leg. The Private stepped back and wished he were invisible.

Ben rushed the doctor, who dropped the saw as Ben's steel hand grabbed his neck and lifted him to his toes.

"I'll have yer balls fer this."

Harley's voice rang out from upstairs. "There's a goddamn woman in the pit!"

The nurse was on her knees in the bloody straw that covered the floor beneath the table. She looked up into Caleb's bruised and bloodstained face and emotion flowed, unchecked, down her sweaty cheeks.

No one moved. There was a woman in the pit of amputated limbs, a doctor about to be executed by a madman, and a distraught nurse weeping on her knees by the makeshift operating table.

"His leg's got to come off," the doctor choked out.

"And so will yer head."

Harley came running out down the steps toward the door to rescue the woman in the pit but stopped short when he saw Ben. He stopped and walked slowly over to his sergeant, and everyone moved out of his way. "There's been enough killin', Sarg. Let it go." His voice was flat and even.

"Like hell," Ben said, thinking that the doc's face had a real nice evenin' glow.

"Let it go, Sarg," he commanded.

Harley's firm words were the kick in the ass Ben needed. He looked over at Harley then back to the doc. He dropped the gasping sawbones to the floor.

"Someone get this man out of here," wheezed the doctor, pulling himself to his feet. The doctor looked at the frozen orderlies. Worthless Privates. He looked at Harley and pointed at the unconscious soldier face down on the operating table.

"Soldier, do you know this man?"

"I do."

"Then perhaps you can talk some sense into your sergeant. There are hundreds more waiting their turn on this table. Your friend's wound is putrid. He won't live to see another day if we leave it. Taking his leg is the only thing to do."

Ben's knife came out. The nurse was on her feet and darted between him and the doctor.

"Doctor, can you excise the wound?"

"I don't have time for this!" He reached for his saw.

Ben lunged across the table, and grabbed the doctor's collar, pushing the nurse on her back over Caleb's prostrate body.

"Sarg!" barked Harley.

"Gentlemen, please!" the nurse exclaimed from her awkward position.

Ben and the doctor looked down into the nurse's distraught face. "Doctor Kenton, I respect your skill, but this soldier belongs to me," she said softly. "Please, try and save his leg."

"Grandma, I hear an angel," whispered Caleb.

The doctor glared. "I don't have time for this!" He shouted again.

Ben pulled the doc close and put the knife's point to the soft spot at the base of his throat. "Make time."

The nurse watched the men's standoff above her.

The doctor spoke through clenched teeth. "Alright," he spat. "Put that damn thing away and take hold of his leg."

Ben sheathed his knife and moved to grab Caleb's ankles.

With the killing moment over, Harley went outside to see about the woman in the pit. Another soldier moved in and took hold of Caleb's shoulders while the nurse took a wet cloth and wiped the swollen wound. The doctor pushed the knife deep into the fetid flesh. Pus and blood sprayed the nurse full in the face. Her stomach lurched and she ran for the door.

"Goddamn cherries! I ask for nurses, and they send me sniveling babies. I need a nurse over here!" the doctor yelled.

Ben watched the nurse rush from the house, holding her mouth. After Caleb was taken care of, he stepped outside to find her. It took a bit, but he finally found her sitting in in the barn, on a pile of straw, where a bit of sun shone from a knot hole in the wall. Her face was swollen from crying.

"Yer his Lydia, ain't ya?"

She met his eyes and nodded slightly. "How is he?"

"Hurtin' like hell. They put him in a room upstairs with a bunch of others."

"Will you take me to him?"

Ben would rather fight a thousand Rebs than go back in that slaughterhouse. Doc was sawing again and the soldier's screams could be heard even down here. Screams like that could shake the stoutest man.

He took her hand and raised her to her feet. Together they walked back to the house. As they stepped in, an arm was tossed across the room and out the window. Lydia swayed.

"Ya goin' down?"

She paused and held her forehead. "I make a fine nurse, don't I?"

Ben helped her up the steps to the room at the end of the hall. The entire house smelled of suffering. Every room big enough for a hatbox was filled to overflowing, even the hallway. They stepped awkwardly between the men on the floor. Caleb lay face down on a cot sandwiched between two amputees. Lydia managed to get near his head and gently wiped the perspiration from his clammy, pale brow. "I'm here, Caleb."

He reached for his illusive butterfly. "Lydia?"

"Yes, Caleb. I'm here."

"Lydia," he mouthed. His thoughts faltered and alfalfa swayed. The field danced with butterflies. One landed on his head. "Look, Grandma, I caught one."

"No, child," said she, "the butterfly found you."

C H A P T E R

NINE

You think I could do better; therefore you blame me already.
I think I could not do better; therefore I blame you for blaming me.
—Abraham Lincoln

L YDIA CHECKED ON Caleb throughout the night as often as she could. There would be no rest, for thousands needed tending. Wagonloads upon wagonloads of wounded were taken into the towns of Perryville and Danville and parceled out to every home, barn, church, and building. Planks were laid across the benches in the church, and wounded men lay shoulder to shoulder across them until the church was a mass of misery. Townsfolk became nurses, surrogate mothers, and burial crews; they gave nourishment, comfort, and penned letters of comfort and often, last words to loved ones.

Mary and Lydia stayed on the edge of the battlefield at the makeshift hospital where the amputations continued for three days. Lydia found a stamina she never knew she possessed, despite the gruesome carnage; she need only look in the soldier's pleading, suffering eyes to become a stalwart of comfort for them.

113

On the third morning, when her rounds took her back to Caleb, he seemed to be resting, and she prayed today would be the day he would come back to her. She kissed his brow. He was clammy and much too warm; he had been fighting infection and in spite of her best efforts, the fever had yet to break. She sponged his brow with cool water and unbuttoned his shirt. The black and blue welts from the bullets that had miraculously bounced off were now turning shades of green and yellow. God wanted him to live, and she could only hope that God had spared him for her. She washed his chest and neck. He shivered, and she pulled the covers up. "I'll be back in a while," she whispered.

She left the house to continue her rounds when a familiar face caught her eye. Sergeant Decker was conversing with a couple of soldiers in dusty uniforms. Despite the fact that their backs were to her, there was a familiarity about them. The taller of the two was well proportioned, the figure of one that commanded respect. Recognition dawned and Lydia's breath dissipated. They were two of her three brothers, Ren and Ethan, but where was her twin, Theo?

Should she run to them? They had no idea she was here. Then again, she felt the snare. Would they try and send her home? Her joy and relief at seeing them alive answered her dilemma and she tossed the what-ifs aside and ran toward them.

Ben stopped talking first as she raced toward them. The prodigal brothers turned to follow his line of sight.

They didn't recognize their phantom sister at first glance, in her three days-old nurse's garb, complete with bloody apron, frazzled hair and smudged face. Ren looked like he was witnessing the second coming.

"Lydia?"

She smiled. "It's me."

"Yee-hah," Ethan yelled and with two large steps had her wrapped in his arms like a Christmas bundle. "My God, what are you doing here?"

Unblemished worry gushed down her weary face. "I'm so glad you're not injured."

"Not so fast little brother, my turn," ordered Ren and stole Ethan's present for a bear hug of his own. "How on earth?" he asked, nearly squeezing the breath out of her. "You shouldn't be here."

Yes, yes, she thought, *here we go*—just like old times. Oh well, it was still heaven to be in her big brother's arms.

"Where's Theo?" she asked. Ren's squeeze froze, and Lydia's heart lurched. He released her. He and Ethan each took one of her hands. She looked at her brothers solemn faces, and hysteria tinged her demanding words. "Ren, Ethan... where's Theo?"

"They're working on him now," Ren said.

"He took some grapeshot in the arm. Tore it up pretty bad," Ethan added.

"Who's working on him?" she asked, pulling her hands from theirs.

Ben stepped forward and gave her the answer. "Sawbones." Her face drained and she started to bolt. Ben took hold of her forearm. "Hold on now, there's no sense goin' in now. Sawbones already done what he's done and there's no changin' it."

Lydia tried to wrench her arm free.

Ben gripped tighter. "Listen to me..."

Ren and Ethan watched the sergeant handle their sister like a skittish filly. They wondered how they knew each other so well.

"Please, Ben. I have to make sure he's alright." She pleaded as the tears began to flow unchecked down her dirty cheeks. Three days with almost no sleep, Caleb and now Theo, the death that surrounded her and the unimaginable carnage all came home to her at that moment, her legs turned to jelly. Ben slid his arm around her waist and led her to a stump by the fire.

"If I'd known yer brother was in the butcher house, I'd have looked after him, but its whiskey done drunk."

Lydia tried to quell the sobs.

"There's nothing you can do now," Ren said.

Ethan took the pot from the fire and poured her a cup of coffee, feeling her pain. She and Theo were thick as molasses.

Her wild tear-filled eyes darted from one to the other. "I can't sit here and drink coffee when Theo just had his arm amputated. I'm a nurse now. I have to go to him."

Ben looked in her puffy, wizened eyes, so young to have seen so much. "I'll go with ya."

Lydia shook her head and choked out a reply. "I'd rather do this alone." Her brothers watched in awe. When did little Sis get so strong? In less than a minute she had pulled herself together and was running off to the hospital. They had been apart less than a month, and yet it seemed like years had passed between them.

"So that little firebrand's yer sister?" Ben asked.

"Can't you tell?" Ethan smiled. "She's such a meek little thing."

"She's got spunk," Ben said. "She's been runnin' round here totin' water, writin' letters and everythin' in between. I don't think she's slept in three days. It's a damn wonder she ain't passed out from exhaustion. She's a worker that one."

"How do you know our sister?" Ren asked, reading Ethan's mind.

"Run into her after the battle. When she found out I was totin' her sweetheart, she near went crazy. She's been by his bedside ever second she could. He'd probably be dead if it weren't fer her tendin'.

She's damn determined to make sure he don't lose his leg, and fer that, I'm in her debt."

Ren raised an eyebrow at Ethan. "Sweetheart, you say?"

Ben looked from one brother to the other. "Ya didn't know?"

"She was supposed to marry the neighbor man a few weeks ago. We thought she had, until today."

Ben rubbed his whiskers. "Ya don't say."

"Who's the sweetheart?" Ren asked.

Ethan piped up. "Caleb Wright, the storekeeper's boy from back home. Better known around here as the Eightieth's brass balls." He looked at Ben then back to Ren. "You know, the one everybody's talking about. He was on that hill collecting Rebel lead for souvenirs. His coat was full of holes but his shirt just had powder burns. I saw it myself. The bullets bruised him but not one broke the skin. Damnedest thing I ever saw."

Ren gritted his teeth. "It's good someone had some guts out there. Wish we could say the same for the Fiftieth."

"Don't be too hard on yerself boys," Ben chimed in. "Most greeners woulda done the same with a yella ass commander like you had. Heard he got relieved yesterday."

Ethan could see Ren simmering beneath the surface.

Ben picked up on it too. "Speakin' of hero, reckon I best go check on him." Things were gettin' mighty interestin', and he was gonna make sure Storekeep pulled through, cause this was a story he wanted to hear.

Ethan and Ren waited till Sarg was out of earshot.

"Give her a chance to tell her story before you go barking at her," Ethan said.

"Sweetheart? Caleb Wright's a damn Protestant," Ren swore.

"Let it go, Ren. You're jumping the gun like always. Give her a chance. I, for one, am damn glad to see her, no matter why she's here. Besides, it's not just Lydia you're fuming about, so don't take it out on her."

Ren glared at Ethan. "We're the laughing stock of this battle."

"Big brother, you did what the rest of us did. How the hell were we supposed to know what to do, with no color bearer and no commander?"

"I should have done something." Ren stared hard at Ethan. "Our little brother ran into the fight, killed two before they got him. What's that say about us? What's Father going to think about that? We send Theo home without an arm… Mother's baby boy for God's sake. We should have at least kept him down or got up and fought with him."

"You can't change what's past, Ren. We'll have plenty of chances to prove ourselves. So, forget it. Let's go check on Theo and then go find out who the new commander is."

Ren kicked at the dirt and followed Ethan back to the hospital.

When Lydia entered the operating room, the house's former living room, Theo's mangled left arm lay on the floor in the bloody straw. She stared at it and thought how many times it had held her, wrestling and hugging. Her head began to spin and she reached for the wall.

The doctor was bandaging Theo's stump. Thank God, the chloroform had arrived yesterday, and Theo didn't have to endure the operation awake. When her head cleared a bit, she inhaled her emotions and walked over.

"I'll finish, doctor. He's my brother."

The doctor looked at her sad eyes. "He should pull through

okay. The infection was contained, but his arm was shattered. I had no choice but to amputate."

"I understand. Thank you, Doctor Kenton." Lydia took the cotton bandage from his hand but wished she'd arrived earlier. Doctor Kenton, like the others, took appendages first, asked questions later. Caleb's leg looked like it was beginning to heal. If Sergeant Decker had not put up a fight, he would be without it. Oh, what did it matter? It was too late, now. Theo's arm was gone forever.

The young handsome doctor laid a hand on her shoulder. "You have been an angel of comfort around here these last few days. Would you consider joining the Sanitary Commission? We could certainly use a fine nurse like you."

Lydia thought about how he had barked at her when he was working on Caleb and his harsh words to others of her ineptness. She had shown him what she was made of since, and now he wanted her to stay. She remembered the humiliation she had suffered at the hands of Miss Crask. What would the snippety old bitty say now?

"I would be honored, doctor."

"Please, call me Simon."

Lydia smiled. "Very well, Simon."

When she finished Theo's bandage and was certain he was in capable hands, she went to check on Caleb. She had spent several hours through the last three nights by his bedside. He had yet to come back to himself since the operation, and he was either unconscious or delirious with fever. Mary supplied her with all of the knowledge and medicines she could to fight the infection. They could only pray it would be enough.

Mary had sent a dozen soldiers to search the woods for honey this morning. She wanted it mostly for the amputees. She said it did wonders to expedite the healing and keep out infection. Lydia hoped they found some, so she could use it on Caleb and Theo. Mary had amazed everyone with her medicinal knowledge and she could give orders like a drill sergeant. Few bucked her—she had improved the poor soldier's conditions more than anyone else. With her for a teacher, Lydia had learned volumes in the short week they had been together.

With her patients looked after, and Ben and her brothers following her, Lydia headed to the cooks fire.

"I don't know about you all but I'm starving."

"I hear that," Ethan chimed.

Ren was busting to get at her, and it wasn't lost on Lydia, she knew him all too well.

"What is it, Ren?"

"This is no place for a woman, Sis. I don't like you being here with all these men. You were raised a lady, you don't belong here."

"Really? I can think of a thousand soldiers that would beg to differ with you on that, and I can think of a hundred more who would be dead if I had not been here."

"That's not what I mean, Lydia."

"What would you have me do Ren, just pack my bag and go home? Home to appease Mother and old man Brenham? Is that the type of man a lady is suited for?"

Ren stared at his hot-tempered little sister. Damn her insolence. "Lydia, you're going home just as soon as I can figure out how to get you there."

"I will do no such thing, and I would like to know why you think that it was alright for you to run away but not for me? I certainly had a better reason than you."

"I didn't run away. I answered the President's plea for volunteers to fight for our country."

"Well, I came to take care of the soldiers that answered that call and that includes you." She had the upper hand and was enjoying the advantage for a change. She wasn't the little girl they left behind in Indiana, and she wasn't about to let them think she was.

"Lydia, you ran away so you wouldn't have to get married."

"Oh Ren, you're infuriating! What does it matter why I ran away? I'm here now, and I'm sorely needed. These soldiers need me and I intend to stay until the war is over!"

"You're going home! And that's the final word on it."

"No Ren, I'm not. For your information, Doctor Kenton offered me a position with the Sanitary Commission just a while ago, and I accepted." *Calm down Lydia, calm down and think.* She took a deep breath and looked around to see that there were plenty enjoying their spat. Until now, no one knew anything about her past. She had been a free soul, respected and loved in a short period of time. She would not have Ren starting trouble for her. She would rather die than go back home.

Ren had an innate desire to put her over his knee and spank some sense into her. "You seem to forget your place, Lydia. You belong at home with Mother and Father. They must be worried sick about you."

"For your information, Papa helped me leave after Bradford attacked me. He even gave me your saddle to put on Dolly."

"I don't believe you."

"Believe what you like. It's the truth."

Ren folded his arms across his broad chest and stared at his red faced sister. "What did Brenham do?"

"Why do you care? You left me to him."

"What did he do, Lydia?" Ren demanded.

"Alright, Big Brother, have it your way. After you all left, he thought I was his, and it seems he wanted me to start my wifely duties early."

"I'll kill the bastard!"

"Yes, that's the answer Ren. Honestly, you miss the point entirely."

"I'm taking you home, and I'll see to him when we get there!"

"You're not taking me anywhere. You seem to forget that you're in the army. You can't just pick up and go. Besides, I already told you that I have accepted a position with the Sanitary Commission. I told Papa I would find the three of you and keep him informed on your health and whereabouts, the best that I could. I intend to send a letter off tomorrow morning and tell him I found the three of you and tell him about Theo's arm. If I go home, it will be to take care of Theo and nothing else."

"You sure seem to be catering to that Wright boy."

"What do you mean by that?"

"He's not Catholic, Lydia. You know that."

"For Heaven's sake Ren, is that all you care about? You're as bad as Mother. I happen to care a great deal about Caleb Wright, and I am intent on saving his leg and that requires a lot of tending. Besides, from what I hear, he's more of a man than anyone in the Fiftieth."

The dagger sunk to Ren's marrow. He seethed. "I won't have no sister of mine trotting after a damn Protestant."

"This may come as a shock to you, Ren, but did you ever think that maybe I don't care what you think?"

Ethan interrupted. "You two haven't been together a full day and look at you, toe to toe in a death roll. Can't we just let it rest and get something to eat?"

Ren was unmoved.

Lydia was exhausted with the argument. "That's a wonderful

idea," She snapped and strode ahead of them.

Ben didn't say a word, he just smiled, rubbed his whiskers and fell into step with the contrary brothers. He was certainly enjoying the entertainment and taking mental notes to razz Storekeep with later.

When they were all sitting with their plates in their laps Lydia spoke first. "Has anyone seen an older nurse with dark hair today? Her name's Mary."

"She was over yonder barkin' orders a while ago." Ben pointed to some tents.

"She sent some men into the woods to find honey this morning. I hope they found some. Mary says it keeps out infection and I was hoping to use some on Caleb and Theo's wounds."

Still fuming, Ren scoffed. "Who's this Mary and where did you meet her?" The interrogation continued.

Ethan watched warily as his siblings embarked again. Some things never changed.

"She's from the Shaker community of Pleasant Hill, not far from here. A place, I dare say, where men still have manners."

Ren ignored the jab. "I know where it is. How did you get way over there?"

If Lydia wasn't so tired, she would never have let that cat out of the bag. What did it matter? He was already seething at her and in her present exhausted state, she simply didn't have the wherewithal to dance around the truth.

"I was running away from a couple of soldiers that wanted to make me go back to Shelbyville. Dolly and I jumped the fence into her garden."

Ethan laughed through a mouth full of beans.

"Be quiet, Ethan!" Ren ordered. "What soldiers? Were they Rebs?"

"It doesn't matter Ren. It's over, and no, they were not Rebels."

"Doesn't matter?" He looked at Ben and Ethan for support. "She says it doesn't matter. She was pursued by soldiers and hooked up with some lunatic that fixes wounds with honey, and she says it doesn't matter."

"It seems to me she's been doing just fine by herself," Ethan said.

"So you think its fine and dandy for her to be here, with all these men, tending their wounds and that it's okay for her to be with that Wright fellow?"

"She could do worse. Hell Ren, he's a damn hero... survived a whole Rebel onslaught and took two dozen out before they took him down. Seems to me, it might be nice to have a hero in the family."

Lydia turned crimson. "I'm only tending him. He's not even conscious, and you already have me marrying him."

Ren had had enough. "Go home, Lydia."

"No."

"Then, get away from us, and go wherever senseless girls go." He made a shooing motion, just like he used to do when they were kids and he didn't want her around. It used to make her cry but now she thought it childish. There was a lot of little boy left in that man.

Ethan knew he should pound the shit out of Renor he would have Lydia running off again. Besides, they were the ones that left her. She had every right to be sore at them, but what right did they have to make her go back and marry Brenham. Ren and Lydia had always been like lard and water. What they failed to realize was that they were two peas in a pod with tempers to match.

"Well, Lydia, what's it going to be?" demanded Ren.

She did a very impressive about-face and walked quickly back toward the hospital without a bite to eat.

"Damn it, Lydia. Come back here," Ren yelled. She paid him no heed.

Ethan spoke, "Another fine homecoming, eh, brother."

Ren swung. Ethan ducked.

"You're so predictable, Ren."

"Well, what would you have me do?"

"Be nice to our little sister. She didn't even eat, you can see she's exhausted; and knock off the shit about Wright. Brass Balls killed more Rebs than all of the Fiftieth." Ethan neither smirked nor smiled as he stepped into Ren's face. "He makes you and me look the fools, and our sister's in love with him. Hell, Ren, you don't give two hoots for church unless it's to spy on the young nuns. And what of him being a Protestant? You can't even spell the word. Besides, how many honeys did you take behind the barn? I don't recall you asking them to say their Rosary first."

Ethan watched Lydia disappear into the hospital. He missed his sister. He could always make her laugh, and she made the best apple dumplings around.

Lydia was by Theo's side when he woke from surgery. Pain creased his face. She sponged his brow. He looked so young, but then, they were only sixteen. He was just beginning to get whiskers, unlike Ren and Ethan's full beards. Why on earth did he have to run off with them? He was white as the sheet he lay on.

"Take it easy, T. I'm here."

Theo opened his eyes. "Lyd?"

"Yes, it's me. Rest now."

"How?"

"Shhh, it doesn't matter. I'm here, and I'm going to take care of you."

"Ren... Ethan?"

"They're here, too. They're fine. Are you hungry?"

"A little."

"That's good. I'll tell Ren and Ethan you're awake, and then I'll get you some broth and bread. But first, let's get some of this good tea in you." Lydia took the porcelain medicine cup. It had a spout and mouth guard so she could give the patient medicine without having to sit them up.

She coddled Theo's neck and helped him lean up while she slowly poured the medicinal tea in his mouth. He struggled to sit.

"Easy, T. Let me help you. You've lost a lot of blood. You need to save your strength and give your body time to heal. You just rest and let me do the rest."

Theo tried to smile, but the pain made it impossible. He had never been happier to see anyone in his life.

Lydia helped him finish the tea and tucked the blanket back around him. With his will to live and her determination to keep the Death Angel away, he would make it. Surely, Ren would come around and see how good it was that she was here, at least for Theo's sake. He and Caleb would be her special charges and she would make sure they had everything they needed and then some. She wished she'd remembered her Rosary; it would help her pray when she was too tired to think. It was rote prayer, but it was a comfort to knead the beads while going to sleep or sitting by a bedside. There were a lot of Catholic boys in the hospital, and she was sure it would give them comfort if they saw her saying a Rosary for them.

Lydia joined her brothers by their fire and gave them some honey cake one of the town folk had baked. Things like this were sheer luxury, and they gobbled it down, licking their fingers clean.

"So Ren, are you still mad?" Lydia asked.

"So that's what the cake was for." Ren took a swig of coffee. "I still think you belong at home."

"I understand why you feel that way, truly I do. But Theo is in desperate need of constant care, and there simply aren't enough of us to care adequately for so many. His chances of recovery would be slim at best, without me to see to him."

"And that Wright boy?"

Ethan watched and waited.

"Caleb's needs my constant care as well. He still has a high fever and is unconscious. I know I can save his leg, but the bandages need changed several times a day to keep infection from setting in and despite their injuries, I can tell you that I've never been happier. This is where I belong, I'm needed here, and the soldiers love me. For the first time in my life, I feel free. I'm doing what I want and I'm good at it. Don't you feel that way now that you're in the Army?"

"I have to say, I do," Ethan replied. "I feel bad for leaving all the work to Father, but I'm glad to be fighting for the Union. I know he didn't understand that, but we were born here. This is our country, and the country I want for my children some day. So yes, I understand what you're saying, but we worry about you, Sis. It's different for a woman to be out here alone. It's dangerous, especially, around all these men. Most of them are good men but you never know."

"Ethan's right, Lydia. This just isn't a place I want my sister to be. We're leaving tomorrow, and I can't rest knowing you're here."

Lydia stared at her brothers; she couldn't believe they would side against her. But then, why should that surprise her. They didn't even bother to tell her they were leaving in the first place.

"I'm sorry you feel that way, truly I am. But I'm staying. This is where God wants me, and you will just have to find your own way to make peace with it. I don't want us parting with hard feelings. So let's agree to disagree and enjoy our time together. I know you're pulling out in the morning and who knows when we'll see each other again."

Her brothers looked at her. She was not the girl of a mere month before. Battle had made men of them, and its carnage had made a woman of her.

"But before you leave, give me as much information as you can on where you're going. I'll write to you about Theo's progress, and you must promise to write to me as well. That's how I'll keep my promise to Papa. He knew you wouldn't write, but that I would. He worries about all of us."

Lydia sat down next to Ren; he put his arm around her, held her tight and kissed the top of her head. "Alright Sis, you win. No more about it."

Lydia kissed his whiskered cheek. "Thank you."

"Well, hallelujah!" Ethan exclaimed. "This place is full of miracles. Now where's my kiss?"

Lydia went to Ethan, kissed his cheek, and hugged him tight.

They talked until the wee hours of the morning. She was sad to see them go but eternally grateful for the time they had spent together. There were no hard feelings. The Weldishofer children were growing up.

C H A P T E R

TEN

)))))⦿⦿((((

Pirate's Cove
May 1939

I OPENED MY EYES. Terror washed over me as the nightmare flooded back. My eyes darted around the cave, but all was still. Peaceful sunlight sashayed through thatched ferns hanging from the mouth of the cave and swaying gently in the morning breeze.

I sat up and tried to make sense of what happened yesterday. My brain throbbed, and every muscle in my body screamed from a night spent on cold, hard stone. Home comforts were calling and I got to my feet, moaning a bit and stretching against the stiff aches.

An image of Grandma kneading her Rosary came to mind and I felt a pinch of guilt. Levi was most likely out combing the woods for me.

At that moment, the cave's sinister voice spoke again and icy fingers brushed my neck. *"I knew you'd come..."*

My heart surged with adrenaline. I yanked my skirts knee high and catapulted myself from the cave, frantically struggling through the tangle of grapevines until I was finally free on the other side. I ran down the familiar trail as fast as I could go, never casting a backward glance.

The swaying arms of the old willow beckoned in the distance. Not missing a beat, I ran, grabbed a handful of branches, swung out over Troublesome Creek and dropped into its icy depths. The frigid water took my breath away, and I shot to the surface with a gasp. My wet dress was dragging me down as I struggled to swim to the bank. I wasn't thirteen anymore. Near panic, I snatched an exposed willow root and clambered onto the mossy bank collapsing in a panting heap in a patch of sunlight. Of one thing I was now certain, I was awake and that voice was real.

I lay there for a long time, going over things in my head. I knew I was awake, but I still wondered if it was possible to have a dream within a dream. A childhood memory came to mind. It was Court Days in Harlan at the end of summer and everyone brought their extra garden produce and anything else they wanted to sell or trade. Khalidah had recently died, and my grief was still raw. I wasn't in the mood to tramp around with Callie Dawn and the other kids, so I wandered away from the crowd and found an old Indian smoking a long pipe and making medicine wheels from pine needles. I stood and watched him for a long time and as if sensing my sadness, he invited me to sit down and began to tell me a story about Dreamtime—a land of spirits where the soul ventures while the body sleeps. He told me that Dreamtime is a spirit land, as real as our everyday reality. Perhaps I was living in Dreamtime.

After that dip in the water, my wet clothes smelled like sulfurous smoke and were smudged with blood from my fall into that pit of limbs. Was this Dreamtime, or was I losing my mind? Could one feel pain in dreams? I pinched myself hard. "Ouch!" It didn't feel like a dream but what were the options? On the way home I smelled flowers, felt the bark of different trees, and tasted a wild onion. I couldn't remember doing those things in a dream before.

I emerged from the woods looking very much like a wet rat. I wasn't even sure what day it was. If I was correct, it was Sunday, which meant most folks would be down at the chapel.

My belly sang a happy tune of anticipation as I strolled up home's green path; it was strewn with vibrant purple violets and sunny yellow dandelions—their simple song a serenade to my anxious soul. I approached Levi's cabin, and he sat in his hickory rocker with Sindbad on his lap—black, fat, lazy and purring beneath Levi's soothing touch. Both of them squinted at me. Sindbad jumped down and hopped off the porch to greet me.

"Miz Mattie, is dat you?" Levi got to his feet and started toward me.

One sympathetic look from my blessed friend sent me running to his arms. I wasn't dreaming.

"Oh, Levi." I buried my face in his brown jacket and breathed deep of earth and pipe tobacco. I was home. "I was afraid you would be out combing the woods for me."

He patted my back.

"No, chil'. The Ancients is lookin' after you. Daise done spoke to me. Is time for you to leap into da fire.

"What?"

"Weez talks about it later. You gots to see Miz Lydia first. She's been jus' aside herself since you lef' outta here yessa-day."

The deep stone steps of Grandma's front porch were warm with mid-day sunshine. Levi left me on the Mercy Seat, one he had made for Grandma before I was born. Carved from oak, the bench was supported on the up stretched arms of two kneeling angels. According to Levi, the Mercy Seat was a place where a person could talk to the Almighty, and He would listen. Over the course of time, many had found comfort there. I was not among them; perhaps it was no coincidence that Levi sat me there, what with his crazy talk about the Ancients. Hell, I needed to commune with someone, a head doctor, most likely. The wood was smooth and warm in the sunshine. Did I remember how to pray? I closed my eyes and struggled with the Lord's Prayer. "Our Father, which art in…" The screen door creaked. I stopped and looked up at Grandma.

"Talking to yourself? Bad sign at your young age," she teased and shuffled to her oak rocker, relief evident on her face. Levi followed, carrying a well-stocked tea tray. My famished body rejoiced at the sight.

"Join us, Levi?" I asked hopeful.

He set the refreshment on the white wicker table and caught Grandma's don't-you-dare stare.

"No, Ma'am. I done had my lunch and I gots to round up da boys. Dat ol apple tree's down from last night's storm." Levi ambled down the steps, using the handrail with more effort than I remembered. I wondered how old he was and supposed only God knew. That's how it was when you were born a slave, your birth unmarked, uncelebrated, your lineage scattered to the wind.

"Frightful storm last night," said Grandma. "Some of the folks over on Greasy Creek swear they saw a funnel cloud." She rearranged her black shawl, and began to rock. "Will you pour the tea, Dear?"

"Gladly," I said, picking up the teapot. The steaming nectar swirled into familiar china to which I added a lump of sugar and bit of cream to each. Grandma's hand trembled when she raised the cup to her quivering lips, and she had to steady it with the other hand. For the first time I could remember, the pinky did not raise.

"Are you okay, Grandma?"

She looked at me over her cup. "I don't believe I slept a wink last night with you out there in that storm."

"I'm sorry Grandma. I didn't mean to worry you." We sat in silence while I devoured six spicy watercress and spring radish sandwiches lathered in sweet butter and three strawberry kolaches, Grandma's favorite pastry. The Greek gods could not have fared better.

"You've been to the battlefield."

I stopped mid-chew. "What?"

"The battlefield." A faraway look stole across her eyes. "You're clothed in it. One never forgets the smell… it stirs the thoughts and resurrects the pain."

She rocked. I chewed.

"You are being drawn to the Shadowlands, Mattie. That was what I was trying to tell you yesterday before you ran off." From her apron pocket, Grandma handed me a small black Bible. An embossed faded gold cross-adorned the worn leather cover. "There is much you need to know."

I licked my fingers and opened the dainty brass clasp, exposing soft worn pages. "It's in German."

"Your Grandfather left it for me…" She faltered. "…during a very difficult time. It seemed that having the Lord's word in my native tongue calmed my fears and worries as nothing else could. I often wondered if perhaps Mother sang lullabies to me in German when I was very small before she became so hard. I have carried that Bible in my pocket every day since he gave it to me." Grandma took it from my hands and stroked the soft pages. "It has brought me comfort on life's many roads. Now, it is time to pass it to you. Perhaps Mattie, it will bring you comfort and peace on your journey."

My chest tightened. "Grandma, you're scaring me. Where are you going, and what journey are you talking about?"

"That is for you to discover. Just as the wise men had to follow their star, so must you. God has a path for each of us, Mattie. Whether you follow yours is up to you."

Seeing this new side to Grandma was more unsettling than the events of the last twenty-four hours. She was my nemesis, the one I blamed for all my troubles, and now she was revealing herself to be a fellow traveler on life's journey; once a woman of fortitude, resilience, and resolve, she now appeared as fragile as hoarfrost.

Most of my life was spent under her roof, yet until now, she had remained a stranger. I grew up an orphan in a place where clan and family ties ran deep. Now, years too late, she was distilling her truth to me.

She moved to rise and stumbled. I leapt to steady her. It was obvious that she was exhausted. I took her arm in mine and walked with her to the door.

"I'm so sorry I worried you, Grandma."

"It's alright, Dear." She lingered in the doorway and pulled a small brass key from her apron hideaway. "There is one more thing I must give you."

She pressed the key into my hand. Again, I felt the surge of energy, just as when she gave me the necklace yesterday.

"Upstairs in the attic, under an old patchwork quilt, you will find a steamer trunk."

We went inside and walked slowly to the parlor.

"It belonged to your great-Grandfather. His father made it for him when he left the Black Forest to come to America. It was passed on to me when your father was a baby." Grandma leaned heavily on my arm. "Perhaps you will find some of your answers among its contents."

I made no reply, intent on getting her to the velvet chaise before she collapsed. Her breathing was labored.

"Grandma, I think I should send Levi for Doctor Lawrence."

"Nonsense, I just need to rest. After all Mattie, I am ninety-three and my time on this earth is nearing its end." I eased her onto the chaise. "What can a doctor do for me when the Lord decides to call me home?" She picked up her rosary from the end table. "I pray every day now, to go home to be with my Caleb. We have been parted far too long." Grandma turned her attention to the robins building their nest in the plum tree outside the window.

I smiled and kissed her forehead. "Alright, we'll wait and see how you feel tomorrow." I wasn't ready for Grandma to leave me alone in this big old house.

In desperate need of a bath, I walked behind the house to the elevated fifty-gallon drum that served as our hot water tank. It was Levi's job to keep the coals smoldering beneath, day in and day out. However, I often ran out of hot water mid-stream and had made it a habit to throw a couple of extra logs on the fire before running my bath.

Grandma never had such problems. She was fastidiously clean and expected hot water in the morning and evening, and that's what she got. Levi would amble over after supper while we sat in the parlor drinking our evening tea. He knew that Miz Lydia would expect her hot water directly, and he did his best to stay on her good side. In his words, she could "peck a feller plumb ta death."

I once overheard Grandma tell great-aunt Francis that she made a promise to herself, when she was a nurse in the Civil War, that if she ever made it back to civilized life, she would never again go to bed dirty and as far as I could tell, she never had.

I wondered for the umpteenth time how Grandma held to her Catholic faith all these years. We lived in the Bible-thumping mountains, and the nearest Catholic parish in good weather was an all-day drive.

Each spring for many years, Grandma and I traveled by train to Lawrenceburg, Indiana—arriving on Fat Tuesday at the home of Grandma's two unwed aunts, Marie and Francis. With no children of their own, they doted on me, and I relished those warm, happy times. We stayed through Easter, and it was the one time of the year that Grandma loosened the purse strings. That yearly trek supplied my wardrobe with much needed dresses, bonnets, and accessories. More than anything though, I treasured the time spent with my great aunts. Aunt Marie taught me the German art of egg decorating, and I always helped Aunt Francis tuck them into the folds of her delicious cardamom-flavored Easter breads.

Grandma's load seemed to lighten while we were there. She often laughed when they reminded her of the childhood mischief she was evidently infamous for, something I couldn't imagine. It was such fun to be with them, and I often fantasized about living with them instead of Grandma.

Grandma said her Rosary at least once a day and usually more. Daddy had built her a stone grotto with a marble Madonna and a bench to sit on in the pines behind the house. I couldn't remember the last time I saw her out there. She used to go nearly every day for an hour or so and pray her Rosary. I guess there were a lot of things that had happened so gradually I hadn't noticed. Melancholy creased my heart. I realized that Grandma was now older than Aunt Francis and Aunt Marie had been when we used to visit.

I on the other hand, held no beliefs. It wasn't that I didn't believe in God, I just didn't feel the need to worship someone who had allowed my life to be emptied of everyone that I loved. I chose instead to live by daily routine and found comfort in the monotony. I felt quite the hypocrite carrying around Grandma's beloved Bible.

Back inside, I opened the valve to the cistern. Luscious steaming water poured forth into the antiquated claw-foot tub; once top of the line, the tub's enamel bottom was dotted with rust. Whenever I broached the subject of replacing it, Grandma turned a deaf ear. She was attached to her things, and this old relic was no exception. I sat on a towel to protect my tender backside and let the water rise around me. The heat immediately penetrated my sore weary muscles, and for a few blessed moments, my mind was still. I lay back and listened to the rushing water, feeling its marvelous healing power. However, as soon as I turned off the water and all was quiet, questions began to intrude. I sat up and reached into Grandma's private stash of imported soaps and shampoos. Normally, I would have settled for homemade lye for my body, and goat's milk for my hair. But for today, my normal routine of in and out was tossed aside as I sought to renew my beleaguered mind with the essence of lavender soap and hyacinth shampoo.

I scrubbed my skin to a rosy glow and lathered and rinsed my hair twice until it smelled of fresh flowers and the last of battle's nauseous odors swirled down the drain.

When I came downstairs, Grandma roused from her impromptu nap, and I helped her back to the front porch, where in the warm sunny afternoon, lilac and honeysuckle perfumed the air.

"Grandma, my head is throbbing with questions."

"Take the key I gave you and have Levi move the wardrobe. I had him nail it to the wall over the attic door, years ago, after I caught you playing up there. The attic is where you will find your answers, Mattie."

I tucked Grandma's shawl about her shoulders. "I'll be back to check on you."

Grandma patted my hand. "I'll be just fine, you go on and find Levi."

When I returned with Levi, Grandma led us up the stairs to her bedroom. I removed the clothes from the massive wardrobe and lay them in neat piles on her bed.

"Lawd, Miz Lydia, I said you'd regret dis, but I's da one doin' the regrettin'," grumbled Levi prying a huge nail out of the back of the wardrobe. From one nail to the next, he worked, shuffling and groaning until the damnable thing dislodged. He pushed, and I pulled, until we moved the monstrosity enough to reveal the narrow attic door. It was much smaller than I remembered.

Grandma's soft wrinkled hand covered mine, and together we opened the door to her past. A stale draft of warm air swept past, breezes in breezeless places, I thought. Goose bumps peppered my skin.

Grandma's eyes grew misty. "The trunk will be up the stairs on your right."

Levi patted her shoulder. "Now, Miz Lydia, why you wanna go diggin' up ghosts?"

Grandma held herself a little straighter and dabbed at her eyes with a lace hanky.

"Its okay, Levi," I said.

"You should just leave it be." He shook his head at us and with heavy steps walked out the door and down the stairs.

"Why is Levi so upset about this, Grandma?"

"Never you mind about him. You just tend to what needs tending." Grandma lit her bedside lamp and handed it to me. "You may be up there a while."

"Will you leave the door open?" I asked.

"Of course, Dear."

Childhood memories had me feeling a bit nervous about this venture, and I wished Grandma were able to go up with me. She shuffled back downstairs as I crept slowly up the dry creaky steps.

Filmy rays of afternoon sun cast a dusty glow over the attic clutter; the trunk was exactly where Grandma said it would be. Despite passing years, she knew the location of every item in this house. I, on the other hand, couldn't remember where I left my shoes.

I swept the quilt off the trunk and sent years of dust swirling. The trunk had a luscious walnut patina that begged to be touched; slowly, I traced the intricately carved butterflies and flowers that adorned the lid with my fingertips. I inserted the key into the ornate silver lock. It turned easily. Slowly, I lifted the lid on a lifetime of memories. The lantern's warm light illuminated several bundles of old letters neatly tied with purple silk ribbons. Lifting out the top bunch, I carefully untied the ribbon and inhaled the faint loose ends of French perfume. The letters were addressed to Private Caleb Wright, Eightieth Indiana Infantry Regiment, from Miss Lydia Weldishofer, 23rd Corps Hospital—postmarked from December 1862 to March 1865.

I gathered them up and dragged the dust cover from an old feather bed. Kicking off my shoes, I climbed in and snuggled beneath musty quilts to read of my Grandparent's private affairs.

Elizabethtown, Kentucky
December 21st, 1862
Dear Caleb,

I was both surprised and delighted by your recent letter. I am so pleased to hear your wounds continue to heal. I too enjoyed our night vigils. I continue to sleep only a few hours at a time, even when my patient load is light. I wonder if I will ever embrace restful slumber again.

Have you heard from home? I received a holiday package late yesterday, from Aunt Francis and Aunt Marie. It has stirred up melancholy and longing for family and friends.

The gray days do little to encourage the holiday spirit. Mary and I are gathering evergreen boughs this afternoon and we hope to find some holly berries as well, to brighten the hospital and in turn, our patient's spirits.

The towns-folk have been so gracious and brought us a cart load of pork, venison, eggs, sugar and flour with which to make Christmas cakes and meat pies for the wounded. I hope you are treated as well.

May God Bless and Keep you,

Lydia

Dearest Lydia,

Thank you for your letter. My leg heals, yet my spirits sag. I miss your words, your eyes and your lovely company. News from home is slow to arrive. Father doesn't write and Mother is ill. Ben tries to keep my spirits up with drills in fighting. He is a fine soldier and I would do well to become as skilled as he.

We train and march in circles all day. We are preparing to give chase to General Morgan and his raiders. How you pursue men on horseback while you're on foot remains to be seen. As terrible as Perryville was, I would rather be a soldier chasing and fighting than sitting in bivouac. Good men become sick daily and vices take control.

We are a long time away from Father's store. I was afraid I shouldn't be seeing you again.

Thank you for uplifting my soul.

Respectfully, Caleb Wright

Eightieth Indiana Inf. Vols.

I held the brittle letters. Bone weary from yesterday's escapades, the attic's old smells tugged at my eyelids. The bed nestled my tired body and with a couple of lingering blinks, I drifted toward faint unfamiliar voices.

ELEVEN

Wright's Mercantile
1861

I EMERGED FROM THE warm brown space between wake and sleep. The bed no longer felt soft beneath me. I blinked and the haze came into focus as I rubbed the sleep from my eyes. My feather bed and quiet attic were no more. I lay instead on a narrow cot and on an itchy wool blanket that smelled of lye soap and wood smoke. I sat up and looked around. Dreamtime again?

I listened to muffled voices that filtered through a canvas covered doorway. A small window above a tower of wooden crates and barrels provided the only source of light in the crowded room. The wide-plank floor was swept clean. Against the far wall, a long wooden table held bolts of cloth—colorful ginghams, calicos, muslins and what I assumed were specialty fabrics wrapped in brown paper.

The voices grew louder and more distinct. I tiptoed across the room and peeked around the curtain into an old-time mercantile. Thick wood shelving lined the walls, chocked full of hardware, dishes, and dry goods. A basket of fresh eggs on the counter seemed to be the object of a heated discussion between a portly middle-aged woman and a young handsome storekeeper. The woman's round face was flushed beneath her brown calico bonnet.

"I'm sorry, Miss O'Malley, but twelve cents a dozen is the best I can do."

"Let me speak to your father, young man. He'll treat me better than that," she snapped.

"He's gone to Lawrenceburg, Ma'am, and he won't be back until the day after tomorrow. I'm in charge until he returns, and twelve cents is the best I can offer."

"Very well, then. Put the twelve cents to my account, but rest assured young man that I will speak to your father upon his return!"

The shopkeeper shook his head as she swooshed out the door and set the bell to ringing.

"You do that," he murmured.

I watched him inspect the brown eggs. He looked up as a pretty girl in a fancy dress paused outside the window to admire the hats on display in the window. They were both distracted—he by her presence—she by a bright blue hat with sweeping feather plumes on top. A richly dressed, severe looking Matron swept up behind her, grabbed the girl's elbow and like a hurricane, propelled her into the store. The door burst open, and the bell jingled wildly.

The shopkeeper fumbled the egg as they burst in, sending it smashing to the floor. Retrieving a rag from his shop apron, he stuttered, "I'll be right with you," and knelt to wipe up the slimy mess.

The girl bit her cheeks and tried unsuccessfully to curb a smile.

"Never mind that now," the Matron snapped in thick German brogue. "I need to see your finest wedding silk. Lace and ribbon as well and they must match."

The shopkeeper straightened and shoved the rag under the

counter. "Yes Ma'am." He smiled at the girl. She flushed and lowered her eyes. "I'll see what we have."

He strode my way. I crammed myself into the recesses just as the curtain swept back.

"Stupid, stupid," he whispered to his reflection in the washstand mirror. He poured a bit of water into the bowl, washed his hands, and ran damp fingers through thick, sandy blonde hair. He smiled, checked his teeth and straightened his tie and apron; a nervous twitch pulsed beneath the corner of his left eye. He moved to the bolts of cloth, picked up one wrapped in brown paper, and returned to the storefront.

Not wanting to miss anything I tiptoed back to the doorway.

"I'm afraid we don't get much call for silk," he said, removing the paper.

The lady inspected the cloth. "I expected as much," she scoffed. "We should have gone to Lawrenceburg." Her ire turned on the girl. "See what a mess you've made of things? Honestly, the way you have manipulated your father in this matter is surely a sin!"

The girl's eyes sparked. "I ought to be married in sackcloth to Bradford Brenham and his thousand acres!"

"That is quite enough, Lydia Elizabeth. This is neither the time nor place for this discussion." The Matron's condescension took aim at the young man. He dropped his eyes and tended to the silk.

The girl's eyes brimmed with tears and her voice shook with frustration and anger. "I want to choose my own husband, Mother. I want to fall in love," she pleaded.

"Lydia. I said we will speak of this later. It is not your decision. Your father and I are making the best choice for you. You will be well provided for."

"The best choice for me? The best choice for you. That's what you mean, Mother."

The young man stammered. "Ladies, perhaps I should look in the back for some lace and appliqués."

"Very well," the Matron snapped. "I want English lace if you possibly have such a thing."

"Yes Ma'am," he replied curtly and walked my way; his face and neck radish red.

I enveloped myself between stacked crates and wooden barrels.

"Old biddy," he snarled under his breath.

He searched through some boxes and retrieved two. He paused by the door until the tirade ceased and stepped into the lull.

Anxious not to miss the drama, I scurried back to my observation point. My dress snagged on the corner of a crate and before I could stop it, the entire tower came crashing down around me.

"Shit," I cursed loudly. In an attempt to pull myself up, I set another tower of barrels in motion. I folded my arms over my head as it rained flour, molasses, and nails. "Ouch! Shit! Ow!"

I looked for escape. None appeared. If I were dreaming, now would be a good time to wake up. I hoisted myself from the crates, busted barrels, and sticky goo and crept back to the curtain, licking molasses from the back of my hand.

"What was that?" The matron's eyes darted to my hole.

"I didn't hear anything," the shopkeeper lied.

"No one plays me for a fool. I heard a trollop back there, doing God only knows what. When your father returns, You can rest assured that he will know how you've been conducting yourself. In his store, no less!"

"Believe me, Mrs. Weldishofer, there is no woman here."

Puffing up like a viper, she snarled, "You see, Lydia, this is why you have no say. You would choose a liar and a fool." The woman sifted through the carton and removed several lace appliqués. "I'll take these, fifteen yards of silk, and twenty of ribbon." She snapped two gold coins on the counter. "Put the change on my account."

"Yes Ma'am." It was obvious that he was doing everything in his power not to lose his temper. He was red-faced, and his pulse was beating the devil's gait beneath his eye.

The girl's blue eyes pleaded with him. He held her gaze for a moment before shifting to the job at hand. His hands trembled as he measured, cut and folded the white silk. He placed the ribbon and appliqués on top, wrapped it all in brown paper, and tied it neatly with a piece of string he pulled from a large ball suspended from the ceiling in a large open weave, cast-iron cup.

He handed the package to the girl. Their eyes spoke volumes as their fingertips caressed beneath the package.

"Will there be anything else, Miss Weldishofer?"

The girl's eyes never wavered from his as tears trickled down her cheeks.

It was obvious to me that their hearts were breaking.

Her benefactor swished forward, her hand a vice on the girl's arm. She looked from one to the other and pushed her charge out the door. The matriarch stopped in the doorway and unleashed a swollen ballast. "I would suggest Mister Wright that you divest your mind of any future thoughts of my daughter." She slammed the door behind her, sending the bell into convulsions.

The shopkeeper slammed his fists to the counter and leaned forward; his chest heaved with anger and misery.

My heart ached for him. As I let the canvas fall back, I suddenly realized that I had just watched Grandma Lydia and Grandpa Caleb flirting beneath a package of silk.

I peeked back into the store and watched Grandpa cut a long

strip from the bolt of wedding silk and shove it deep in his pocket. His eyes looked my way.

"Who in the hell is back there?" He demanded. Pulling an ax handle from a barrel he strode my way with a bull's fury.

I stumbled backward, tripped over a barrel and fell into the molasses mess. The curtain swept back.

He looked at the calamity, then at me. His gray-blue eyes congealed, and he slammed the ax handle into a crate above my head.

I scrambled backwards. "It was an accident!"

CHAPTER
TWELVE

Grandma's Attic
1939

"MIZ MATTIE, wake up."

"I'm sorry. Please don't hurt me!"

"Hush child, is just ol Levi."

I opened my eyes to see Levi's golden-green ones peering into mine.

Breathing relief, I sank into the bed.

"You bin travelin' again," he said. His hand wiped my face with his ever-present rag. "You is a mess."

I tasted flour on my lips.

"Damn it to hell, Levi. What's going on?"

"There, there Miz Mattie. Calm yerself."

"Calm myself. Calm myself? In less then forty-eight hours, I've been covered in blood and pus and now in flour and molasses." I cowered in the bed. "Make it stop, Levi. Dear God, make it stop!"

"I cain't. You is walkin' the Shadowlands. You the chosen one, Miz Mattie. Does you remember the prophecy my mammy told you?"

"I was ten, Levi. Ten!" I remembered more than I cared to admit.

Levi sat on the bed and rested his head in his hands. After a few moments, he sat back and looked at me. His face was troubled. "Is time, Miz Mattie. Time for you to know yer destiny. Only ting is, Miz Lydia's gonna be powerful mad when she finds out I tole you."

"Why would she be mad? She's been talking about crazy stuff for the last three days. Travels, sights, things yet to see, and all kinds of…"

Levi shook his head emphatically. "Is not the same ding. She's talkin' about her past and a promise your Grandpa Caleb made to her. I is talkin' about Pangari… da ancients… yer birthright."

"I'm sick of these goddamned riddles, Levi. I don't care what you and Grandma want. I want my life back!"

"You has to know that yer Grandpa Caleb was part of da prophecy but Miz Lydia won't have nothin' to do wid it. And she'll have my hide fer talkin' 'bout it."

"I'm not afraid of Grandma, Levi. Besides, what does Grandpa have to do with all of this?"

"Yer Grandpa Caleb's Grandma Hannah was my grand-mamma too."

I stared at Levi, now nothing was making sense, absolutely nothing. "How is that possible?"

"That's a story fer another day but the short of it is this… Caleb's Grandma Hannah was married to a slave owner, a cruel man and ever month when she went wid-out child, he'd beat her. So, she gots to spendin' time wid the slaves, tryin' to better dere life da best she could.

She fell in love wid my Grandpa and dey had a son, name of Amos. Now Massa dought she was a carryin' his child but she knew it was Moses baby and dat when it was born and Massa saw it was black, he would kill dem all. The Ancients was a lookin' out fer my pa and Massa was off gettin' drunk when Hannah gives birth to my pa, Amos. She run off dat very night and lef' da baby wid da slaves.

Massa ran a breedin' farm and day was so many a bein' born all da time, dat another gal took my pa as a twin to hers so Massa would never know. So you see Miz Mattie, we is related, we has da same blood. Is time fer you to know yer destiny. Day is no escapin' it."

"Levi, this is all too incredible to be true. Am I dreaming? Are you here right now? Am I here?"

Levi's orbs glittered, their gold flecks a sojourn of stars in orbit. "Real as the sun dat rises ever mornin'. Now I is gonna tell you what Mammy told you when she was a dyin'. But first I have somethin' to give ya."

I sat up and wrapped my arms around my knees.

Levi reached deep in his shirt pocket and pulled out a ring. It was a gold ring, fashioned like a snake with a head on each end of its body. The heads lay side by side, each had one eye open, watching the other, one a ruby, one a diamond. "Dis was given to Mammy by da Ancients when she was given her birthright, before da white men took her. Somehow she kept it hid or it hid itself when danger was near. It's yers now. You is da Chosen, Miz Mattie and you needs it more dan me."

With a shaky hand, he slid the ring onto my index finger. I felt a ripple of knowledge and a vision of a seashore of the whitest sand lay before me, and there were countless black children playing in the waves beneath an azure sky. I watched them laugh and play as Levi recited the timeless story.

"My Mammy, Khalidah, was born under da Shadow of Pangari, far across da ocean on da island of Pemba and she was da seven daughter of da seven daughter of da seven son. The Pangari legend say, to da hundred generation da Shadows come. She was to be da next priestess of da Tambookie tribe but da great ship, Sultana, landed on da shore and dey spirited her away, brung her to dis land to live beneath da shadows as a slave. I is her seven son, I have the eyes of golden green just as you have, day is only given to da heir of da prophecy. Mammy had dem, I have dem, and I gives dem to you Miz Mattie. I had no babies of my own, so da night you was born, I stole you from yer crib and me and Mammy took you to da sacred circle. We chose you to be the bearer of da prophecy and da one to fulfill da ancient promises. You is da hundred generation, Miz Mattie. We took you to da Ancients and dey pass my veil to you, you feels it like I does, da memories is in yer blood. Just like you is seein' the children play. Open yer mind and listen for da whispers, den you will understand."

Levi took my hands in his, rolled back his head and began to chant. "In da days of da darkness, da spirit come, and dey called da spirit, Pangari."

Murmurs filled the attic and images seized my mind.

"Mwana Saba, open your eyes to the tumult and hear our call. The lamp of life grows dim. You must continue the circle that will set straight the darkness."

I sat alert and scared. "I don't want to be chosen, Levi. I want my boring miserable life back. Make it stop!" He held my hands tight in his as a fast and wild wind began to blow, swirling Grandma's letters about the attic. I gripped his hands in terror.

The voices continued to murmur. "When Pangari wills, when the time of fulfillment draws near, the portal to the past will open."

There was a shriek and a wail and the glass blew out of the window. I squeezed my eyes shut.

"Da portal is open, Miz Mattie."

The voices chanted louder. "Mwana Saba, step into the great

darkness. You must bind-up the threads of time for the deliverance of future generations."

Levi gripped my shoulders, and shook my eyes open. "Miz Mattie, if you fail, if Pangari's seed is not sown before da portal closes…" Levi's eyes were on fire with emotion, and then he pulled back into himself, released his grip and bowed his head in exhaustion.

The attic calmed. *Thank God.*

"What? What is it, Levi?"

"You control yer destiny, Miz Mattie. You must listen to da whispers and embrace da Shadows of what was."

"And if I don't?"

"You must!"

"What is it Levi? What happens if I don't?" I was terrified. I had never seen Levi like this. Maybe he doubted the choice he made so long ago—doubted me—was it any wonder?

"Our skin be different, but our souls be da same. We is of da same soul line. Just like yer Grandpa Caleb and his Grandma Hannah. You must listen to da Ancients and let dem guide you."

The attic grew dark. We sat in silence for a long while. I shivered. "What time is it?"

"After seven, I reckon."

"Can we leave?"

Levi looked hard into my eyes. "Don't you forget what happened here today. You cain't hide beneath da shadows no more! You is of da light and you must bear da light for dose not yet born."

Quietly, like a scolded child, I followed Levi's slow steps down the stairs into Grandma's dusky bedroom. The sun had dipped behind the mountains.

"Levi, what do I have to do?"

"First ding is to go see to yer Grandma. She sent me up to fetch you down."

"That's not what I meant."

Levi looked back at me. "Listen."

"Listen? That's what Grandma said. What in the hell am I supposed to be listening for?"

Levi put a hand on my shoulder. "You better tend to yer Grandma. She's on da porch."

I could see there would be no more answers tonight.

I stepped outside; sweet evening air greeted me. Grandma's eyes were transfixed on the silhouettes that ran the perimeter of our yard.

"What are you looking at, Grandma?" I asked, softly touching her shoulder.

Her hand reached up to cover mine. "Just thinking I guess. Would you like a cup of tea?"

"More than you know."

We sat in silence and sipped our tea while the crickets played us a melancholy tune, and a moth flitted about the oil lamp, casting wild desperate images across the porch. I felt just like that moth. Drawn to something I didn't understand, banging myself into it again and again, out of control, gaining nothing. We were both immersed in our thoughts when I noticed Grandma shiver in the cool night breeze. I rose and tucked her tired black shawl around her thin shoulders.

She looked up at me. "What on earth have you been into, child?"

I had completely forgotten to clean up from my recent foray in the molasses. "I'll explain in a minute, but first I need to know something."

Grandma's eyes went back to the yard shadows.

"Levi told me about Pangari, about stealing me in the night

when I was a baby. Is that true?"

"That old poop should learn to keep his mouth shut."

Lydia remembered the night Levi stole Mattie from her cradle and he and Khalidah took her to their voodoo forest. She had trailed them with lantern in hand and blood on her mind. When she reached the circle in the forest, her lantern fizzled, and the air sang unearthly notes. Filled with terror, she had watched her newborn granddaughter rise out of Levi's elevated hands, on a swirling white eddy. Up, up, Matilda went into the night sky, up to the height of the tallest trees.

Giant shadows came from the forest and moved into the circle, forming a second ring around the swirling white mass. Strange songs emanated from everywhere, and slowly the baby descended, landing softly in Khalidah's outstretched arms. The shadows dispersed, and her lantern relit of its own accord. She had rushed forward and scooped Mattie away from Khalidah.

Whatever Levi bestowed on Mattie that night, plagued the child with nightmares and daydreams. Lydia had done everything in her power to keep them at bay; she felt certain at the time, that if she refused to acknowledge them, they would go away, and until now, she thought they had.

"Don't you listen to none of Levi's voodoo nonsense, you hear?"

"Levi doesn't practice voodoo, Grandma. He's the most spiritual man I know."

"Voodoo," repeated Grandma.

Lord, there she went again. If I didn't find a way to change the subject, she'd harangue me till the Second Coming.

"Now tell me what you have been up too. Making molasses cookies?"

I smiled weakly.

"I was reading your letters to Grandpa back in 1863, and I fell asleep on the feather bed in the attic. I dreamed I was in this old general store kind of like Mister Bailey's in Harlan."

Grandma made no response so I continued.

"There was a handsome young man keeping the store, probably about twenty or so, and this girl came in with her mother." I paused, hoping she'd jump to my conclusion, but of course she didn't. She sat unresponsive, except to adjust her shawl. "It seemed they were buying silk for the girl's wedding gown."

"Did you see the young man drop an egg when we came in the store?"

"What do you mean, we?"

Grandma stared through the blackness. The squeaks from her rocking chair ruminated in our strained calm. "You were not dreaming, Mattie. I don't know how it is happening or why, but you appear to be traveling back in time. I was the young girl you saw. My mother had taken me to buy silk for my wedding dress. She was going to marry me off to Mister Brenham, a man more than twice my age, widowed with five children. His oldest daughter Camilla was just two years younger than I."

Grandma's eyes went back to the forest's boundaries. "He had a large farm that adjoined ours. Mother had dreams, big dreams."

I listened quietly. Was I dreaming again, or was she opening yet another parcel from her past?

"Father pitied my predicament, but he was no match for Mother's relentless determination." Grandma's lips quivered with each sip from her precious pink china. I understood the china now. It fit the fancy dressed girl in the general store. Old curiosity renewed. I wanted to know more about her past, about Grandpa.

"The War wasn't long in coming, but Mother maintained— in fact, insisted—that it was not our war. My brothers felt differently, as did I, perhaps because we were young, seeking adventure, thinking glorious thoughts… they of fighting, I of escaping my loveless fate."

Painful memories floated across her face.

"Finally, Papa had seen enough of Bradford Brenham. He gave me his rainy day money and helped me make my escape. I never saw Papa again. He dropped dead behind the plow the next spring, trying to do the work of four men."

"Oh Grandma, that's awful."

Grandma dabbed at her eyes with a hanky. I refilled our cups with tepid tea and waited for more.

"I was ill-prepared for the realities of war, and I felt pressed to help in any way that I could. No one of authority beckoned to me… only those poor bleeding boys… the weather so hot and dry. I did all I could for them but it was so little, and their needs were so great. They were the best boys, so grateful for a gentle word, a sip of water, someone to hear their last words."

I touched Grandma's arm. She laid her hand on mine.

"The suffering on a battlefield is beyond human comprehension."

I thought of all of those hands begging for help as I strode across that field carrying that sweet little boy.

"Yes, I know," I whispered.

THIRTEEN

Pine Ridge Settlement School
May 1939

I SLEPT SOUNDLY AND woke early. I snuck up to the attic and gathered the strewn letters, stowing them in my apron pocket. Anxious as I was to get back to them, I cooked a breakfast of fried ham, potatoes and buttermilk biscuits, served hot, with fresh strawberry jam and butter.

Grandma wasn't up yet—a first in my memory—so I went to check on her. To my relief she was sleeping peacefully and I drew the heavy brocade curtains to hide the day. I glanced at Grandpa's portrait and could swear he winked at me. I winked back and tiptoed out, closing the door quietly behind me.

I set the table for two and ate alone reading the letters. I tidied the kitchen, fixed Levi a plate, and stuffed the bundle of letters in my apron pocket.

Levi was on his porch sipping coffee. A heavy mist hung in the valley, the air cool and fresh. The day was waking, birds twittered and the sun's morning rays illuminated the fog hovering over the mountaintops. It was going to be a beautiful day. Levi took the steaming plate, stuck his nose close, shut his eyes, and inhaled.

"Why thank you, Miz Mattie. I ain't cooked none yet."

"My pleasure, Levi. Enjoy."

With everyone occupied, I walked toward the little stone Chapel. I had not set foot in the Chapel since my baby was carried from it in a tiny pine box. Inexplicably, I was drawn there this morning to read the letters. Perhaps, as Levi said, I was beginning to feel the need to put those heartaches beneath the shadows, once and for all. I was emotionally exhausted and looking forward to a long lazy day.

The beautiful morning gave me a happy heart and the craziness of the past few days seemed a distant dream as I paused at the thick limestone steps of the Chapel. My eyes traced the overgrown trail that wound up the mountain to the family cemetery. The upkeep of the family plot was the one job I refused to do.

I opened the thick wood door and stepped into the cool darkness; it felt safe and peaceful, with a holy stillness. I sat in a pew by a curved, cathedral window through which I could see the valley below and mountains beyond. I picked up a letter, but the subdued light was not yet bright enough to read by. Patiently, I waited for the sun to crest the mountaintop. I smiled to myself. No one would look for Mattie Wright in the chapel and I could read undisturbed for hours.

Within a few minutes, the crimson orb rose silently above the farthest mountain range and transformed the gray sky into a creamy watercolor sea. It was a magnificent daybreak, and my quiet mind basked in its glow.

A curious effervescent mist began to undulate across the mountaintops and I walked outside, letter in hand, to see it better. I wished Levi and Grandma were there to watch it with me. It was the kind of rare occurrence that you wanted to experience with someone so you could talk about it later. Before I realized the true nature of the phenomenon, it rolled across the valley and up the hill at lightning speed. It looked harmless enough, a rolling multi-colored cloud.

Wrong again.

It swept me away to a warm sunny day where I appeared several yards beyond a Union encampment. A young soldier was reclined against a thick hickory; it was the storekeeper of yesterday. I moved closer. He had a blue cap tilted on his thick blonde hair and had traded his shop apron for Union blue. He was using his knee for a writing table, composing a letter on a dismantled envelope; he dipped his pen into an ink bottle encased by a miniature oak barrel and began to write. The pen made tiny scratching sounds and he talked as he wrote. "I hope this doesn't anger her."

I jumped when a boisterous voice rang out from inside a nearby tent. "Anger her? Hah! Ya shouldn't be writin' that firebrand in the first place."

"I don't care. I'm lonely and I miss her."

"Ya don't know that one." A burly, muscled man spouted as he emerged from their tent. "Ya don't know any woman the way ya should."

The men exchanged eat-shit glances. Soldiers around them chuckled.

"She's a hellcat. I'm a tellin' ya Storekeep. Ya git tangled in her web and she'll suck the blood right outta ya."

"What in the hell are you talking about?"

"Yer life, Boy. Yer apt to lose yer life."

The letter writer laughed. "It's pen and paper. I never heard of anybody dying from that."

"Damn it Storekeep, what don't ya understand? After all my

careful instruction, I thought you'd learnt somethin' by now."

Fire flared in Caleb's eyes. "I can hold my own with the best. You're the only one in camp that doubts it."

"You'll burp."

The letter writer looked sideways at his nemesis. "Belching will cost me my life?" he smirked.

"A hiccup, ya might call it. That heifer, she'll make ya hesitate, fill yer thoughts with her instead of where they need to be. Watchin' yer ass and mine."

"That's the craziest fool thing I ever heard."

"I'm a tellin' ya. Ya best let her go. If ya make it home, find her then."

I looked to the letter I still held in my hand. It was written on a disassembled envelope.

> *My Dearest Lydia,*
>
> *Please excuse this letter but I have no proper paper and no way to get any as we are on the move. But I wanted to write to you again. My wound aches with all the marching but it is better than being left behind. It makes me think of the battles that lie ahead but also of your gentle, persuasive spirit. It's quite remarkable.*
>
> *Every morning and night I relive all of our moments together. When I left Indiana, I thought I would never see you again. And when I did, my prayers were answered. At first, when I saw your tear filled eyes, I thought that I must be in heaven. In them I saw your love and concern for me. It was then that I determined to live and to love you. To have you for my own. I long for the day when I can wake up next to*

you and kiss you awake.

I like referring to you with "dearest" as you in calling me dear in your last letter. It sent shivers of joy down my spine. Thank you for having the courage to speak your heart, it allows me to speak mine as well. I want to marry you, Lydia and I want to raise a family with you by my side.

I think of you often. That's not true, for I wonder of you continually. This world of killing has allowed us to correspond this way. And how peculiar this is! Back home I had to steal glances of you walking the boardwalks. I made the mistake of telling Father this. He scolded me terribly saying that good English do not associate with those Germans who butcher our language and rob our businesses. A full-grown man had to listen to this, but I didn't believe it.

Do you know "Ode To Psyche" by Keats? It makes me think of you...

They lay calm-breathing on the bedded grass; Their arms embraced, and their pinions too;

Their lips touch'd not, but had not bade adieu, as if disjoined by soft-handed slumber, and ready still past kisses to outnumber

At tender eye-dawn of aurorean love: The winged boy I knew; But who wast thou, O happy, happy dove? His Psyche true!

"Psyche" means soul and this you are for me. I read and reread your letters and I'm afraid they

are becoming tattered and soiled. But I keep them next to my heart, knowing they passed through your hands to mine. I love you Lydia—I want to hold you and kiss you, search your senses with my own. Do you want the same?

I must go. Ben's yelling for me to stop writing that nurse and git off my ass.

Your loving servant, Caleb

CHAPTER

FOURTEEN

The dogmas of the quiet past are inadequate to the stormy present.
—Abraham Lincoln, December 1, 1862

C ALEB FELT BEN'S eyes on his writing paper and gripped
his pen tighter.

"Ya shouldn't send that letter, Storekeep."

Caleb stiffened. "Tell me then, oh wise lover of women, why
shouldn't I mail this letter?" What did Ben know of loving? He saw
women for bedding, dogs as friends, and killing as a trade.

Ben sat next to Caleb and watched the men in camp. Any
that caught his gaze, quickly turned theirs elsewhere. Sarg was not
one to be crossed; a sideways glance might get you killed, at least
that's what they believed, and that was the way Ben wanted it. He
treasured their fear. Smiling inward, he scowled outward and
lifted the letter from Caleb's knee.

It was the first time in weeks that Caleb had been able to sit
long enough to finish a letter. Between marches, skirmishes, and
relentless drilling he had yet to finish a letter. Time and again, he
had to tuck and bundle his emotions. It had been nearly a month
since he received her last letter and with no other outlet, his fears

and frustrations spewed onto the page.

Ben skimmed the letter front to back.

"It ain't a gonna do."

"What's wrong with it?" Caleb snapped.

Ben shook his head and chuckled. "Ya send this, and you'll have hell to pay, I mean, looky here, Corporal Shithead. Ya hear what ya wrote? Like she's got another man. What do ya think she's a doin? Havin' a social while we kill Rebs? She's workin' her ass to the bone, that's what. And ya go a waggin' yer finger at her."

"Let me see."

Caleb jerked the letter from Ben's hand. He was tired, and he didn't want to hold his feelings any longer—especially after that last letter she sent. He wanted her more than he'd ever wanted anything, and just when he thought she felt the same, she looped a knot in his tail, telling him they would be fools to think of marriage until the war was over. Then there was that Mary woman and that damn doctor, spending their evenings with Lydia while he sat on picket duty waiting for some nutcracker Reb to breech their line.

"I've got to say what I say."

Ben reiterated. "It don't matter yer reason. If ya want hell down yer back, go on and mail it."

"It's said, and that's the way it's going to stay." Caleb folded the letter and stuffed it in his shirt. "I read you her last letter. She's making me crazy."

Ben rolled the chaw out of his mouth and pitched it. "I've taught ya all I know 'bout stayin' alive when the bullets fly, but yer heifer—she's a hell-cat. She may bitch about her mother's ways, but yer Miss Lydia picked up traits from that same she-cow, and it don't mean a lick whether it's good or bad. It's there and I'm a tellin' ya when she gets that there letter, she'll cut yer heart out." Ben breathed deep the waft of a hundred cook fires. "And fry it up for supper."

Harley was riding mailbag today and Caleb grabbed his gun and stomped off to give him the post. The smell of frying meat made his stomach growl. Successful foraging at nearby farms yesterday had gleaned enough hams that they would have a chunk of meat with their sloosh tonight. Sloosh, that handy concoction they'd learned from the Rebs, was a mixture of flour or cornmeal fried up with grease. He couldn't remember the last time he'd had a good piece of meat.

Harley was finishing his meal when Caleb walked up. He watched Caleb carefully address the post and drop it in the mailbag.

"For your lady friend?"

"Yep."

"I'll drop by their camp, save some time."

"Drop it by?"

"They're camped just outside of Perryville. Didn't you know? Reckon a fight's comin'. The General sent out a request a week ago for them to get down here and join us before we head on south. They set up camp late last night. You must have been on picket when all that scuttlebutt was going around."

"Ben knew?"

Harley smiled and tied down the mailbag.

"Reckon so."

Shit-to-high-heaven. Caleb strode back to the tent. "Why didn't you tell me she was that close?" he demanded of Ben.

Ben took a big bite of ham and talked through it. "Damn it, it ain't no dumb luck that the hospital's travelin' this close. Get yer head outta yer ass, and back where it belongs and that's a goddamn order! Eat yer supper and git on out to the pickets."

"This is bullshit."

Ben focused on his food but kept one eye on his steaming subordinate. "Get yer plate."

Caleb's boots didn't move. "I ought to punch you."

"I'd like to see ya try."

Caleb thought hard about it. He had an innate desire to lunge at Ben and knock him off his log; he stared hard at him but thought better of it. Sarg would kill him. Besides, he was hungry and bullets and beans came first to a soldier's heart. Caleb swallowed his anger and dug into the supper Ben had fixed; sloosh, green apples, and ham—a feast by soldier standards. Damn that woman. He'd never acted like this before. Maybe Ben was right. Maybe he should just let her go. He wolfed down his supper, grabbed his gun, and prepared for a long cold night on picket. He hated the duty because it gave him too much time to think, and all he could think about was Lydia. She kept him in a state of controlled hysteria, and that was a poor and dangerous place for a soldier to be. Ben claimed Rebs lurked behind every hill and holler, and with the hospital so close, he just might be right; he usually was. Then again, after Lydia read his letter, she might just leave him to bleed to death on the next battlefield.

At daybreak, Caleb walked into bivouac. Breakfast was cooking and the coffee smelled like heaven. He didn't miss a beat getting to it. While he ate, he watched Ben clean his gun, his head full of a night's worth of thinking. The worst part was that he thought Ben might be right.

"The men must be laughing behind my back."

Ben looked at his charge. "About what?"

"Everything."

"If they are, they do it with respect. They know them stripes cost a couple hundred Razorbacks their lives. Hell, yer a livin' legend."

Caleb poured more coffee and finished off the last piece of ham. "Maybe so, but I had no choice in what I did."

"Like hell! Ya wanted yer ass dead, tryin' to redeem yerself, that's what."

"How do you know what I wanted?"

"Cuz I put that hole in yer leg."

Caleb stared at the cup in his hands. He had known it, felt it, but to hear Ben say it was a knife to his heart. He knew Ben gave him what he deserved and should have shot him dead, but it still hurt like hell.

"You gave me what I deserved."

"Yep."

"Do the men know?"

"Nope."

"Guess the Lord wants me alive."

Ben dislodged a piece of pork from between his front teeth with the tip of his boot knife. "Jesus tell ya somethin', did he? I'd like to know myself how yer coat got them holes and yer body just got bruised."

Caleb rammed the cleaning rod down the barrel of his Springfield. "Maybe he's saving me for Lydia."

Ben smirked a reply. "If'ns he was, ya blew that to hell when ya posted that letter."

Caleb's chest tightened. "Has Harley left yet?"

"Rode out twenty minutes ago. Yer good as dead. She'll be a readin' that letter before breakfast."

FIFTEEN

Your dispatch of yesterday has been received, and it disappoints
and distresses me. ...I am not competent to criticize your views
and therefore what I offer is merely in justification to myself.
—Abraham Lincoln

LYDIA SAVED THE letter all day and now opened it by lantern light. She knew Caleb would have words to say after her last letter. He had talked about marriage, a family and his ardent love for her. It was her heart's desire to marry him someday, but with the sickness, death, and pain that surrounded her every day it seemed impossible. The war had stolen her ability to dream—there was only the now and the now took everything she had.

Today began with the death of sixteen year-old Jeremy Smith. He had been with them since the battle of Perryville and Lydia had become his friend and confidante. She knew he was taken with her, but she treated him as if he were one of her brothers. He would only eat for her, and to everyone's astonishment, he had held on despite a severe abdominal wound. All these long months, she had tended him as one of her special charges. Each day she made sure she had at least five or ten minutes to sit with him and he loved to make her laugh with his silly jokes. He was so homesick and while he never learned to read or write, she took faithful dictation for him and sent dozens of letters home to his mother, always enclosing one of her own. He was his widowed mother's only surviving child. His father had been killed at the Battle of Fredericksburg in December, and Lydia was determined to send Jeremy home to his mother alive. In fact, Doctor Kenton had said just yesterday that he might be well enough to travel home as soon as the weather warmed. Yet today, after a week of steady improvement, his fever surged, and within two hours, he was gone. She had just finished writing the sorrowful letter to his mother through tears of her own. Jeremy had been a bright spot in her weary days, and tomorrow they would bury him alongside his comrades that fell on that same battlefield last October.

When she thought the day could get no worse, a courier arrived with a month old letter from her cousin Vera. Papa was dead, sweet, wonderful Papa, dead behind the plow, trying to do the work of four men. She wondered if her brothers knew. Theo left her in March, not to go home but back to his unit, with the hope that his new commander would let him stay on and help with the horses and courier duties. He couldn't fight anymore, but there was plenty to do in the Army that didn't require the use of a rifle.

Lydia's unbearable grief was compounded by the hatred she felt for her mother. Had the War not come, had her brothers not left, had she been able to stay, Papa would still be alive. There was no reason to send letters home now. She had no home without Papa.

Papa's replies to her letters had been few, and she often wondered if Mother intercepted them; it would be like her to punish him that way—angry at him for helping his daughter escape. Lydia blamed them all. Even more, she blamed herself. Leaving Papa alone with Mother, she might just as well have hammered the nails in his coffin.

Mary and Doctor Kenton came looking for her when she didn't come to dinner. Wishing only to be left alone with her grief, she feigned a sick stomach. Now she sat alone in her tent and opened Caleb's thick post. She unfolded the paper and stared at his words. Angry words. Accusing words.

> *Dearest Lydia,*
>
> *I'm deeply hurt by your remarks. It's more than a lonely soldier talking here. Yes, I read more into your letter than what was written. I presumed to see through your words and straight into your heart. If I was wrong, I apologize but I've looked beyond the way it should have been with months and perhaps years of correspondence and courting.*
>
> *I fear another has gained your affections. No, that's not quite true, is it? There is someone else, isn't there? You demand the world of me, and what can I expect from you? Criticism, fear, and betrayal!*
>
> *Your sense of propriety runs deep and your temper is quick. I live with that, but I also live with daily death, of myself and others. Seeing these things, as must you, I beg you to let go of your heart, Lydia. In a few weeks, we will meet and after that, while we chase Morgan and his raiders, it may be months.*
>
> *I live with fear, disease, and damnable weather. You can run home anytime you wish. I enlisted and you volunteered. All I have for comfort is Ben*

and my dreams of you, whereas, you have all kinds of soldiers and doctors to choose from.

As for your German kin and my English ones, I didn't mean to insult you. I was trying to say how our cultures keep us apart. It's one good thing of this War, many are learning on the battlefield that we all bleed and die the same.

My English ancestors believe God ordained them to rule the world! All hogwash! We must get past this, for there is no separation of people in the Lord's kingdom. Ben is a scoundrel but he treats all people the same, usually bad, but at least it's the same, and there's merit in that! But you, my sweet Lydia, twinkle your eyes and swish your hoops to get what you want.

Lydia did not finish. She tossed it aside—how old she felt—how she longed to sleep a dreamless sleep. Yesterday, she turned seventeen. No one knew except Theo, wherever he was. She had begged him to stay with the hospital, he was a lot of help around the camp and she desperately missed his company.

Soul-weary, she felt the salt of Caleb's words. Where was her anger and the strength it could give—the strength she needed to let him go? She saw beneath his words, felt his frustration and loneliness—accusations based on what little he knew. Still, she reasoned, before Papa's death, she would have lashed back, chewed him up, and spit him out for speaking to her that way. Now there was only the immobilizing weight of her grief.

She would allow Caleb to see what he wanted. Maybe then he would put an end to their foolish dreams. But she knew in her heart that Caleb Wright was a common man, and common men fought when causes died. She saw it daily, in the dead and the living, in the

Union Blue and Confederate Gray. Their General's would drive them forward until there were none left to fight and they would willingly go, like "lambs to the slaughter."

Lydia was hampered by her staunch German upbringing and the unspoken conformity required by the Catholic Church and propriety a brutal master. It was all so confusing. She and Caleb should be waltzing to a lover's melody but instead, they struggled to learn the uncharted steps in a world gone awry. How foolish it would be to open her heart to desires and dreams in this crazed world of war. How vividly she remembered watching him struggle for life against fever and infection. How many nights had she kept vigil by his side, praying that God would not whisk him away. Night after night, day after day, she bathed his head with cool water, spooned broth into unresponsive lips, and dressed his wounds. Caleb was oblivious of the hours she had spent gazing upon his handsome face, memorizing every nuance, or how carefully she shaved and bathed him. What would he think if he knew she kissed his lips when all around were asleep? Even after he was well enough to stroll the camp with her, he had never tried to kiss her, and now his letters implied physical pleasure and ardent desire. Her face flushed when she read them, and his words throbbed moist between her legs. Things of that nature were simply not spoken of in her life, not even suggested at, that was, until Bradford Brenham came along. Her last encounter with the old boar was seared in her mind along with Mother's words to Papa. "She'll find out soon enough what marriage and men are really all about."

She supposed Mother meant for her to think on that, since she would soon be a child bride and expected to perform her wifely duties. She had no one to learn from. Vera knew no more than she did and probably less. Why was it such a sinful thing to talk about? Children abounded so obviously something was going on. Was it always a sin or only until you were married? Was it painful or pleasurable, or both? Surely, she wasn't the only girl to wonder these things.

Caleb had been so shy back home. Now, having survived a brush with death, there was no stopping his words and thoughts, most of which involved her body as an object of desire.

Yet, the war raged, and Caleb remained a soldier. She would be a fool to let go of her heart, let alone anything else. If he knew of her love for him, she would be as guilty of his death as if she shot him in cold blood. A distracted soldier was a dead soldier. How well she knew the truth of those words. It was better that Caleb be alive and alone than lying cold in his grave because she let him love her. No one would know of her heartache and if God blessed her with a stray bullet on the next battlefield, so much the better.

SIXTEEN

The occasion is piled high with difficulty,
and we must rise to the occasion.
—Abraham Lincoln, December 1, 1862

"CORPORAL WRIGHT," Harley hollered walking in long strides across the compound.

Caleb stepped out of his tent. He was about to get a nap in before another night of picket duty, but Harley was smiling like a shit-faced drunk, waving a letter in the air.

"It's from that lady friend of yours."

Caleb snatched the letter and tore it open. Harley stayed to see his reaction. Caleb's exploits were as close as he'd ever gotten to a woman. Harley was a handsome, tall, well-built man but insufferably shy around the opposite sex and it was the bane of his existence.

Dear Corporal Wright,

I received your letter by courier and it raised a few eyebrows. Mary doesn't leave my side, like a guard-dog that one. I was shocked and angered at your response to my letter, yet having agreed to meet you when your company arrives I will hold my tongue until then.

I have a soldier in my ward that belongs to the Eightieth and he keeps me up on your movements. He's a strange one and has yet to explain his current wounds and state of affairs. He goes only by Private Stahler. Do you know him? Regardless, he tells me that you are camping nearby. I will meet you by the large stand of oak trees near Doctors Creek down the ridge from the Russell house. I will arrive at noon tomorrow.

I do care for your thoughts and feelings Caleb Wright and have my own to deal with as well. I believe Ben is influencing you and that does not bode well for me or our continued correspondence. On the other hand, Doctor Kenton thinks I waste my paper and ink on you. Suffice to say that I won't be unjustly accused and have you wag your finger at me.

Until we meet again,
Lydia

Damn. "Hang on Harley. Is Gensler running courier today?"

"Yeah. He's jawin' with Sarg."

"Go catch him. Tell him to wait. I need to send a note back."

Harley hurried off while Caleb turned the letter over and wrote a quick reply.

Dearest Lydia,

I know I didn't explain myself well in my last letter. I was angry because I split my heart open and showed you what I feel for you and you gave me nothing but a slap on the hand in return.

*I know I blurt my emotions out like grapeshot, but
at least I allow it to fly and show you what I am. Time
to have a soothsayer read your mind is not in the cards
for me. The world moves forward and I go with it.*
      Your servant,
      Caleb

Gensler took the letter and rode off.

Caleb hatched a plan. Fate had brought them together again, somehow, someway he would get to her and explain his feelings better. If the Captain wouldn't approve a pass, then he would sneak out after nightfall and hustle back before morning. He strode to the Captain's tent; no one was getting passes nowadays—not even officers; he was a fool to ask but he had to try.

Captain Challand, a barrel-chested man of medium height, dark eyes and hair—moustache and goatee neatly trimmed—was sitting at a makeshift desk studying a map and marking areas in ink when Caleb knocked on the tent pole. The Captain looked up.

"Come in Corporal."

"Thank you, Sir." Caleb removed his cap and stepped into the tent.

"What can I do for you?"

"I would like to request a twenty-four hour pass. My lady friend is a nurse with the hospital, now camped, near here."

The Captain leaned his fancy chair back on two legs, knitted his fingers together over his iron gut and patted the tips of his thumbs in concert.

"Corporal, you're a good man and as deserving of a pass as any in my command." He rocked.

Caleb was sure the Captain was going to topple backwards. Perhaps thinking the same, the Captain plopped the chair to all fours and stood up. His hands behind his back, he walked around the table, his voice solemn.

"As a soldier, you must know that after the mutilated bodies we found on that farm this morning, I cannot spare one man for even an hour."

"But Sir…"

"No, Corporal. Gravemaker is in these parts, and I need every available man to find that son of a bitch and string him up."

"I realize that Sir, but I…"

"This is a war, not a goddamn dance party, Son."

"If I could just…"

The Captain's voice spewed steel. "That will be all, Corporal. You've got first watch, tonight."

Shit. Caleb saluted and snapped his heels. The Captain returned the salute.

Caleb's platoon had been on the Gravemaker's bloody trail since the battle at Perryville. Most of the soldiers considered the murderer to be Satan incarnate. The bastard eluded them like a night phantom, leaving only mutilated bodies for them to bury in his wake. Ben gave rise to the notion that he might be the ghost of that Rebel spy they strung up in Munfordville.

The Gravemaker pillaged, burned, and slaughtered all in his path with an emphasis on the slaughter—he murdered men, woman and children but his real delight seemed to be the ruthless torture, rape, and killing of innocent girls and women.

Caleb had almost forgotten about the new victims the scouts found that morning and Lydia wasn't but three miles from there. She had to be warned. He walked over to where Ben sat sharpening his double-edged blade on a stump in front of their tent.

"Capt'n won't sign off on a pass."

"Didn't spect he would," Ben said running the blade the length of a leather strap anchored under his right foot and stretched taut across his knee.

"He gave me first watch."

Ben smiled and rolled his chaw to the other cheek. "Capt'n hates yer pretty face."

Caleb didn't doubt it. "Will you take it for me?"

"Watch yer picket boys?"

"I'll double up on yours for a week if you'll do it."

"Yer gonna get us both demoted with yer fool-ass ideas."

Caleb persisted. "You don't give a shit about promotion. So, will you do it?"

Ben spit on the strap and slowly ran the Bowie back and forth. "What I care 'bout is my business. That she-cow's got yer head nestled a'tween her rosy tits like a horse with blinders on."

Caleb bristled. "What would you do if it was your woman? She doesn't know about Gravemaker and those bodies they found this morning. That farm can't be more than three miles from where they're camped."

"Fact is, I don't have no heifer and there's plenty a reason for it."

Caleb checked his weapon. "I don't know why in the hell I thought you'd understand."

"I understand just fine. I understand yer runnin' on half past two. What makes ya think it won't be you a meetin' up with Gravemaker? Now, that'd be a fine kettle of fish fer me to explain when they bring yer mutilated body back to camp in the mornin'."

"Damn it, Section Hand, I can watch my back but Lydia…"

Ben threw his Bowie into the tree next to Caleb's head. Caleb flinched as the breeze ruffled his hair. For a breathless moment, Ben's beaded eyes looked hard into Caleb's. He wasn't sure he liked Caleb's new name for him.

After a few tense moments, Ben's iron façade broke into an ornery grin. He walked to the tree and jerked the knife out with ease and slid it back in its bloodstained sheath.

"Ya better have yer ass back before the cock crows or it'll be me yer a dealin' with."

"I owe you one."

"Damn straight."

Ben picked up his rifle and headed for the pickets without a backward glance.

Caleb's heart picked up a beat. He could go. He grabbed his rifle and headed in Ben's direction. When he was out of sight of camp, he made a sharp right and hoofed the five miles to the Army's makeshift hospital.

The assemblage of tents, wagons, campfires, and cooking kettles that made up the hospital sat in an unplowed field, bordered by dense woods. Caleb heard Lydia's soft laughter amidst friendly male banter. His jealous trigger tripped, and he walked stealthily through the rows of tents until he could see her from where he stood in the recesses. Her distinct curvaceous silhouette effectively drew audience. *Damn her comely ways.* He moved closer, one slow heated step at a time.

He saw the doctor that wanted to take his leg, standing tall and straight next to her, sucking on a glowing pipe. She had neither acknowledged nor denied his accusation of there being another man in her life and maybe that was because he was right.

"Gentlemen, it is time to take your leave and let the lady get some rest," the doctor said.

The fellows gave no lip, tipped their hats, wished her a good night, and ambled off toward their campfires.

"Was that really necessary, Simon? Honestly, I wish everyone would stop making decisions for me. I was enjoying myself, something I sorely needed today."

The man laid his hand on her shoulder. "I was only thinking of you, Lydia. You weren't well at dinner and I didn't want you to tire yourself out entertaining the troops. We can't have you getting sick now can we?"

"I will get along, Simon. Really, I'm fine. It was just such a shock losing Jeremy."

"You shouldn't get attached, Lydia. You know that."

She snapped, "Sometimes Simon, it can't be helped. I am human, you know."

Simon guided her arm into his. "As we all are." He gave her arm a sympathetic pat. "Perhaps an evening stroll would do you good. There's a lovely full moon tonight."

"Maybe she would like to stroll with me," Caleb said, stepping from the shadows, his voice low and flat.

Lydia jerked her arm from the doctor's. "Caleb?" she stammered. "What are you doing here?"

He stood with arms crossed, his face poker straight.

"I didn't expect you so soon."

"Or maybe you didn't expect me at all. It seems there are plenty of others to entertain you, or should I say, for you to entertain."

She simmered. "How long have you been standing there?"

"Long enough."

"You were spying on me?"

"I was surveying the situation."

Lydia's face iced. "Leave me be, Caleb. Go back to your camp." Her voice shook with emotion. "If you could think for one minute that I…" She stormed past.

He grabbed her arm. "Lydia, wait."

She tried to jerk free. He held fast.

"Let go," she cried.

"That will be enough, soldier," Simon ordered.

"Stay back, sawbones. This is none of your concern."

"Then, I will make it my concern," retorted the doctor, taking Lydia's other arm.

"Stop it! Stop it, both of you," Lydia scolded, tears running down her tired face.

Instantaneously, the two men released her, and she stepped away from the two-man snake pit.

"Simon, I will speak with Caleb. Please leave us."

The doctor glared first at Caleb, then looked tenderly at Lydia. "I'll be close by if you need me."

"Thank you, Simon."

The doctor walked a few yards away and lolled against a tree. His pipe smoke billowed while he savored Lydia's silhouette. He would win her away from that non-com just like he gained the charms of that girl at Pleasant Hill, beautiful, innocent Clarice sang like a nightingale.

Lydia's delicious tongue cut the soldier down to size. Kenton swelled. He pushed at his hard discomfort and buttoned his coat. They were within ten miles of Pleasant Hill. He would leave at dawn and be in Clarice's larder by noon.

Caleb looked into Lydia's teary eyes.

"I'm sorry, Lydia, I shouldn't…"

"You're right, Caleb. You shouldn't have, but you did."

"Please. Let me explain."

"I'm tired, Caleb. It has been a very difficult day."

"What happened?" Caleb asked. His jealous thoughts turning to concern.

"We'll talk tomorrow as arranged. Now, please Caleb, go back to your camp and leave me to mine."

She whisked past without apology, leaving him alone to deal with the demons of the night.

CHAPTER

SEVENTEEN

As our case is new, so we must think anew, and act anew.
—Abraham Lincoln, December 1, 1862

BEN RAISED AN eyebrow when Caleb, well nigh before dawn, strolled up the hill.

"Just checked on the boys. All of em's awake. Things bin pretty quiet." Ben's voice was low. "Didn't speck ya back this early."

"I made an ass of myself."

Ben chuckled. "Wha'd ya do?"

Caleb propped himself against a tree, his rifle resting on his boot. "She thought I was spying on her."

"Were ya?" Ben looked at his friend's forlorn face.

"Ah hell, Ben. She was talking to that shit-faced sawbones, you know, the one who wanted to take my leg. I hung out between the tents for a while. That's all."

Ben snickered. "Ya let her catch ya. Thought I taught ya better en that."

Caleb watched the darkness. Someone was watching them from the trees. He checked his rifle. Ben cocked his pistol.

Caleb whispered. "Hell, I didn't even get to say hello, you know, proper-like."

"Let it go. War ain't no time fer courtin'," replied Ben, his voice low and cautious.

"I can't. We've agreed to meet tomorrow by that bridge over Doctors Creek."

They stared back at whoever was staring at them. Satisfied that the Reb was having second thoughts, Ben lowered the pistol's hammer.

"I know I already owe you Ben, but would you square it with Top? Make up some bullshit, some way to get me a horse?"

"Vail owes me plenty, but it's me he owes." Ben passed wind, loud and strong.

"Shit, Ben."

"Might need to at that."

Caleb moved north of the smell.

"Let me think on it. I'll let ya know when ya get back to camp." Ben picked up his rifle. "Stay awake. That damned bastard's out there. I can smell him."

"Thought that was you."

Ben snorted and disappeared in the woods without a sound. Caleb wondered how in the hell he could walk so quiet, he must be part Indian.

Caleb squinted at the trees across the meadow. Quiet moonless nights were hell on the eyes. He decided to walk the line and make sure his boys were awake. As he walked through the dark, a thought exploded in his mind. He had completely forgotten to tell Lydia about Gravemaker. How could he have been so stupid? Damn his jealous mind! In a few short hours she would ride all the way to Doctor's Creek, traveling alone through dense forests and long stretches across open fields. Even without Gravemaker, it was a risk a lady shouldn't take. Especially with all the troops about.

The long uneventful night gave him too much time to think. At first light, he headed back to camp with hopes of getting a jump on Lydia and meeting her, a mile or so, south of the hospital. Perhaps he could find another spot for them to talk, one closer to camp and away from where his cowardice memory mocked.

Ben had the courier's horse saddled and ready. "There's some vittles in the saddlebag and a full canteen, but it'll cost you a full month of watchin' my pickets."

Caleb shoved the rifle into the buckskin sheath that hung from the saddle. "Done."

Ben looked at his weary comrade. "Watch yer back."

Caleb mounted the frisky black beast.

"I'll be expectin' ya back afore the sun sinks."

Caleb wanted to tell Ben of his blunder, forgetting to warn Lydia, but he knew Ben would never make such a mistake. He would never get so caught up in his emotions that he forgot the mission.

"I'll do my best," was all Caleb said as he galloped out of camp.

Except for the rhythm of hooves, the morning was serene. Caleb thought of the meeting place that Lydia inadvertently picked. Under any other circumstances, he would have refused. It was where he should have died a coward and while he made a stand, it would never erase the hole in the back of his leg. A shameful memory and yet without it, there would be no Lydia in his life. It was her diligent care that saved his leg and most likely his life. As he drifted in and out of consciousness in those first pain and delirium filled days, he dreamed she kissed him and ran fingers through his hair. He hoped to get a taste of the real thing today. He had been a selfish fool to send that letter and then accuse her last night. He had a lot of fixing to do.

He watched for her all the way to their meeting place and when he was within half a mile, she was still nowhere to be seen. Maybe she changed her mind. If he rode back to look for her, he might miss her if she came in from another direction and it would be just like her to do that sort of thing.

Once at the creek, he dismounted and tethered his horse to the bridge. His soldier eyes surveyed the area; the landscape bore few signs of battle and autumn's leaves and bleeding streams were no more. Doctors Creek was flowing clear and cool, and the day was warming. Winter's icy shadows had mummified comrades and enemies alike in shallow graves. Many were buried where they fell, nearly four thousand in all. The labor was over and earth's womb was, once again, giving birth; tiny purple violets and yellow dandelions speckled the hillside. The battlefield's greening sod betrayed his fallen brethren; gunfire, cannon retort, and the moans of injured and dying soldiers lingered among the spring blossoms and dancing butterflies. Budding trees stretched and bound the contours of the Kentucky landscape like a vigilant serpent guarding her dead. Pain struck hard in his chest. One bullet branded him a coward, that would never change. Yet he was a man now, his boyhood left far behind in the fields of Indiana.

Caleb couldn't shake the feeling that someone was watching him, and he looked up the rise. Where was she? Images of some of Gravemaker's victims, particularly the women, played across his mind, and his heart and eye beat the rhythm of fear. While he would rather greet a hailstorm of Rebel lead, than Lydia in a temper, he wanted the worst she could dish out right now. If only she would crest the hill.

He looked at the creek flowing unconcerned beneath the bridge. The liquid glass cast his reflection, no longer October's battle weary coward but a soldier—proud, tall, and confident. His hand rubbed a two-day beard, and he wished there had been time to wash and shave. His chest was in knots, a thousand Rebel Enfields paled in comparison to these love aches and worries.

His mind folded back to the smoky haze of battle when the Eightieth had been pinned down, caught in the crossfire of deeply entrenched Rebel troops. Harley told him that they were so desperate for water that they drank from this same stream, but on that sweltering day Doctors Creek ran red and tasted of earth and mortality. He had not been with them—of that, he would be forever ashamed. Today he would gladly die for those same men and looked forward to standing with them in the next battle.

Lydia came over the hill at full trot, immediately spotting her wayward soldier below. She scanned the landscape and thought of all the soldiers buried about. She hoped she wouldn't see any bones protruding from shallow graves.

"Whoa, Dolly."

She shifted to sidesaddle as she didn't want Caleb to think she was anything less than a proper lady and after last night, it was obvious that he had his doubts.

Dolly pranced down the hill and Caleb looked up in anxious relief. His warrior-angel sat the saddle well, prim and proper, in black skirt and white blouse fastened at the neck with a cameo broach. The black shawl fell from her hair as she bounced down the hill. Her flaxen locks were parted down the middle and pulled back into a bun. Caleb longed to let her hair down and run his fingers through it. How desperately he wished last night had never happened.

Lydia halted by the bridge, the waters beneath, a pirouette of sunlight and leafy shadows.

Caleb extended his hand. "I was worried."

"You needn't have." Lydia took his hand and slid from the saddle.

"I didn't get a chance to tell you last night about Gravemaker, but we think he's in the area. I tried to meet up with you this morning, but somehow I missed you.

"Who's Gravemaker?"

"He's a murderer that we've been searching for since October. We call him Gravemaker because that's all he does. He leaves bodies behind, and we dig their graves. Some of our scouts found five more bodies yesterday at a farm not far from where you're camped."

Lydia's eyes flashed with empathy. "Were there children?"

Caleb thought for a moment before answering. "Four."

"Dear mother in Heaven. How old were they?"

"I don't want to give you the details, Lydia. I just want you to be aware that he's out there. Did you take a different route today?"

"I was enjoying the morning. I guess I took a longer ride than necessary but the field was so pretty with the wildflowers blooming, I just had to ride through it."

Caleb raised an eyebrow. "It's dangerous for a woman to travel alone Lydia, you have to keep your wits about you. Please don't do that again. How did you get away without an escort? I thought Mary would make sure you had one."

"Caleb, I'm with men all day." She didn't want to be lectured and why did everyone think she was so vulnerable. She had proven her worth with these soldiers, and there wasn't one of them that would do her harm.

"I left at daybreak while Simon was making rounds, and Mary was busy retrieving the kettle of beans we set to cook in the ground last night. I told her I was going to Perryville to see about provisions and rode off before she could protest."

Caleb gazed at his headstrong lady. "I'm sorry I didn't warn you last night, Lydia. Please don't travel out alone again."

Lydia said nothing; her thoughts were not of lurking dangers but of Papa, her protector. "Please Caleb; don't treat me like a child. Let's talk about why we're really here."

Caleb had no illusions; she always cut straight to the heart of the matter. He just hoped she wouldn't leave him to bleed.

"I was afraid you wouldn't come," he said.

"After last night, I almost didn't."

"I'm sorry. When I got back to camp last night I was on picket duty and had plenty of time to think about what I did. I didn't come over to spy on you. Harley told me about your camp being so close and I couldn't stand not seeing you. So I used the fact that I had to warn you about Gravemaker, to get out of camp. Ben saw through it, but he let me go anyway."

"I wanted to see you too... I just wish it hadn't happened the way it did." Should she tell him about Papa?

"I'm sorry, Lydia, can you please forgive me?"

"Oh Caleb, of course I forgive you. It's just that I'm so tired of this war, of the killing and the dying. Is it so wrong to want some propriety in this piecemeal world we live in? To try and feel like a Lady and want to be treated as one?"

Caleb's thoughts folded back to the acrid scent of black powder and the screams of dying men. He closed his eyes. They should not have met here. It was too soon. Beneath his boots, the Eightieth's altar stood, and the earth continued to drink from their sacrificial chalice.

"Are you alright?" Lydia asked.

Caleb tried to will the vision away. "Why do you ask?"

Lydia placed her fingers softly beneath Caleb's left eye.

"You have a twitch." She knew what was happening to him, even if he didn't. How often she had seen soldiers' memories triggered, by a smell, a sound, the sight of something from the past, and it would throw them back to the horror, just like they were there all over again.

Caleb put his hand over hers, and Lydia waited for it to pass. When it was over, his face was bathed in perspiration; his eyes full of pain and guilt. "I love you Lydia. I'm sorry for my jealousy, I just need you more than anything and I don't want to lose you."

Lydia held him tight and listened to the beat of his heart. She wished she could be with him all of the time and give him comfort against these demons of war. As he held her secure in his arms, thoughts of Papa flooded in. She didn't want to hold back the truth or her love any more.

He felt her muffled sobs. "Sweetheart, what's the matter?"

Thoughts of Papa, Jeremy and the hundreds of others she had watched die was too much to carry alone. With Caleb's love wrapped around her, she wanted to hold on forever. The thought of losing him was unbearable.

"I want to love you, Caleb. Truly I do. But if something should happen to you…"

Caleb cupped her face. "Listen to me, Sweetheart. Soldiers are dead even as they live. We can't fight if we're thinking about living. I've seen it in myself, and I've seen it in others. When you stop thinking about killing and start thinking about staying alive, that's when the bullet finds you." His lips kissed the tears from her cheeks.

With trembling fingertips she touched his face. His words were too much a dream. "If I let you love me, you will die. A distracted soldier is a dead soldier. You know it, Ben knows it, and I know it."

"Let me take that risk," he pleaded, kissing her quivering lips.

Lydia shook her head. "I would rather live alone and know that you are alive than to know you lie cold in your grave because I let you love me."

Grandma's butterfly necklace warmed in Caleb's pocket. *Marry the one that mends your wounds, touches your soul, and speaks to your heart.*

"You think too much."

"I'm scared."

"Listen to me. When I was at that oak tree, I wanted to die. I shot those Rebs because they were killing my friends. I didn't care if they killed me, but I was sure as hell taking some of them with me. When I didn't care, I had nothing to fear. I take the strength of that oak tree with me wherever I go." His hands wrapped tightly around hers. "You are like that oak for me, do you understand that? You give me a reason to live, to make it through this crazy war. When I survived all of those bullets, I knew God was keeping me alive for you."

Lydia was stunned. He spoke what was in her own heart. "If I say yes to you, I open my heart to pain and…"

"Possibilities?" he interjected, smiling the smile of the store-keeper's son.

Her moist eyes looked earnestly into his. That was the smile that had made her look over her shoulder that day on the boardwalk back home. It seemed a lifetime ago. It was that same smile that melted her heart and sent her chasing after him. He was the one that waltzed through her dreams every night; the one she prayed she would see smile again as he lay unconscious and delirious for days on end.

"Promise to come back to me." She said.

Could any man promise what God controls? "Close your eyes, my Darling."

"Why?"

"Trust me."

Lydia closed her eyes and listened to Caleb rustle through his coat pocket.

He fastened Grandma's keepsake about her neck. "Accept this as my promise. It was my Grandmother's and her mother's before that."

Lydia opened her eyes and lifted the silver butterfly. It glittered in the sun. "Oh Caleb, it's beautiful."

"Grandma gave it to me before I left. She said to give it to the one who mends my wounds, touches my soul, and speaks to my heart. You do all of these."

Lydia smiled at her handsome soldier.

Caleb took her hands in his, his face solemn. "Grandma has a special gift. She sees things before they happen. She knew I would be injured, and she knew you would mend my body and soul."

Lydia's heart fluttered as his fingers caressed hers.

"Grandma said it would keep me safe and now I give it to you. It will hold you in an angel's cocoon and keep you safe for me."

Lydia's hand went to the butterfly. "Then I can't take it. You'll need it more than I ever will."

"No Lydia, it's yours. You are my dream and my butterfly. Keep it as my promise that I will return to you. The good Lord will keep me safe."

"Dreams can die, Caleb."

"Our dreams won't die, Lydia, and neither will I."

CHAPTER

EIGHTEEN

Fight him when opportunity offers. If he stays where he is,
fret him, fret him.
—Abraham Lincoln, June 6, 1863

MARY WAS SILENT that evening. Lydia's deception had brought their friendship to a crossroads.

"Nothing happened, Mary. I just needed some time alone with him, time to talk about the future."

Mary poured two cups of coffee and motioned to her tent. "There are too many ears about, especially, that one."

Lydia followed Mary's gaze to Doctor Kenton. He was watching them from the shadows, puffing on his pipe.

"He has been barking at everyone today. His sour mood is just one example of the pain and worry you have caused this camp today."

"I don't know what else I can say, Mary. I'm sorry you were worried, and I'm sorry that someone had to take up my work for the day, but I'm not sorry that I went to meet Caleb."

"Lydia, this is not about propriety. It's about your safety. Did you know that the Eightieth has been tracking a killer as well as Morgan's Raiders? And that killer, the one they call the Gravemaker,

is in this area. They found more of his cruelty yesterday morning…
a woman and her four children. God rest their souls." Mary's concern
was not lost on Lydia. "And you were out there alone today."

"Caleb accompanied me back to camp."

"Did he approve of you riding alone to meet him this morning?"

"It was already arranged. How was he supposed to warn me?"

"Did he tell you about Gravemaker?" asked Mary.

"Yes, he did," she replied curtly and began to tidy up. Busy
hands, quiet mind, her mother used to say.

"Well, you can rest assured that he knew about Gravemaker's
whereabouts last night when he was here. If he really cared about
you, he never would have agreed to you being out there alone today."

"It was my idea to meet," Lydia snapped. "I arranged it. Caleb
was only taking my lead." She straightened the cloth on the table
and knocked the vase of wild flowers over. Her hands shook as she
set the leaking vase upright and reached for a towel.

Mary sipped her coffee and watched her smitten charge.
She thought of her own daughter. She would not make the same
mistake with Lydia. "Men want what is under your skirt. Make no
mistake about it. Caleb is just a young buck in rut."

Lydia put the flowers back on the table. "You make it sound so
cheap. How can you judge him? You don't even know him."

"Can you tell me that he did not touch you today? That he
would not have bedded you if you were willing?" Mary's remarks
planted a fertile seed of doubt to fester in Lydia's soul.

"I'm tired, Mary. It's been a very trying day. I'm going to my
tent." Lydia's head throbbed. "Goodnight."

Lydia turned the lantern low. Her curvaceous shadow danced
against the canvas of her tent as she released her corset. Her bosoms
fell soft and full as she donned her nightgown.

Simon savored the revue, carefully calculating his next move. His crotch bulged. She had foiled his plan to visit Clarice without even knowing it. Her moment would arrive; they all succumbed in the end. He watched her lean over and blow out the lamp. The performance was over, but his ache needed attention. He extinguished his pipe and stepped into the trees. With her image in his mind and some well-applied strokes, he gained release. The day would come when the storekeeper would die and Lydia would come to him for comfort. He would show her how to lose her sorrow in passion and pleasure.

Lydia dozed fitfully all night. Around four, she gave up on sleep and fixed a cup of tea. She preferred tea to coffee, but it was nearly impossible to get these days. Occasionally, Vera would send her some from home. Lydia saved it for special occasions and savored each cup.

She opened the tiny door on her nurse's lantern and lit the oil lamp within. The lantern resembled a portion of stovepipe with a domed lid and nose-shaped vents on either side. She removed the lid and the two tin cups stored beneath. Filling one with water from her bedside pitcher, she placed the cup over the low flame. How often she had heated medicine and broth for Caleb, Theo, Jeremy and so many others, during late night hours.

She sifted through her small black trunk for the cup and saucer. She no longer felt guilty for taking them. They were a bit of civilization in her war torn world. Carefully, she unwrapped them and held the cup to the light while the water simmered. The translucent pink porcelain had a magenta rose and a cerulean butterfly hand-painted on the inside of the cup beneath the gold rim. How she longed to blossom like the rose and take flight like the butterfly, yet she remained bound in a cocoon, a withered bud on a drought-stricken vine. If she lived by Mother and Mary's rules, in ten years she would be no different than them. Why didn't anyone care what she thought or felt? Her brothers would have gladly seen her married off to Bradford and Mary had stepped in, uninvited, as a surrogate mother, never trusting, always watching. She was suffocating.

Only Papa had listened. He knew her heart, saw her gifts, loved her fiery disposition, and they laughed together behind Mother's back. Dear sweet Papa. She saw his face, felt his strong arms, and warm hands helping her to the saddle that last night. She remembered the pride shining in his damp eyes when she mounted like a boy. She imagined his death face, withered, and ashen. Had anyone come to say goodbye? Her one true ally was dead. The one who listened and loved was gone forever. She no longer had a home and she belonged to no one.

Sobs rose from deep within—a tidal wave of grief rushing up and out, in body shaking, choking sobs. Her stomach lurched with the ferocity of her anguish and she dashed outside to spew the bile that was her life.

She cleansed herself at the rain barrel and slowly walked the perimeter of the camp, recovering in the cool night air. Snores sifted across the stillness accompanied by an occasional groan or cough. What was she doing here with all of these men? They treated her like royalty, but perhaps Mary was right and they all just wanted the same thing as Bradford.

If only there was another woman her age, someone she could talk to about things. Several times she had written to Vera, begged her to come and join her, but Vera simply had no reason to leave. If Aunt Esther were her mother, she wouldn't have left either. Vera's packages came once a month like clock work when they weren't moving around and her letters kept Lydia up on happenings back home. The longer she was away the less the home-town happenings mattered. The gossip paled in comparison to the reality of her life and she felt like a boat without oars on the sea of war. Vera was still an innocent and Lydia felt old by comparison. Once they had shared all of their secrets, now they had little in common. Still a letter was a letter, and Caleb and Vera were the only ones who knew where to send them too, except for her brothers, who knew, but never bothered. She was grateful for Vera's consistency and dependability.

With the hem of her gown soaked with dew and her bare feet freezing, she hurried back to her tent. The sky was beginning to lighten in the east and the birds twittered in the trees. Lydia poured the tea and bathed her cold feet. Donning fresh petticoats, she snuggled back under the covers, closed her eyes and allowed her thoughts to sift hazily over to Caleb. His letters were poignant and full of passion; his sorrowful eyes and caressing fingertips beneath that damnable package of wedding silk gave her the courage to flee and the desire to find him. Now here they were, miles from home and religious condemnation—free to choose. But were they? War dictated caution and discretion. Ben and Mary chaperoned and disapproved. Had she simply swapped one prison for another?

She retrieved Caleb's letters from the nightstand, lit her bedside lamp and read them again; his words were warm and sincere. Yet even he seemed not to listen, but put forth his own mind; judging and condemning. Did he really love her or only his mind's eye view of who he wanted her to be? She had to know for sure.

Daybreak was at hand, soldiers stirred with snorts, coughs, growls, and occasional laughter. Lydia missed her brothers, especially Theo. He had been her playmate for the first twelve years of her life, up to the moment that Mother decided it was time for her to begin conducting herself like the well-bred young lady she was. After that horrendous day, her time outside was restricted to early morning and after supper—to protect her ivory complexion from the sun. Mother stood over her shoulder day in and day out as she struggled to master embroidery, knitting, crocheting, quilting, and tatting. She hated it—all of it. She longed to be out with her brothers in the field and tending the animals. The only household task that gave her pleasure was cooking. In the kitchen, she could create, experiment, and reap the praise from the men in her life. It gave her great satisfaction to watch them devour her delectable creations and beg for more. No matter how she wished it different, she was more at ease with men than women. Men said what was on their minds and women talked around things. Men talked of events. Women talked of other women—and she had always hated the gossip they seemed to treasure. She could care less about who looked at whom in church.

Vera saw to Lydia's needs, sending her toiletries and clothing when needed and reporting on her well-being to the relatives, but she never gave away Lydia's location. If Mother knew where to find her, she would send a marshal to bring her home. Now that Papa was gone, Mother could just marry Bradford Brenham and his thousand acres herself. If he tried with Mother what he had tried with her, Mother would hack off his hand with a dull butcher knife. They deserved each other.

Lydia wondered if she would ever have a home of her own. If so, where would it be? Not in Indiana. If she married Caleb, their prospective faiths and families would ostracize them and condemn their union and their children.

Lydia struggled to envision a world without war, but all she could see was an empty gray slate. She might as well wish for the moon. Even if she could go home, who would be left to go home to? The little girl in Lydia wanted to retreat to her cave and never

LEE ANN NEWTON • JAMES A. BENSON

come out. Unfortunately, that was something Lady Lydia could never do. She would never shirk her duties to the wounded, the Army or the Union, and as much as she hated the war, she knew that dear President Lincoln was doing the only thing he could. If the Union remained fractured, nothing would matter; the country would soon come under siege by a despot ruler from somewhere over the sea.

Private Stahler told her the rumor that the Eightieth would join the Spring Campaign and march south to Tennessee and Georgia and be part of the push to Atlanta. Then what? How long before she saw Caleb again? Would she ever see him again? Why couldn't she love him? Who was going to stop her? Wasn't it better to have some memories than have nothing? He was all she had, but for how long? There were issues to resolve and it couldn't be done in a letter.

Lydia began to emerge from her cocoon in the transient dawn, her beautiful wings drying as she prepared for flight. She opened her trunk and carefully removed all of the items; at the bottom was the blue Paris dress. Its gilded silk felt like heaven against her skin compared to the nurses clothes she had been wearing. She cinched the bodice up tight until her breasts were snug with a smooth valley between. She looked at her reflection in the washstand mirror; her sapphire eyes married the blue of the dress like a bright autumn sky; the silver butterfly hovered above her exposed cleavage—choice flowers, smooth and white. With a mischievous smile, she brushed her hair up into a French roll and secured it with the butterfly comb. She left a few well-chosen curls fall loose about her shoulders and bosom. She did a final check in the mirror, spritzed on a bit of perfume, and strolled into the sun-dappled morning. She thought of what Caleb's reaction would be when he saw her. *You're mine today, Caleb Wright.*

Mary sat on a stump peeling potatoes by the fire.

201

"I'm riding over to the Eightieth's camp," Lydia stated.

Lydia's estranged friend looked up at the defiant young woman. "Goodness gracious. What are you doing, trying to give the entire Union Army a heart attack?" Mary rose and wiped her hands on her apron. "You can't go looking like that, and you most certainly can not go alone."

"Mary, I was not asking permission. I am going."

Mary sighed; there was no dealing with this one when her mind was set. "Very well, but at least wait until I can get a soldier to escort you."

"Very well, but I'm leaving as soon as I get Dolly saddled." Lydia whirled and headed for the corral. Doctor Kenton was there saddling his horse for his tryst with Clarice.

"You look magnificent, Lydia. I'll saddle Dolly for you."

"Thank you, Simon."

"Would you like me to accompany you on your morning ride?"

"I wouldn't be much company I'm afraid."

"It really isn't safe for you to go alone, Lydia."

"I'll be fine Simon and I won't be far from camp. Truly."

"Stay within sight."

Lydia smiled and let Simon give her a hand up to the saddle.

Mary scurried through the camp, wooden spoon in hand. She snapped at two privates eating breakfast.

"Take two horses from the corral and escort Miss Lydia over to the Eightieth's camp." The men eyed her like a preacher to sin. "Well, what are you waiting for? She has already left. Move quickly, and I'll save you each a double helping of potatoes and ham." She stuffed an apple in each of their hands. "Now go!"

The privates jumped to their feet and headed for the corral.

Lydia held Dolly to a walk, taking time to gather her thoughts and enjoy the morning. Her escorts had little trouble catching up, albeit from a safe distance. They respected and admired Miss Lydia so long as her ire wasn't directed at them. When she was riled, she could make Mary look like a Sunday picnic.

The soldiers spoke in low tones, grateful it was Corporal Wright she had her pinions set on. They chuckled. Wright's morning was just about to get real interesting.

"Ya best git up, Corporal Darlin'," sang Ben from the campfire outside their tent.

"Go to hell."

Ben stuck his bearded face in the tent. "Yer Honeysuckle's waltzin' into our beddy-bye with two privates in tow."

"Knock off the shit, Ben. You know I'm pulling double duty."

"That's right. Ya owe me. But I ain't shitin'. Yer man-eatin' heifer's a comin' this a way." Ben whistled low. "And she's lookin' fine, mighty fine."

Caleb heard horse hooves.

"Shit."

He sat up and yanked on his boots.

"Damn that woman."

Lydia walked Dolly to the middle of camp and halted. Morning's low rumble of activity erupted into a barrage of whistles and catcalls. Her escorts rode in close to keep the gawking soldiers at bay. The flamboyant Princess appeared unnerved. She spotted Ben and waved a gloved hand.

"Sergeant Decker."

Ben swiped his grizzly face and tipped his cap. Lordy, lordy, Storekeep's heifer could waylay Beelzebub.

"Would you please inform Corporal Wright that I'm here to see him?"

Ben walked toward the crowd. The soldiers parted as if he were Moses and they the Red Sea. Hat in hand, he made a broad bow. "Yer Highness, I'd be obliged to do that, and mind ya, I'm not much on sassin' a filly of yer graces but when it comes to he'in and she'in, I leaves that up to the principles involved." Enjoying his part in Caleb's castration, Ben continued. "Yer just gonna haf to fetch him yerself."

The men whooped and shouted. "Come and get it, Wright! If you don't, we might."

Caleb stepped from the tent and wiped the sleep from his eyes. The hollering tapered off as the show began. Caleb's cap rested on uncombed hair, and he was in desperate need of a shave.

Ben grinned and stepped away from the Princess.

Lord, help me now. Lydia was in full blossom for all to see.

Lydia clucked to Dolly and sauntered over. The entourage followed. Caleb saw the eyes of comrades perusing his landscape and he felt his jealousy surge.

"Lydia, what are you doing here?"

"Well, good morning to you too, Corporal," she teased. "You seemed bold enough to my presumed affections yesterday."

The men hooted.

Caleb's mind raced. What did he do? Miss Spitfire had a burr in her saddle and had obviously come to remove it.

"I don't know what you mean." His mind struggled to wake.

"I'm not sure what you meant either, and don't you assume I know. If you want to know what I know, then ask. I am not one who suddenly knows what she didn't know, and I'm not sure I know you at all."

Caleb's face screwed into a knot. "What in the hell are you talking about, Lydia?"

"I am talking about talking with you. I have words to say, and I do not want to delay in saying them."

"Sweetheart…" He tried his best to whisper but his voice kept rising. "…we're standing in the middle of a circus, and I'm the main attraction."

"Yes, I know." Prim and proper on her mount, she was ringmaster.

Caleb stepped closer. He challenged her boldness and put a hand on her thigh. Impulses surged for both, but neither gave it away.

Soldiers prodded one another and encroached with caution.

Caleb kept his voice low. "Can we talk later today as we planned?"

"We cannot."

"And why not?" *Lord.* God sure played men the fool when he created women. He made them the jesters in His great celestial minstrel show.

"I changed my mind. Now please go tell your Captain, God, or whomever you must that I am not leaving until we talk." Lydia bent over. Caleb got a full view of her luscious hills. She purred. "While you are attending to the Captain, I will dispose of these guardian angels Mary sent along."

Determined not to fall prey to her charms, Caleb stood his ground.

"I can't do that, Lydia. I'm only a lowly Corporal. Top would shit a brick and bounce it off my head if I ask for another pass."

"Watch your language, Corporal. I am a lady, in case you have forgotten. Now, do what you must, but make it happen."

Damnable woman.

"I apologize for my words, Lydia. I didn't realize that a lady displayed her charms quite so vividly." His wolfen eyes browsed her milky flesh.

Storm clouds swept her face.

Caleb's mind back-peddled. "I'm sorry. I didn't mean that. But I can't wake the Captain."

"Your Captain is already up."

Shit. Caleb's shoulder blades tensed. The Captain stepped from his tent and assessed the situation in his enraptured camp. His gaze paused on the Princess then on her pawn. The soldiers did little more than shuffle their feet. They hoped the Captain would let it play out.

Lydia waved to him. He tipped his hat in return and ducked back into his tent. He expected the Corporal to bring an explanation and a good story.

"Everyone knows you should be dead, Caleb, and your living-legend status opens doors. Doesn't it, Sweetheart?"

God, she stroked sarcasm with ease. "It's not like that, Lydia."

"If you wish to see me at all today, you will find a way to make it happen."

Caleb had no illusions to Lydia's tenacity. If he didn't agree to her demands, she would most likely leave horse prints on his ass and confront the Captain herself. Or worse yet, she'd leave and never look back.

Caleb offered his hand. "I'll do what I can."

Lydia took his hand and glided from Dolly's saddle in a cloud of blue silk.

"Stay with Ben while I talk to the Captain."

Satisfied, she smiled and tucked her arm into Ben's. She thought he blushed a bit under that thick beard of his.

"Hot damn!" Ben said to Harley. "Looks like I get to keep her." If Storekeep didn't know what do with this lovely thing, he was an idiot.

Caleb stepped into the Captain's tent.

"What is it this time, Corporal?" the Captain sat at his makeshift desk, drinking coffee and composing the day's orders—

same as always.

Caleb stood in the triangle of sunlight that streamed in the door. "Sorry for the interruption, Sir."

"From the rumble in camp, and if I were a betting man, I would say you have a heap of woman problems." The officer kept to his chores.

"Yessir." Caleb simmered. He didn't like the camp knowing his business.

The Captain placed his pen on the table, poked at the tobacco in his pipe, and struck a match. He held the fire to his pipe and sucked several times until he was puffing smoke like a dragon.

"Let's have a look-see, Corporal. I've heard your lady's quite a pleasure to behold."

Caleb followed the Captain into the waning morning. Even the Captain played him a fool. Caleb knew damn well he had already savored the view like everyone else.

"Where did you hide her?"

"She's with Sarg." Caleb pointed, although her whereabouts were obvious by the crowd of men gathered around; her golden hair shimmered in the sun.

"Ah, yes." The Captain took a long drag on his pipe and blew the smoke out the side of his mouth. "Can't say I've seen any finer. You're a lucky man, Corporal. Tell me more about your beautiful problem." The Captain took three quick puffs. The embers glowed orange and he blew the smoke out of the side of his mouth. He watched his men flirting with the angel in their midst. A beautiful woman could boost sagging morale in no time.

Corporal Wright was a treasure trove of surprises; coward turned hero—alive with over twenty bullet holes in his coat—and now this. He hoped the Corporal had some wonders left that would lead them to Morgan and the elusive devil Gravemaker. Propelled to folklore status, the men respected and revered Wright, and there was mighty power in that. The men would follow him off a cliff if he told them they could fly. The Captain watched the men revel in the presence of the lovely lady that knew Wright's Achilles Heel.

"So it's a pass you want?

"Yessir."

"Have you gone to Vail with this?"

"No time, Sir. If I don't get one right now, that woman is going to barge in here and demand one herself."

"Is she now?"

"Yessir, she'll come in here and give you a bloodletting."

The Captain thought of the beautiful women he had known and could think of plenty to do with Wright's gal if she chose to come into his tent.

"You've got duty. Who's going to watch your pickets?"

"Decker. Sergeant Decker, Sir."

The Captain poked at the tobacco in his pipe. "Does he know this?"

"I believe so, Sir."

"Does he or doesn't he?"

"He does, Sir."

The Captain watched Wright watching Lydia entertain the troops; she was a natural.

"It'll get you killed," the Captain goaded.

"Sir?"

The Captain rekindled his smoke.

"A jealous mind. It's a distraction."

Caleb steamed beneath his stiff façade. How many times would he have to listen to that same crap argument. "I can't give her up. Back home, I couldn't even talk to her, I'm Protestant, she's

Catholic, know what I mean, Sir?"

"It's the way the world's built, Corporal. I can't even get new boots for my men, and you want to change the way people think. Noble ambition, but a fool's mission in a country at war." The Captain crossed his arms, one hand holding the bowl of his pipe. Thin lips sucked the stem and blew smoke from the side. His gaze never wavered from the jovial crowd. "We slaughter our own countrymen because their beliefs are different than ours."

Caleb's eye started to twitch. He didn't have time for some asinine, philosophical discussion. "If I could just have a pass through tomorrow morning, Sir, I'll pull a full week on picket with the men. I just need some time to square myself with Lydia, that is, Miss Weldishofer."

The Captain observed Wright's blue-eyed filly, a beautiful spirited lass. He married a good woman. She wasn't beautiful like Wright's, but she worked hard, cooked well, and blessed him with two fine sons. He remembered his father telling him once, that the beautiful highfaluting kind were hard to keep happy and if a man chose foolishly, he could expect to spend the rest of his days jealous and broke. The Captain drank in the panorama of the filly's young firm breasts. His father failed to mention the pleasures of the night.

"Are you going to marry her?"

Caleb absorbed the same scenery as the Captain. Lord, she was beautiful. He had never known such desire, but God almighty why must she tease him so?

"I asked if you're planning to marry her."

"Yessir," he replied, with hesitant words. "Just as soon as it becomes her idea."

His commander chuckled. "They're all like that, Corporal. Every last one of them." Challand took a drag. "Without them, though, we'd be mean and dejected. Course then, we'd whip them damn Rebs inside a week just to get at their women."

Caleb's loins agreed.

"You've got one chance, Wright. Fillies like that one, have too much spunk to wait. Understand?"

"That means I can have the pass?"

"You got your damn pass. Now, get your amorous ass out of my sight and your brain back where it belongs."

Caleb saluted. "Thank you, Sir."

"Keep your wits about you, and watch your back. We haven't bagged that sick, son of a bitch killer yet."

"Yessir!"

The Captain returned the salute and went back in the tent to finish his waylaid chores. She sure had wholesome breasts.

NINETEEN

)⟩⟩⟩◗◖◖◖◖◖

Blessings on the brave men who have wrought the change
and the fair women who strive to reward them for it.
—Abraham Lincoln, April 18, 1864

BEN WALKED a saddled chestnut gelding around the tent with two rolled blankets fastened behind. The saddlebag was full and a rifle hung in the front. He handed Caleb the reins. "I had to make a pact with the devil to git this horse from Vail. Yer checkin' my pickets fer two months."

Caleb swung into the saddle, the leather creaked. "Thanks, Ben."

"Hope ya still feel that way tomorrow." Ben eyeballed Lydia like he would a pork chop. He wondered again if Caleb knew what to do with all that. "Watch yer back."

Caleb walked his horse over to where Lydia still sat, surrounded by would-be suitors. He couldn't figure out what on earth he had done to set her off. He left her with a kiss yesterday, and everything was fine. Hell, it was more than fine.

Harley helped Lydia back in her saddle. She waved at the boys and followed Caleb down the dirt road. It was her turn to do some

211

admiring. He sat the saddle well. He should have been cavalry, his strong broad back and tight buttocks in form-fit wool made her tingle. She thought of his fiery eyes in the camp, his wanton stare, and his hand on her thigh.

Caleb's body was poised and alert, angry and confused, aroused and anticipatory. He listened and watched for anything amiss.

Lydia felt his anxiety. She kicked Dolly to a trot and came up beside him. "There's something I have to tell you."

His face said, please tell me, but he said nothing.

"I'm sorry, Caleb. I deceived you."

"Deceived me?"

"Well... yes." Lydia was feeling worse. Caleb's humiliation was obvious.

"I didn't plan it exactly like it happened. I guess I wasn't thinking of what it would do to you."

"I don't understand."

"I needed to get you out of camp, and I didn't know how else to do it."

"Good Lord, Lydia. Is that what you were doing?"

"I knew you had a pass yesterday and the day before, and I knew you wouldn't be able to get another one. I was desperate."

He sighed but couldn't help smiling; she had gone to a lot of trouble just to get him alone. What on earth was she up to? "Sweetheart, don't you respect me enough to ask? I'll find a way to make it happen. Gensler, Johnson, or Ben will do most anything I ask. It comes at a price, but they do it."

"I couldn't wait."

"Wait for what?" Silky dogwood petals cascaded with each breath of wind. One fell to rest on Caleb's blue cap. Another landed softly between Lydia's breasts. She left it there.

"Where shall we go?" she asked.

"Do you trust me?"

Her lips formed a flirtatious pout. "I'm here, aren't I?"

Caleb leaned over and kissed the pout away. Browsing fingers removed the dogwood petal from between her breasts. He sat back and tucked the petal in his pocket. Lydia put her hand on his thigh. His hungry eyes fell to her lace-lined ivory hills and then rose to her full rosy lips. He shifted in his saddle.

She nudged Dolly's flanks and with a tease galloped ahead. He pursued. A chase ensued, and she laughed out loud. It was a glorious spring morning. Her heart felt young again. New leaves unfurled in the warm sunshine, and flowers of every hue blanketed the hills and hollows, trillium, jack-in-the-pulpit, tiny violets, bloodroot, and forget-me-nots sang spring's anthem. When the road left the woods and opened to reveal soft rolling hills, Lydia stopped. The sun was warm, and the sky was a brilliant shade of blue accented with a single puff of cloud.

Caleb galloped past, off the road and down the valley over to the next rise where he dismounted beneath a massive oak tree. Lydia followed; she knew where he was taking her now. He wanted to show her his oak tree. The limbs had been sheared off, and hundreds of lead balls remained embedded. He helped Lydia from her saddle.

"This is where you sought your death?" she asked softly, placing her hands on the bullet-ravaged tree. Her heart quaked as she realized that each of these bullets was meant for him. How many more found their mark but were stopped short by a wondrous guardian angel?

Caleb wrapped his arms around her waist and nestled his face in her hair. "When I fought here, I had no purpose. I wanted to die because I was so ashamed." He looked into her eyes as sensations of that day and all its inglorious turmoil and dishonor washed over him. His pain was excruciatingly visible.

Lydia spoke softly. "Ashamed of what?"

"I kept it from you, from everyone, but I have to be honest. You have to know what kind of man I am. I was a coward that day." He looked for shock on her face or disappointment; there was none, only empathy. "I killed a man, my first. He was close, and I blew half his face off, and he didn't die. He just lay there clutching his face and screaming. I got scared, and I ran. Ben stopped me with a bullet in the leg."

"Ben shot you?" Lydia was aghast.

"I got what I deserved"

"You almost died because of that wound."

"Coward's are usually shot dead, Lydia. He did what he was supposed to do, only not quite."

"You've never been a coward, Caleb. You were just a boy then. Who wouldn't be terrified with something like that? You went back to the line and faced the Rebels alone that day. You saved lives. That is hardly the act of a coward."

"I was trying to end my life. I was no hero."

Lydia looked into sad gray eyes. Her heart writhed with his pain.

"I left you in Indiana because I was too big a coward to confront your mother."

"That's not true. You came the night you left. That took courage, Caleb. You're not a coward. You're more of a man than any other I've met. You have more courage than I do. You've bared your soul to me, and I've showed you nothing. You're strong, humble, and courageous. God has a plan for you Caleb and I hope it includes me."

Caleb seized the moment and went down to one knee. He took her hands in his and watched her eyes as he asked. "Will you marry me, Lydia? Will you be my wife?"

Lydia was shocked, amazed and deliriously happy. She wanted

him more than anything else. She wanted to give herself to him, to love him, to sleep with his heart beating next to hers. But where could they possibly get married, and who would marry them? If there was no Mass, it would never be condoned by the church. She would be excommunicated. Did she care? Did God? Caleb would be going south to the fight, and she and the hospital would soon follow as the dead and wounded piled up. She wanted to answer him, but her voice seemed to have dropped to her toes. What could she say? Had she really thought this through? Did she want too? She wanted to dissolve herself in the world she saw spinning in his eyes, lose herself in his arms, his kisses, in all that he could give and forget the war, the death, everything.

In answer to his question, she removed his cap and let her fingers course a familiar path of days gone by, through his hair, down his face to his lips. "I came to Kentucky to find you. You're all I've ever wanted, Caleb. When you left me, I had to follow."

His eyes registered surprise.

"When you were unconscious, and everyone was sleeping… I kissed you."

Caleb stood and gazed into her soft unsure eyes.

"I want to marry you, and I want to be your wife, but right now I want you to love me," she said in a barely audible whisper. She looked to the farm below. "Let's go down there."

Caleb was in awe. Who was this woman? Was she really asking what he thought she was asking?

"Do you think anyone lives there?" she asked.

"No, it was torn up during the battle."

Caleb helped her to her saddle, mounted his own and led the way down the hill to the farm. Cannon and gun had made the house a sieve for wind and rain. It was no place for lovers. He took her to the orchard behind the house and spread the blankets on soft green grass.

To his perpetual surprise, she wanted no more conversation. She stood before him and slowly began to undress. He moved closer and kissed her, eager and exploring. Without hesitation, she responded in kind and surrendered her fears for the pleasures he could give. Caleb's mind released. His thoughts blurred as he unwrapped her porcelain body. She purred, and with each pleasure he imbued, she responded in kind. He stroked her shimmering shell and luscious interior, and together they flowed from course to course.

When their passion slowed and the sun was high, Caleb spread their simple meal and dreamed of dessert. They spoke little, and while they ate she tempted and teased with her lips and tongue.

Was he dreaming? If he was he never wanted to wake up.

"Caleb, I need to know something."

"Hmmm?"

"Why did you accuse me in your letter of having affections for another?"

This wasn't the conversation he had anticipated after making love. But who could figure a woman's mind.

"I shouldn't have done that, but when I'm alone I think about things and I see how other men look at you. I know they would take you away from me, given half a chance."

"I'm with men all the time. They can't take me unless I'm willing to go." She took a bite of apple and teased with her eyes.

Caleb smiled. "Sweetheart, my jealousy is not like a lantern that I can turn on and off at will." He took her apple. "I tried my best to shut if off that night. A man can't do that but a soldier can. When I saw Kenton with his hands on you, I forgot I was a soldier.

I'm sorry." His hand caressed her smooth thigh.

She lay back. "Doctor Kenton is my friend as are most of the men in camp. I love you Caleb, but I don't know how to abide jealousy. It wants to own, conquer, possess."

He kissed her. "I understand that, but when I saw you going for a moonlit stroll arm in arm, it seemed like more than that."

"I know how it must have looked, but it wasn't what you thought. The reason he was there was because I hadn't come to dinner. He came to check on me."

"Perhaps I assume more than I should, and I know that I get jealous, but I'm working on that."

He tried to quiet her with kisses and for a while it worked, but her mind didn't still. Before his passion was uncontrollable, she rolled away and smiled. "I'm not done talking yet," she said.

Caleb retreated. "What is it, Darling. What do you need to tell me?"

She closed her eyes for a moment. She wanted to tell him about Jeremy and Papa without crying, but when she opened her eyes, it was to the concern in his. This wasn't going to be easy.

"I lost a patient the day you came to camp. His name was Jeremy Smith. We were very close. He should have died months ago, but he kept going. I wrote letters home for him, read to him, prayed with him. I sat up nights when the pain kept him awake. Then, when I made rounds that morning, he was burning up with fever and within two hours he was gone. He was his widowed mother's only living child."

Caleb listened. "You loved him?"

"Like he was my own brother."

"This is what you don't tell me in your letters. This is what you deal with every day. You love all of your patients."

"Not quite, not all." Lydia thought of Private Stahler, the way he watched her when she changed his bandages and shaved his face. *No, definitely, not all.*

"There are a few, like Jeremy, that I get attached too." She thought of how he winked at her right before he would tell her a joke. "He was taken with me, and he was dying, slowly dying, and he was only sixteen. His father was killed at Fredericksburg." She looked in her lover's eyes. "I would have kissed him if he had asked me to, to give him that one small pleasure before he died." She caught a glint of jealousy in Caleb's eye, but admiration as well. "He never asked."

Lydia's eyes welled. "There's more."

Caleb waited patiently.

"I received a letter from my cousin Vera that same day. It was nearly a month old."

Caleb looked at her tormented face and the tears that threatened to overwhelm her voice. "What is it, Sweetheart?"

"Papa's dead and I killed him."

"What are you saying, Lydia? You didn't kill your father."

"Yes, I did. When I ran away to look for you, I left him alone. I was all he really ever had. He was trying to do all the work and put up with mother as well. If I hadn't run away, he would still be alive. I know it."

"Lydia, you can't possibly believe that."

"Well, I do believe it," she cried. "It's just like the fools who try to argue that this war is not about slavery. Well, it is. If there were no slaves, if the Southern States didn't demand the right to take their evil filth with them into the new territories, there would be no war. It's because of slavery that the states could not settle their differences. It's because of slavery that boys like Jeremy die, and men like you seek their death on the glorious battlefield."

"I'm so sorry, Sweetheart." He pulled her to him as tears fell like raindrops on her breasts. "I want you to marry me, Lydia. I want to take care of you, protect you."

She needed that now, needed something, anything to stay afloat. "I want that too." She looked into the expectant face born to her each night in her dreams. What guarantees did they have? Did anyone have? "Love me, Caleb."

The afternoon spilled into a moonlit night. Hunger and passion rose and fell in soft swells, finally slowing to tender kisses and long embraces, their bodies entwined. As night neared dawn, they savored a bittersweet loiter, and having released love's result, time and again, Caleb lay next to her heart. Exhausted and content, they slept beneath the blanket to await God's predawn serenade.

Lydia woke to gentle strokes on her brow.

"How is it possible that you've chosen me?" Caleb asked.

She didn't want to talk. She took his hand and placed it over her supple breast.

"Sweet Jesus," he mused. Her breasts were untamed, nipples erect. He let his lips follow their dream, and she rose to his desire.

They rode to the within a hundred yards of the hospital camp perimeter.

"When are you breaking camp?" Lydia asked.

"Soon."

"Will I see you before you leave?"

"I'll find a way to see you. I promise."

Lydia kissed him slow and long until he moaned and pulled away.

"Damn, you don't make this easy."

She flicked her tongue at him. He shook his head and rode away.

"Wake up." Ben kicked Caleb's bedroll. "I don't wanna listen to ya swoonin' bout no she-cow."

Caleb rolled his ass to the voice. Disoriented and warm with passion, he reached for her, "Lydia, where are you?"

"Right here, Sweetheart," Ben sang and gave the bedroll another swift kick. "Git up," he ordered.

To Caleb's dismay, his cobwebs evaporated, warm and sensuous, his hand on Lydia's angel-silk belly, naked as morning dew, leg draped over hers, face cradled on her feather-down breast, fingers stroking long golden tendrils, askew from lovemaking.

The horrendous baritone boomed, and Ben's boot met ribs.

"Ow!" He tried to hide from the dream stealer. "Damn it, Decker," he growled sitting up and rubbing his side. "What time is it?"

"Sun's full up."

"You're a son of a bitch! I ain't had but two hours sleep, and you know I got double-duty."

Ben snorted. "I knew where that dream was headed. Ya spout like a loose-lipped mockin' bird when yer sleepin' and ya was a makin' me sick."

Caleb stretched and flexed. "I can't help it. Hell, I don't want to. Beats waking up to your ugly face."

"The way ya snuck yer ass back in the tent this mornin', I'd say you've been doin' more than dreamin' bout it."

"What's left to eat? I worked up an appetite."

Ben chuckled. "Is that a fact? It's about goddamn time you figured out what to do with a woman. Now maybe I'll be able to get yer mind back where it belongs. Start the fire and I'll round up the grub." Ben moved outside. "They give out pork and taters yesterday."

Their bellies full, Caleb and Ben sat by the smoldering fire. Their rifles were gritty, and they lazily set to cleaning them.

"Ya been sowin' yer seed and if ya ain't careful, you'll be lookin' back when the bullets are flyin' forward.

Caleb rammed the cleaning rod down the barrel. "I know my job."

"Damn it Storekeep, I know it. But ya get daydreamin' on duty and yer gonna be dead and maybe take some of us with ya."

An approaching horse fractured the conversation. A woman in nurse's dress galloped in. She rode straight for Caleb and reined in hard, throwing dirt in their conversation. Ben threw Caleb a questioning glance.

"Where is she?" the woman demanded. She sat erect and furious on a dapple-gray mare. Caleb knew Mary immediately.

"Who?" replied Caleb, poker-faced. What game was Lydia playing now?

"Lydia. I know she was with you last night. Now, where is she?" she demanded loudly.

Her chill hit hard and a hush fell over the camp. Soldiers stared from every corner. Wright was certainly keeping the troops entertained these days.

"If you'll dismount, Mary, we'll discuss this in private." Caleb extended his hand.

She took his hand and dropped ingloriously to the ground. "What have you done with her?"

"I left her at the perimeter this morning around daybreak." Caleb's eyes surmised the fiery woman; she was about Ben's age, an attractive woman with wavy brown hair secured in a bun behind a rosy face and violet eyes.

"You haven't seen her at all?" Caleb asked, concern laced his words.

"If I had seen her, I wouldn't be here."

"Did you ask around camp?"

"Believe me, Corporal Wright, I turned every tent and cot inside out, and Dolly hasn't been seen either."

"What are you saying, Mary?"

"I am saying that she has not returned to camp since she left yesterday."

Ben met Caleb's glower. He stepped in their tent and within a breath was back with weapons and ammo. He tossed Caleb a pistol. "I'll git some horses and let the Capt'n know we're goin'."

"Going where?" Mary asked.

Caleb's heart pounded. He donned his gear and checked his guns.

TWENTY

After reading the letter, the had mist come and swept me away, not back to 1939, but to another place. I found myself standing in a budding forest of lemongrass leaves. The flora and fauna sang of spring and rebirth—May Apples covered mossy animal paths, a perfect place for mushroom hunting. Instinctively, my eyes roamed beneath the foliage looking for Morels.

Stepping from the forest's shadows into the transitory dawn, I was struck by the beauty of the morning. Yellow daffodils and purple violets waltzed on a grassy knoll above an unplowed field. Shafts of lemon colored light streamed heavenward behind rolling green hills.

Several feet away, a handsome young man in Union blue rested a shoulder against a poplar. A smile played on his clean-shaven face and a gentle breeze lifted his long, wavy hair.

Unseen and unheard, I felt like an intruder, as I watched him through the trees and his beauty compelled me to stay. He seemed a fellow sojourner. Old feelings stirred. This sort of man could not be found in my neck of the woods. The folks along the Cumberland Gap had no wanderlust. When they saw earth and trees, they envisioned house timbers and gardens.

He was tall, lean, and muscular like a feral cat. His face was strong and finely structured, his lips firm, his hair long and wild. Sensual sensations rippled under my nightgown, and I smiled. I would have happily shared a Harlan Friday night with this man; he brought to mind some better times. It had been a long time since Chester Dunaway and I ran wild together. He taught me the finer pleasures of the flesh. I never loved him like I did Stephen, but we were good together. He liked to drink, gamble and dance. The dancing was what I liked and of course, the sex that followed. Grandma wouldn't allow him in the house, and I think she was actually relieved when he was shot dead over a dime, in a poker game. He was the last man I let in my bed. And it had been a long time since Chester. Until now, I hadn't given it much thought. Maybe I wasn't a lost cause after all. I just needed some new bucks in my mountains.

I looked back to the handsome man in front of me and followed his gaze to approaching riders. He moved behind a tree and watched them through the budding branches. The riders were a Union soldier on a roan and a young woman riding sidesaddle on a chestnut mare. She was wearing a gorgeous blue dress and her golden hair lay long and loose about her shoulders. A twinge of envy nudged my heart; they were a vision of two people in love, sharing a beautiful morning.

The stranger's gaze was riveted on the riders, his face no longer complacent but with the look of a wolf on the prowl. I had misjudged him. His hand massaged the handle of a large blade, sheathed by his side while the other hand fondled the bulge in his pants.

I knew his type, and I knew the riders. Was I helpless to intervene?

C H A P T E R

TWENTY-ONE

*In this sad world of ours, sorrow comes to all; and, to the young,
it comes with bitterest agony, because it takes them unawares.*
—Abraham Lincoln, December 23, 1862

L YDIA WATCHED CALEB gallop away. Life's perfume danced on the morning, and she raised her face to the sun, welcoming the early warm rays. Lulled by Dolly's sway, Caleb's caresses were fresh on her mind and she wasn't ready to go back to her other life—to face the stares and questions, she knew awaited her. She turned Dolly around and galloped back into the morning, her preoccupied senses lost to the steady approach of another rider.

Fingering a blue bandanna, he rode the courier's black gelding into her quiet reverie. Dolly pranced, waking her mistress to the invasion. The rider stopped a few yards away. Lydia looked at him.

"What are you doing here? You nearly scared me to death!"

He ignored her rebuttal. "So pure... so chaste. You fool them all."

He swiped the edge of his mouth with the bandanna and

leaned over the saddle horn.

"No one knows where you are, Lydia. The camp's a buzz, and there's talk among the boys of lynching your corporal. You've created the perfect diversion. Just as I knew you would."

Lydia's heart fluttered; this wasn't right. "That is quite enough." Her voice betrayed her fear. Father's warnings came unbidden. *Trust no man, ever.*

He walked his horse within three feet of Dolly. "I didn't get the first lick like that bastard corporal, but I mean to have the second."

Lydia's instincts took control. Her heals careened off Dolly's flanks. Dolly bolted. The man countered. Dolly reared. Lydia tried to get her leg over the saddle so she could hang on but before she could get it all the way over, the man drove his horse into Dolly's side, knocking her sideways and throwing her mistress into a rag doll spin to the ground.

"Need some help, Ma'am?" taunted the soldier, circling Lydia as she vied for footing. "Take my hand." He coolly observed her search for escape.

She hiked her dress and attempted to circumvent his prancing steed. With every attempt at freedom, he countered with his four-legged beast. Unlike the surreal quality of nightmares, this soldier's guile was transparent and his intentions clear.

"Take my hand," he demanded.

"Never," she panted. Dodging yet again, she made a run for it.

The hammer clicked. "If you don't get your ass up here, I'll put a hole through your rosy tit." He moved up behind her.

She looked up at her captor and wondered if Caleb was still close enough to hear her scream. The soldier's eyes were devoid of pity.

"Caleb!" she screamed as loud as she could.

"Take my hand, Lydia," he demanded again.

"Never!"

He removed his foot from the stirrup. "We can do this the easy way or the hard way, but you are coming with me."

Lydia's mind raced. How was this happening? Where was Caleb? If she ran now, he would shoot. If she took his hand, she would give in to whatever lay ahead. If he shot her, she might live. If she went with him, she would have time to think of a plan of escape. *Help me, Jesus.*

"Take my hand," he demanded.

She looked into his empty eyes. There was no way she could make herself give in to his demands. He would have to shoot her. At least then, someone in the camp might hear and come to her aid. She darted away from the horses prancing feet and ran down the hill. He galloped after her, grabbed her arm, jerked her from the ground, and threw her over the saddle. She kicked and twisted, but his grip was a vice. The saddle horn dug into her chest just below the ribs and he pushed his elbow into her back. She screamed in pain. He cinched her mouth with the bandanna and her cries became nothing more than muffled moans.

"You've taunted me long enough. Now it's my turn." He grabbed her ass with rabid glee and kicked his horse to a full gallop. He would have Wright's woman. His cock surged at the thought of the fight she would give him. He wouldn't lose his composure this time. He would make it last.

His hand rummaged beneath her skirt.

Papa if you can hear me, help me, please! What had she done to this man? She had tended him in his time of need, bathed and bandaged his mysterious assortment of wounds, poured broth down his throat when he could not do it for himself. She had saved him from death. Would he take the life that returned his?

She dug her fingers into the wound on his leg, a wound she had so carefully tended, and one she knew was not wholly healed.

He groaned. "You'll pay for that bitch." He spurred his horse and the pounding gait knocked the wind from her lungs.

She struggled for breath, tried to right herself, but his steel arm held firm. The earth-colored collage swirled beneath her—weeds slapped her face. How far had they gone and where was he taking her? She tried to look up, but the galloping horse made that impossible. The saddle horn drove into her chest with each gait, making her want to retch. Had Caleb heard her scream?

She had to do something—anything was better than nothing. She eyed the leather strap that held the saddle in place. If she could just work it loose from the steel ring. The ground moved past at dizzying speed; the horse tossed her up and down bruising her screaming body. She focused all her strength and determination on the strap. Her fingers ached with the effort. The leather began to loosen. Her escape was at hand.

His knee bludgeoned her ribs as the saddle slid. Struggling to stay upright, he let go of her. She pushed against the horse's heaving sides with all her might. The ground spun toward her as she fell. The horse's hind hoof grazed her temple.

Momentarily stunned, her thoughts became an incoherent jumble. Caleb was there, wounded in the distance—poised against a lone tree with a thousand rifles leveled his way. He wanted to die. She desperately wanted to live.

Lydia stumbled upright. The farm where she and Caleb had frolicked lay but a few hundred yards away. She chanced a look at her captor; he stood by his horse, tightening the saddle. Like a rabbit doomed, she ran, dizzy, disoriented and in so much pain. Caleb would come. He had to. There was nowhere to hide.

Help me, Papa!

She heard the horse closing in behind her. She ran faster, but he grabbed her arm and jerked her from her feet, half carrying, half-dragging her to the farm.

Look beneath, Lydia. Find his weakness.

They approached the farmhouse, and he dropped her like a sack of grain to the ground, turned his horse sharply, and jumped from his mount. Before she could react, he kicked her crumpled form. "That was a stupid thing to do," he hissed.

Lydia twisted away as he hoisted her to her feet. She wanted life, but her body could sustain little more. Her belly screamed from his boot. She knew now that he was the one Caleb had warned her about. *God, I want to live.* She kicked at the wound beneath the bloody trouser. His reaction was immediate. His fist bashed her to the ground followed by another boot. Ribs cracked. Her eyes welled.

"Stop it…" she sobbed. "…please, stop."

He grabbed her hair and dragged her toward the porch steps.

"Stop," she screamed. "You're hurting me!" She struggled to get her feet beneath her.

He jerked her up the steps and kicked in the door.

She caught hold of the doorframe. He laughed and hurled her inside like a rag doll. Her dress caught and ripped on the splintered doorway.

This man, this demon that possessed her was one of the Eightieth. That was why he had escaped their scrutiny. He was at Perryville and every skirmish in between. He was going to kill her and Caleb would find her mutilated body. He would never forgive himself. She couldn't let that happen. This demon had to have a weakness. She knew him and tended him. There had to be something she could say to stop this madness!

"Get up, bitch."

She wrestled the bandanna from her mouth. Her voice rasped. "Please don't do this. I tended you, fed you…"

"I saw you last night in the moonlight," he whispered, "I

watched Wright mount you."

"You're making a mistake."

He smirked. "There's no mistake. I've waited as long as I intend to. I want what Wright had and so much more."

There would be no reasoning. She bolted out the door, her eyes scanned up and down, left and right, searching for a weapon, a place to hide; something, anything that would give her a chance. *God help me, please help me.*

The demon smiled and watched his prey through the dirty broken window. Let her think she can escape—that she stands a chance. When she disappeared behind the smokehouse, he unsheathed his knife and strolled out the door. He paused on the porch and savored her desperation.

She found a broken hoe protruding through thick dead grass. "Thank you," she whispered. She flattened herself up against the building. *Please God, send Caleb. Hurry God. Please hurry!* She crept up to the corner and peered around into the abandoned barnyard.

He came up behind her. "Did you really think I would let you go?"

She turned and swung as hard as she could. The hoe spun a horizontal arc and cut him across the temple. He swayed from the blow and a river of blood streamed down his cheek. She swung again but he caught the hoe mid-air and ripped it from her hands.

"My turn," he said, taking a step toward her.

Lydia prayed for time to suspend as she turned and ran into the overgrown field, toward the orchard. If she could just buy some time until Caleb discovered she was gone.

Gravemaker watched Lydia's blue-silk form move across the field. *She thinks she has a chance. Like fucking hell.* He walked to his horse and swung into the saddle.

She heard his rapid advance. She ran faster, though her body screamed in protest. *Where are you, Caleb? He's going to kill me. My God, he's going to kill me!* She saw horse and rider's shadow, saw the rifle swing toward her head. She felt the thud that cracked her skull. The world went black.

He dismounted and threw her limp form over the horse and mounted behind her. He'd been patient long enough. She's gonna feel it all. She'll beg. He smiled—they always did.

He tethered the horse in the barn, slung her over his shoulder, carried her inside the house and dropped her to the floor. She sounded like a busted melon hitting sod. He went to the well and filled the bucket.

"Time to wake up, bitch." He tossed the full bucket in her face.

Lydia coughed and gasped and rolled to her stomach.

He knelt, and with practiced efficiency sliced through layers of petticoats. With a knee pressed against her spine, he groped within her silver thighs.

"Stop it, for God's sake stop!" She begged through pain and tears.

"I hadn't thought of taking you on your belly but since that's the way you want it." She tried to right herself. His knee pushed harder.

"Don't move, bitch."

She couldn't. She tried to breathe.

His hands groped. They prodded, poked, slapped, and pinched. He undid his fly. His red cock lumbered out.

"Raise your ass, bitch."

"Oh God, please don't do this. You don't know what you're doing," she pleaded between sobs. "I took care of you." His hands were vices now. "Thank you kindly for that." He shoved his cock between her trembling legs, deep into her soul.

"Caleb," she screamed.

"He can't help you now. I killed that son of a bitch before I came for you," he grunted with sickening pleasure. "You'll see him in hell soon enough."

Sweet Mother Mary let me die.

Day turned to night and Papa's voice spoke no more. Rescue would not come. She was in the grips of a rabid man. Teeth, fists, and knife left his marks. She struggled to stay afloat. The more she died the stronger he became.

When she fought no more, he dragged her naked into the black rainy night, bent her over the well, and fucked her goodbye. He started to push her into the well but thought Wright might not find her there. So he dragged her across the barnyard to the cellar, trussed her like a branded calf, and pitched her down the limestone steps. "Enjoy hell, you fucking whore."

The door slammed on her tomb. Lydia did not hear. She was enveloped in Papa's waiting arms.

TWENTY-TWO

)))◗●◖((((

Are we degenerate? Has the manhood of our race run out?
—Abraham Lincoln, September 1863

"**N**O TIME FOR the saddle," Ben yelled and tossed the reins to Caleb.

Caleb mounted the roan, snuggled against the withers, and freed the horse of all restraint. Nostrils flared as rider and horse hurtled down the rutted lane and damp earth spit up behind them like demon's dung.

"Where is he going?" asked Mary.

"Go on back to the hospital, Ma'am."

"I will do no such thing!"

Ben loaded his horse with rifles, canteens, blankets and two bulging buckskin pouches. The horse pranced in restrained agitation. The air pulsed. Ben grabbed the saddle horn and put his foot in the stirrup. "Hah!" he bellowed. The horse leapt forward, propelling Ben into the saddle, his body molded to the leather as he lay low to catch up to Caleb.

"Best let the men handle it, Ma'am," Harley said.

Mary took the reins. "Like they handle this war?" With a

mother's determination, she undid the sidesaddle and pushed it off. "Get me a man's saddle, private."

Harley cinched the saddle tight and gave her a hand up. Mary bundled her skirts knee high as she had seen Lydia do the day she sailed over the fence and into her life and she kicked the horse to action.

"Hah!"

They rode all day searching every farm they passed. It was early evening when Ben made a suggestion to make camp for the night. Caleb turned a deaf ear.

Mary protested. "We must rest."

Neither made reply but rode on.

Mary's body ached, but the men continued undaunted. At this pace, they would drive the horses to their death. Night fell and a storm burst through the clouds, pouring down lightning and rain. Their search continued, stopping at every house, riding through every woods.

Mary was soaked and nearly asleep on her mount when the sky began to brighten, and bits of blue sky began to show through the departing grey clouds. They came over the rise and crossed the Mackville Road. Simultaneously, they saw Dolly grazing in the cornfield below.

"Hah!" Caleb yelled; slapping the reins he galloped ahead. Doctors Creek meandered near. Caleb knew the place well; it was where the Eightieth made their stand. The trees where he turned tail stood between them and the abandoned farm. The oak lay just beyond. Caleb's mind filled with images of Gravemaker's gruesome work as he galloped through the woods. Maybe she just came back to their love nest to think on things.

The house sat amid thick gnarls of prairie grass, thistle, and milkweed. Shreds of blue silk screamed at him from the splintered doorframe; the battered door was ajar. His heart raced as he jumped from his horse, drew his pistol and ran to the house. Without stopping he burst through the door, pistol cocked.

A bucket lay on the floor near the stone fireplace along with Lydia's bloody clothing.

Ben was a heart's breath behind and exploded through the door. Caleb wheeled, pistol cocked.

"Whoa, it's me, Storekeep."

Slowly, Caleb lowered his weapon, his face grieved beyond any Ben had seen. His gaze moved to the pile of bloody blue silk. "Let me do the searchin', Storekeep."

Mary came in and gasped. "Dear God in heaven."

Caleb pushed past them out the door. "Where was God when this was happening?"

Mary started after him, but Ben touched her arm. "Give him time."

Mary lashed back at him. "There is no time. Every moment counts."

"There's no helping her now, Ma'am."

Mary snapped, "You speak as if she is already dead."

Ben laid a gentle hand on Mary's shoulder and went to check the barn. "He ain't left one alive yet."

Caleb knelt by the well and pinched blood and earth. He looked at his fingers then to the sky. "Damn you."

The sun was shining through Caleb's oak tree on the hill, casting its shadow in the direction of the root cellar where his lady lay. Caleb followed heaven's reply and walked over to the cellar. He couldn't think of what lay below. It was only his soldier's training and experience that kept his legs from giving way. He grabbed the cold metal ring, pulled the door open, and laid it back. Lydia's laughing eyes and sweet kisses flitted through his tormented mind as he began his ascent into the dim, stench-filled cellar; it reeked of rotten potatoes. Shards of light embodied his greatest fear. The air emptied from his lungs, his muscles knotted and his eye pulsed beyond control.

Lydia's swollen and bruised face was unrecognizable. Her body lay bound and bleeding on the cold dirt floor, her veil of silken hair a mash of mud and blood. Angry blue welts and deep cuts screamed at him.

Caleb cut her bindings and stripped off his jacket. He covered his angel and gently gathered her into his arms. Slowly, he walked up the stairs where Ben and Mary waited, his face contorted in anguish. Tears stung his eyes.

Ben grabbed the blankets from the saddle and ran ahead to make a place inside. Mary followed solemnly and prayed. Never had she seen a woman desecrated by such violence. While Ben worked to start a fire, Mary felt for the beat of life and prayed for the impossible.

"She's alive, praise the Lord, she's alive." Mary removed Caleb's coat from Lydia's naked body. She gasped. "Dear Jesus in heaven, what kind of man did this?" Together she and Ben stared in shock and anger at her mutilated body.

Ben looked at the broken lovers. "Twarn't no man, Ma'am. It's the bastard I'm gonna murder." Caleb's face was pale as Lydia's— sick with guilt, fear, hatred, and revenge. Ben knew it all. Images of Rosita came unbidden to his mind and stabbed at his heart. Her screams had jarred every fiber in his body. There had been no goodbye, and their son never took his first breath.

The fire crackled while the three fought to save what life was left. Ben picked up the bucket, took Mary by the arm, and moved her outside. Caleb would have his chance to say goodbye.

Mary's eyes questioned but Ben gave no reply. He wasn't talking, but she could sense the pain he felt deep within. She wondered if some day she might get the chance to help him talk about his past and get to the hurt that was buried so deep beneath his tough soldier veneer.

"I'll bring in some wood before I leave," he said.

"Where are you going?" She wanted him to stay.

Ben handed her his loaded Dragoon. He kept the Colt. "If ya need me, fire this. It'll kill anythin' twice over. I'll be close enough to hear it."

"I am a woman of peace. I bear no weapons."

"I don't give a shit what ya are," he threatened. "Use it, ya hear. I'll bury no more women. Not in this life."

Mary considered this stalwart man and thought it better not to argue. They were all weary and emotionally spent. "Very well, but before you go, I will need a travois made. We need to take her to the hospital as quickly as possible."

Ben assessed the worthy woman and wished back fifteen years. "She won't live long enough to get there, ya know that."

"It is in God's hands," Mary said softly.

There ain't no God, he thought walking to the well. He tied the rope to the bucket, dropped it in the well, hoisted it up, and carried it back to Mary.

Mary stopped just inside the door. Her heart broke at the sight of Caleb's shaking body hovered over Lydia's still form. Ben left to make the travois, and she carried the bucket over to where Lydia lay and began ripping her petticoats for bandages. She dipped a piece of cloth in the cold water, rung it out and handed it to Caleb.

"Clean her head wound with this. I need to examine it."

Caleb took the cotton, never looking away from his love. His words were mangled as he spoke and clutched the cloth. "Why didn't I see her to her tent?"

Lydia's heart beat to a dead man's gait. He'd seen it too often and with the bloodstains on the floor and in the cellar, he knew she was dying. If only he could give her some of his blood, his life.

"It's my fault," he said through bitter sobs. "I should have protected her, I should have been here, I should have known."

"Caleb, you are no good to her, thinking that way. I've seen worse on the battlefield and miracles aplenty. We must pray and believe, but we must tend to her at once. This is no time for berating yourself. It will change nothing. Only action and prayer can make a difference now. Ben's making a travois. We'll take her back to camp at first light."

Caleb could not pray, but only curse the one that didn't help. Where were the angels when she needed them? Where was he?

Ben finished the travois, threw out the bloody water, and drew fresh before leaving Mary and Caleb to the doctoring while he went to sorting footprints and signs. He separated the marks without difficulty. He understood all types—from sniper Reb to cold-blooded killer—every goddamned one left a telltale and this one had a limp.

He nursed a suspicion. The devil-man's killing followed their movements. No doubt, Lydia knew his name before today.

TWENTY-THREE

Pine Ridge Settlement School
May 1939

S UNLIGHT STREAMED THROUGH my bedroom window.
I opened my eyes and squinted in the bright white light. My
mind moaned. Had I been on that hilltop, or was it just
another dream?

Moving from the bed to the window, I savored the magnificent
view of Rebel's Rock. It was a towering cliff of limestone, sparse,
except for a few spindly pines that grew in the bits of earth that had
lodged in crevices of the shallow outcroppings. The trees changed
regularly as the strong mountain storms ripped them out by their
shallow roots and sent them tumbling to the forest below.
Undaunted, nature would replace them by the following spring.

Rebels Rock was legend in this part of the country. Old locals
claimed a Reb from Tennessee leapt to his death, rather than be
captured by the Yankees. They swore he was buried on top and
haunted it still. I never believed it, but it was a good story to keep
the little kids from playing up there.

A deep narrow path wound its way around the base and up the backside of the rock. After a leg-burning climb, one gained the Rock's spectacular view. Despite the legend, it remained a favorite make-out spot with Harlan's teens. Stephen and I had consummated our worthless love up there many times, always under the light of a full moon when it was bright enough to see the steep worn path.

My mind skipped to the deviant man on the hill. If it had been a dream, I was suddenly reliving it in vivid relief. Thankfully, I was rescued by the comforting morning smells of coffee and sugar-cured bacon wafting into my room from the kitchen below. I splashed some water on my face, ran a brush through my heavy hair, and hurried down to breakfast. Grandma was in diligent pursuit of potato flesh with the rosewood-handled peeling knife that Levi kept razor sharp at her behest.

"Do I smell coffee?" I asked.

"I thought you might need some," she said, her cup already half gone.

"You thought right." The steam curled as I poured the wondrous black brew into a heavy clay cup that Levi had fashioned for me years ago.

"Did you have trouble sleeping?" Grandma asked.

I stole a piece of raw potato from the wooden bowl. "Why do you ask?"

"I looked in on you around midnight. You weren't in your bed and I didn't hear you return this morning."

I sighed and sat down at the table. "In that event, it would appear that I have been to your world, watched the sun rise, am back ready for breakfast, and all before seven."

"What did you see?" Grandma asked, as if this were normal breakfast conversation.

"There was a young soldier standing on a hill watching the sun rise. Then two riders... another Union soldier and a woman in a beautiful blue dress... came across the meadow below." I watched Grandma's face for any clue.

She gave away nothing.

"The soldier on the hill hid behind some trees and watched them. I think he was up to no good." Then I did something I had never done. I told her the rest, of his wanton eyes, the bulge in his pants, and the knife in his hand. Grandma fumbled the wet potato and the knife slipped and sliced her finger, spreading blood across the potato starch.

"Fiddlesticks," she mumbled. "I've spoiled the potato."

"I'll get a bandage." I scurried off to the medicine cabinet. When I returned, the color was gone from Grandma's face and I thought she might faint. I knelt to doctor the wound she held bound in a dishcloth.

"Are you alright?"

"I'm feeling a bit tired all of a sudden. Would you mind finishing the breakfast?"

"Of course not." I finished bandaging her finger and helped her to the parlor. "I'll bring you a plate."

She made no reply but sat wearily by the window. I was sure she knew in full what I had only seen in part. I hit the raw nerve she carried still.

In the days that followed, Grandma reverted to her old habits and asked me to return the necklace, Bible, and the key to the steamer trunk in the attic. I ignored her request as my journeys continued without my consent. No amount of denial on her part and no amount of wishing on mine could turn back the clock to a simpler time. Grandma's gifts were my only validation that I was sane. According to her, our conversations never happened and my excursions back in time were simply nightmares. She was so adamant about these things that I began to question my sanity and the craziness that had become my reality. Grandma's enigmatic and cryptic request to unravel her threads and put them right was at a dead end. Without her cooperation, I was clueless to clues and could go no further.

In that long month of May, I was swept away on multiple journeys. Between them and Grandma's renewed silence, a new foe emerged, a recurrent nightmare in which I stood on the crumbling edge of a bottomless precipice. Each time the stone gave way beneath my feet, I tumbled head over heels toward a raging river of fire.

The weather turned sultry and the nightmares and journeys persisted. June was hotter than hell, and many any were the nights I lay naked and restless between damp cotton sheets. Most nights, I slept not at all, stealing instead, a few hours before dawn when the air finally cooled a bit, only to wake to another day of insufferable heat. Much to Grandma's chagrin, I often slept through breakfast but her routine never wavered.

She frowned at my unkempt hair and clothing. I didn't care. I was frazzled inside and out. Grandma had shared too much for me to go back to the way it was and whatever force had been put in motion, obviously had no intention of giving me a moments rest, in body or spirit. With the children released until fall, I spent most of my days hiding in the springhouse—that wondrous cool burrow in the mountain—reading Grandma and Grandpa's letters by lantern light, in search of a clue, an answer, something to give me a new direction.

Then I came across a letter buried at the bottom of the trunk and tucked inside the sheath of a wicked, antler-handled knife.

My Dearest,

Mary has agreed to keep this letter safe until you are able to read it with your own eyes.

I have been ordered south and my soul is torn. To leave you lying shattered, there are no words for the pain and guilt that I feel.

It was you who showed me the way to my true soul and upon my return, I shall restore yours to you.

When we touched and loved, it was like stepping from the shadows into the light. Your love I have always sought, even in my dreams and yet I never believed it could be.

I shall not die, Sweetheart. For as you continue to cling to life, so shall I. Hold the course until we embrace once more.

Your Loving Servant,
Caleb

I read and reread the letter. Something awful had happened to Grandma, and I was convinced that it had something to do with the sandy-haired devil on the hill. In fitful frustration, I reached into the deep trough of cold spring water and pulled out the never-ending jug of Sassafras tea. With the jug in one hand and two glasses in the other, I went in search of Levi's council. I found him dozing in the maple tree's deep shade.

"Levi?"

One eye opened to a slit. He smiled and took the sweating glass I offered. His deep burgundy lips parted slightly and emptied half the glass in an endless swallow. A visible sigh of cooling contentment moved through his body. He had a seamless satisfaction with life, and I wished I could have the same.

Though my mind pulsed with questions, I forced silence and drank the first glass without interruption. When I could stand it no longer, I began my probe.

"Levi, I think I'm losing my mind. I don't know if I'm living in a dream world or if these things are really happening or both.

"Does dey feel like dreams?"

"I don't know," I moaned. "Maybe it's just my wretched life catching up with me. Maybe it's that mid-life restlessness folks talk about."

Levi held his glass out for more. "By da Lawd above Miz Mattie, Providence tain't no illusion." He reached into his sagging shirt pocket and removed a leather tobacco pouch, soft with wear, and his ancient bamboo pipe. "You is dealin' wid powerful forces. Da spirits live on beyond dis earth." He buried the pipe in the pouch and pushed tobacco deep into the bowl.

I thought of Khalidah, her stories, and her gentle ways. How I loved listening to her mystic tales. She became the door through which I was allowed to dream. When I spoke of leaving the mountains, she didn't scold. Instead, she told me of her life on the far away island of Pemba. Sometimes that story would lead to a deeper darker story—a story I never tired of. Her face would set like stone, and her eyes became the ocean, the wind, and the sky. Through her eyes, I would see the mighty ship, Sultana; feel her devastation as it took her away from all she knew and loved. She would tell me of the prophecy and her birthright—how Levi was saved by the intervention of the ancients at the breeding farm in Kentucky. He was her seventh child, the six others had been sold away and she never saw them again.

Her words chilled, and her body swayed as she danced the story of being cast into the impenetrable darkness of slavery, a darkness that dwelled beneath the shadows—so complete—so depraved—that were it not for her belief and contact with the ancients, she would have been lost to herself forever. With wild gesticulations and fervent words, she howled and tossed the story until it soared in my mind like a wild magnificent storm.

Grandma sought to dissuade me from spending time with Khalidah—in fact punished me repeatedly for that very offense, but I adored the stories and the way they made me feel when I sat by her hearth and she acted them out. Her eyes would grow wide as her hands swept wildly in front of me. It was unlike anything else in my life. Her stories were exciting, magical, untamed, and no matter what punishment awaited, Grandma could not keep me from Khalidah no more than you can keep ants away from a picnic. She was a feast for my soul's imagination. I had not thought of those stories in many years, and they rushed back to me with the crispness of a newly printed book.

Levi struck a match on the side of his shoe and brought the flame to the tobacco. I watched his ritual as I had thousands of times before; he puffed a couple of times until the tobacco embers glowed and every once in awhile he would inhale the thick fragrant smoke. It was this exhalation I subconsciously anticipated. The scent was linked to my deepest memories. It spoke to my inner self, the self that was so confused these days. To be here with him, in this familiar way, was like a pleasant sedative.

"Remember da prophecy?"

I thought of our time in the attic and Levi's magic flowed over me like ocean's tide, opening my mind to a lush, fertile land scented with cinnamon and clove. Music sailed across crystal waters and ebony spirits danced.

Compelled to my feet, I followed him to the secret path of his sacred place. It was protected by a forest of treacherous hawthorn trees whose long cross-shaped thorns grew thick and vicious on trunks and limbs.

Callie Dawn and I often asked Levi about his forest. We were always curious how he managed to escape into the thorn trees without being noticed and return unscathed. We tried once and came out bleeding and crying.

Levi remained close-lipped about many things in those days. So we settled for the old-timers tales of shadowy giants and strange music that came from within the forest—stories Levi neither denied nor confirmed. The mountain folk remained suspicious yet respective of the old black man and his Tambookie Forest.

I was in a stupor. I knew what was going on, but I could not shake the verdant-scented valley from my mind. With each step Levi took, the trees seemed to lean back to reveal a well-worn footpath. Our journey ended in a sea of soft green grass surrounded by a thick wall of towering bamboo. I remained suspended between two worlds while Levi made a fire from hawthorn branches. A tree he said was sacred and could cure many spiritual and physical ailments. Purple puffs of clouds began to boil as the sacred smoke spiraled upward and my world fell away into a storm of lightning, thunder, and wind as Khalidah's words spoke to me again.

When the moons fullness embraces rebirth, the Chosen One must leap into the great Darkness. If the Chosen One should fail. If Pangari's seed is not sown, before the moon wanes in winter's dawn, mankind will be destined to live beneath the shadows.

I was speared upon her liturgy as the ancient bells of Babylon struck the resounding tones of all of the lost heroes. Once again, I heard Khalidah's last words. *You are the Chosen. You must fulfill the prophecy. It is your destiny.*

TWENTY-FOUR

And the promise being made, must be kept.
—Abraham Lincoln, August 26, 1863

C ALEB RODE SLOWLY into the hospital camp, dragging the travois that held his tightly bundled angel. Soldier's stared, cursed and kicked the ground. When Caleb stopped in the middle of camp, Doctor Kenton rushed to Lydia's side.

Caleb dismounted and pushed him away.

"Now see here, Soldier…"

Caleb extracted his knife and knelt to cut the bindings that held his precious mangled cargo. Gently, he cradled her in his arms.

"Take her to my tent," the doctor huffed.

Mary rode up beside them. "No. Bring her to mine."

Caleb followed Mary while Kenton strode off for his implements. Mary held the tent flap back while Caleb ducked inside.

"Lay her on my cot."

Caleb's body functioned on demand. He was living in a state of controlled hysteria. He wanted to help, to do something, to kill the bastard responsible. Violent twitches pounded beneath his eye.

Mary poked her head out of the tent. Numerous soldiers stood

247

silent, watching, waiting, hoping, praying. She stepped from the tent and spewed a flurry of orders. The camp jumped to life. Everyone wanted to help save their angel—the one who listened, mended, fed, and put pen to paper for them. She had always considered them before herself, and she was loved by all.

Caleb poured water into the basin and dabbed at Lydia's seeping wounds while Mary sorted through bottles in her apothecary.

"I need roasted onions to make poultices and lots of boiling water. Can you get someone to do that as quickly as possible?"

Caleb nodded, kissed Lydia's unresponsive lips and left.

Mary spoke to her charge while mixing Blessed Thistle and Lady's Mantle, some for tea, the rest to be added to the roasted onions. "This is going to relieve some of your pain and hopefully stop the bleeding." Mary stopped what she was doing, she sat beside her friend and held her limp cold hand between her own. Lydia had become like a daughter to her, and for a moment the grief welled up. She sent another petition heavenward, dried her eyes, and took a deep breath. "Now you listen to me, Lydia Weldishofer. You are going to hang on to life, and you are going to come back to us. Do you hear me? You must not let that devil win again!"

The tent flap lifted, and Doctor Kenton stepped inside.

Mary tucked Lydia's hand back under the quilts and went back to her task.

"How is she?" he asked.

"Alive. That in itself is a miracle. God only knows what she's been through."

Doctor Kenton lifted the quilt. "My God! What kind of a man did this?"

Mary's voice was soft and solemn. "It was no man. It was Gravemaker."

Days cascaded. Caleb kept silent vigil and slept little. He spooned White Willow Bark tea into Lydia's unresponsive lips.

"What is this for, Mary?"

"Pain. If she can feel, it will help her keep her strength."

Caleb took Lydia's limp hand in his. "Is she aware, Mary? Does she know I'm here?"

"I do not know, Caleb. I simply do not know." She rested her hand on his shoulder. "We are doing everything we can. She is in the Lord's hands now. She walks the land between heaven and earth, and we can only pray that she will stay with us."

Caleb stood guard at Lydia's side, determined to keep the Angel of Death from stealing her away. His prayers were angry demands, and he could find no peace. Grisly images of vengeance began to consume his thoughts.

One morning Mary entered the tent with a cup of coffee for him. "Ben is outside. He wants to speak with you."

Caleb put Lydia's hand on her stomach and tucked the covers snug around her before emerging into the bright bustling day. Ben was on the courier's horse with a piece of paper in his hand. Their eyes met.

"Time to go, Storekeep."

"Like hell."

"We've got orders."

"To hell with your orders."

Ben dismounted. "Corporal, I'm takin' ya back. What kind of shape yer in, is up to you."

"I'm not going, Ben."

Ears around camp perked. Bets were in the making.

"Damn it Storekeep, I'm givin' you a goddamn order."

Caleb's anger focused on his friend.

"I'm staying until she wakes up, and nobody's saying different."

"Guess we'll see 'bout that." Ben dismounted, removed his hat, and hung his knife sheath on the saddle. He squared his shoulders to Caleb. "We don't have to do it this way but if that's what ya want, yer gonna get yer ass kicked." Ben wanted the fight; he wanted to see how prepared Caleb was for vengeance. Sides, the boy needed to get rid of some of that anger and guilt. Could be that Storekeep would kick his ass.

"I'm not going, Sarg."

"You denying a direct order, Soldier?"

"Guess I am."

Ben spit on his hands. He and Caleb squared off. Caleb landed the first punch and Ben rammed his shoulder through Caleb's stomach, taking him to the ground. The camp erupted into cheers and jeers as the fists flew. Caleb dug into what flesh he could find in Ben's hard stomach and rolled them both head over heels.

"Eat this, Decker."

Caleb put his all into the right cross, but Ben rolled out of the way and came back with a hook from the left hand of God. Caleb went prone; his brain rattled.

Ben sprang to his feet.

Caleb rose in slow motion. He wasn't going to leave Lydia.

Ben knew he wouldn't give up that easy and landed a right foot in Caleb's short ribs, lifting him two feet in the air. Caleb fell back with a groan.

"Stay down, Boy. It'll only git worse."

Caleb lunged for Ben's legs.

"I'm no boy!"

He latched onto Ben's lower legs and thrust upward and back. They hit the ground in a harmony of groans. So—Ben was human after all.

Caleb jumped up and turned, fists in the air. "Like I said, I ain't going."

Not since he'd tussled with Vail years ago had Ben had such a good fight. Storekeep had learned well.

"Gimme a hand, boy."

"I ain't fallen for that shit."

"Ya got my word. I won't stomp ya."

Ben's word was as good as Jesus'. So, Caleb extended his hand and jerked his friend to his feet.

The men were disappointed.

"We'll be breakin' camp at first light," Ben said.

"I said I'm not leaving her."

Caleb never saw the lightning, iron right hook that sent his ass back where he started.

"I expect ya back before dark," Ben said mounting up.

Five minutes and a bucket of water later, Caleb lay awake starring up at the covey of men holding meeting around him.

"Hey Corporal, you awake?"

Caleb's cow-eyed expression said, "Not quite".

"You shouldn't have trusted him."

He wrestled out a couple words. "What in the hell happened?"

"He cold-cocked you."

Caleb dusted himself off and went back to Lydia. His face burned at the laughter behind him. Damn them all. Mary was changing the dressing on his darling's head. "How is she?"

Mary looked at Caleb's busted lip and disheveled appearance.

"What have you been into?"

"Benjamin Decker."

"Oh, I see. That's not a good thing, is it?"

"No Ma'am, but it got me a few more hours with Lydia."

"Wash your filthy hands first."

Mary stepped from the tent and waited for the sound of water trickling into the basin. "Lord, help us all."

Caleb stroked Lydia's hair. "I'm sorry, Lydia. I'm sorry I didn't warn you." His voice caught on the growing lump in his throat. "I'm sorry that I didn't protect you, that I didn't listen. That I didn't hear your screams." He looked at her pale thin face. "I promise you, Sweetheart. I will come back. As God as my witness, I will return, and we'll have a proper wedding like you deserve." Caleb massaged her hand and kissed her unresponsive lips. He took off his boots and carefully snuggled up next to her. He needed to hear her breath and feel her heart beating against him one more time. Would she ever wake? Would she think he abandoned her if she did?

Mary handed him a cup of coffee when he came from the tent an hour later. He sat close to the fire away from the growing chill.

"I have to go, Mary."

"You must not worry. I will stay by her side, day and night."

Caleb's storm-swept eyes peered into hers.

"You must stop torturing yourself so. Stay focused on your duty so that you may return when the battles are over."

Caleb gripped his cup. "If she would just open her eyes then I would know she still lives. How long can she survive on broth and water?"

Caleb's tortured face hurt Mary's heart. He needed absolution, yet he would not accept it. If he left like this, he might never make it back.

"Doctor Kenton and I are working on that. She has a very bad head wound, Caleb. There is nothing you can do. Your duties are elsewhere and it is imperative that you remain focused on them, not on Lydia. She's made it this long and that is a good sign."

Caleb tossed his remaining coffee in the flames. A hiss of steam rose in reply. He reached into his coat pocket and handed Mary an envelope and the dead soldier's German pocket Bible.

"When she's well enough, see that she gets these." Mary took the letter and Bible and clasped Caleb's hand.

"It's not your fault."

His eyes gave away his shame.

"Oh Caleb, don't do this to yourself."

Caleb pressed her hand and walked out of camp. He was glad he had five miles to compose himself. The men would all know. Some would find fault, some would console, and others would take up arms and attempt revenge. To none would he respond. To them, he was a living ghost, and so be it.

That evening Mary read Caleb's parting words to Lydia by lamplight. She hoped Lydia could hear and that it would give her hope and courage to fight her way back from hell.

> *My Dearest,*
>
> *Mary has agreed to keep this letter safe until you are able to read it with your own eyes.*
>
> *I have been ordered south, and my soul is torn. To leave you lying shattered. There are no words for the pain and guilt that I feel.*

Far off, Lydia heard Mary's voice speaking Caleb's words. Near, she saw an angry soldier, face contorted in pain, supported by a lone tree. Pieces of cloth burst into dust when bullets struck his unprotected chest. She reached out for him.

C H A P T E R

TWENTY-FIVE

)))∙∙𝄐((((

Let us have faith that right makes might; and in that faith let us,
to the end, dare to do our duty as we understand it.
—Abraham Lincoln, February 27, 1860

A T DAWN, the Eightieth marched toward Tennessee. Caleb's heart and soul stayed behind even as his feet moved forward. Ben told no one of his suspicions, and Gravemaker remained unidentified. Camp life dragged for one and all.

Caleb received no word of Lydia and his demeanor quickly soured. He drilled his men from dawn to dusk until their morale was as low as his.

Ben gathered his gear and bunked elsewhere, leaving Caleb alone to deal with his miserable thoughts and bitter moods.

General Burnside took command of the Army of the Ohio that September, crushing all hopes of furloughs. The Eightieth knew of Burnside's debacle at Fredericksburg, and the canceled furloughs did nothing to endear the General to his new command. Boredom—the soldier's worst enemy—took root and with no reprieve in sight, the men bristled. Fistfights broke out daily and some soldiers deserted.

255

Burnside was hell-bent on restoring his reputation among the senior commanders, and he was sure he could do it with the farm boys that made up the Eightieth, and their sister units. Born in Liberty, Indiana, he trusted the boys fighting ways and innate ability to rout Rebels. "To hell with West Point ways," he often remarked to anyone who would listen. In his opinion, he knew the best way to fight in the mountainous terrain of Kentucky and Tennessee, and he kept his men moving back and forth through the two states in pursuit of Morgan and his Raiders.

The General sent a cavalry brigade to retake the Cumberland Gap Garrison, a formidable stone fortress, manned by twenty-five hundred Rebs. The Confederates put up a staunch fight and held their own. Undeterred, Burnside sent the Eightieth to pass a little "love note" to the Rebel commander. The soldiers cursed the horrific pace in their boots worn thin. Few words were exchanged as they marched, double-quick, nearly seventy miles through the Appalachian Mountains.

The letter was a ruse. General Burnside informed the Confederate commander that he had brought a prime fighting division to take out the Rebs, when in fact, he had only a few hundred. With no decent lookouts in the thick mountains, the Confederate commander folded his cards and surrendered.

With blistered feet and no fight when they got there, deportment suffered and the soldiers were near rebellion. Captain Challand sent Ben out to round up some musicians to break the monotony and soothe the dreadful beasts stomping around his camp, dressed as soldiers.

Later that evening, the soldier's sang familiar tunes to the home guards mandolin, fiddle, and banjos. They even managed to drink some homebrew, and for once, the commanders turned a blind eye.

Ben left the festivities to jaw with the Captain. Caleb stayed to himself and watched from a distance. He knew he was a thorn in everyone's side. He snapped at comrades, was curt with the officers, and drilled his men without mercy. He clung to the one identity that could keep him sane, that of a soldier. He watched for Ben to come out of the Captain's tent. Since Ben left their tent for another, he was no longer privy to his inside information.

Ben came out and walked over to Caleb. "I need ya to git a dozen men together. We're headed up the Laden Trail to take down a Rebel lookout at first light."

"We took out the garrison. What's left? They can observe all they want. They've got nothing to back it up."

"Look-a here, Storekeep. I'm given ya a goddamned order and I 'spect it to be carried out. Now git yer gear together and round up a dozen men. Make sure Johnson and Stahler are along. We've got sharpshooters to flush."

"I know my job," Caleb snapped.

"Coulda fooled me the way you've been drivin' the men in the ground."

"Why are you in charge of this mission, anyway?"

"My home-place is two ridges over and I've hunted every hill and holler within twenty miles a here and there. I can take ya cross these mountains blindfolded. I'll smell them Rebs before ya ever see em."

Caleb glared. He wanted to take down Ben's arrogant ass.

"Git crackin', soldier. Ya got yer orders."

Caleb felt the heat rise to his face and passed his rancor to the next in line.

"Johnson!"

Harley Johnson was nearer Ben's age, tall, gangly, and handsome. He looked up from cleaning his rifle to the rhythm of the banjo.

"Get your ass over here."

Harley sat his gun aside and walked long-legged over haversacks, bedrolls, and lounging soldiers.

"Whatcha need, Wright?"

"That's Corporal to you."

Harley's face went poker straight. There was no room to play with Wright of late, not since Gravemaker got to his girl, and who could blame him?

"What's the order, Corporal?" Harley asked with a slight emphasis on Corporal.

"Round up Stahler, Roberts, and nine more. We move at daybreak to take out a Rebel lookout."

"Hot damn. It's about time we got a little action. I know just the men to take."

Caleb's cheek pulsed. "I don't give a rat's ass who you get. Just get it done. Tell your men to draw five days rations and a hundred rounds. Understood?"

"Yessir." Harley hesitated; he wanted to say something to ease his one-time friend.

"Well, Johnson? You want a hug and a kiss? Get it done." Caleb opened his father's broken pocket watch. "You got thirty minutes, and it's ticking."

Harley's face fell.

"Yessir, Corporal."

Caleb watched Harley walk back to the singing. The men were getting drunk, and he wished he could. The Captain was sending them on a pointless mission, a waste of energy for weary soldiers. What they needed were furloughs, but instead of marching north to Lydia, he would be marching south to some damn rock and a handful of worthless Rebs. From the thunder rumbling in the distance, it would be raining before daybreak, just in time to muddy things up.

Morning broke to a cold drizzle.

Ben barked. "Git em in line, Corporal. Light's a wastin' and I 'spect to be eatin' Mary Belle's vittles by sundown tomorrow."

"How about some arsenic pie," Caleb muttered. "Stahler, take the point. Johnson, the rear. Move out!"

Stahler smirked and checked his attachments. Caleb didn't like the man, but he was a crack shot and would be a good one to have at the point.

The landscape was a hunter's paradise. Ben thought of past trophies; his first whitetail at age eight, taken with Pa's long rifle and his first black bear at twelve; it would have ate him alive if Pa hadn't backed him with a head shot that dropped the charging beast in its tracks. The bear fell so close to his feet that he felt its last hot breath.

They marched double-quick up the Laden on a two-day trek to the mouth of the Hannah River then veered north to the sheer limestone bluff, the reputed Rebel lookout. Careful to stay out of the Rebs' view, Ben led his men up the backside of the mountain— a perilous deer path that wound through thick growth, carved by mountain contours in a steep upward climb. For hours, they pushed up the muddy slopes. They were nearly spent when they reached the Laden Trail. It knotted an unruly course along nature's rough-hewn topography littered with rockslide debris from the heavy rain.

Caleb tried to focus on what lay ahead, but Lydia waltzed through his mind; visions of her moonlit silhouette, laughing and teasing with dancing blue eyes, soft kisses and passionate embraces. These images were soon transposed with mutilated and bloody ones. Revenge reared its ugly head.

He didn't even know if she ever woke up. Hell, he didn't even know if she was still alive. He picked up the rhythm of soldiers on the move: marching feet and the rub of crossed leather straps on wet gear—the sounds could numb his thoughts if he let them. Months of marches got one dreaming to the monotonous beat of soldier's feet. He and others learned to sleep on the move by watching the set of boots in front of them. The body was an amazingly adaptable machine. He thought of Lydia and chanced another demand of God for his lovely lady. The response was a vision that came in a torrent; a man he knew, but could not identify, stood gaunt and emaciated on the hurricane deck of a burning steamboat above a great chasm of churning, black water. In its wake bobbed the heads of hundreds of drowning men. Flames lapped at the man's feet despite the pouring rain.

The image dissipated as quickly as it came, leaving him shaken. It had come unbidden, time and again, since the first night he left Lydia's side. He spoke of it to no one and instead scoured Grandma's Bible for answers, but truth hid within the Scripture, and God took refuge elsewhere.

The haunting vision tangled his senses, and he sought relief by spilling endless confusing letters onto Lydia's nightstand. His disjointed ramblings could provide no balm of Gilead for his lovely. His precious Lady, did she live still? He dreamed last night of lying beside with her with a baby sprawled between them, a son whose breath was sweet with mother's milk. In his dream, Lydia laid in peaceful slumber, uncovered and unafraid, her milk-laden breasts exposed to the heavens.

"Wright, stop here," Ben shouted over the dozen blue caps spread down the trail.

Caleb's mind was elsewhere and he kept marching.

"Wright!" Ben bellowed. "Git yer mind off them tits and ass and back where it belongs. I expect a goddamn answer when I talk to you."

Stahler heard Ben's rant and cut loose on Caleb. "Wright, get your head out of your ass. Didn't you hear Sarg? I ain't planning on taking no bullet for a fucking distracted coward."

Caleb snapped back to the task at hand and lunged for Stahler's throat and taking him to the ground.

Ben had, by then, reached the two combatants. "Knock this shit off," he said, jumping in the fray. As he pulled Caleb off, he ducked a right. "Settle it another time, but not on my watch." Ben spat. "Stahler, get back to the point and pay attention. We're gettin' close. Caleb, you take the rear."

Stahler shot Caleb a smug smile and trotted past the others.

Another hour down the trail, and Ben's hand shot up; they stopped until he waved them forward. "We're not but two shakes from the Rock." Ben's voice was quiet and low. "My Grandpap's homestead is at the bottom of this holler." He sniffed the air and took a deep breath. "I can smell Sis' biscuits from here. It'll be dark in an hour. How 'bout we get some home cookin' tonight and rout them Rebs in the mornin?"

The tired men agreed.

"Keep yer wits about ya. Them damn Rebs might be dinin' in and Mary Belle packs a gun and the will to use it."

"Reckon she would, bein' your sister," teased Harley.

"Alright, let's git some supper. Pan out and keep yer mind outta the kitchen and on yer backside until we git there. We'll gather at the creek." Ben waved them down the mountain into the thick woods.

Caleb wasn't happy about the delay. If Ben screwed up another furlough, there'd be hell to pay. He hung back to voice his dissent to Ben but waited until the men were several yards down hill.

"Ya got somethin to say?" Ben challenged.

"I do."

261

"Git on with it. I'm hungry enough to eat a grizzly's ass."

"We're here to do a job, and I'd just a soon get to it. We could get in behind those Rebs tonight and be on furlough by week's end."

"Reckon that's so, but I ain't a passin' this close to my kin without stoppin' in. And that's the last word on it."

"You're a son of a bitch, Decker."

"Reckon so."

Little light reached the ground through the dense canopy once twilight closed. Caleb and Ben stayed on the down-slope and followed the sound of running water. They caught up to the others as they were wading across the rocky creek.

Ben's voice was sharp. "Johnson, you and Roberts set the perimeter. Stahler, check the outbuildings for any uninvited guests."

The soldiers stalked through the recesses, weapons drawn. The home place was quiet except for the occasional moo of a cow. The light went out in the cabin as they got close. Ben sidled up to the window; his fingers gripped his Colt as he crossed the porch. Slowly he pushed the door open.

"Speak yer name," a woman challenged.

"Damn it, Mary Belle. Ya gonna shoot yer own brother when I just dropped by fer supper?"

"Say yer name so I can hear plain, stranger."

"Fer God's sake Mary Belle, its Ben."

Mary Belle listened hard. "Jefferson Benjamin Decker? Is that really you?"

"Reckon a man could git some vittles round here? Hells fire woman. Course it's me!"

Mary Belle uncocked the gun, put it in its place, and relit the lamp. Ben put his pistol away and stepped into the kitchen, his grizzly bear arms open for her sweet embrace. She squeezed him like the prodigal come home.

He had forgotten how good the softness of a woman could feel.

"Lord above," gushed Mary Belle. "I done give ya up fer dead, Jefferson." Tears rained relief, a wish seldom granted in these troubled times. He smelled, but Lordy, he felt good—alive and in the flesh. "I ought to beat ya silly. Have ya done forgot everythin' I taught ya? I know ya can write."

A couple of gawking soldier's meandered nearby.

"Those yer boys?"

"Yessum."

"How many'd ya bring along? Those out there looks mighty tired and hungry. I'll get the girls busy rustlin' some vittles." She hugged him again. "Lord, Lord, I'm glad yer here Jefferson."

"Git them nieces a mine a cookin' and me and the boy's will throw some planks together outside fer a table."

The back door opened and a red-haired Lily came in toting a full bucket of fresh milk. She squealed, "Uncle Jefferson." The milk sloshed as she sat down the bucket and catapulted herself into Ben's arms. Near eighteen, she was full-sprouted.

Ben barely recognized his favorite; his arms held woman not child. Seven years was too long away. He hated the name Jefferson, but he loved his nieces, and only they held the privilege to call him that. A thirteen-year old Emma appeared not a minute later and greeted him with equal ferocity.

Caleb stuck his head through the door.

"Who's this handsome buck?" asked Mary Belle. This one made her warm inside.

Ben didn't turn around. "That one's the hero—part devil, part mule—bullets won't kill him."

Caleb didn't want to socialize. "Corporal Caleb Wright, Ma'am." He offered his hand.

"And a gentleman, too," she fairly sang.

Ben stepped aside. The girls clung to their ol Hickory Uncle.

"You're as beautiful as Ben is ornery." She motioned Caleb to a chair beside a table cluttered with cooking utensils.

Caleb took off his hat but stayed in the doorway. "Thank you Ma'am but if you'll beg my pardon, I'll stay out here and see to the men."

"Nonsense, come on in here and let me get a good look at 'cha. In the last two years, I got but one letter from this wayward brother of mine. He talked only of a Caleb, the Storekeep that the Rebs couldn't kill. He scrawled four pages worth. I ought to know. I've read it a hundred times."

Ben ignored Mary Belle's disclosure.

Caleb looked at Ben's poker face. Some day he would crack into that layer, the one that wrote the letter, the one with a hidden past.

"Ya heard the woman. Git in here and sit yer ass down."

Caleb wasn't in the mood for conversation and as nice as the gesture was, he'd rather be outside. He glared at Ben and Ben's eyes ordered back. He came in and sat at the table.

"Thank you, Ma'am."

"If yer Ben's friend that makes you family. Call me Mary Belle."

The weary soldiers congregated around the door. The room smelled of fresh apple butter. Mary Belle noticed Caleb favored his left leg—some wound, likely. She admired the strength of his body and the knowledge in his eyes. That didn't come from Ben's instruction—that came from living, making tough decisions and learning hard lessons.

"The men and I need to clean up before dinner, Mary Belle," Ben said. "We'll be back directly, but could ya spare some of that bread and apple butter? We're plumb starved to death."

"Why, you know I can. Y'all scoot on out to the well and I'll send one of the girls with it. We'll fix you a meal you'll not soon forget." She leaned out the back window and with the high pitch of a mother called her chicks in. "Gene-veeve! Est-errrr! Lov-elllllll! Git on in here. I got a surprise."

Within seconds, the girls bounded through the back door and nearly laid Ben over with their affections, a cluster of loveliness around a crotchety old badger. Four of the five were full-blossom, and their stares were man-hungry and hopeful.

"Ma'am, I think we ought to stick to the barn," Caleb said.

"I'll not hear of it," Mary Belle retorted. "We haven't had the company of men in God knows how long. Sides, a man needs more than bread and butter to fill his belly, and a woman needs more than woman folk, and that's the Gospel truth."

Images of Lydia in cool moonlight waltzed behind Caleb's brow. "Ma'am, these aren't boys. They're hungry, lonely, and longing in every way a man does. I believe it would be best if we stayed down at the barn."

Mary Belle laughed. "Ya can't hold back them feelin's no more than ya can stop a ragin' river." All Decker-stubborn, she was.

Caleb surveyed Mary Belle's girls. Lily was the epitome of her name—fair and green-eyed, tiger-lily hair, and built to please. Besides pretty little Emma, he wasn't sure who was who. He listened for a while to Ben joke and tease and their identities soon became clear. Genevieve was tall and svelte, small-breasted but breathtaking beautiful. Her mouth was a half-opened rosebud, her eyes a liquid sky; a man could lose himself in those. Lovell was a bit of a thing, not as beautiful as the others, yet her black hair and black eyes shimmered like ebony and she had a smile that would melt a man's heart. Ester was red-haired and voluptuous like her younger sister Lily but more contained. Caleb was sure she would have snared a man by now if there were any to be had. She was aloof—probably smarter then the rest—her freckled skin radiant and sun-kissed. Her hands showed the life she led, calloused with small cuts and scrapes but scrubbed clean; most likely, she handled many of the heavier chores.

Caleb got up and followed the men to the well. Once their stomachs were full, they would be sparring for the girls' attentions. He would have to keep a tight rein.

Lily grabbed the towels and bolted after the Corporal.

"Where's she goin', Mary Belle?" admonished Ben.

Mary Belle ignored the snorting bull. "Ester, bring in enough apples for that stack cake receipt, and Emma go gather some eggs. Lovell, git a ham from the smoke house, and Genevieve cut the bread and take it out yonder to them hungry men with plenty of yer apple butter. That should tide them over till dinner's ready."

Emma bellyached. "Oh, Ma. I haven't seen Uncle Jefferson fer so long. Cain't Lily git the eggs?"

"He'll be spendin' the night. You'll hear enough from him and everyone else. Now, off to the henhouse with you."

"Yessum," she mumbled and sulked out the door, basket in hand. She knew a one-time reprimand was Ma's limit, and Ma punished with a firmer hand than Pa ever had.

Ben waited for the youngest to exit. "Maybe sendin' the girls out there ain't such a good idea. We got fightin' ahead and my men don't need to be distracted with no damn petticoats."

Mary Belle overlooked Ben's child-raising intrusion and tended to the wherefores of making a large meal. "I know the girls seem over anxious, but ya need to understand. The only men left round here are the home guards, and they're all married. Why my Lily's just been a cryin' fer a baby of her own."

"We stay on more then a couple days and she just might git

her wish."

Mary Belle pushed a wooden bowl of potatoes and a paring knife across the table. "Worse things could happen."

Ben swore under his breath and started peeling. "What happened to John?"

"Ain't heard a word since Shiloh," Mary Belle said, cutting onions. "Do you think he might be rottin' in one of them Rebel prisons?"

Ben knew the full carnage of that bloody battle, the mass graves, thousands unidentified. "Might," he said. He'd be damned fore he'd tell her any different.

He listened to her prattle about all the news from the holler while he finished the potatoes. He shoved the bowl across the table. "I'm gonna check on my men."

Mary Belle watched Ben amble out the door and stick a wad of tobacco in his mouth. Too bad he never got over his Rosita. A man like that needed a woman's warm arms and soft kisses to keep him from getting too hard, and he needed children of his own to bounce on them big knees of his.

Supper came as promised, served in the light of a full harvest moon and a few well-placed lanterns. The night was warm and still when the girls filed outside with their feast. The men whistled their appreciation and lusted for the lovely lasses with meadow flowers in their hair. The platters were heaped high and the soldiers dreamed of dessert in the form of sweet ruby lips.

Lily carried tender buttermilk biscuits, piled high, and slathered with fresh-churned butter. Emma carried a large bowl of assorted wild greens and onions, wilted with sizzling bacon grease. Ester manhandled a monstrous wooden platter of thick slices of ham and tender-skinned potatoes.

Mary Belle had also prepared Ben's favorite—Kentucky red

cob corn and fresh goose beans cooked up with fatback and smoked hog jowl. She sat the towering bowl in front of him.

He grasped her hand, and his manly demeanor gave way to boyhood delight. "Ya remembered."

Mary Belle rubbed his back. "Course, I remember Jefferson. This may surprise ya, but there ain't a day's gone by that I ain't wished fer this night. Yer big Sis don't forget the important things."

Ben snatched the deep wooden spoon and took a heaping helping.

When the men thought they could eat no more, Lovell brought forth her masterpiece: a thirteen-layer apple stack cake with a pitcher of fresh cream to pour on top. If the girls were looking for husbands, they could each have two.

Ben watched his men relish the vittles and worried for his girls. They were flirting with all the comeliness mountain lasses could give, and his men were drinking it up like it was corn whiskey.

Mary Belle flitted here and there, tending and flirting with all the men. She soon shooed Emma inside to make coffee.

The decision to delay the assault had been sound. His men needed a night off and a good rest after their hellish march. He just had to make sure they didn't have too much fun.

When the makeshift table was cleared and all content, Ester, Lily and Lovell brought out the dulcimer, mandolin, and fiddle. The men hooted when Lovell went to playing the fiddle with such vivacity that the horsehairs began to split. Then Lily coaxed a sultry haunting melody from the dulcimer while Ester accompanied her sisters on her cherished mandolin. Just when they thought the entertainment could get no better, Genevieve broke into song, her voice as sweet and warm as a mid-summer's night. It was nearly two in the morning before Ben succeeded in chasing the girls off to bed and corralled his men in the barn.

Caleb took first watch. The night turned cool as it often did in the mountains. He hunched over his small fire and stared through the flames, his thoughts filled with promises and regrets. He took one of Lydia's old letters soft with wear, from his pocket. His heart hurt more than he thought possible. *God, is she alive?*

When the men's snores came loud and long, Ben brought him a cup of coffee. "Slide yer ass over," he grunted.

Caleb moved a bit. An owl hooted. Ben put another log on the fire and it crackled and popped, sending orange bits of ash spiraling skyward. Carefully, Caleb folded the letter and nestled it back inside his jacket.

Ben sat down. "You remind me of somethin' my Grandpap used to say. When he was havin' a bad spell with the farm or the brew didn't turn out right, he'd say that if it was rainin' pussies he'd step outside and git hit with a big ol dick."

Caleb couldn't help but smile.

"What's eatin' yer ass, Storekeep? It's been months now and yer still sour as a green apple."

"I haven't heard anything about Lydia since I left. Hell Ben, I don't even know if she's still alive."

Ben poked at the fire. "Life's a bastard, that's shore."

"It's that and these damn promises I keep making." Caleb's hands wrapped the warm tin cup. "I've never broken a promise."

"I don't make promises. Not to God, not to myself, and damn shore not to anybody else."

"That supposed to make me feel better?"

Ben shrugged. "Can't change what's done. Thinkin' too much makes a man crazy. Time to let it go."

Caleb sought Ben's black eyes, the flames reflection flickered in them. "I can't."

Ben stood and tossed the coffee grounds in the fire. It hissed a reply. "Gotta. There's demons yet to kill and one past due."

Caleb listened but made no reply. The fact that the bastard responsible for Lydia's mangling was still drawing breath was not lost on him. He had killed the faceless Demon in his mind a thousand times over and savored each one.

"I'll send yer relief in a couple hours."

Ben disappeared into the shadows. Grandma Hannah's long ago words sifted into Caleb's bitter thoughts. *Live every day the good Lord sees fit to give you. It's a gift.* Seasons came and went, he grew up, and she grew old. He missed her. If anybody could sooth his guilty soul and vengeful mind, it would be her.

An hour or so before dawn, Harley poked Caleb with the butt end of his rifle.

Caleb jumped, his pistol cocked.

"Sorry, didn't mean to startle you. I could see you were thinking. Someone should've been out here before now, go on and get some rest. I'll take it to daylight."

Caleb went to the barn and slept past rise and shine. He woke to wondrous breakfast smells. Light streamed in as Lily opened the barn door with a plate of flapjacks, sausage, and sunny-side eggs balanced on a mug of coffee. Caleb sat up, rubbed his three-day beard, smoothed his dusty unkempt hair, and wiped the sleep from his eyes.

"Are ya hungry?" she asked soft and quiet.

"You bet." Caleb took the plate from her and the cup of coffee. Warm melted butter ran down the sides of the tall stack along with lots of thick sourwood honey.

"Your Ma sure knows how to please a man."

"I cooked em."

"She must be a fine teacher." Caleb smiled at the red-haired girl, fair as a river nymph, and took a mouthful. "Mmm."

Lily blushed and sat nearby. She watched the handsome soldier devour her sweet treat. Caleb licked his sticky fingers and took a drink of coffee to cleanse his honeyed mouth.

"Want some more?"

"No, Ma'am, not another bite. But it was delicious. Best I ever had."

Lily moved closer. "Want me to shave ya? I shaved two of the boys this mornin' with Pa's straight razor. They said I done a real good job."

"Is there anything you girls can't do?" Caleb asked.

Lily moved deliberately so that her petticoats showed. "There ain't nothin I cain't do." Her warm breath sent his thoughts south, where the sun doesn't shine and trouble begins. In his hurry to move away from the amorous lass, he spilled the remnants of his coffee down the front of his drawers.

Lily moved toward him. "Want me to wipe that up fer ya?"

"No, Ma'am," he sputtered getting to his feet. "Thanks again for the breakfast. I best go see to the men."

"Uncle Jefferson's already done that. Yer the last one up. They've done gone off 'cept for the one splittin' wood and Uncle Jefferson."

Caleb moved quickly toward the door. She dodged in front of him and put her hands on his chest. "Sure ya don't want a shave?"

Caleb lowered her hands. "Lily, you need to get back to the house, and I need to find your Uncle." It was definitely time to go.

"Can't ya just kiss me?"

Caleb stared at her sweet virgin lips. He thought of his last moments with Lydia and pushed past. "I've got duties to tend to."

Stahler was chopping wood. Lily watched Caleb move toward the cabin and decided to work on the other one. He looked up as she headed his way, her hips swaying.

Ben barked something across the barn lot and chased Lily off for the umpteenth time.

Caleb glanced back and shook his head. The sooner they left the better.

Mary Belle was hanging wash on a line strung between two trees. Ben sat nearby. "She's got an eye for that one," Mary Belle said.

"She's an eye for anythin' with a sack tween its legs."

"Jefferson Decker, that's filthy talk and I won't have it spoke round here."

"That's not talk. That's the truth."

Lily watched hungry-eyed as Stahler lifted a log to the chopping block and swung the ax with precision. The crack smacked the air.

Ben had to get the boys gone before nightfall.

Mary Belle smiled. "If I was younger, I might do some chasin' of my own. It's been a long time."

Ben ignored the comment. He'in and she'in was something he didn't want to think about where his sister was concerned. "We'll be leavin' tonight."

"You cain't. Why yer men are havin' such a good time and just look at my girls. They haven't been this happy since John left."

"Exactly my point. Nothin against their happiness but these boys are leavin' fore nightfall. Ya don't need no more babies to feed."

Mary Belle wagged her finger. "Like I said Jefferson Decker, there's worse things could happin'."

Ben's red-cheeked, round-faced sister amused him, but he gave nothing away. "Courtin' and fightin' don't dance," he mumbled. "I'm ridin' over to Big Laurel and talk to Sam. Is he still at the livery?"

"Till he dies, I reckon," Mary Belle said. "He knows about every Reb that slithers through here."

"Specked he would. That's my aim. Mind if I take Blue?"

"He's too old, Ben. Take Lily's Moonwalker. He's full a vinegar but rides like a dream."

Ben's face screwed into a grimace. "Moonwalker?"

She laughed. "They're girls, Ben. Romance? Remember?"

"Nope."

"What about Janice Dunaway?"

Ben ignored her tease, walked to the corral, and saddled the frisky chestnut. He cantered over to Caleb.

"The men are out on picket. Keep Stahler away from the girls till I git back."

"Where are you going?" asked Caleb.

"Big Laurel."

"We leaving tonight?"

"Yep."

Ben nudged Moonwalker's flanks. He would enjoy the morning ride through familiar places, the spot where he landed his first whitetail and another where he first tasted love. There was comfort in the familiar. Something he'd had precious little of since a lifetime ago.

The town was quiet, empty of horses and men. Sam's anvil rang a familiar tune. Ben trotted over.

"Well I'll be goddamned," Sam said. His ugly face lit-up, unchanged except for a crooked nose and a few more missing teeth.

"Sam," Ben said casually.

"Ben Decker. I thought you were dead."

"Haven't found the bastard that could get it done. But plenty's tried." He eyed the meager pickings of horse stock in the split-rail corral.

Sam's leather apron bounced a belly laugh. "Bet they has at that." He reached deep into the cooling barrel and extracted a stoneware jug of corn whiskey. He popped the cork and handed it over. "It's a damn good batch."

Such were the ways of the hills. Ben missed them. He hoisted the jug to his shoulder, chugged the liquid fire and breathed smoke. "Shit-fire Sam, that's better'n a bow-legged whore."

Sam took the jug and drank deep. "Ain't it though?"

The men sat in the shade and worked the jug, made small talk, and caught up on lost years.

"What's the word, Sam?"

"Home Guards left this mornin' up the Laden for Lover's Leap."

"Where ya got the good horses hid?"

"Ain't none. Morgan took 'em, least ways, some bushwhackers bent on joinin' him. Came through four days ago. Took ever decent horse I had and saddles too."

So much for getting mounts for the men. "Gentleman horse thief they call him, my ass. Morgan, a goddamn burr under the Union's mighty ass saddle. They've had us chasin' that sumbitch nye on a year now. Where were they headed?"

"Tennessee, but ya won't catch em on foot. I'd be more worried about that cannon them Rebs are a pullin'. They're aimin' to put it up on the Leap."

"I'd like to see that," chuckled Ben. "Can ya see em tryin' to pull a ton a brass up that rock? It's rough enough gettin' a girl up there for some stumpin'."

Sam chortled and took another drink.

"That may be, but there's no tellin'—yer boys hurt 'em deep when they routed the Garrison and tricked their General into surrenderin' em without a fight. They're hell-bent on gettin' even. They get that cannon up there and you'll be breathin' fire ever time ya come up the Laden which is might regular as I sees it. I wouldn't take it to lightly. They've done some pretty amazin' things this far."

"Who's in charge of the Home Guard?"

"Kelsey. He left with the boys this mornin'. Ya can catch up to em on horseback. They're on foot. Most of their mounts were here when Morgan's boys came through."

"Much obliged, Sam."

Ben tried to swing into the saddle, but it took two tries and a hand from Kelsey to get his drunk ass seated.

"Good to see ya, Ben. Watch yer back round that rock."

"Always do, Sam. I got eyes 'tween the blades."

Sam didn't doubt it.

Ben caught up to the Home Guard within the hour. Kelsey had Ben in his sites long before he recognized his old friend's familiar flow; horse, man, and weapons all in accord. Ben Decker always had sat the saddle well. Beat Kelsey in more ways than one in years past.

Kelsey turned to his young sergeant. "Couch, give the men a breather."

Ben rode in tall and oblivious, his head happy with whiskey. "Kelsey. How in the hell are ya, ya son of a bitch?"

"Liable to be dead if ya don't keep yer voice down."

Ben laughed and stumbled off his mount.

Kelsey's cheek bulged with tobacco, beneath a thick black beard. "See ya been to Sam's place."

"Damn straight. He's got a good batch." Kelsey handed Ben a plug of Kentucky tobacco. Ben bit off a piece and rolled it into his cheek. "Who broke yer nose again?"

Kelsey grinned. "Too much of Sam's shine, that's what did it.

Darryl Meehan and I swapped fists. He got in the last lick and it was a good-un, but when his Lizzy found out we was fightin' over a whore, she took a fryin' pan to him and liked to killed him."

Ben hee-hawed.

"Laugh now, but let me show ya somethin'." Kelsey motioned Ben to follow him through the wood to an adjacent trail.

Ben knelt and examined the deep ruts in the earth.

"I'll be damned. Sam was right. They're haulin' a goddamn Napoleon."

"They're determined sons-a-bitches. There's been nothin' but trouble since they got here. Seems y'all smashed their peckers, takin' their garrison."

"They bought the ruse. We just offered it."

"Whatever bee they got up their ass, left three of the Simpson boys dead. Their old man's so broke up he's sure to follow 'em to the grave."

"What happened?"

"Them damn Rebs come through and took their plow horse and most everythin' they had in the smoke house. So, the boys tried to sneak in on em about nightfall. Hell, they didn't have a chance, didn't get inside thirty yards of the pickets. Them Rebs ain't no cherries."

"I got the Union's best," Ben said. "We'll lead off the advance."

"Nothin doin'. My men want first crack at those Gray bastards for a pound of flesh and retribution. Them Rebs ransacked every farmstead within thirty miles a here and we aim to git even. This is our fight, Decker."

"Damn it Kelsey, you'll lose half yer men before ya can get close enough to do any damage. Let us take the lead on this."

"No sir. They'd shoot me if I did 'em that away even if you are a Decker."

Ben saw that there was no dealing with his friend on the particulars. "Who ya got?"

"The Cantrell's, Dunaway's, four of the Reese brothers, the Bailey five and the Thompson twins. A few others joined up from 'round Hyden."

"Alright then. Meet us at Mary Belle's at sundown."

Kelsey's neck tightened. "We'll be there."

They walked back through the woods. "Janice died. Did ya know?"

The woods glazed over. She was Ben's first love—stolen by Kelsey while Ben was off fighting in Texas. "When?"

"Two years ago. Lost her and the baby."

Ben saw Kelsey, bloody and beaten, lying unconscious behind the barn. That was seven years ago.

"Where's she buried?"

"On the ridge under the mountain laurel. She loved the way they smelled. Used to fill the house with em."

The hate had left Ben when he found Rosita in Texas. Strange—he and Kelsey were back on equal terms—alone.

"Will ya check in on Mary Belle now and then?"

Kelsey whistled. Moonwalker's head jerked up. Her mane rippled as she trotted over to nuzzle Kelsey's hand. "Already do."

"Shoulda known." Ben grabbed the reins and mounted.

"Think John's dead?" Kelsey asked.

"Nope." Ben met Kelsey's stare. "When I'm in hell, ya best bury me in a hickory box and nail it down tight, cause I'm gonna haunt yer ass if yer in Mary Belle's bed." Ben drove his heels into Moonwalker and trotted off through the woods. Old thoughts of vengeance made for a short trip. The Corporal's dozen watched their noncom ride in. Caleb continued checking the ammo and weapons; their haversacks and bedrolls were stacked against the tobacco barn.

Ben ignored the troops and galloped up to the porch. He bounded off and barged into the house.

Mary Belle scolded. "Heavens to Betsy! What are ya tryin' to do? Scare me to death?"

"When Kelsey gits here, tell him we're at the Rock."

"Lover's Leap?"

"He'll know." Ben aimed to get the Rebs to deal their cards early. Wipin' ass was for Kelsey's greenhorns, not Ben's vets. "I'm takin' the horse. I'll swing back after we clean up them Rebs. Keep the gun loaded."

"Jefferson, I can take care of myself. Ya ain't been round for seven years. Reckon I've got on just fine."

"Shit fire woman, just shoot first and ask questions later." He was out the door and shouting to the men. "We're movin' out. Ya know the tune."

Caleb barked, "Stahler, you're point. Johnson, take the rear. Let's move."

Ben trotted ahead. Caleb fell in behind Stahler.

It had been four months since he left Lydia, half of them spent on the march, half in camp. Before bad thoughts could settle, the Rock loomed across the narrow valley, a couple hundred feet high and thirty yards across—a stretch for their rifles—but they could get close enough to make the Rebs real uncomfortable.

Ben waited for the men to catch up and peered through his monocular. Caleb joined him. "Looks like a mother of a cannon," Ben said.

"How many men have they got?"

"Them Johnnies are gruntin' like they can't pass wind," whispered Ben. "Looks to be a dozen or so." He motioned the platoon to be silent and lay low. "Gotta give 'em credit fer tryin'."

"Why don't we start this dance now?" Stahler asked none too quiet.

"Wanna wait till Kelsey's close 'nough to hear the firin'. He'll be good backup."

Stahler persisted. "We can do this ourselves. Give me four men, and I'll show you what we can do."

Ben raised the monocular to a few sparse pines on top of the Rock. From that vantage, two Reb's watched the progress of the cannon, shaking their heads and laughing.

"Stahler, slither yer ass back with the others," Ben ordered. "We do this my way."

"I'm point man," he argued.

"Move it, Stahler," Caleb ordered. "You heard the Sarg. Get to the rear with Johnson. We wait for Kelsey." Caleb watched to make sure Stahler followed orders then turned his attention back to Ben.

"There's two on top, and maybe one bedded down with a rifle." Ben said shifting the glass. "With the other twelve below we might need Kelsey." Ben moved the monocular along the Hannah. Kelsey's men were sneaking along the creek. "I'll be damned. Git the men primed, Kelsey's about to blow our cover. I'll be back."

Like a mountain goat, Ben picked his way down toward the Home Guard. Before he was halfway, a sniper spotted the guard and fired. Kelsey's men answered with an arsenal and a little bit more.

Caleb barked and his platoon ran the narrow path with the echoes of gunshots popping below. The Rock jutted from the mountainside. Rifle fire and men's shouts rang below the towering mustard-gray limestone, the sulfuric scent of black powder carried on the updraft.

Kelsey's men were pinned fifty-yards straight down behind a few measly boulders.

"Times a wastin' men," Ben yelled. "Let's send them Rebs to their Maker."

The Yankees let out a war cry that echoed through the valley. Slipping and sliding down the mountain, they clamored through the trees, over rocks, and into chaos. Their cry of support bolstered the Harlan boys who jumped from their cover and gave chase to the scattering Johnnies.

Ben watched a couple Rebs sheer off into the woods and barked at his men. "Stahler. Head them two off. Roberts. Gensler. Go see what's left up on that damn lookout. Johnson, you stay with Wright and rattle the bushes. The rest of ya come with me, we're goin' up the backside."

Ben and his worked their way to the top while Caleb and Harley crept further downhill into a crumbling limestone enclave beneath the rock's shadow. Sniper fire whizzed nearby.

Gensler's men fired in rapid succession while Ben gained maybe ten feet nearly straight up to fresh shelter. He wedged himself between two rock warts and sparse scrub.

A Rebel sharpshooter put lead into Robert's shoulder. Ben's rifle cracked and silenced the threat. He gained ground slowly while his boys contended with the rebel sharpshooters. He made the crest under heavy cover from his men. He picked off two, but the last Reb was barricaded between rock waves and sparse pines. He was trapped, clinging to the southern precipice and laying fire into Caleb and Harley two hundred feet below.

"Give it up Reb," Ben shouted.

"Go to hell!" was the terse reply, accompanied by a ricocheting shot that spat rock close to Ben's face.

"Damn it Reb. Give it up. There's no one left up here but you."

"And waste away in one of yer goddamn Billy Yank prisons? Nothin doin'." The Rebel's voice echoed frustration more than fear.

"Ya take the oath to the Union and give me yer weapons and we'll let ya be on yer way."

A shot screamed through the scrub and chipped more rock. "That's what ya can do with yer traitor Yankee words. I signed on fer Tennessee and I reckon I'll stay on fer Tennessee."

Ben admired the man's gumption. "Reckon I'll have to kill ya then."

"I'll take ya with me, Yank."

The Reb fired again, and Ben returned the volley while working his way closer. Ben was less than twenty feet away when the Reb's rifle ran fallow.

The Reb had little left. He knew it, and the blue-bellies knew it. He watched the rolling gray clouds move across the sun devouring the soft blue sky. He thought of his sweet Irene. He could see her waving a tearful goodbye, standing there by the blooming magnolias along the creek that ran past their home, holding baby Bessie in her arms. Three-year old Peter stood by her side, bravely waving his daddy off to war, hot tears running down his sweet pink cheeks. He had shed a few of his own after he turned and walked away.

Ben's voice boomed. "C'mon out Reb. Ya got no where to go."

"Go to hell, Piker." The Reb inched closer to the seam of the precipice. The tops of pine trees beckoned below, but they were at least twenty feet out, maybe more. If he could get to the trees, he might have a chance. He knew these Yanks. They'd met in a Kentucky battle last fall. With all that fightin' under their belt, he knew a tick couldn't move without bein' seen. He lay on his back tucked behind a wave of smooth gray rock and gripped the deer horn handle of his knife. He knew the Yank was closing in.

If he closed his eyes and tried hard enough, he could almost believe he was laying by the Mississippi where he and Irene used to picnic with the children. He could almost taste her fried chicken and light as air biscuits. He wished the power of Jesus would send him all the way back to Memphis and his family.

He looked off to the left, down a seamless valley. They'd been routed from the Garrison alright, but despite the Yanks assumptions, not all of them had surrendered, they got away to fight another day and it looked like this was the day. Jacob's legs flexed. He'd knife the Yank and take them both to hell if it came to that.

Caleb and Harley checked the rock's periphery for snipers. Spring and Enfield rifles stopped talking overhead. Caleb stepped from under the enclave and peered up, wondering if Ben and the boys were pinned down or visa versa. His thoughts were answered by a Rebel yell. Caleb's heart skipped a beat. A man leaped from the rock directly above, twisting and turning, grasping at wispy pine boughs in his deadly descent. The Reb hit the ground with a sickening thud.

Harley scurried up the steep bank. "I'll be damned," he panted. "Ya think Sarg tossed him over."

"I'll find out." Caleb ran over to the dying man.

The Reb's eyes fluttered open, and a crooked smile formed on his face. "Know me, Yank?"

Caleb knelt. Perryville's killing field and a stranger's canteen came to mind. He looked at Harley. "Check on Ben and the boys."

Harley ran off and Caleb turned his attention to his unlikely battlefield angel. "You're Jacob Eggleston from Tennessee."

The Piker was dying fast. "Looks like I'm gonna beat ya to hell after all, Yank. A damn shame too... My Irene's bound to be heartsick over it."

Caleb took off his canteen, lifted Jacob's head and poured a bit of water into his mouth. Jacob swallowed and coughed up blood.

Caleb found his handkerchief and wiped it away. "My men toss you?"

Jacob struggled against his broken body. "Like hell. I was fightin' yer Sarg. He was gettin' the better of me, so I ran and jumped." Death seeped into his eyes. "Thought I could make it to the pines."

Caleb cradled his head. "You dumbshit. You saved my life. I would have let you go."

"Guess ya owe me, Yank."

"Guess I do."

"Ya seen my blade anywhere?"

Caleb twisted his neck. An antler handle protruded from the dirt. "This it?"

Jacob's pupil's lit up like the steel was Holy Scripture.

"Pa made the handle from the horn... of my first whitetail. Guess I'll... be... seein' him... today." His eyes began to close. "Take care of it, Yank. There's killin' left in it... I'm sorry to say... no Rebs mind ya."

"No Rebs?"

Jacob tried to grin. "Can't feel a thing, Yank. Promise you'll give it to my boy." Caleb started to stand, but Jacob's hand grasped his. Eyes fluttered open again. "Bury me on top of this rock, Yank."

"Like hell."

"Ya owe me Yank. 'Sides, it's close as... I'll ever get to heaven." Jacob half-smiled. Death's pallor was stealing Life's light. "When the war's over—git the knife to my boy, Peter, down by Memphis. He'll be missin' me shore."

Caleb's throat constricted. "Damn, Reb."

"Promise me, Piker." His hand clenched Caleb's shirt.

"Promise." The Reb's eyes glazed.

"I promise, Jacob." *Damn.*

Caleb held the one who saved his life and watched the sun move behind towering gray clouds, illuminating the edges. God's breath blew the clouds away, and the sun broke forth in shattering light. An angel-breeze swept down to take the spirit of Jacob Eggleston, Reb from Tennessee, up and out from beneath the shadow of the Rebels' Rock.

Caleb thought of his promise to Lydia and wondered if Jacob had promised the same to Irene. He maneuvered Jacob's deer-handled knife into its sheath and slung it across his own chest.

Ben, Harley and the Harlan boy, Howie Dunaway, watched from a few yards away. Caleb didn't know how much they heard and wondered why he cared. He hoisted Jacob over his shoulder and headed up the steep path to the top of the Rebel's Rock.

Ben looked to Harley. "Take the boys and gather the gear. Find a place to camp and set Stahler and Roberts on picket."

"Got it, Sarg."

Ben followed Caleb up the laborious trail—there was no point in trying to change Storekeep's mind. Ben yelled once more over his shoulder to those lagging back. "And bust up that cannon and push it in the creek."

TWENTY-SIX

Pine Ridge Settlement School
May 1939

I WOKE BENEATH LEVI'S shade tree beside a warm
half-empty pitcher of Sassafras tea. Levi was gone, and my
mind was a conundrum. Would I ever have another crisp
coherent thought?

Levi was not to be found, so I spent the rest of the day moving
alongside Grandma in our age-old routine. I picked a bushel of peas,
and together we hulled them on the front porch. They would be
delicious cooked together with freshly dug new potatoes and green
onions, smothered in my buttery white sauce. It was a dish I
dreamed of when the snow was piled a foot deep and there was
nothing green in sight. It was the epitome of spring fare, and I made
it almost every night while the peas lasted.

After a glass of ice tea, I went back to the garden for an hour or
two of weeding, training the shelly beans to the growing cornstalks,
staking the half-runners and then picking the strawberries that had
ripened since the morning. I returned famished with Mama's red-
rimmed bowl heaped full.

Thankfully, Grandma had started supper and had a fine loaf of bread baking. The smell was heaven. I went upstairs to change, and the thoughts that followed me through the day's chores intruded once more.

Khalidah's voice played again. *If Pangari's seed is not sown, before the moon wanes in winter's dawn, mankind will be destined to live beneath the shadows.* I had to find Levi tomorrow and get him to tell me the whole prophecy again. It had something to do with the full moon, but I couldn't remember exactly what. Was the prophecy connected with Grandma and Grandpa, and if so, how? Or was it completely separate from the things Grandma spoke of, like Levi said. But what about Grandpa? If he and Levi shared the link of Hannah's blood, was Grandpa part of the prophecy or just me? I had a million questions and no answers.

I had to get back up to the attic, but Grandma couldn't know; she had made it clear that she didn't want me up there anymore. Her strength was just beginning to return and I didn't want to upset her again but I needed to look all the way through that trunk and there were things in the bottom I hadn't gotten too yet. Somehow, I had to convince Grandma that everything was back to normal. However, that would be hard to do if I continued to sleep through breakfast every morning. Hopefully, Levi had some kind of tea that would help me sleep.

I changed and went downstairs. Dinner was the kind of meal that made the garden worth all the work: hot fresh bread, home-churned butter and fresh black-raspberry jam, served beside creamy peas and potatoes, a lovely salad of garden and wild greens topped with lots of green onions and wilted down with a hot bacon-vinegar dressing. Dessert was simplicity at its finest—buttermilk biscuits split and topped with fresh strawberries lightly sugared and topped with a mound of fresh whipped cream.

I took Levi a dinner plate and he gave me some of his secret teas. Not only did they boost my energy level but the night tea made me sleep like a baby—no travels, no dreams, and no nightmares for two whole weeks. Grandma began to believe I was once again living in nineteen thirty-nine and relaxed.

The summer solstice arrived with a fury and the Ancients beckoned once again. Visions, nightmares and time travels were my lot. The time had come to find the rest of my answers.

I finished the breakfast dishes, wiped off the table and hung my apron on the wood-peg by the door. I saw Grandma through the window, sitting on the front porch, sipping her tea and watching the morning prosper. A doe foraged in the thick green grass where the yard met the woods, several young rabbits nibbled sweet clover blossoms and hopped about in the heavy dew, and a blue jay's throaty "J-J-J" announced his descent to the feeder, scattering the more gentle songbirds. I pushed open the squeaky screen door.

The part of me that craved the old complacent days had vanished. For the first time in years I felt happy and alive, and although my questions far outnumbered my answers, I was ready to embrace the challenges ahead. Time to put my plan into action.

"Grandma, I'm feeling ambitious today. I'm going to take down the curtains and give them a good washing. Do you need anything before I get started?"

A smile creased Grandma's relaxed pose. "No, Dear. I want to sit here while the morning shadows linger."

I kissed her cheek. "I'm going to start with the bedrooms upstairs. If you need me, just tap on the railing, and I'll come down."

Grandma patted my hand. "Thank you, Mattie."

I rubbed her frail shoulder, departed inside to the kitchen, retrieved the oilcan, and zipped up the stairs to her bedroom. I laid her robe on the bed and quickly oiled the hinges of the attic door. The screen door squeaked. I froze. Grandma's cane tapped across the floor, hesitated at the stairs, and then to my relief, moved in the direction of the parlor. In haste, I gave the door a few quick, back and forths, hung the robe back in its place, and tiptoed across the hall to take down my dingy cotton curtains.

The day turned into an arduous one. Grandma insisted on laundering the curtains herself, as I knew she would, and had me take down several more pairs. Her industrious German blood kicked in and she instructed me to pull the carpets as well—no light task and one for which I needed Levi's help. After I had beaten the carpet for the third time, I began to think my plan had backfired but Grandma's fatigue mirrored my own, twice over. She would sleep soundly tonight especially with an extra dose of valerian and chamomile in her nightly tea.

We parted company at nine, and I lay in bed until midnight, listening to the whippoorwill sing its nightly tune. A refreshing breeze rustled the freshly starched curtains. It was the first pleasantly cool night in forever, and I had to force my weary body from the bed. I stuffed the unread bundle of letters into my robe and snuck into Grandma's bedroom. She looked small and frail in her big bed with Grandpa standing guard above her.

Quietly I opened the attic door and crept up the dark attic steps pulling the door shut behind me. Once in the attic, I lit my lantern; its soft yellow light flooded over dusty relics. Shadows frolicked in the flickering flame and Khalidah's ancient words urged me on. My skin tingled as I lifted frayed quilts, and old sheets from ghostly statues of lost forgottens. I pulled the dusty coverlet from a velvet fainting couch; the faded cushion was worn smooth except in the deep creases. Here, among Grandma's things, I hoped

I could figure out the clues that lay between the lines of Grandpa's cryptic letter. I sat on the couch and curled my legs into the folds of my comfortable misshapen robe. I turned up the wick on the lantern, and the flame surged, sending a wisp of black smoke swirling up the chimney.

> *15 June 1863*
> *My Darling,*
>
> *I pray in earnest every conscious minute for your recovery. I have failed you. Duty be damned! I left you in your darkest hour. I kill men while you lay suffering. Sweetheart, it is a miracle that you still live. Know that I shall return to you by and by and hold your heart to mine.*
>
> *Closer and closer, we think we get to Morgan and his Raiders, but they are ghosts. We've marched too many miles with little to show for it. Alas, I think only of you while we continue to chase a mirage.*

A breeze stirred and the lantern light danced. I ignored the shivers and read on.

> *I need you by my side, and yet I sit here alone. Ben bunks with Harley and wags his finger at me, but how can that help? My dreams are nightmares. I'm so lonely. I long for your sweet words. I'm confused. My irresponsibility with you pounds me continually.*
>
> *Sweetheart, do you still love me? Are you well enough to write? How is Mary?*
>
> *I yearn for your words in letter as I long to see your eyes and taste your lips. Please write. Soon we*

shall corner Morgan, and then by hook or crook, I
shall lie by your side.
  Your devoted servant,
  Caleb

I closed my eyes. What happened to Grandma? My mind shifted to that moment on the hill, with the sandy haired soldier. My weary body slipped toward slumber and time's shifting sands swept me away.

I woke not under attic rafters but to colored leaves whirling on autumn wind and a gray squirrel standing on hind legs, flicking his tail and scolding me from a nearby tree stump. Running footsteps and crunching leaves sent the squirrel and me scurrying for cover. Two Rebel soldiers came into view and a shot rang out behind them. They darted past me, jumping fallen limbs like the devil was on their tail. They were my kind of men—rugged, with tanned skin, dark hair and three-day whiskers. They wore homespun Confederate uniforms.

The tallest soldier chanced a look behind in his fleet-footed escape. Another bullet whizzed. Instinctively, they lowered their heads and ran faster, disappearing down the hill while I watched for their pursuer.

A blue-clad soldier trotted into view, his right hand brandished a revolver, it was the sandy-haired devil from the hill. Intuitively, I held my breath and prayed he couldn't or wouldn't see me. His attention was on the fading footsteps and he fired another round in their direction before jogging after them.

I started after him, but my clothing snagged on a bush. I reached to untangle myself and realized that I was still in my nightclothes. *Great, this is just great.*

Men cursed in the distance and guns erupted. I hurried down

the soldier's path and prayed I was invisible. Something caught my eye—it was the Union soldier's haversack. He must have tossed it aside for the time being. I picked up the leather pouch and slung it over my shoulder. I wasn't about to pass up the opportunity to see what was inside. "Nosey," Grandma would say. How often she had lectured. "Genius creates, goodness does, and ignorance lives on gossip." *Be quiet Grandma. I'm looking for clues, nothing more.*

Sometimes when I traveled, I was merely an observer and no one could see me. Other times, like in the general store, I was there in flesh and blood. The problem was, I never knew which, until someone gave an indication that they could see me.

I left the path for fear of being seen and ventured into a vaguely familiar stand of young pines. Angry voices battled over the next rise. They were at Pirate's Cove, by the cave. I knelt in the soft pine needles, quickly loosened the leather ties and upended the haversack. My blood chilled. This was no ordinary soldier's knapsack. I scooped the treasure back in the bag and paused to caress one I knew so well. I put it back in the haversack, slung it over my shoulder and jogged down the path. I veered to the right, and climbed to the bow of the rock ship where I could observe unseen. I crept to the edge and peered over.

The sandy-haired devil was shouting into the cave. "You Rebs, come on out. We got you cornered."

"Like hell you do. Come in and get us."

"Chicken shits," challenged the devil. "Still sucking Mama's tits?"

Silence replied, and I wondered what the Rebs were planning in the cave's darkness. Ancient implements from the Revolutionary War lay below, entwined with weeds and rocks. The rusting iron and rotting oak shards gave testament to the cave's once valuable commodity of saltpeter, mined by a different group of soldiers that fought for freedom of a different sort.

My heart beat to the tempo of my rancor; in my reality, war loomed once again in Europe to the drum of another tyrant. Would there ever be peace and understanding among God's creatures? Could I really play a part? Were Khalidah's words truth or myth? How could I be the Chosen One here in these isolated hills?

A rifle cracked. Smoke spewed from my childhood haunt and the bullet careened through the trees.

The Yankee hugged the side of the cave entrance and taunted. "That all you got? Nothing but a worm beneath your petticoats?"

The Rebs fired a double volley. He drew his knife. No Rebel surprise would take this one. He would kill the Rebs if they came out and go in after them if they didn't. After finding Grandma's necklace in his bag, I knew he was the cause of whatever had happened to her. After all these years, he still had some kind of hold on her. A hatred of a kind I had never felt, surged through me. I wanted the Rebs to win this fight.

He looked like a wolf on the hunt—focused and intent on the kill, he would take no prisoners. Could I save them? Was I here or was I only a mirage?

The Confederates burst from the cave in a rage of bullets and a cloud of sulfurous smoke. The Yank snatched the first one out and with lightning precision slit his throat. The poor Reb grabbed his neck and folded to the ground gasping for breath. His partner dropped his spent rifle and extracted a knife with a brass guard over the handle, and charged into his assailant. The Yank's pistol fired. The Reb groaned but fought on. I cheered when his knife sliced the devil's shoulder.

He ignored the strike and drew his blade across the width of the man's back. The Rebel arched, and in that instant, the devil buried his knife in the Reb's gut. I turned away from the scream and the blood. Tears bit my eyes.

I looked back to see the Yank gathering the dying men's discarded weapons and pilfering their pockets. He held up the Reb's tintype of a beautiful woman. "That one would be a pleasure. Maybe I'll pay her a visit on the way to Atlanta, seein's how you won't be there for her. When I've finished fucking her, I'll tell her I killed her Darlin' and fucked him while he died."

"Bastard!" The gutted man lashed at his executioner, only to have his own throat slashed. The Yank rolled him over and slit his trousers.

The killer straightened to unbutton his fly. I scrambled to my feet. "Stop it, you Bastard!" I screamed.

The devil looked up. Without hesitation he grabbed his gun and knife, and started up the hill after me.

Shit. He can see me. I grabbed his haversack and bolted up the western ridge, angling back toward the Laden Trail. Khalidah's words echoed around me. *If the Chosen One should fail…* I ran through the haunts of my youth; they streamed past in a torrent of yellows and browns. I leaped logs and wished for shoes. Khalidah's voice surrounded me, …*destined to live beneath the shadows…*

An iron hand grabbed my arm and spun me round. I swung wildly at my captor. "Let go of me, let go!"

The grip tightened. "Whoa there, little lady. Easy now."

"Murderer!" I yelled, swinging all the more, pelting his muscular form.

He caught my wrists and twirled me around, wrapping my arms tight across my chest. "Whoa now. I'm not going to hurt you." His grip was a velvet vice. "Calm down, Missy. I'm not going to hurt you."

It was then I saw my pursuer. He stood on the crest of a leaf-covered hill thirty yards distant, tucking his weapons away.

"He's going to kill me!" I yelled hysterically. "He just killed two men, and he's after me."

"Who, Ma'am?"

"Him… on the hill!"

"Ma'am?"

"Shoot him," I screamed. My head spun. My legs were going to jelly. The man cradled me to his chest.

"Are you alright?"

My vision was blurring. "Him, up there. Shoot him!"

"That's Private Stahler. He's one of us."

"He's not! You don't know what he is."

"Stahler?" yelled the soldier. "Get on down here and straighten this out."

Stahler stared, unmoving.

My firm-chested protector sat me down and stepped onto the trail. "Stahler!"

Stahler stepped backwards toward the heavy cover of trees, turned and walked away.

"What's the matter with him? Is he deaf?" he asked.

"Stop him," I demanded with my head between my knees.

"I best wait on Sarg and the Corporal."

I looked up, my head swimming. The man hoisted me to my feet. His arms gathered me as I swooned. He smelled of wood smoke.

"You okay, Ma'am?" His gentle baritone rolled over me.

"I'm telling you, that man is a killer."

The man's hazel eyes looked into mine, his voice soft but firm. "We all are, Ma'am."

Quietly I asked, "What's your name?"

"Harley Johnson." He searched the landscape past my head. "Sarg and the Corporal are coming. Tell them what you told me."

I turned around. Two soldiers were coming down the Laden, and one of them was Grandpa. I looked down at myself. I was still in my robe.

Harley mumbled, "I can't understand why he walked off like that."

I slung off the haversack and shoved it in his chest. "Here's your answer. Give this to Caleb and tell him it belongs to Stahler."

Harley held the haversack. "You know the Corporal?"

"I can't explain right now. Just give it to him." Grandpa was just twenty yards off. Harley took a couple of steps in their direction. I took the diversion and darted for the trees.

"Matilda? Matilda Hannah Wright, are you up there?"

I woke with a start; the gray morning light was seeping through the new attic window and my lantern was out.

"Matilda?" Grandma's voice crackled with worry.

My game was up. Her cane lit on the first step. "I'm here, Grandma. Don't come up. I'll be right down."

There was no reply, only movement away from the door. I waited in the hope that she would go downstairs and give me a chance to come up with a good excuse.

TWENTY-SEVEN

I think that one of the causes of these repeated failures is that our best and greatest men have greatly underestimated the size of this question.
—Abraham Lincoln, March 6, 1860

HARLEY WALKED TOWARD his comrades.

"That woman wants me to give you this." He held out the haversack.

Caleb grabbed the pouch. "What woman?"

"Her," Harley turned. "Where'd she go? She was there just a second a go."

"Well, she ain't there now. Dump the haver," Ben commanded.

Caleb upended the bag. A pile of ribbons and jewelry tumbled out. His heart caught as he picked up a silver butterfly dangling from a broken chain. *It will keep you safe.* His blood boiled.

"Who's haver is this?" he demanded.

"She said it belongs to Stahler. She was a rantin' and ravin' about him goin' to kill her. He was standin' on that hill over there and I told him to get down here and straighten this out, but he just stood there like he didn't hear me and turned and walked off."

"Where to?"

"I don't know."

"Which way did he go?" Ben barked.

Harley pointed over the rise.

Ben stared through Caleb. Caleb's fingers clenched the necklace. Sarg darted off toward Mary Belle's, with Caleb and Harley on his heels. In the world of war, butterflies drank blood and friend turned foe.

Ben kicked in the cabin door. Mary Belle fumbled a plate she was drying, and it crashed to the floor.

"Good Lord, Jefferson, what on earth's the matter?"

"Where's the girls?"

"What's the matter?"

His face was flint. "Answer the damn question, Mary Belle."

"Genevieve and Lovell are over at the Simpson's, and they took Emma with them. Ester spent the night with Betsy Reese, and Lily's out gatherin' persimmons. Now, tell me what's goin' on?"

"No time. I'll explain later. Stay here in case the girls come back. If they do, keep 'em inside till we get back. Git the shotgun and if Private Stahler comes by here, shoot him first, ask questions later."

"Shoot him?" The words echoed to an empty door.

Caleb and Harley were by the barn. "Wright, Johnson, fan out." The order was loud, meant to be heard. "I'm goin' to find Lily. The rest of ya shake the bushes."

Ben ran the steep cow path, dodging cow-pies. It was nearly a half hour before he found Lily, bare as morning's dew, her arms and legs wrapped around Stahler. She was feeling the pleasure only a man can give, and Stahler was hard at giving it.

This was a hell of a note. If he shot Stahler, he'd fall dead on

Lily, she'd never get over that, it wouldn't be much better, if he pulled him off and slit his throat. *Shit.*

He fired a warning shot. Stahler yanked up his pants. Lily scrambled to cover herself but Stahler wrapped his hand in her long hair and jerked her to him.

"Ow! Uncle Jefferson!" she cried, her face a mass of pain, confusion and fear.

"Stay where you are Decker!"

Damn. "Leave her!" Ben yelled.

Stahler laughed and dragged her naked and screaming into the woods.

Ben ran after them. Caleb and Harley heard the shot and came running. The bastard was moving in the direction of the cave. When they caught up to Ben, he was behind a massive boulder that protruded from one side of the cave, the dead Rebs lay outside where Stahler had dropped them.

"Where is he?" Caleb demanded, as revenge beat a tyrannical rhythm in his head to images of his broken, angel.

"Inside."

Ben looked at the Reb with his ass exposed to the sky. There were no words in Ben's prolific profane vocabulary for a bastard that could do that to another man. His mind ran with options. He examined his implements. A long gun was useless in tight places, so it would be a pistol and knife fight. Stahler had Lily, and he was responsible for bringing the wolf to her door. He would get her out if he had to die doing it.

Caleb looked at Ben's weapons. "He's mine."

"He's got Lily." Ben's black eyes shone with guilt and worry.

Caleb nodded and checked his pistol. "Guess it's you and me then."

Ben pulled the Bowie and checked the edge of the blade with

his thumb. He tucked his revolver in the front of his trousers and gripped the killer blade. His skinning knife was shoved between ankle and boot.

Ben looked at Caleb and saw his own reflection. "Ya best be in a hell-bent fever to kill him cuz he's the bloody devil."

Twice in his life, Ben hesitated, and twice someone died—his brother, Jeremy and sweet Rosita. He rolled the chaw from his mouth and tossed it aside. Each life needed its day in Hell. Today was Caleb's. Let it not be Lily's.

Caleb withdrew Jacob's blade. *There's killin' left in it… no Rebs mind ya.* Stahler was no Reb. How in the hell did he miss it? *Did you ask Ben of Stahler? Did he know him?* Hell, they all knew him. He was in their unit.

"I'll fire some down range to cover ya gettin' in. The cave splits about five yards in. On the left, ten yards further, is devil's hole. Watch fer it. It goes clean to hell. Come in from the right, find a hunk a rock fer cover, and close yer eyes and listen. When yer eyes adjust, move on in. I'll be behind ya. I figure he's got a short gun and a couple knives, maybe a Reb's rifle. One thing's shore… he's got plenty of ammo. There'll be no angel to save yer ass this time, Storekeep. Ya git a hole, it's gonna bleed. It's Satan in the flesh in there. Just remember—we get Lily out first."

Caleb removed the broken necklace from his pocket and handed it to Ben.

"See Lydia gets this if I don't make it back."

"Nothin' doin'. Put it back. You'll have to give it to her yerself."

Harley put a hand on Ben's shoulder. "We'll get her out, Sarg."

"Alright then, Caleb goes in first. I'll cover him and you cover me. I want ya to wait out here for Lily and if we don't make it out, kill the bastard when he comes out. No mercy."

"You got it, Sarg."

Ben opened fire and Caleb darted inside, to where shadows relinquished their cast. He hid behind a hollow in the cave wall and did as Ben instructed. At first, he heard nothing but a trickle of water from somewhere deep within. In his mind, Stahler was a serpent, curled up somewhere, waiting to strike. Caleb cocked his Colt and gripped Jacob's knife in his other hand.

Stahler's voice taunted. "I smell chicken-shit. Just like at Perryville, eh Wright, yella as the piss running down your legs."

Lily whimpered, "Let me go."

"Shut-up!"

Caleb breathed slow and even. *Patience.*

Harley started shooting. Ben came in and Caleb moved toward Stahler's voice. It was hard to judge with the echo. A breeze radiated from the pit's core—Ben's hole to hell.

"Not much beneath your petticoats, is there Wright? I showed your gal the size of a real man just like Decker's niece here."

"Help me, Uncle Jefferson!"

A slap echoed. Lily cried out. "I told you to fucking shut up!"

Caleb heard Lily crying. His blood pulsed. *Patience.*

Stahler's hammer made a distinctive double-click, one known by every soldier, anytime, anywhere. Caleb's boots dislodged earth and stones as he moved along the cave's cold rough wall.

"You coming in or am I gonna have to take you down like I did your whore?"

Caleb's mind pounded.

"She fought like a badger, but I got her down on her belly and fucked her. Did you hear her screaming your name?" He laughed. "She thought you'd come riding in and save her, like some fucking white knight. I told her I killed you and I will."

Caleb thought of Lydia praying for him to come while Stahler tore her up. His teeth locked; his hand clutched Jacob's knife.

"She gave up on her yella belly savior while I used her for my whore. She knows what her body's for now. All of it."

Caleb could barely contain his rage, visions of Stahler taking her, making her—he knew—felt it—but to hear it from the bastard's lips was more than he could stand. Satan needed a new tenant.

"Your bitch fought like a wildcat. I fucked and cut her and fucked her again. She was good, best I ever had."

Caleb's rage would not be contained. He took the devil's bait and rushed from the shadows. Stahler's gun exploded on cue and put a lead ball in his left shoulder. Caleb raised his pistol and sprayed six bullets toward the gun flash. Stahler sprang from the shadows and knocked him to the ground.

Ben dashed past.

"Uncle Jefferson!"

Caleb and Stahler rolled with flying fists and slashing knives. A shoulder caught Caleb beneath the jaw, rattling his teeth. Jacob's knife met a mark somewhere, and Stahler groaned and came back with one of his own.

Caleb rolled away and got to his feet. Stahler straightened and Caleb dove in for the kill. He wedged his arms around Stahler's waist as the demon's knife filleted his back. Caleb rammed him into the stone wall and jumped back.

Stahler lunged.

Caleb shoved Jacob's knife in the devil's lung. He pushed Stahler back against the wall, pulled out the blade and put it to his neck. "I'm going to carve you up piece by piece, just like you did my Lydia."

The devil laughed while Satan's invisible henchmen loomed. "She'll think of me... every time you fuck her... She'll see my face, feel my hands."

Jacob's blade slit tender flesh.

"She'll never be rid of me." He gurgled and gasped. "You took her cherry. I took her soul."

"She lives and as God is my witness, you'll have no hold on her from Hell!" Caleb watched Gravemaker struggle for a last breath. He threw him over his shoulder and pitched him into the gaping pit, all the way to Hell.

Ben and Harley's weapons were leveled at the mountain's mouth when Caleb emerged, a bloody mess. Lily stood nearby wearing Ben's coat, her face bruised and wet with tears.

Ben looked at his prodigy with pride. "Best get ya back to Mary Belle's before ya bleed out."

Caleb flinched as Mary Belle swabbed his lacerated back with her mountain concoction. "Ben, there's too much damage here to stitch. Some of these holes and cuts are clean through the muscle. Best send Genevieve to get Doc Bowen.

"Just do your best, Ma'am." Caleb grunted through the pain. He was light headed from blood loss.

"I ain't never worked on a mess like this. He's got a bullet in the shoulder, a knife wound in the side and his back looks like he's been flogged. It might get infected if it ain't done right. Ben, get the doc."

Caleb gripped the pillow as Mary Belle poked and prodded. Ben looked up from his supper plate and forked half a pork chop in his mouth. His eyes assessed the pulp that was Caleb's back.

"I'll fetch him." He grabbed his Union cap, strapped on his pistol and was out the door.

Lily came behind Mary Belle and wrapped her arms around her back.

Caleb twisted his neck to see the girl. Her eye was swollen shut where the bastard landed a fist.

"Sorry, we didn't get there sooner, Lily."

Lily smiled weakly. "You got there soon enough."

TWENTY-EIGHT

Pine Ridge Settlement School
June 1939

W HAT HAD I DONE with Grandpa's letter? I searched everywhere and finally, in desperation, asked Grandma about it. Of course, she denied any knowledge of it. "Gone is gone," she said. "You can move forward or not at all, Mattie. Leave the past behind, where it belongs."

Easy for her to say—she wasn't traveling to the past every other day. She found solace in whispers, prayers, and sleep.

Despite Levi's tea, sleep again became a mirage for me, and my dreams were becoming more and more of my reality. Frustrated, I filled a quart jug with water and went outside into the hot humid day. My feet led me up a forgotten path behind the chapel where birdsong serenaded and young rabbits nibbled at the strong green blades of grass that had pushed through winter's bowed clumps of brown fodder.

The ancient oak's spacious arms came into view long before the stones that slept beneath. I stopped on my upward trek and took a deep drink from my jug. The sun was beating down and sweat trickled between my breasts. Was I ready for this? I thought of turning around, of how much easier it would be to walk back down the hill and continue to ignore the pain and the past. Unfortunately, the time was gone for such indulgences. I looked down the hill and beyond to the towering green mountains. I traveled, not beyond them, as I had so often dreamed of doing, but within them to another time.

My shallow roots were reaching far beneath the shadows of these mountains, grasping for the life-giving water of my ancestry. How could I have been so blind to the spirit, heritage, comfort, and flowing grace of these Appalachian Mountains? I wiped my damp brow, took another long drink, and with a deep cleansing breath of pure mountain air, climbed with renewed vigor.

The squeaky iron-gate announced my presence to the dead, weeds and grass grew high around the headstones. Rose brambles completely covered the small stone set in place that cold rainy day when I buried the last of my dreams on this hill. The heartaches of my lifetime lay before me. A stone angel holding a baby in the cusp of her wing was the cold sentry of this hallowed place. Years had splotched her white marble with lichen and moss. Daddy sent to Italy for the angel after the fever took Mama and Ruthie from us. I ran my hand down the angel's wing to the face of the baby she held. The rose-covered grave behind me beckoned.

I refused it and knelt by the grave of Jefferson Benjamin Decker instead. Levi said Ben preferred war to quiet Kentucky Mountains and that he left his land to Grandma, provided she build a school on it and teach his kin and the other mountain children how to read, write, and cipher. He wanted his kin to learn to use their minds as well as their guns. Grandma had definitely risen to the challenge, had in fact, devoted her entire life to it.

Then there was the enigma—a slab of bluish rock with three simple words "I Love You" carved on it and above those words, a butterfly hovered, frozen in flight. How many times had my fingers traced the words on this stone; how many hours had I sat in this same spot, longing for Mama—for her loving arms and soft warm kisses. My eyes watered with pity for that child of yesteryear.

Grandma and Levi would give no explanation for the blue stone and after a while, I accepted their silence and made up my own stories. Now, at thirty-five I wanted the truth about the stone and everything else. How could I succeed on my journey if I didn't know who I was or where I came from? I knew little about Grandma's kin in Indiana, except for the infrequent visits from my childhood and even less about Grandpa Caleb's. Now that I knew Levi and I had a blood tie, I wanted to know everything, every last sordid detail.

I went over to Mama's grave and began to pull winter's dead grass away, to my delight there was a mass of wild pink roses blooming beneath—roses Callie Dawn and I planted as children. We had packed a picnic early that morning and spent the entire day up here, playing make believe. In our fantasy world, we were kidnapped by handsome pirates on fast ships and taken to enchanted ports where they gave us magnificent gifts of jewels, and we were rich and happy. After our picnic, we lay on our backs and made sky paintings. I remember Callie Dawn pulling the withered rose roots out of her apron pocket. "For your Mama and Ruthie," she had said, handing them to me. In silence, we had dug at the soil with our hands and ceremoniously planted the tiny offering. It had rained all that night and the next day. When again I came to the cemetery, new leaves had sprouted and tiny pink buds greeted me, kisses from heaven.

The sound of rustling feet and a tapping cane disrupted my reverie. Like a disobedient child, I half-leapt, half-rolled over the cemetery's rusty iron fence, a barrier entangled in vine and brush. I lay in the prickly weeds staring up at the sky wondering why in the hell I reacted like that. Of course, I knew the intruder had to be Grandma; she seemed to be moving in the same thought pattern as me. She hadn't been up here in months and I couldn't imagine what possessed her to walk up here when it was nearly a hundred degrees. Through a pinhole gap in the thick vines, I watched her shuffle through the tangled carpet of weeds, relying heavily on her cane. She poked and prodded around the heavy grass clumps. Patience and progress were Grandma's trademarks. She held no contempt for nature's ancient ways. *"It matters not, how long the journey, only that one makes progress,"* she often said to my impatience.

She sat on the stone bench beneath the sentinel oak and removed her crystal rosary from her apron pocket. From that vantage, she could survey the entirety of the family plot. It was then that I saw my water jug. Grandma's eyes must have followed mine.

"Matilda?"

My heart beat as fast as that winter's day long ago when she caught me in the attic. I hunkered down and hoped she'd think I'd gone off and forgot the jug.

"Matilda Ann Wright, show yourself this minute." She stood and looked around.

Storm clouds rolled over the sun, and a strong gust of wind blew through the trees. A huge raindrop hit my nose. It seemed that even the gods were conspiring against me. Hidden from view, I crawled around the fence to the open gate and Grandma's backside.

"Grandma," I said. The wind lashed at us; it was going to storm. Damn these mountains. There was never any warning.

You couldn't see it coming. Just boom and there it was. And here we were on top of this damn hill.

"Grandma, what are you doing up here?" Wind lashed at us. I took her arm, and as quickly as we could, we left the cemetery and started down the hill. The rain started with thick drops that became blinding horizontal sheets within seconds, lightning flashed and thunder shook the earth.

Levi met us at the garden in his oil slicker. "I was jus comin' after you." He covered Grandma's other side, and together we propelled her to the chapel where we waited out the tempest storm. We sat there in awkward silence and watched the pines blow about in the wind and rain. Lightning flashed, and a magnificent peal of thunder made the chapel tremble around us. Grandma closed her eyes and shivered; we were soaked through. I didn't want her catching a chill, so as soon as the sun broke through and the rain was a mere sprinkle we moved toward the house.

"Levi, stoke the wood under the hot water tank. I want to get Grandma in a warm bath as soon as possible."

"Dat's a good idea, no need fer her to catch cold."

"Grandma, let's get you out of those wet clothes and I'll make us a nice cup of tea."

Grandma said nothing but moved slowly with her cane through the foyer and up the stairs. I put on the teakettle, thanked Levi for his help, and went upstairs to change.

Dry and dressed, I pity-patted to Grandma's bedroom door, where I heard muffled sobs, quietly, I opened the door a bit and peeked in. She was still in her soaked clothing, lying on the bed, lamenting to the soldier in the picture.

"Darling, why must you torture me so? Can the past not remain between us alone?"

309

In the gray afternoon light, I saw tears travel the carved paths of Grandma's anguished face.

"I don't know what you and the Lord are conspiring, but I beg you to leave Mattie out of this. Let me take my nightmares to the grave."

Surrounded by shadows, a lucid voice whispered in my ear.

Patience.

TWENTY-NINE

I say try; if we never try, we shall never succeed.
—Abraham Lincoln, October 13, 1862

C ALEB'S MIND QUIETED for the first time in weeks as
he rode for the hospital bivouac. The crisp cool air and
trees robed in fall splendor betrayed the Perryville of last
when the hot dry earth parched all who fought upon it. He had
become a man in the year hence, battle wise and weary, but his
heart was strangled with guilt, he had been gone so long when she
needed him most.

Ben's words made their infamous trot across his mind. *I don't
make promises. Not to God, not to myself, and damn shore not to
anybody else.* Ben savored the fight. It was all he knew. Caleb
wanted it done and over with. He wanted to move on to another
life and put this one behind him. Would that time ever come and
would he be alive to see it? Would any of them? These were the
questions that haunted when he had time to mull. No one knew,
he kept his feelings submerged, locked away from his men for
appearance sake.

He heard voices in the distance. His pulse jumped with

anticipation and dread as rows of white tents, lining the freshly harvested tobacco field, came into view. Soldiers sat convalescing outside where they could enjoy the fresh autumn air and warm sunshine. He trotted in on a borrowed mare and hastily surveyed the camp, hoping for an early glimpse of Lydia, out and about, being the nurse he knew her to be.

Mary stood where he hoped to see his betrothed. She was speaking to Doctor Kenton who apparently had also just arrived on horseback, the bastard doctor had been with Lydia while he'd been off doing what soldiers do. Mary's frantic body language told an anxious story. The doc dismounted, barked at a nearby noncom to take his mount, and fast-stepped to a tent, set apart from the rest, with Mary on his heels.

Caleb dismounted, tied off his horse, and walked to the center cook-fire for a cup of coffee. After the long chilly ride, the fire's warmth felt good. The soldiers waited and watched. Within a moment, Mary reappeared and rushed to her tent. Her eyes immediately found Caleb. He was unable to tell if she was displeased or just startled.

Caleb tipped his hat. "Hello, Mary." With a soldier's scrutiny, he watched her eyes. She looked at the tent then back to him.

"I'll be right back, Caleb. I have to take the doctor something." She disappeared in her tent, came out with two apothecary bottles, and swept back to the other tent.

Caleb held his composure to all while he sat on a stump by the fire and sipped the steaming black brew. Coffee was for him what whiskey was for most, though it did nothing to ease the voices shouting in his mind.

It was twenty minutes and two cups later when Mary finally reappeared. She strode to him with false courage pasted on her face. "I'm sorry, Caleb, you have given me quite a start. Did Ben know you were coming?"

Caleb stood and the tick below his eye began to play. "I didn't know I was coming myself until this morning. Ben got me a four-day furlough. Things are all quiet, for now at least." His sixth sense warmed. "Where's Lydia?"

"Would you like a cup of coffee? There's some on the fire."

Caleb held up his cup, "I've already had two."

Mary looked at the earnest soldier blocking her path. There was something different. He seemed taller, stronger than she remembered. More like Ben. She'd seen it before. The strong grew stronger with life's adversities, and the weak mostly got killed or died of a sickness. Then there were a few, a select few, who overcame their weakness and became the mighty. Caleb was one of those.

"There is something you should know before you see Lydia."

Caleb stood grounded, his arms folded across his chest.

She touched his arm. "Please Caleb, let's speak in my tent."

"Just tell me, Mary. I'm not going anywhere except to see Lydia. Now what is it that you don't want to tell me?" Caleb studied her countenance as one studies the enemy. She was hiding something, of that much he was sure, and he made up his mind to get it out of her as quickly as possible.

Mary made motion to a stump. "At least sit down."

He ignored the request. "I came to see Lydia, Mary, and I have waited as long as I intend to. Where is she?"

"Very well, I can see there will be no dealing with you." Mary struggled to find the right words and her hands trembled. What could she tell this man? That the damage the demon inflicted was more than they could have possibly imagined. That he had tortured her in ways beyond human comprehension. "It is only by God's grace that she lives."

His eyes never wavered.

She took a deep breath and released the painful truth. "Two

weeks after you left, she woke. It was another few days before the memories began to surface and when they did, I thought it would kill her all over. At first, she was too weak to leave her tent. She sat there hour after hour hugging her knees, rocking back and forth, crying—wailing. I thought she would never stop."

Mary studied Lydia's blue-eyed soldier. His expression remained stoic except for the pulse beneath his eye, which had begun to twitch violently.

"She was afraid to be alone, afraid to go to sleep. She grew frantic if the lamp oil grew low. She couldn't be in the dark or left unattended." Mary's eyes grew moist. "Oh Caleb, it was the most pitiful thing I've ever seen."

Caleb's heart felt like gnarled vines were squeezing the blood from the soft spots, but he remained silent, intent on hearing all.

Mary removed a hankie from her pocket and wiped her eyes. If he would only speak, perhaps then, she would find the courage to tell him the rest. "I stayed in her tent on the worst nights, Doctor Kenton on the others."

Color surged to his face. She had struck a nerve. "Why didn't you send for me?"

"Oh Caleb, how could I? What could you have done, that we weren't doing?"

"It might have made a difference."

"Perhaps." Mary was finding her footing. "Or it might have made it worse."

Caleb's ire reared. "Why do you say that?"

Mary sat down. This interrogation was giving her weak knees. "I really wish you would sit down."

Caleb remained entrenched.

"You are exasperating."

"So I've been told."

Mary watched the faintest crease in the corner of Caleb's mouth. Perhaps he wasn't a lost cause. She breathed a bit easier and quickly threw the awful truth at him.

"We were finally beginning to make some progress when she realized what I already knew." Mary looked hard into Caleb's molten eyes. "She hasn't spoken since."

Caleb tried to hold his resolve though daggers pierced his soul.

Mary held his stare. "Ben and I have been writing. He is a good man and a good friend—to you and to me. We were afraid that if you knew how bad she was, you would desert and get yourself hanged trying to get here. Ben knew you couldn't get a furlough with your unit campaigning into Tennessee, and I thought that if we could convince you all was well, by the time you arrived… it would be."

Caleb's composure softened. "And my letters?"

"I read them to her, but she's been like a mummy. She won't read, won't respond, won't talk. I am so sorry for the deception, Caleb. Truly, we were thinking only of you. You must believe that."

"Mary, I don't understand. I know she's been through hell but…"

"She is with child, Caleb. She believes it is the demon's seed she carries." Mary's words hung like ice in the frosty air.

Caleb had known it, felt it, dreamt it. But to hear it, to know it as fact, took his breath away. "Where is she?"

Mary studied him as she stood. "In her tent with Doctor Kenton." Concern creased Caleb's brow as he searched Mary's eyes.

"She won't eat. I called for the doctor to return to camp. Despite all that we have done and all of the progress she has made, we will lose her if something doesn't change soon. I've tried everything I know, but it's as if I am not even there. She lies there hour after hour, day after day, staring at nothing. Sometimes tears slip down her cheek but that's all."

"Dammit, Mary, you should have sent for me." Caleb tossed the coffee grounds on the fire, handed Mary the cup and strode across the camp to the offset tent. He reached it just as Doctor Kenton was coming out.

"You can't go in there, soldier. She needs her rest. I think you've done enough already."

Caleb grabbed the doctor's collar and lifted him to his toes. Instinctively, his hand found the handle of Jacob's blade. "Why haven't you done more, you swine sucking bastard?"

Mary ran toward them. "Caleb, don't."

Without a word, Caleb shoved him away and disappeared into Lydia's tent.

Caleb eyes took a moment to adjust to the dim light. Stale air hung in the tent like a mantle of despair. His eyes misted as he looked at his lady. She was a mere whisper of the beautiful women he had lain with just six months before. His fingertips and voice trembled as he knelt by the bed and stroked her sleeping face.

"Sweetheart, I'm here. I've come back like I promised."

Lydia's eyes fluttered open. Her beautiful blue eyes were a dismal shade of gray. With the tenderness of a dove, he slid his arm under her back and gathered her to him. Her bones protruded through the thick black dress.

"Oh, Lydia, what have you done?"

His hand traversed her swollen belly and unfamiliar emotions took command. Months of unspoken anguish screamed in the silence. Lydia's whimpers filled the unbearable void and she shoved his hand away.

A voice whispered in Caleb's ear, *patience.* He rocked and kissed her forehead. Her whimpers quieted, and she drifted off to what he hoped was a dreamless sleep. He kissed his angel and lay her back in the bed. He removed his boots and weapons. Months of longing evaporated as he curled his body next to hers.

The smell of coffee, potatoes, and onions frying in bacon grease woke Caleb. When had he eaten last? Hunger gnawed his stomach. He looked at Lydia, she was so pale—but he was here, really here, holding her. He laid his head next to hers on the pillow and held her tight.

When his hunger would be quiet no longer, he rose and stepped into the chilly evening. The sun was bidding farewell amidst an opaque sky of pink and orange brush strokes and delicious aromas enticed him toward the fire. Convalescing soldiers hovered around the cook pots and cots creaked from the hospital tents as the infirm stirred, craving nourishment and a reprieve from the boredom of hospital life.

Caleb walked up behind Mary. She was busy stirring a huge black kettle, and as with most women, had eyes in the back of her head, reaching for the coffee pot, she turned to hand him a steaming cup.

"Thank you, Mary."

Caleb sipped the black brew and stared at the sizzling potatoes mixed with salt pork and onions. The smell was tantalizing. Lydia would start eating tonight, as much as he hated playing the hard nose—especially having just arrived—he could not indulge the senseless starvation she was inflicting upon herself and their child. She would need to be strong when their son decided to leave his seclusion and enter this war-torn world. A recurrent dream had often filled his nights—images of a boy child conceived in moonlit shadows on meadow's grass, brought forth in pain and tears, cleansed by fire and water. The fire and water part troubled him mightily. Grandma Hannah would know what it meant and he wished he had her gift of discernment.

Mary handed him a heaping plate. "I had a cot set up for you in the sergeant's tent."

Caleb took the plate, ignored the inference and went to sit with some other soldiers, where he ate with greedy relish. After finishing the first plate, he returned for another. Mary dished him up more. This time he ate and savored each bite.

"Did you hear what I said?" she asked.

"I'll be taking a plate and a cup of coffee to Lydia unless you've got some milk stashed around here somewhere."

Mary didn't like being ignored, but she appreciated his determination where Lydia's health was concerned. She dipped inside her tent and emerged with a pitcher of milk. "I was going to make butter, but I would rather you take it, if she will have it."

"She will," Caleb said with a determined glint in his eye. "As for the cot, I'll be sleeping in Lydia's tent. I promised that I wouldn't leave her side, and I don't care what anyone thinks. I'll marry her today if she'll have me."

The smile drained from Mary's face. "Caleb she can't be— you can't..."

"Dammit, woman. I didn't come here to fill any carnal urges. Give me her plate."

"I'm sorry, Caleb. I didn't mean to imply..." Mary's words trailed off. Caleb took the plate, grabbed the milk, and strode back to Lydia's tent, focusing his ire on the doctor standing guard outside.

"Out of my way, sawbones," Caleb demanded, never breaking stride. He was a mere six inches from Kenton's too handsome face when he stopped.

"Have you no decency, man? Miss Weldishofer cannot be subjected to your manly urges. What kind of bastard are you?"

Caleb stared a killer's stare. "The worst kind. Now step aside."

"As her personal physician, I order you back to your unit, Corporal. She cannot be bothered by the likes of you. If it weren't for your lack of judgment, she wouldn't be in this condition. I hold you entirely responsible."

Caleb glowered and spoke through clenched teeth. "You murderin' son of a bitch. If I have to set this plate down, it'll be your heart in my haversack. Now move aside."

The stand off continued. Caleb sat the jug of milk on a stump and moved to open the flap of Lydia's tent.

Kenton grabbed his shoulder.

Caleb dropped the plate and spun, drawing Jacob's blade. In half a heartbeat, the battle-tried soldier had the doctor by the hair and his throat exposed—the doctor's oversized Adam's Apple bobbed up and down as Jacob's blade lay cold and steady beneath his chin. Caleb whispered in the doctor's ear, unaware of the hundred sets of eyes riveted on them. "The Reb that I got this knife from, said I couldn't kill no Rebs with it and I haven't. I killed Gravemaker with it, and I intend to kill you."

Mary thought Caleb's move manly bravado until she caught glimpse of the knife's edge, glistening on both sides. He had honed a killer's blade and was obviously adept at using it. Seconds cascaded as she ran for him. He was crossing the line.

"Corporal!" she barked in her best Sergeant Major imitation. "At ease!" Kenton's back arched as Caleb pushed the blade to tender skin. Piss trickled down the doctor's leg. Soldiers rose from their campfires and sauntered over.

Caleb sensed Mary's extended arms and felt a descending calm that comes only from earnest prayer. "You so much as touch the hem of Lydia's gown, and there won't be a next time."

Lydia stirred and the killing moment waned. Caleb released the doctor and sheathed Jacob's knife. "Mary, I'll need another plate." He picked up the pitcher of milk and disappeared into the tent.

Lydia was awake. "I thought you were dead," she whispered.

Caleb set the milk on the table and took her trembling body in his arms. "I'm so sorry. I came back as soon as I could. I sent letters."

"I couldn't believe they were from you, not after what he did. He said he killed you... and... and..." Her lips trembled.

"Shhh, I'm here now, and I'm not going anywhere."

Mary entered cautiously and handed the fresh plate of food to Caleb.

"Thank you, Mary. Can you have someone bring an extra cot?"

Mary nodded, smiled at Lydia, and left.

"Can you forgive me for not coming sooner?"

Lydia reached for his hand and brought it to her lips. "You came, that's all that matters."

Caleb sat next to her, the steaming plate on his lap. He kissed her forehead and stroked her limp hair. "We'll talk in a while, but right now, I want you to eat some of these fine potatoes Mary cooked." He lifted a fork with a single bite of potato on it.

She clenched her lips and shook her head.

"Please Lydia, eat for me, for our son."

Lydia's face distorted in torment. "How do you know it's our son?" she cried out through shaking sobs.

Caleb set the plate aside. He held her wasted body and felt her fear and grief with every fiber of his own. He wished he could kill the bastard a hundred times over again. She sobbed until he thought she would faint from exhaustion.

Tenderly, he leaned back and searched her troubled eyes. "I had a dream, Lydia, after I left you, when you were still unconscious." Lydia took the handkerchief he pulled from his pocket. "I was holding a baby, a boy child and I knew he was our son, yours and mine." Lydia's eyes welled again and she blew her nose. "Our love will live beyond this war, with or without us. You must believe—it is my seed that lives within you."

"I wish I could feel it like you do," she whispered.

"Leave the believing to me, Sweetheart." Caleb removed his coat, rolled it up and put it behind her pillow. Gently he eased her back, poured a glass of milk and held it to her lips. She met his eyes and stared reluctantly into the thick white liquid.

"Please Lydia, you have to live. I can't even think of a world without you in it."

"Only for you," she whispered and reluctantly sipped at the milk until it was half gone. Only then did Caleb remove the coat from beneath her pillow and tuck the covers around her.

"Rest a while."

"Stay with me," she implored.

"Shush now, Sweetheart. I'll be right outside your tent standing guard against your demons." He kissed her brow. Lydia smiled a half smile and breathed a shallow sigh. He held her hand until she drifted off to sleep.

Mary sighed and watched Doctor Kenton walk quickly to his tent—to change his soiled pants and have a drink, no doubt. Men. Perhaps the Shakers were not as wrong as she originally thought. With a vow of celibacy, there was no reason for jealousy.

Harley rode into camp while Caleb stoked the fire outside Lydia's tent. "What's the word, Johnson? My furlough extended?"

"Major says you got two weeks. Colonel will sign off on it."

Caleb poked at the fire; he had hoped for more. He would have to push her harder than he wanted to. "It's late, you might as well stay the night. I hear there's an extra cot in the sergeant's tent."

Harley tied off his horse, sat by the fire and poured a cup of coffee. The flames fit Caleb's persona. "I think I'll do that, Lieutenant."

Lydia emerged from the tent, teetering and Caleb rushed to catch her. He swept her up in his arms; she couldn't weigh more than ninety pounds. "And where might you be going, Sweetheart?"

She ignored his question and attempted a smile. "Did I hear someone call you 'Lieutenant'?"

Harley piped up. "Yes, Ma'am. That's Lieutenant Wright. Got promoted last week after he killed the Gravemaker..."

"Johnson! When I want your courier services, I'll ask for them. Is that clear?"

"Yessir!"

"To the sergeant's tent, Corporal. If they have any questions, send them to me."

Harley saluted and tipped his hat to Lydia. "Ma'am."

"Good night, Harley," she said and turned her attentions to the man at hand.

Caleb's face was taut.

"Why did you snap at him?" she asked.

Caleb looked in the fire. "I killed your demon, Lydia. I sent him to Hell."

A gruesome weight lifted from her soul. She was safe, and Caleb was alive. She pulled his mouth to hers, surprising him with a long passionate kiss in full view of the camp.

"Mmm," he said. "You're not going to make this easy."

She smiled and huddled close to his chest. He carried her to a fresh tent, one he had ordered set up earlier in the day while she slept. He secured a clean sheet and nightgown from Mary and gathered a bouquet of crimson and yellow maple leaves for the table by her bed. He laid her on the fresh cot and covered her with the butterfly quilt Grandma had sent for her. Caleb had told her only that she was ill.

"It's a beautiful quilt, where did you get it?"

"Grandma Hannah made it for you."

"She knows?" she asked alarmed.

"No Darling, she only knows that I found the one that tended my wounds, touched your soul, and spoke to your heart. It is her way of welcoming you into the family."

She smiled at her brave, thoughtful soldier. "I've missed you."

Caleb tasted her lips again. "Don't move. I'll be right back." He stepped outside, withdrew his saber, scored a line in the rocky soil six feet in front of the tent, thrust the saber in the ground outside the door, and hung his cap on it. He sensed Kenton watching him through a sliver of open tent flap. Caleb removed his Colt from its holster and pointed it straight and true in the direction of the good doctor's head.

Kenton stepped back in disgruntled haste and took a deep swig from his near empty flask.

Caleb put the pistol to bed and went after hot water, soap and towels. He had no home, no dowry to give and his pocket carried a sum total of two dollars in loose change; it would be some time before his officer pay made any great difference. He thought of Lydia and their child, how would he provide for them? Then he thought of the doctor and the better life the bastard could offer.

His doubts vanished on his return; it was his name she called. With loving eyes she watched him as he carefully disrobed her and discarded each soiled garment. Slowly and meticulously he washed every pale blossom. While her body lacked substance and vitality, the bruises and welts were gone. Bright pink scars were all that remained. A flicker of life kicked beneath his gentle touch, he smiled and tapped back. He helped her into the fresh white gown and knelt beneath her swollen belly, his hands caressing each side. The babe's resonating patter greeted him, and he kissed each tap. His enraptured eyes perused her roundness and maturing breasts. "You're so beautiful."

Lydia gazed upon her lover. "How can you still love me?"

"Shhh," he said to her uncertainty. "How can I not?" He longed for more kisses. "Take me into your darkness Lydia, let me conquer your demons."

She swayed into his utterance and invited his hands to journey across her soft skin, up to her full breasts.

He reminisced of a moonlight feast and Grandma's prophecy. His breath abated. She was too fragile. They couldn't do this. He pulled back and reached into his pocket for Grandma's repaired necklace. He fastened it back in its rightful position, upon his angel's neck.

Lydia felt it with her fingers. "Where did you find it?" she whispered. "I remember the day you gave it to me. You said it would keep me safe…"

Caleb's eyes pained. Lydia rushed to cover her errant words. "I didn't mean that," she said. Her eyes glanced downward for a second. "What I meant…was that I thought you would die without it, and yet here we are. We live when we should be dead, just as you wanted to die by that tree, I begged for death and yet I lived. God must have meant for us to be together."

THIRTY

Pine Ridge Settlement School
June 1939

T
HE STORMS WERE over, and I walked to the barn for
a couple of bushel baskets. A lengthy visit to the garden
followed, yielding three bushels of tomatoes and two bushels
of half-runner green beans. I sorted, cleaned, and canned into the
wee hours of the morning.

Bright white light from the full moon streamed down, when at
long last I threw logs on the fire beneath the hot water tank and
went inside for a nice long bath. Grandma had joined me briefly for
a haphazard dinner of green beans, fresh tomato slices, and morning's
leftover biscuits and ham. Her attempts at conversation were a
rambling of distracted thoughts, and I worried over her health. I
sighed audibly when I stepped into the steaming hot tub. The
washstand mirror reflected a firm body and I paused a moment to
examine my well-proportioned physique; my breasts still sat high
despite my age as I had suckled no young. How often I observed
the young women of twenty-five with bodies more worn then
mine, a baby on the hip and three or four in tow. This firm body

was my lonely reward for having no children. Grandchildren would be theirs. The heat penetrated every fiber of my body as I slid beneath the steamy surface. I leaned my head back and closed my weary eyes; my tired muscles began to relax as I replayed the day's events in my mind.

Grandma would not speak of the venture to the cemetery, or why was she crying. I needed to find that letter. Had I left it somewhere or did she find it in my room and take it?

In the wink of an eye, these questions quickly became the least of my worries. My heavenly puppeteer was at it again. *Shit!*

I stood butt naked and dripping wet in front of a strange man in some dank canvas tent. My eyes bulged as the man lunged for my breasts.

God, this isn't funny! I slapped at his hands.

He looked at the flask in his hand then back to me, took another drink and swaggered forward. I shoved him away. He stumbled backward and fell over a small table with a groan. I yanked a wool blanket from his cot and covered my assets as best I could. His lusty cow-eyed stare devoured me as he stumbled to his feet.

"I'm not an illusion from that whiskey bottle, Mister. I'm real, and you must believe me when I tell you that I am a proper lady."

He was on his feet, a look of happy bewilderment and shameless intent on his face; he wasn't buying it, least ways, not the part about my being a lady.

"Listen Mister, don't get any ideas. I don't know how I got here but you have nothing to do with it. Understand?"

He lunged. I waltzed out of reach putting the cot between us. He stammered, "I don't care who you are or how you got here." He lunged again and staggered. "Dammit woman, quit moving." He swayed my way. "You're my illusion, and I intend to have my way with you," he slurred.

I dodged again, but I was out of places to go, except out of the tent, and he was blocking that escape. By the bulge in his pants, I realized my plight was desperate. He got a sly look and walked across the cot. I tried to outmaneuver him, but I had no place to go. He seized my blanket and took me to the floor. Twisting and turning in my mummy wrap, I tried to wrestle free as he covered my mouth with his sour whisky one. I was fighting with a lion, intent upon his supper. Lucky for me, he moved into position, and I gave him a quick knee to the groin. His eyes rolled, and he groaned. I pushed him off and scrambled to my feet.

"You'll regret that," he moaned grabbing my foot.

I dropped the blanket and lurched toward the overturned table grabbing the flask. I dumped what was left in his lusting eyes. He clutched his eyes and cursed me.

"How's that for an illusion!" I shouted darting out of the tent. My triumph was only seconds long, when I found myself stark naked staring into a camp full of open-mouthed, hungry-eyed soldiers.

The joke's over, God. Get me out of here.

The men gravitated toward me as I looked for escape. Whistles and lewd remarks began to fill the still air. I stepped against the tent, wrapped my nudity with the flap, and faced my horny brethren. The wool of their breeches grew tighter, as they inched my way. "Looks like doc's got a live one," said one stepping ahead of the rest. "I could take a turn at that."

"Yeah, where's he been keeping her?" another questioned, rolling the chaw from his mouth.

"Guess he didn't wanna share."

The salacious comments came at me like popcorn. *Take me back. Take me back, God.* My tormenters were close enough for me to smell the wood smoke on their clothing and see the hunger in their eyes.

Then miracle of miracles, I saw a familiar face push through the crowd. He walked slowly toward me, his face one of confusion and amusement.

"Who is she, Harley?" a soldier shouted. "You been holdin' out on us?"

The man ignored the banter. "You okay, Ma'am?"

I nodded. He was my rescuer twice over. He unbuttoned his shirt and handed it to me.

"Put this on, and I'll take you over to Mary."

The willful camp erupted with anger. Harley faced his berating comrades. "This woman is a lady. Now get back to what you were doin'."

"Lady my ass. She's doc's whore," said the one in front.

My fumbling fingers hurried to button up the wool shirt. "Thank you," I whispered to the back of his head. He smelled of hard work and resolve.

He turned. His gaze fell to where the shirt ended—not far enough. He sucked air and grabbed the shirttails with both hands and yanked. "The boys have been without for a long time."

I gazed helplessly into his deep hazel eyes and looked at the cast of soldiers.

"We better keep movin'," he said in a half-order, half-suggestion.

I nodded. A few soldiers encroached ready to challenge his authority.

"We best get you to Miss Mary's tent, second from the right. Just stay with me," he commanded.

My attacker stumbled from the tent at that moment, waving my blanket in his hand. Hooting and hollering commenced, rising to a crescendo.

"Who's first?" he shouted jerking the flap from my hands. "She's on the house."

This started the stampede. Harley jerked me from the onslaught, and together we darted from tent to tent. Somewhere in this madness, he pulled me into one.

A woman looked up. "Oh, my!"

Instinctively, I tried to stretch Harley's shirt.

"Miss Mary, I'll leave this lady in your care while I take care of the men." He let go of my hand.

"No, stay, please," I begged.

"Ma'am, don't you worry none. I could rough them boys up pretty good, and they know it, but Miss Mary here can send them to hell with her Scripture words." He grimaced a little at Mary. "Beg your pardon, Ma'am." He looked back at me and winked.

I loved his smile and twinkling eyes. If I weren't being chased, I might do some chasing of my own. The soldier's had not been thrown off so easily, and they were outside the tent voicing their displeasure—to put it mildly.

"See to the soldiers, Private Johnson and I will take care of this young woman." Mary's mothering eyes scolded and her voice was serious as midnight. "You must stay out of sight. If you show yourself again, in this manner of undress, I will be unable to save you. Do you understand your grave predicament?"

"See what I mean?" chimed Harley. "You'll be fine under Miss Mary's wing. Now do as she says, and I'll check on you after bit." My earthly savior vanished out of the tent and into the angry melee.

"I better help him. It sounds like you have stirred the Devil's pot."

Before she could exit, my assailant entered, swaying with drink. I wrapped my torso with a bedspread from Mary's cot. The disgruntled, disoriented man charged my way. Mary stepped between us and shoved him back.

"Doctor Kenton, you are drunk. Mind your manners and take yourself and these men away from here."

"Not without her."

"She is not your possession, Doctor. Now please leave."

The doctor balked, and the others lingered outside, despite Harley's damning orders. The fracas grew louder as they demanded their bootie. I wanted my nice warm tub.

Mary's face was growing redder by the second. The doctor stood there eyeing me but backed up a couple of steps. Mary scowled at him and went straight to a large black trunk. She threw open the lid and extracted long white pantaloons and a black dress and shoved them in my arms. Her ire turned on me. "One can hardly blame them. It is not every day that a woman meanders through camp in Eden dress, or should I say undress?"

"No, I suppose it isn't," I said softly, holding the clothes. I felt ashamed for something over which I had no control.

The law laid and admonishment given, Mary swept out of the tent, dragging the inebriated doctor with her. I was under the distinct impression that she was not to be ignored. She began spewing Biblical epithets like a drill sergeant giving orders, and it wasn't long before the soldiers quieted down and began to drift away.

After an hour or so, I peeked out. The doctor sat on a stump smoking a pipe and watching our tent. I ducked my head back inside. Mary returned a short while later with a plate of food and some fresh water.

"Are you hungry?"

"A little. What year is it?" I asked bluntly.

She looked at me with new concern. "Have you been wounded?"

"If I were to tell you where I've been and the things I've seen, you would most likely consider me insane."

"I already do, but no mind. War is insanity." Mary came around behind me, got a comb and brush and sat to work on my tangled damp hair. "You are to see the Captain within the hour. You have some explaining to do."

She parted my hair down the middle and swept my damp hair into a simple bun at the base of my neck. "To answer your earlier question. It is the thirteenth of October in the year of our Lord eighteen hundred and sixty-three."

"Eighteen sixty-three?"

"A forgettable year for you?" She handed me stockings and shoes. "These should fit you well enough."

"Where are we?"

She tilted my head back and looked into my eyes. "You must let me examine you later. I fear you've taken a blow to the head."

"Truly, I'm fine." I wanted to change the subject. "Harley called you, Mary."

"Mary Buchanan, recently of the Pleasant Hill Faithful community."

"You're a Shaker?"

So, she could smile. "One doesn't hear that term often. It was given to us by people from the outside. For a time, they were invited to observe our worship services in hopes of recruiting them into our community. That, I'm afraid, was not one of the wisest choices the Elders ever made."

"I'm sorry, Mary. I meant no disrespect. It seems that I can't get anything right, today."

"No offense taken. I left the community when the war came to Kentucky. I wanted to be of greater service to the wounded soldiers."

"Will you go back when the war's over?"

"I don't know. I must listen for the Lord's instruction."

"As must I." The words fell from my mind like a wayward breeze.

She took my hand in hers. "I am sorry. I haven't asked your name or what it is you seek."

"My name is Mattie." I dared not say more for fear that she might put me on bed rest for a head injury. I wasn't sure myself what I was seeking so I said, "truth," and nothing more.

"Mattie Truth?"

I smiled. "Yes, my name is Mattie Truth."

"Has He spoken to you?"

"The Lord?"

"Of course."

"We don't talk much. It's mostly my own voices I hear."

"Do you think the Lord is limited to words?"

"I suppose."

"There are no supposes with God, Miss Truth. The one you seek is the Lord. He is the truth and the way."

"He's my tormentor, and he has a horrible sense of humor," I said. Mary frowned. "I'm sorry Mary, but I don't know who or what to believe these days."

"Miss Truth, I have seen enough death and miracles to know water from wine, and you are less of one and more of the other."

"I don't understand."

"You will in time. Now you must stay inside. My duties abound beyond this sanctuary. I will come for you when it is time to see the Captain."

I hoped I'd be gone by then.

The Captain came to see me that afternoon. Mary thought it best that he come to her tent as the troops were still a bit riled. He was a nice man, but his tactics weren't much different from Mary's, and it was obvious that he thought me less than a lady. He asked me all the same questions as Mary; questions I could not answer for fear of being thought mad, and I wasn't sure what they did with crazy women in the 1800's. He told Mary to keep me under wraps until he figured out what to do with me.

So, I remained cloistered in the hospital camp. I was content to reflect and observe from the shadows while the camp readjusted to the normalcy of 1863. As it turned out, Mary was only three years older than me—not the ten I judged her to be. Weather and work had taken their toll on her simple beauty, but her stamina put mine to shame. She left the tent two hours before dawn and after making and serving the patients' supper, she made rounds to change dressings, write letters, and listen to the laments of lonely hearts. If that were not enough, she diligently rose twice during the night to repeat her daytime course. By the soft light of her nurse's lantern, she offered medicine and warm broth to those in need.

Despite my recluse status, Mary kept my hands busy peeling baskets of onions and potatoes and darning endless pairs of socks by lamplight. I stoked the tent stove on chilly mornings and when it warmed into the day, I sat in the tent recesses with the flap open and observed life outside. However interesting life in 1863 might be I despised the confines of the many layers of clothing I was required to wear for propriety sake. Mary's nurse's uniform did little to complement my physique and complexion.

Try as I might, I could not get her to tell me about the patient at the far end of camp, in a tent set apart and always under guard. She visited this tent four and five times a day, sometimes not returning until morning. On those mornings, she was solemn, her forehead creased with worry.

Then the day came that I was sure would usher me back to 1939. Handsome young Grandpa rode into camp. Mary seemed taken aback and flustered, she said something to him and came into the tent for a couple of medicine bottles.

"Who is that, Mary?" I asked.

"I can't talk now, I have a patient to tend too," she snapped and swept back out.

I watched Grandpa pour some coffee and sit by the fire. I propped open the tent flap so I could observe him, unseen. After about a half an hour, Mary came back out of the tent and went to him. I could hear nothing of their conversation but Mary was wringing her hands, and it seemed like he was drilling her for answers. Finally, he swore loud enough I could hear.

"Dammit, Mary. You should have sent for me." I watched him toss his coffee grounds in the fire and stride toward the tent set apart. I didn't see him again until the next day and then only briefly. He stayed inside that tent for the most part or sat outside keeping guard. I didn't know who was in the tent, but I had my suspicions and it was giving me fits not knowing for sure. Finally, I made up my mind to see for myself, but I didn't get far before I was intercepted by a rider coming into camp.

My loins tingled, and my heart raced as he rode toward me, his eyes riveted to mine. I knew I should run back to the tent, but my feet refused to obey.

My Knight Templar tapped his brim and smiled. "We meet again, dear Lady."

"I believe I owe you a debt of gratitude two times over," I stammered.

"Two times?" His eyes smiled with mischief.

"In the doctor's tent and at the ridgeline with the soldier chasing me."

"I would have rather had an explanation. Where did you go? I had a heck of a time explainin' that one."

Mary came out of her tent. It was nearly time to start cooking supper. "I thought I heard your voice, Private Johnson." She looked from him to me and back again. "Do you know one another?"

"Yes, well sort of," I said. "It's a long story."

"Not so long," he teased and looked at Mary. "She came flyin' out of the woods straight into my arms and then just disappeared, leaving me holdin' the evidence that proved Private Stahler was Gravemaker."

Mary's breath hung for a second. "So, it was Private Stahler? I heard the rumors and could scarcely believe it was one of our own."

"Who's Gravemaker?" I chimed.

"The Devil himself," Mary whispered.

"The man who chased you, Ma'am." Harley interjected, dismounting. "It was Stahler to be sure. He would have killed Sarg's niece if it hadn't been for you bringin' us the evidence when you did."

Mary asked with hopeful restraint, "Is he dead?"

"Lieutenant Wright field dressed him to be sure. Took some good licks himself, but Sarg's sis and the local doc sewed the Lieutenant up. We left the bastard's body at the bottom of a pit in one of those god-forsaken caves. Fittin' place for the Devil, don't you think?"

Mary tried to be indignant, but it was obvious that she was relieved by the news. "You should not rejoice in the killing of another, no matter what the reason."

Harley saluted in an attempt to agree to disagree. "Where might I find the Lieutenant, Ma'am?"

"When did Caleb get promoted?" Mary asked.

Harley's smile lit the sky. "Just a couple days ago, he doesn't have his new uniform yet, but he's been promoted just the same for killin' Gravemaker. And they promoted me to take his place." He pointed to the new stripe.

Mary's cheeks lifted. "Congratulations to you and your Lieutenant. May the Lord have mercy on us all."

Harley laughed. "Indeed."

"You will find your Lieutenant in the tent set apart," she said, then turning to me, "Mattie we must start dinner."

My eyes sparkled at Harley. He grinned wide. My heart fluttered; I desperately wanted to be back in those long muscular arms. I was long over-do for a good dream.

Mary led me in the opposite direction. "I do not recommend that you keep company with Private or rather Corporal Johnson," she said in undertones. "He is a lonely man like all of the rest. You would do well to keep to yourself and pray for discernment. You must discover why you are here. We will be moving to our winter quarters in Elizabethtown soon, and you will have to decide to come along or stay elsewhere."

Despite praying for my return, I woke the next day to the sound of a Civil War camp—and the next and the next. I seldom saw Grandpa and when I did, it was only from a distance. His routine never varied. He filled two plates at the cook fire and disappeared into the mysterious tent. He spoke to no one, and no one spoke to him except for Harley. Doctor Kenton took a furlough to Indiana, and I was glad to see him go.

At long last, I began to explore the small encampment. Despite the thrill of seeing Harley, the monotony of camp food and camp life was wearing thin. My straw cot was nightly torture, and I longed for my feather bed. I wanted to pluck fresh vegetables from my garden and cook them on my stove and eat them with Grandma in our kitchen. Yet, I was powerless, held captive in 1863 by a force I could not identify, for a purpose I could not discern.

"Mattie," Mary asked one evening while we sat by the campfire, "how can you possibly be going on forty years when you look to be less than thirty?"

"Oh, it's easy. I haven't been born yet," I confided, pouring myself a cup of boiling black coffee. The coals snapped sparks into the night sky, like fireflies dancing to the stars.

Mary stared at me as if to determine my intent. "Your words are as mysterious as your arrival."

"At least I gave the boys a break from their tiresome routine. How do you stand this monotony, day in and day out?"

Mary's face showed disappointment. "I didn't know you were unhappy. Perhaps I can arrange an outing for you."

"With Harley?" I asked hopeful.

She was not pleased and stood to make her rounds. "I'll see what I can do." I hadn't meant to hurt her feelings. I sat by the fire until the embers turned gray.

From a distant century, Grandma's voice admonished, *Idle hands, idle mind.*

Harley arrived at my tent one morning shortly after daybreak, his tall lean figure silhouetted in my doorway. "Excuse me, Ma'am."

My pulse jumped at the sound of his deep soft voice. I sat straddled over a washbasin, washing my long thick hair with my eyes squeezed shut against the soap's caustic lye. I fumbled with the water pitcher. "I'm afraid you've caught me in a compromised position."

He stepped in. "Here, let me help you." His large firm hand released mine from the awkward pitcher. "I used to help my sisters back home."

I searched blindly for my towel. My stomach fluttered. He placed it in my roving hand.

"Thank you."

Cool water poured forth onto the base of my neck and it streamed over and through my hair to the basin below. He gathered my mane like a horse's tail and twisted it into a rope wringing out the excess water. I wiped my face and handed him the towel, deftly he wrapped my wet head.

"There, that should do it."

I looked up into his tanned, and ruggedly handsome face. I wanted those hands on my body, those smiling lips on mine.

"Sorry to interrupt you, but I saw the tent flap was open and Mary said you wanted to see me."

"No, it's okay. I didn't sleep much last night."

"How about a walk after breakfast? It's Indian summer, warm and sunny."

"I would love to."

"What about your hair?"

"I'll let it dry in the sun."

Harley took the hairbrush from my bedside table. "How about we find a nice sunny spot, and I'll fix it for you."

I stood and stared into his happy brown eyes. He had thick chocolate-brown wavy hair, strong cheekbones, thick whiskers several hours old, and a dimpled chin. His smile showed two slightly crooked teeth in an otherwise perfect mouth. In that moment, I saw it all again. "You were in the window," I whispered.

"Ma'am?"

"The battlefield. The pit beneath the window."

His look was incredulous. "You were the woman in that pit at Perryville, the one I clunked with that arm?"

Emotions reeled as my legs turned to jelly. It was a surreal moment that catapulted me between past and present, from Levi's forest, Khalidah's bedside, to Grandma's attic and back. My hands went to his shoulders for support and his to my waist.

"You goin' down?"

I rested my swimming head on his chest.

"Who are you?" he asked softly.

My hands moved down the taut sinew of his arms. His fingers unconsciously caressed where they sat. "What were you doing in that awful pit and where did you go?"

What could I say? Oh, I travel through time—I really live in 1939?

"It's a long story."

His smile gleamed. "I'd like to hear that story sometime."

"I bet you would."

He laughed. As I stepped from his arms, his eyes paused on my protruding nipples. I'd totally forgotten that I was still in my thin cotton gown. "Perhaps you'd better wait outside while I change into something decent."

"Yes, Ma'am," he blushed and stepped out.

I looked at my swollen breasts. Was it from the chill or Harley? I thought back to another day.

"I'm tired of waiting for you, Mattie," Stephen complained that night on Lover's Leap.

"Do you love me?" I had asked my aggressive lover. "We're to be married in a month. Why can't we wait?"

Stephen gave me his don't-start-that-again groan. His hungry fingers couldn't get where they wanted to go fast enough and he popped two buttons from my blouse. Desperate for affection and tired from the months of holding him off, I surrendered. It was a new beginning and pleasure soon became my regular escape, a drug of intoxication, pungent like cheap wine and cigarettes.

I stepped from the tent in my nurse's garb. "Where shall we go, Harley?" I asked, desperately wishing I had something more attractive to wear.

He extended his arm, and I gladly took it. Jealous eyes watched from every corner. Mary peered our way from the cook fire. I felt a twinge of guilt for not helping with breakfast and decided to make up for it when I got back.

Nevertheless, the morning begged to be embraced. "Let's go that way." I pointed down a leafy path. We strolled away from camp, arm in arm, beneath a vibrant-blue sky. The warm yellow sun kissed my damp brow, and I squeezed his arm. I looked up at him, he glowed contentment, just like me.

Was I responsible for my actions in this bent time? Was it real? There were no decipherable rules. Was I the first? And if so, why couldn't I make my own rules? I desperately wanted to seduce him. Would he be willing? Were there consequences for my actions? Was it real? Could I change history, or was I a pawn of the gods? I decided that it was my delusion, and I was going to have some fun for a change.

Out of sight of the camp, I turned into the woods and picked a semi-secluded spot. Harley followed, apparently comfortable in my presence and the day.

"Where are your kin?" I asked.

"Ohio. They have a small farm in Ripley County."

"And you?" he asked.

"Pine Ridge."

"Where's that?"

I found a sunny spot where the trees parted above us. I wished I'd brought a blanket. I sat on a carpet of crunchy leaves and began picking the twigs from our bed. Harley hesitated but a moment, and sat beside me.

"Kentucky."

"Near here?"

"Maybe."

I looked again into his beautiful strong face. His eyes questioned. I could see the wheels turning at locomotive speed.

"Harley, I would love to tell you my story. Really I would, but I don't quite understand it myself."

We sat in silence, him puzzling things over in his mind—me watching him do so. I began to brush my hair.

"Let me do that. I always liked braiding my sisters hair when they would let me."

I sensed his nervousness, but he was trying hard to cover it. I handed him my brush. "Harley, I don't know if today is real. I don't know if I'm dreaming or if I'm really here with you." He took the brush and looked at me, waiting for me to finish. I looked at him for a moment and then said exactly what was on my mind. "I desperately want to kiss you."

He put the brush down and looked deep in my eyes. I think he thought I was joking or that he was dreaming. I answered his disbelief by moving into his arms. I stood on my knees in front of him and kissed him. He responded awkward and unsure. I sought more, his breath quickened, and he began to keep up. My fingers went to his bulge. He groaned. I worked the buttons loose and continued kissing him, searching his depths. Nature was taking over, his hand moved to my breast, the other to the buttons of my dress.

It was obvious that he had the tools to please—as I knew he would. I had one button to go and while kissing him, pulled him to his feet. He eagerly followed my lead. I released his wondrous towering manhood and plummeted to my knees and without hesitation took him in my mouth; his eyes caught mine in wonder, confusion, and obvious pleasure. He moaned. Did women do this in the 1800's? Did I care?

When his body began to tremble, I probed the depths of his mouth and stroked his pleasure. When he had taken about all he could stand, I stood and undressed in front of him. He watched in amazement as I stepped out of the pile of clothing at my feet and straddled him. I teased by swaying lower and lower until the tiger pounced; he rolled me to my back and plunged to my depths. It was my turn for amazement; had anything or anyone ever felt this good? The feel of his lips on my nipples, the mating dance, the erotic sharing of physical pleasure—we plunged ahead though questions remained.

That was the last coherent thought I had until we lay exhausted and spent. We had shared the intimate of intimates, spoken words of the flesh, but knew little of each other's lives or minds. We lay naked on our clothes, dappled sunlight dancing across our bodies. He perched on one elbow and looked into my face, his desire already rising. Without question, I took him again. There is definitely something to be said for a tough rugged man. When I could take no more, I rolled away laughing.

"You must think I'm a whore, Harley."

"Never had one."

He was serious. *Oh my God.* "You mean you've never…"

It was his turn to laugh. "Guess I had some catchin' up to do."

"Well damn, Harley. I never stole a man's virginity before."

"Did you mind?"

Heat rose to my face. "When can I see you again?"

"Don't know… might be a long while." He looked over my highs and lows. "Guess we should stock up."

"I'll be walking bowlegged back to camp if you jump me again." I laughed. "I thought we were done."

"Not hardly." He grabbed my ass and took me from behind. It

seemed he wanted to try out every conceivable position his virgin mind had conjured over the last umpteen years. Who was I to argue?

It was nearly dark when we returned and probably a good thing. My clothes were wrinkled, my lips chapped, and I probably still had leaves and twigs in my hair. It never did get brushed. We snuck into my tent. Judging by the chatter echoing from the common area, I knew that Mary was busy serving dinner. Harley moved a long wavy strand of hair out of my face and tucked it behind my ear. "Can I come for you after dinner tomorrow?" he asked. "I've got guard duty back at camp tonight."

I made love to his mouth, pushing my way inside. There was no fight, and for a moment, I thought he would take me again.

In a heave of visible effort, he stopped and shook his head. "Damn woman!" He chuckled. "I gotta go, or I won't be worth two cents tonight."

"I'll see you tomorrow after dinner then."

He retrieved his hat from my cot and turned to go just as Mary swept in.

"Corporal Johnson," Mary's voice accused. Harley jumped like he'd been caught with his hand in the cookie jar.

"What are you doing in here?" She smacked at his leg with a wooden spoon.

"Where have you kept Miss Mattie all day?"

"Oh, Mary, leave him alone," I said in jest. "I was the one that kept Harley out."

Harley hurriedly tipped his hat and made a backward waltz out of the tent. "I'll be by for you at seven."

My face glowed as Mary's gaze settled on my crazy hair. Thankfully, her impending questions were delayed by the approach of steady footsteps.

"Mary?" It was Grandpa's voice. My heart jumped when he poked his head inside. He looked at me and back to Mary.

"Please Lieutenant, come in," Mary said, her eyes cutting me down.

He hesitated a moment, removed his hat and stepped inside. My eyes locked on Grandpa's. Mary looked from him to me and back again.

"Lieutenant Wright, this is Mattie Truth." We stared at each other, flesh tingling. "Mattie, this is Lieutenant Wright. Do you know one another?"

My soul vibrated. Words failed.

Grandpa stared at me, puzzled and confused.

My mind raced. Had I told anyone my real last name? I purposely withheld that information from Mary and Harley, or so I thought, but what of the others whom I tended to daily? I couldn't be sure. I prayed I hadn't woven a web in which I would soon be ensnared.

"I don't believe we have," I squeaked.

The silent crevices of Grandpa's assessment brought my nerves to the surface like a cold breeze on a warm wet body. In him, I saw my father's image right down to the nervous twitch beneath his left eye. Broad and tall, Grandpa stood strong and confident. He was the spitting image of the man in the portrait above Grandma's bed. I could see why she kept him there.

Recognition leapt to his face. "I know you. You're the woman who made that mess in our store, and you're the woman from the woods at Perryville," he exclaimed. "I wasn't daft. I knew I saw a woman in the brush!"

Grandpa was the man I saw shot in the back of the leg. "I'm sorry, Lieutenant," I sputtered. "But I'm quite sure we've never met." My lie hung limp in the air.

"Not so," he countered. Mary attempted to dislodge his questions, to no avail. "Johnson told me you were the one that gave him Stahler's haversack. I want to thank you for that."

Why had I been such a fool? Of course Harley would tell him. It was his duty to inform his officer and besides it appeared they were friends as well.

"But I need to know, Miss Truth. Where are you from and for which side do you carry sympathies?"

Mary stammered. "Lieutenant, you don't mean to imply?"

Grandpa's eyes hardened. "Why else would she keep popping up in Federal positions?"

My mind tumbled.

"Lieutenant, I think it best that we speak outside," Mary said.

Grandpa looked at me as if trying to look inside my head. "I'm taking her over to headquarters in the morning," he said before stepping outside.

I caught Mary's hand as she started to follow him out. "What's going on? Who does he think I am?"

She crossed her arms. "He thinks you are a Confederate spy."

"What? That's ridiculous. I may seem peculiar, but I'm no spy. You have to believe me."

"I believe you, Mattie, but Lieutenant Wright can do as he pleases when it comes to Army matters."

"Can you help me out of this dilemma?"

"Mattie, this is no dilemma. If they find you guilty, you would be put in prison or worse."

"I'm not asking you to help me escape. I just need you to ask the Lieutenant to give me a chance to explain."

"Were you the woman that Lieutenant Wright saw at Perryville?"

I'd already decided, as far-fetched as it was, to answer the rest of Mary's questions with the truth and nothing less, despite what she might think. "Yes, I was that woman." Mary's face was stoic and concerned. "I was in the brush at Perryville and in the pit of amputated limbs later at the field hospital. I was also near the cave when Private Stahler murdered those men and later Harley saved me from him."

Mary's face went white.

"Why do they call him Gravemaker?"

"I'd rather not speak to you of the Devil. He was the worst humanity could produce."

"Did he have anything to do with the patient that is in the tent at the end of camp?"

Mary looked uneasy. "She's the only survivor of his wickedness, and she's barely hanging on."

Mary searched my eyes.

"Is her name Lydia Weldishofer? Is she from New Alsace, Indiana?"

Mary pointed at me, her face hard. "Who are you?"

"Mary, my last name is not Truth. I am searching for the truth. That is why I'm here. My last name is Wright."

"Are you related to the Lieutenant?"

"Yes, but he doesn't know me."

Mary was aghast. "Wait here."

"No wait!"

She dashed out.

Holy shit, now what? I damn sure couldn't tell them everything. They'd hang me for sure. If I was trapped here, I wanted it to be with Harley not in some Federal prison.

"Caleb, I want to come," Harley said. Mary stood silent.

"That's fine with me." Caleb softened his tone. "I don't like this, Harley. I know what this woman means to you, but I have no choice. It's my responsibility to get to the bottom of this, and I have to presume she's a spy. It just doesn't add up."

"Just listen to what she has to say."

"Normally in this kind of matter, I wouldn't, but for you, I will. Let's get this over with."

Thank you, Jesus, thought Harley. *Thank you, Jesus.*

The three stopped in front of Mary's tent.

"Mattie, the Lieutenant would like to speak with you." Mary said. There was no reply. "Mattie?"

Caleb removed his revolver.

"There's no need for weapons, Caleb." Harley said.

Caleb brushed him aside and stepped in. "She's gone."

I woke to find myself immersed in my own bathtub. The water was cold and I was still wearing a Civil War nurse's dress. *Thank you, God.*

THIRTY-ONE

Important principles may, and must, be inflexible.
—Abraham Lincoln

L YDIA GRIPPED CALEB'S hand as the buggy jostled to a stop. "Please don't leave me here," she whispered. Caleb turned and cupped her face in his strong gentle hands. Tears shone in her beseeching eyes.

"Don't worry, Sweetheart, everything will be fine. I promise." He sounded confident, but his mind tumbled. Her bulging belly looked like a giant melon on a fragile vine. The hollow gray eyes that peered at him a mere week ago, once again, danced blue. Her stamina had improved daily under his diligent care, but his heart strangled with the task that lay ahead. Mary assured him that Lydia would be well cared for by the Shakers of Pleasant Hill. He wished he could send her home to Grandma Hannah; she would tend Lydia's spirit as well as her body. Yet winter was nearly upon them, and there was no time with duty calling him south.

Lydia cowered against him as he helped her from the carriage. A cold November air whipped at her skirts, and he gathered her to him like a forlorn child. Together they walked through the gate into the village where she would live and give birth to their son; he knew she would be alone among these strangers and their peculiar ways.

Mary left camp the day prior to make arrangements with the Elders before their arrival. Caleb trusted Mary's judgment, but he also relied on numerous reports from soldiers whom the Shakers had tended both before and after the battle of Perryville. Pacifists, they took care of all—the Blue and the Gray.

Mary was waiting at the gate to usher them through. She took them to a small, white clapboard building, a type of town hall. A long slim table of perfect proportions sat in the center of the sparse room with twelve matching chairs.

"Please sit down," she instructed and took an adjacent chair. "You are my dear friends, but our village is neither inn nor hospital. We are committed to a life serving Jesus Christ, without the burden of carnal desires. Your presence here may be unsettling for some of the Believers, as they have separated themselves, man from woman, for a higher good and spiritual enlightenment. An espoused lady in their midst might stir up yearnings and breed temptation."

Caleb's mind lashed; they had taken away God's gift of children and to what end? Didn't they realize that without children and God's ordained order, their days were numbered? It was true that they tended the Blue and the Gray, but was it right to live in this country and avoid the greater responsibility? In the distance, he saw several strong able-bodied men, and he had to restrain the urge to press them into service. The sooner he left this place the better.

Mary told Lydia and Caleb about life as an expectant mother in the Pleasant Hill community. Lydia would have to live apart, near the novitiate house and she must not wander the grounds except in specified areas. She would not be allowed to associate with the Faithful of the community and would take her meals alone. She would be fed and clothed and a local mid-wife would check on her from time to time. A bell was mounted on a post in the front yard of her cabin and she could summon the Faithful in this way, should an emergency arise. Mary assured Caleb that she would stay at Pleasant Hill until the baby was born and Lydia could go home to Indiana.

Lydia appeared resigned, but Caleb bristled within, but with no other choice at hand and duty calling him south, his soul began to disengage. Separation was imminent and self-preservation tactics once again began to take control. He needed to make a quick exit, lest his resolve crumble beneath the sadness of her gaze. There could be no compromise and her intuition would soon discern his reservations.

His quick exit was thwarted—it seemed the Faithful were not without compassion. They refused to hear of him taking leave on an empty stomach and arranged a private dining for the young couple for "sustenance and farewells."

The hearty meal consisted of braised beef and savory winter vegetables served in a rosemary butter accompanied by robust wheat-berry bread for sopping the wondrous juices. Caleb's thoughts brightened. If Lydia ate like this every day, she would regain much needed mass and strength before the baby came. He ate with relish, his appetite that of a soldier, untarnished by unpleasant circumstances.

Lydia ate slowly, deliberately, forcing every bite down under his concerned gaze. She committed his eyes and face to memory; his steel-blues were sad and concerned, his well-sculpted jaw in need of a shave and his finger-combed, thick, brassy blonde hair beckoned her touch. His Union cap rested beside his plate. These images would be her only company in the long lonely weeks ahead.

Caleb finished his meal and tilted his chair back on two legs. Her thin features sang of tender springtime flowers.

Lydia smiled, blushing beneath his ardent gaze. She poked a bite of rutabaga in her mouth and watched him watching her. His eye-twitch two-stepped, and she thought back to their meeting by the bridge at Perryville.

She speared a carrot and chewed with feigned determination.

Caleb laughed. "Stop, please." She stabbed a hunk of meat. It sent Shaker sin pulsing through his loins.

"Can you stay the night?" she asked. "It's already late, and I have an entire cabin all to myself."

Soldier duties made for hardtack decisions. "I can't."

"It's going to storm, Caleb, and it's getting late," she countered. "You'll be caught out in it and catch your death."

He remembered how much better prime rib tasted than his daily fair of salt pork. "And what of Mary's Shaker rules?" he asked. Even his beautiful espoused lady could not quell the morbidity lodged in his gut. "Besides, I've already stayed longer then my furlough allowed."

Lydia knew he spoke the truth, but she longed for one more night with comforting words and sensual touches. "You won't make much headway if you leave tonight. You'll sleep cold and wet when you could be lying next to me in my nice warm feather bed."

Good God. Didn't she understand? Just drive the knife in, Lydia. Go ahead. "You're not making this easy, Lydia."

"I don't intend to. Why should I? I may never see you again."

"Don't talk like that," he said.

"Why not? It's the truth. You may die, I may die, that's the way it is." She pushed away from the table. "We should find Mary. I'm feeling tired."

Caleb rose. "Don't be angry," he pleaded. "I'll come back, I promise. Everything's going to be just fine." She might as well be a Johnnie. She'd shot him straight through the heart. He followed her into the brisk afternoon, his hand resting on the small of her rigid back. A biting wind swept the dirt and leaves swirling up about them.

"Winter's coming," he said.

"In so many ways," she whispered.

Mary appeared as if on cue, she must have been watching and waiting, Caleb thought wryly.

"Let's get you to your cabin," Mary urged.

"I'll get her trunk." Caleb turned toward the carriage.

Lydia looked at him with those puppy dog eyes and followed Mary down the stone path.

"Damn her," he sputtered and wrestled the trunk from its position. He slung it to his shoulder and followed the skirts in the distance. Lydia had him feeling like a drop of water hopping in a hot skillet. She might as well just cut him open and rip his heart out with her bare hands.

The cabin was sparse but comfortable; it would be cozy enough against the blustery, winter winds. The stone hearth held a small cast iron kettle, suspended above a crackling fire.

Lydia was pleased to see a small oven built into the stone alongside the fireplace. She would be able to bake her own bread and perhaps an occasional pie or cake. A large wooden mixing bowl and two smaller ones for serving graced the maple mantle along with an ingeniously crafted, seamless, wooden water bucket by the door. She had never seen such quality craftsmanship.

The double bed was made of golden maple, its simple clean lines polished to perfection. Three handcrafted quilts covered the thick feather mattress and the down-filled pillows looked like a cloud of comfort. Caleb would stay the night, Lydia decided. If she could get him to sleep here one night, his scent would linger.

Mary helped Lydia to a straight back chair. "Caleb, would

353

you bring in some water before you leave?" Caleb avoided Lydia's eyes and gladly took the bucket to the well. "The weather is moving toward winter," Mary remarked. "There is a nice stack of firewood outside your door, and I will have Caleb stoke the fire before he goes."

Lydia didn't answer. What did she care of the weather? It was fitting that it was cold and gray, just like she felt. "I hope Caleb rides ahead of it."

Mary patted her shoulder. "He is a tower of strength, he will be fine."

It wasn't the sort of thing Lydia wanted to hear. "Yes, he is strong, but even the strong falter."

Caleb came through the door, a full bucket in hand. The winter air swept in with him.

Mary looked from one to the other. "I will be down the path at the last cabin if you need me. God be with you, Caleb. Give my regards to Benjamin."

"I will, Mary. Thank you for everything."

Mary stepped into a whirlwind of falling leaves and scurried down the path.

Caleb set the bucket near the door and positioned a chair in front of Lydia so that they sat knee to knee. He took her complacent hands in his and searched her face for forgiveness. "I shall miss you terribly, my Darling."

Lydia looked down at his brown calloused hands. "Why must you go tonight?"

"It's better that I go." Soldiering destroyed reason. "The longer I stay…"

Lydia got up abruptly. Caleb held her hand, but she pulled free and walked to the window. Dead leaves rolled across the yard. It didn't appear that she would come back to him; he waited; she remained. *Lord Almighty.*

She spoke to the glass. "Please stay," she said softly and turned to him with tears in her eyes. "Leave in the morning if you must, but please stay with me tonight, Caleb. We've had no time, and I'm so scared. I don't want you to go. I don't want you to leave me here, not like this."

He knew he should protest—should leave this moment.

She saw the hesitation. She had one chance to entice him further and then he would surely stay. She untied the ribbon at her bodice and pulled the comb from her hair: It fell long and loose about her shoulders. "Take these memories with you, Caleb—love me tonight. Leave in the morning if you must, but I need to know that you still want me. I need to know that I can still be a wife to you."

Oh God. He sat mesmerized, tucking away every image, storing them deep in his mind so that he could retrieve them in the days to come. But for now, it was real. She was here, laying herself bare to him in the soft glow of firelight—her crimson nipples full and firm, her belly protruding and round. She was still thin but beautiful in every way. Her eyes teased with passion as the last of her petticoats fell to the floor. He looked past the scars and all they represented. He had to show her that she had not changed in his eyes, not at all.

He drew a ragged breath, his pants suddenly tight and uncomfortable. While his instinct was to move to her, he paused to savor the view. How long until they would be together again? She stepped into the circle of his legs, her breasts level with his mouth. There was no question, his tongue caroused the sweet softness; his hands caressed her back and buttocks. He would stay.

A wild Kentucky storm raged through the night. It was nearly dawn before the lovers lay entangled, exhausted and content, snuggled deep within the downy mattress beneath the heavy quilts.

Caleb stared into the flickering flames while Lydia dozed beside him, naked and warm in his arms. Ice pellets battered the windowpanes. The baby moved against his belly. At that moment, he hated being a soldier. He laid there, his refuge murmuring softly beside him, his son speaking from within. The image came again of water and fire—the true battle raged in his heart.

When morning broke through the frosty prism-glass window, he kissed her forehead and got up to stoke the fire before she woke. He donned his socks and pants. He wanted the cabin warm for her; she was still so fragile and couldn't risk taking ill. Not that she acted fragile last night, but he had been gentle and reassuring even though he'd been afraid he might hurt her. He pulled the covers over her shoulders so that all he could see was her tangled hair and smiling lips. She laid her heart open afresh last night; his hands had felt every scar, kissed and caressed her fear and pain away. It was he she saw when they made love, not the Devil.

He stoked the fire and added fresh kindling. It crackled to life, and he laid three logs on the flames and swung the kettle over. If only he could take her home to Grandma Hannah, be her man, stay and care for her. He sat on the bed and she woke to his tender caress. "I have to go," he confessed, kissing her lips.

"Not yet," she murmured. Her hungry kisses chased all thoughts of leaving away.

His vixen kept him through noontide. Mary waited and watched the cabin from another. She breathed relief when she saw them come out and walk to the stable. They emerged a short while later with horse in tow. The cold winds whipped Lydia's cloak and skirts as she took shelter beneath the heavy wool hood of her cape, snuggling close against her soldier. They walked slowly down the path to the road that would separate them, perhaps forever.

They stopped at the gate leading to the outside and Lydia turned into the circle of Caleb's arms. "You have to come back to me. Promise."

Caleb's gut churned. She knew the risk, the impossibility of what she asked, but he could not deny those beseeching pools of blue, the morning's lovemaking still fresh in their hearts.

"I promise."

The wind whipped her hood off, tangling long blonde tendrils of hair about her face. He tucked one behind her ear and caressed her chilled cheek.

"I love you, Caleb Wright. If it takes a lifetime, I will wait for you to come back to me."

He lifted her hand to his lips. "No matter where I go or what happens, I will come back for you." Caleb's voice caught.

An intimate final embrace, a savored exchange of warmth and passion, it was time.

Lydia watched Caleb mount his horse. He gazed long at her tear-streaked face, thrust his heels into the horse's flanks, and galloped away down the wintry road.

He never looked back. She never looked away.

MORE ABOUT
"BENEATH THE SHADOWS"

Dear Reader,

The book you hold in your hands is the result of many strange and unexplainable coincidences. The journey that created *Beneath the Shadows* began long before God brought Jim and I together to write.

Great human trials and bloody battles of anger, anguish and passion leave energy upon the earth. Jim and I have often felt that we were taking dictation from the lost heroes of the Civil War, (those who perished on the battlefields and those who suffered through at home and in the ranks.) Today we are again living through monumental change as a nation and a people. One must wonder if Abraham Lincoln pondered the power of his words or knew how eloquently his words would speak to us today.

On December 1st, 1862 in an address to Congress he said, *"Fellow citizens, we cannot escape history. We of this Congress and this administration will be remembered in spite of ourselves. No personal significance or insignificance can spare one or another of us. The fiery trial through which we pass, will light us down, in honor or dishonor, to the latest generation."*

With humble hearts, we pray for and remember the men and women of our Armed forces who continue to sacrifice for our freedoms. With our story we pay homage to the Lost Heroes of every generation, so that others might know and remember them.

If you wish to know more about the authors, their appearance schedule, upcoming books or to read Lee Ann's blog, visit their website. www.newtonandbenson.com

Printed in the United States
71417LV00002B/513